a nov
by Ellen Cass
Shelter
Me
D0612600

SHELTER ME

ELLEN CASSIDY

For Diana—my first reading partner and confidante, whose love of romance novels inspired me at sixteen, and continue to, at fifty-six. Our friendship was a gift from God in so many ways. Until we meet again, my dear Danusia, somewhere over the rainbow...I always hold you close to my heart.

ACKNOWLEDGMENTS

Cover art credited to Lisa Van Plew Clid, of Starlight Studio & Art School, Three Oaks, Michigan

SPECIAL THANKS

To my husband John, without whose support my writing would still be languishing unread in various notebooks. I'm forever grateful.

1

When Kathleen and her best friend Summer were teenagers, their favorite pastime was cruising the mall, but what they liked even more than shopping was sitting on the cobalt-blue iron benches in front of Sears and wondering about the love lives of the strangers walking by. They'd discuss who looked besotted, who didn't, if one was cheating on another or about to break up, and who might be spectacular in bed. They were especially fascinated with anyone pregnant. Some women looked happy; others looked ready to expire, with their bloated ankles and wobbly gaits.

"I read, somewhere, that your boobs go up, like, three cup sizes when you're pregnant," Summer said. Kathleen had looked down at her own less-than-blossoming chest, as if she needed to be reminded of its seemingly dormant state. "That could be cool. I could finally ditch the training bras."

Summer grimaced. "No way! I'd need a crane to hold mine up."

Kathleen remembered that conversation so vividly because they'd laughed hard at the idea of a boob crane lift. So hard that the mall security cop kept circling around their bench suspiciously, convinced they were high or drunk on something. As it happened, they weren't. Not that time, at least. They'd whisper and giggle as couples strolled holding hands (or sometimes, the couples' hands in one another's back pockets), "That guy can't wait to get her home, I bet." Or seeing men with bellies hanging well below their belts, "How can they even *do* it?" Not to mention chittering about how anyone would want to "do it" with someone so grossly fat and ancient. Kathleen laughed when she thought of these times; so easy it had been to crank out the judgment as they'd sat there with their sleek, virginal bodies and clueless selves. Funnier still, this habit of visualizing strangers' peculiarities was one she couldn't shake. And twenty-five years later, working in a brand-new hipster brewery presented endless opportunities for rumination.

Of course, there were the regulars, who became too much like friends or family to visualize that way. Rather, she'd ponder what her customers' lives were like outside of the pub, what led them to spend all night or even all afternoon drinking their cares away. When it was slow, which wasn't often, she might do some prodding. She learned that Donny, a foreman for the Road Commission, didn't want to be asked when the car-swallowing cracks on their local highways were going to get filled; instead, he wanted to ask her things like why did women leave their husbands. Specifically, why his wife. And now he'd revealed he was overlooked for a promotion because he was too old.

"Screw'em, all of'em," he said. He tipped a glass back and Kathleen stared at his big hands. They were a workingman's hands, the cuticles permanently ingrained with grease. He smacked his lips. "Pretty good, pretty lady." Donny was somewhat new to the craft beer scene and quickly became a convert. "Man, this stuff has flavor," he said, holding the glass of gold up to the light. "Maybe if I'd had this stuff ten years ago, I'd still be married."

Kathleen mopped the bar around him with a white rag. "Yeah? Why?"

"I dunno. It sure relaxes the hell out of you. We mighta had a lot more sex."

She laughed. It was true that people said things all the time to bartenders that they wouldn't to others. Part of it was booze loosening the tongue; another part loneliness. But mainly, it was that a good bartender knew how to listen and keep their own mouth shut, qualities that were in short supply in the year 2018. "I'm sorry to hear about the promotion business."

He waved a hand. "Ahhh. The hell with it. Probably just ride the retirement wave onto shore, now."

"How much longer before that happens?"

"Ten years, maybe."

She folded the rag up and put it below the bar. Ten years sounded like a long time to be miserable, but what did she know of the real workforce? A series of waitressing jobs, married at twenty-four, and then her job was being a wife to Steve. She managed to convince herself, over time, that'd been enough and what she wanted. Then he became sick and she became a widow, much sooner than she'd imagined. Her current situation was the proverbial "when a door closes, a window opens" scenario. A new beginning, of sorts, bartending and waiting tables at a place called HopCanon in the obscure little town of Mount Simon, Michigan. Population: 2,400.

Summer Martin, still her best friend, and her husband Jeff were the owners, and had convinced her to join their team. On the first day, Kathleen was as nervous as a caged cat; her beer experiences had been limited to limes squeezed into bottles on hot summer beach days. After all the caretaking with Steve, it was like coming out of a time warp. She'd been so immersed in the world of Parkinson's, of therapies and meds and appointments, she'd had to school herself on the current trends just to keep a conversation going.

"I don't know about this," Kathleen said to Summer at her orientation. "Do you really want a server past thirty with spider veins? I feel like I'm not the right demographic for this scene."

"Don't be ridiculous. You'll be great. Lord knows you're acquainted with waiting on people hand and foot. You're fast on your feet, attractive, and because you've listened to me blab on for years about nothing, you got that covered for all the Chatty Cathies you'll encounter." Summer hauled out a flight tray, which was what customers ordered to try different beers, and filled eight glasses at four ounces each. "C'mon, bottoms up. For training purposes."

Kathleen chose their signature imperial pale ale, referred to as an IPA, which they'd christened with the name "Betrayal." The taste was surprisingly good: bitter, but piney. She downed two more glasses, another IPA brewed with honey and the other a brown ale, in quick succession.

"To address your assertions," Kathleen said, "The last time I was considered 'fast' was in fourth-grade track. My attractiveness meter falls on the dishwater-gray-church-mouse level. And you have most certainly not blabbed on for years about nothing. My brain has turned to mush. I'm afraid that the computer keypad is enough to cause a seizure. What happened to good ol' cash registers?"

Summer laughed. "Out with the dinosaurs." She ran a hand through Kathleen's ponytail. "Your color may be dishwater, but you are hot, honey. Look at your boobs, for God's sake. Remember how we'd constantly compare, back in the day? You could pass that pencil test, still!" She pointed to her own ample chest. "Unlike me. I could stick a twenty-four pack of Ticonderogas under these babies and they wouldn't budge. See what breastfeeding does? Those La Leche crazies always leave that fun fact out of their little meetings."

"Who? Why are you talking about pencils?" Kathleen was wishing she'd eaten a heartier lunch. "God, your beer is strong."

"Never mind. Now, Beer 101, lesson number one: you don't toss them back like a shot. They're called samples for a reason. You sip, my dear." Summer cleared the tray away. "Anyway, I was trying to say you're gonna rock our tiny tees, even though this is hardly Hooters. Stop worrying. We'll get you introduced here comfortably. It'll be a breeze."

What an introduction it had been. HopCanon stood out from the rash of breweries cropping up all over Michigan, due to its unique beginnings: a few years ago, it was a decommissioned Catholic church, and sat vacant for a time. An experienced homebrewer, Jeff jumped on the idea of marrying his beer with a religious theme, and in his hometown, no less. They'd tried to stay true to the essence of the place, while putting their own spin on the décor and atmosphere. The black cushiony board which had previously held the day's hymns now held the day's featured brews, and the former pews served as community benches. They'd turned the pulpit into a waitress station and added on a circular bar. But the crown jewels were the stained-glass windows that filtered sunlight into the sinners' pints below.

The job was every bit exhausting as it was fun, and Kathleen felt like a baby emerging from the womb with the newness of it all. She supposed her excitement at going to what most considered menial work, even drudgery, was a reflection of how boring and unrefined she was, but so be it. The minute she put on the (yes, very snug) rust-colored work tee, she was energized. She couldn't wait to ask about waitress Megan's latest dating adventure, if bartender Zack was going to grad school or not, if salad guy Eric was still moving out of his parents' basement and in with his boyfriend. Their lives were fascinating to her, open maps yet to be trod upon, their paths unsullied by unrealized dreams and paralyzing losses.

Her extremely devout mother, Peggy, was less than thrilled with her daughter's employment, calling the whole affair heathen-ish. Kathleen had prepared for the backlash. "Monks have been brewing for centuries, Mom. It was safer than drinking the water."

"Did they serve it up to crowds of atheists, who sat around probably mocking Christians?"

Kathleen drew in her breath for patience. "It's not like that at HopCanon. But, yes, the monks brewed for hospitality. To all walks of life, in fact."

Peggy's still-attractive face clouded. "Well. Your father, God rest his soul, would be appalled at this ... this development. On sacred grounds."

On the contrary, thought Kathleen. The man had kept whiskey hidden in his home office for years. She couldn't understand why, as her parents drank socially and were hardly teetotalers. She'd found a pint of Jack Daniels when she was a junior in high school, along with dozens of hotel-sized liquor bottles, all while rummaging for stamps in a desk drawer normally kept locked. But the motherlode of excavation among the alcohol paraphernalia was the tattered Bible with a rosary tucked in the middle. On top of a well-worn copy of Playboy, no less. She'd quickly rifled through the pages, cursed her flat chest, and pilfered a handful of the miniature vodkas to choke down for that night's football game. She reasoned that, even if her father noticed, he'd never dare mention their disappearance.

Peggy dropped the subject of the blasphemous brewpub, thankfully. At almost forty, Kathleen was not about to let her mother stamp out the silver lining that had managed to poke through the dark of the past few years. Finally, she had little to no responsibilities other than taking care of the dog and the cat, and house maintenance. Her stepdaughter was grown and freedom beckoned, waiting to be tasted like the beer that flowed from the taps.

Kathleen went to the back to clock out. She yawned, relieved her Friday shift was over. Sleeping well had been a challenge for years, and it was only nominally better since beginning the job. Summer came bustling in just as she went to get her purse.

"You have to stay for a while. I want you to hear the new guitar player I hired for Friday nights. Well, for a few of them, anyway. And he's starting in ten minutes."

Kathleen rubbed her eyes. "Ah, I'm so tired. I'm sure he's great, but I gotta go let the dog out and—"

"I'll text Sam. He loves Hugo. He won't mind."

"The kid is eighteen. I'm sure he has plans on a Friday night."

"I don't care. I'd rather he be out exercising dogs than smoking weed somewhere, boning his girlfriend in the back of his car. Did you know I caught them half-naked, the other day? I swear, if he doesn't get her pregnant, it'll be a miracle." Her phone dinged. "See here, he messaged that he can do it." She looked up at Kathleen, alarmed. "Jesus. What if she comes with him and they go to town at your place?"

Kathleen laughed. "Have at it, I say. At least somebody would be getting some action."

"Bite your tongue. I'm telling him to go alone. Order a

beer and meet me at table six." She did a double take, studying Kathleen's hair. "Did you get highlights done?"

"Yes."

"Looks great. Okay, see you in a few."

Kathleen hesitated. It'd been ages since she'd heard good live music. When she and Steve had gone to such events, it was jazz festivals, the majority of the attendees aging geezers lounging in lawn chairs and struggling to stay awake. But that was life with him; what he liked ruled. What she preferred had been relegated to a dusty back shelf whose location she had trouble recalling. She ordered a freshly-tapped stout named "Doubting Thomas" from bartender Zack, and went to table six, on which Summer had placed a "Reserved" sign. The beer was decadent, smooth, with hints of chocolate flavor that disguised its higher alcohol content. This drink could be checked into her newly discovered preferred box, that's for sure. She sighed, contented, and sat back in the chair, taking big sips. She was happy to note the place was packed. Her friends had worked hard for this and she was glad to be a part of it.

The evening's new entertainment was setting up not far from her, arranging speakers and an array of cords. He glided around the equipment like a panther, dressed head to toe in black, but she noticed within his gracefulness there was a slight hitch to his gait. He had a black V-neck sweater on, loose-fit jeans, and boots. He passed her and she got a good close up at him then, the mahogany-colored whisker shadow and thick hair. The locks were a shade darker than his shadow and long enough to tuck behind his ears, but not quite long enough for a ponytail. He was slim, possibly more than was healthy for his tall frame, with skin paler than hers. And that was hard to achieve. The main difference was the contrast of shades: her face was ghostly and wan ("Put some damned make-up on. You look like a Victorian-era child sick with the flu," Summer would tell her), while his complexion looked like the Pond's cold cream she used to dab on from her mother's makeup bag, with a touch of rose-gold CoverGirl blush thrown in. *That's how it is when you're in your twenties*, she thought, taking another swig of Doubting Thomas.

"What a day," Summer said, pulling up a chair next to her. "This is a great crowd. Wonder how many follow him."

"He must have groupies, and I haven't heard him sing a single note. He's gorgeous," Kathleen said.

Summer squinted. "He's so ... skinny. I don't remember that when I met up with him. He looks like a damned anorexic."

"Stop. He does not."

"He does! Look, his clothes are literally hanging off of him."

"He makes a fine closet, then."

Summer leaned forward. "Does he have a limp or something?"

"Something. Maybe a sprained ankle."

"You always did go for weird-looking guys. Personally, I couldn't fuck anybody skinnier than me. Good thing Jeff's a big man."

Kathleen laughed in spite of herself. "You're terrible. All I said was he's cute. I didn't say I wanted to sleep with the guy. This is why your son is fruitfully multiplying, if he's as bad as you say. Sam's inherited your dirty mind."

Summer guffawed, "I don't deny it. But grandma-hood cannot be in my cards, yet." She waved to the panther and he came over to their table.

"Hi," he said, shaking Summer's hand, "Good to see you again."

"Likewise. Thomas, this is my buddy, barkeep, and trusty server, Kathleen Brooks. Kathleen, Thomas."

Their eyes and hands met, and a rush traveled down Kathleen's belly. "Hello," they said at the same time, smiling, and he didn't look away. She flushed and forced her head to turn. He and Summer discussed the night's agenda and freebies, while Kathleen risked a peek as he chatted. He had large teeth, unstained, with a slight gap in the front, and his bottom lip was fuller than the top. And, dear God, was that a dimple in his right cheek? She could not pull her eyes away, nor reign back in her rapidly releasing inhibitions.

"I'm getting another beer," she announced, standing up next to him. "May I bring you something?"

"Sure," he said, his gaze moving ever so briefly down her too-tight HopCanon shirt. A small silver hoop earring in his ear flashed as he shifted.

"What would you like?" Her face blazed ridiculously at the question she'd asked customers a hundred times.

"I'm easy to please. Surprise me."

The shiver returned. Innocent enough comments, but she was suddenly fifteen again sitting in front of Sears and wondering what it would be like to touch the Pond's-cold-cream-skin under the black sweater, pressing her finger to the dent in his cheek. "Surprise you. Maybe I will," she said, appalled at the flirty tone in her voice.

Are you nuts? He's a baby. What do you think you're doing? Besides, what makes you think he's interested?

But he was, if the traditional signals hadn't changed any. He was watching her every move with those amber-colored eyes, and not making any attempt to hide it.

He wrapped the leather guitar strap around his chest, as she approached with his beer. "Thanks," he said, their fingers touching as she handed it to him. "A stout?"

"Yes. A pint of Doubting Thomas for Singing Thomas," she said, hoping she sounded witty and not slightly drunk.

He laughed and his wide smile lit up the area as if he was on a real stage. "Quite appropriate. With a name like that, I hope it's good."

"So good I'm on my second one." She held her glass up, as if to confirm.

"Sweet. Cheers, then," he said, and they clinked their glasses together. He drank, watching her again with that same intensity. She didn't know what to do next; her body and tongue felt spongy and immobilized. "Have a good set," sounded like something you'd say to a child leaving for school.

Move. The command made it to her feet, so she finally turned and walked back to the table. One of the other servers cued to silence the bar music, and he adjusted the microphone.

Summer appeared and elbowed her. "I'll be back in a bit. I gotta take a call."

Kathleen nodded. Her attention was drawn to the entertainment.

"Hi, everyone. I'm Thomas Hart, and I'm psyched to be here, tonight, to share some tunes. When I'm not performing with my band, I mostly do soul-type covers, with an original thrown in, now and then." He looked up at the recessed lighting, which cast a brilliant sheen on his hair. "And what a cool place. I think I might be sitting in the choir's spot, so that's fitting. Let's hear it for HopCanon, for hosting live music."

Kathleen looked around as the crowd clapped, and her eye caught an older couple wading their way slowly through the people. The woman, tastefully dressed and her silver hair in a chic updo, was stooped behind a walker. The man was behind her and craning his neck for an open table.

They got closer to Kathleen and she could hear bits of their conversation.

"Let's just go home. This was a bad idea, coming out on a Friday night," the man said irritably.

"No. We sit at home all day and night, for Pete's sake. I think I see a spot right by the young man, there—"

"That's too close. I can't eat dinner with a bunch of goddamn noise blasting at me."

Kathleen rose swiftly and tapped the man's elbow. "You two can sit here," she said.

They both turned, the relief on their faces obvious. "Are you sure, honey?" the woman asked, concerned. "We don't want to inconvenience you. Where will you sit, now?"

"I don't mind standing," Kathleen said, even as her achy feet screamed for respite. "Please, take it."

"I think it's still too close," the man said, gesturing to Thomas, who was just beginning to strum. He smiled in their direction.

"Nonsense. This is perfect. Thank you so much, my dear."

Kathleen expertly folded the walker and rested it against the table. The woman's face stretched in surprise. "My goodness, looks like you have some experience with those wretched things."

"I do, I'm afraid." She held out her hand. "I'm Kathleen."

"Imogene Schmidt. And this is my husband, Bill." The husband in question was still surveying the place with a critical eye, and as he swiveled around, his hearing aid caught the light. "Bill!" his wife snapped.

He wrenched his neck back to them stiffly. "What?"

"This nice lady is Kathleen."

They shook hands. "Sorry. Bill Schmidt."

"Nice to meet you both," Kathleen said in a hush, hoping to limit the conversation, or at least get the volume down.

"I'll get the attention of your server, but I can bring you a drink if you'd like."

"Oh, you don't have to do that—"

"That would be very nice," Bill interrupted. "I don't suppose they've got Heineken at these fancy beer places."

"No," Kathleen smiled. "They have something similar, though. And for you, Imogene?"

"I'd better just have water. These medications my doctors have me on don't mix well with alcohol."

Kathleen had a momentary flash of a particularly bad bathroom episode with Steve, who'd consumed three drinks one evening, knowing full well the consequences later. Parkinson's meds didn't mix well with alcohol, either. "Okay," she said brightly, "I'll be right back with refreshments."

She ordered "Layman's Light" for Bill, a lager that was pale in both color and taste. Bartender Zack raised an eyebrow. "Not for you, I am guessing."

"No. For a newbie friend. Put it on my tab, please." Kathleen weaved back to the table and served the two just as Thomas was jamming to a Stevie Wonder song.

Imogene took the water gratefully. "Thank you so much, dear." She raised her voice, "Bill, look, Kathleen brought you your beer."

"Come again?"

"Your beer! Give her some money."

"Ah, yes." He fished out a ten-dollar bill and tried to give it to Kathleen.

"It's on me. Enjoy the show," she said, leaning up against a post to finally do the same.

She caught Thomas' eye as he sang. *"Ooh, baby, you set my soul on fire—"* He shook his head, his hair swinging out, and a rush bolted through her core down to her toes. Her enjoyment was not to last. Within minutes, there was arguing and hints of desperation at the table she'd given up.

"No. Just get me the walker, please."

"By God, you're a stubborn woman. You can't go by yourself," Bill's shout could be heard over the music.

Kathleen sighed and left her post. Observing the two was like looking in a queasy funhouse mirror; it was her former life, accompanied by a flood of relief that the image wasn't real. "Do you need to use the restroom?" she asked Imogene, gently. "I can go with you. Like I said, I've had some experience."

"We've now managed to intrude completely on your evening." Her voice was shaky, close to tears.

"You haven't. Come, it's fine."

But it was a twenty-minute ordeal, after which it was plain the woman was exhausted. They left the restroom and Imogene stopped and leaned against the wall, her bony knuckles gripping the walker's handles.

She smiled weakly. "You've been so kind to an old cranky couple, it won't be forgotten. Did you say you work here?"

"I do. Just started a couple months ago. The owners are good friends and I thought I'd try my hand at something new."

"I love what they've done with the place. We were married here, a million years ago. Did I mention that?"

"No." Kathleen grinned. "Does it feel strange to see it like this?"

"Not really. I'm glad the building is in use. To think it seemed old back then!" she chuckled softly. "But that's youth for you. Clueless, romantic. Let me tell you, in those days, Bill was the bee's knees, handsome as could be. He wasn't so crotchety, either." Her eyes, still a vibrant blue, seemed to beg Kathleen for understanding. "He's a good man, loyal and hardworking. My condition has taken such a toll on him. I can't even begin to say what he's sacrificed to take care of me." She flitted a hand in the air. "Oh, Lord, listen to me prattling on."

Kathleen touched her hand. "I understand. I took care of my husband for a long time before he died."

"I'm not one bit surprised. And you, so young. I hope he was appreciative."

"In his own way. Like you said, illness takes a toll."

"Yes." Imogene sighed deeply. "Our daughter ... she tangled with Bill over me, and now there's this horrible rift. She can't see that everything he does is out of love."

"Families can be difficult. I'm so sorry."

"No need. It is, as they say, what it is." Imogene shifted, then tried to straighten herself. "Now, may I ask one more thing from you? Then we shall leave you in peace."

"Of course."

"Could you tell Bill I think we need to go home? I can wait here. I'm just so ... tired."

"Absolutely." She didn't have to get him, because Bill was already there, jostling behind a couple of oblivious girls dancing to the music.

"Is she all right?" he asked Kathleen anxiously, loudly.

Kathleen bent close to his ear. "Yes, I think so. She wants to go home, though. I was just coming to get you."

"Okay. Thank you for helping." His face softened, showing Kathleen a glimpse of the man Imogene described earlier. "Ready to go, Genie?"

"I am. But one more thing." She turned toward Kathleen. "What's your last name, honey?"

"Brooks. Kathleen Brooks. Why—?"

"Never mind. Thanks for indulging a doddering old lady. Time to enjoy your night, now. And your fella, up there." She pointed to Thomas.

Kathleen flushed. "What? Oh, you're mistaken. I met him for the first time tonight."

"Is that right? He hasn't taken his eyes off of you since we walked in. I'd say you should get to know him." She peered behind her glasses. "Good-looking, though he could use a few good meals."

They bid goodbye, and thankfully Kathleen spotted Summer at the table the couple had vacated. "Hey, what happened to you?" Kathleen whispered, sitting down.

"Shit went to hell in the kitchen. It's all good now, though. Who were the old folks?"

"I'll tell you later."

Thomas slipped into an Otis Redding medley. He had that deep huskiness perfect for the genre and for doing Otis homage; so perfect that heads turned and mouths closed. Kathleen took several deep swallows of her forgotten pint and leaned back. She closed her eyes as the melancholy lyrics reverberated, drowning out any remaining background chatter.

"*... You were tired and your love is growing cold ...*" His voice was both a sweet balm and a reflection of her own exhaustion. The alcohol and the words swirled together, bringing latent emotions to a reluctant surface.

Oh, God, please. Please, not now.

Dammit, she *would* have fun again. She wouldn't be sad tonight, even if Doubting and Singer Thomas and Imogene and her walker were making it so. Anyway, where was this silly reaction coming from? Lately, she'd felt nothing but the weightless joy of fewer responsibilities. It was like being let loose in Candyland and deciding what treat to try next, to see what path led to the sweetest new adventure.

"Good, isn't he?" Summer examined her phone. "Listen, I gotta go. The home front is calling."

"Okay."

"Are you alright? Do you need a ride?"

"I'm fine, and no. I feel great, actually." It was true. Her limbs were loose, the threatening tears a memory already.

Her friend stared. "Call me if you need to."

"Will do." Kathleen fluttered her fingers. "Buh-Bye."

Summer laughed, "You're such a lightweight. Drink some water."

"I will. After this next song."

Which was, appropriately, "Brown Eyed Girl." Though Kathleen's eyes were more hazel than brown, it never seemed to matter. Everyone danced to Brown Eyed Girl, and that everyone included her, tonight.

"So, seeing that Valentine's Day is only two days away, I think I should help set the mood, if you don't mind," Thomas said. The crowd cheered, clearly not minding. "This is from Irish songwriter Foy Vance. Here's 'Feel for Me.'"

He wasn't kidding about setting the mood. The tempo was exquisitely slow and the guitar chords and his voice replete with longing. The cords in his neck bulged with the effort, and the incessant pub chatter nearly ceased, as did Kathleen's breathing as he repeated the song's title and lyrics about hearts on fire.

She glanced at the throng of people. Surely, this aching ballad had to be for a girlfriend, somewhere, perhaps in the audience. There did seem to be a table of rather enthusiastic folks with a few women, and after the song, he stopped for a brief break and talked with them. *The girl must be one of them*, she was thinking, feeling absurdly disappointed, just as he approached her table.

"May I?" he asked.

She lurched forward too quickly, almost upending a glass of water. “Sure.”

His long body filled up the empty space, and a blush bloomed on her cheeks and extended down her neck like a spreading wine stain. “Hi,” he said, slightly slouching back with his knees apart.

She swallowed. “Hi. Hey, you sound fantastic up there.”

“Thanks, but with these songs, I’m really just a good imitator. Hours of practicing pays off that way.” He leaned in. “I hope you’re sticking around?”

“I am. In fact, if I have much more Doubting Thomas, I might need a ride home.” The words flew out, the effect the same as if she’d erroneously pushed the send button on an electronic device. “Um, I mean, I wasn’t hinting. I guess that sounded bad.”

Shut. Up. Now. The irresistible urge to giggle launched upward, killed into oblivion as he stared at her.

“I think it sounds absolutely fine,” he said, and at that moment, the server, Deirdre, appeared and asked, or gushed, as Kathleen heard it, if Thomas would like another drink.

“Yes, thank you, another Doubting Thomas. And one for you, too?” he said, gesturing to Kathleen.

“Maybe just a five-ouncer. And some water, please.”

He continued with his quite unsettling direct perusal, and she tingled and fidgeted under its strength. To feel seen by someone so obviously attractive was a wonderful, foreign sensation to her.

His deep voice interrupted her thoughts. “You’re liking the show?”

“Very much. That is, what I’ve seen of it. There was an older couple—”

“Yes,” he chuckled, “I heard them. And I saw what you did.”

"I didn't do anything, just let them sit, that's all." Kathleen commented on the nearby table, "You have some fans, it would appear."

He turned, "Oh, those guys. They're all friends from work. My previous day job."

"Ah. And what was that, if I may ask?"

"I was a nurse in the psychiatric unit at St. Anthony's."

Her brow raised in surprise, "Is that right?"

"Yeah."

"How long did you do that?"

"Three years. And then I officially burned out. Or my body did, rather." He laughed a bitter laugh. "Pretty sad, isn't it?"

"No. Isn't it a risk for the profession?"

"I guess."

She finished off her pint. "One thing you always hear about nursing is how rewarding it is."

"And one thing you also hear about is how compassionate nurses are. I tried to be, but I wasn't."

"I find that hard to believe."

His neck jerked back slightly. "Really? We just met. I could be a horrible person, for all you know."

"I doubt it. Working in the service industry automatically qualifies me as an excellent judge of character. And you strike me as ..." *What, Kathleen? Magnetizing? Talented? The Solution to Celibacy? Check all of the above.*

She swallowed nervously, "As ... I don't know, warm?"

"Warm, huh?" he laughed, "That's a first."

She could feel the burn creeping up her neck again, "And not the last to say it, no doubt."

Deirdre appeared with their drinks. They both sipped, looking at each other while trying not to be obvious.

"So, how did you end up on the musical path?" Kathleen asked, gesturing to the stage.

He shrugged, causing the V in his sweater to shift and reveal a tuft of hair, and never was a dismissive movement so alluring. She tried not to gawk.

"My dad was a doctor and he wanted nursing for me. In his eyes, pursuing music was in the same category as becoming a tree-hugging yoga instructor. 'Pointless and empty-pocketed,' I believe were his words. You can imagine the resulting shitshow. Excuse my French."

"I actually like the idea of teaching yoga." She impulsively placed a hand on top of his, "But what I know for sure is that nurses are angels on earth. When my husband was dying, they literally saved my life. I'll bet some would say the same about music, too."

"I'm sorry for your loss." His expression belied the trite phrase, loosening her own thoughts.

I'm not. Not anymore. Steve could be a nasty, selfish prick. The forbidden voice was gone as quickly as it came, and she withdrew her hand, already missing his warmth. "Thanks," she murmured, then brightly, "On a lighter note, I'm glad I stayed after work to catch your act. What've you got planned next?"

"Mmm, let's see, a little John Mayer, a few other bluesy numbers. Any special requests?"

Oh, I'd like to request, all right.

For one terrifying second, she wondered if she'd said it aloud. No. He was still waiting for her answer.

"Just do what you do," she said, hoping she sounded nonchalant. He smiled and got up. He floated across the floor and her mind wandered, picturing his lithe legs wrapped up in hers, arching his back up and down like a cat and pressing inside of her, and she ground a fist to her forehead.

Sitting in front of Sears with Summer, all those years ago, had definitely left its mark.

2

After the set, he came back to the table, bending down close to talk since the taproom had returned to its noisy levels. He smelled woodsy, and his lips brushed her ear accidentally as someone pushed from behind, knocking him off balance.

"Sorry," she heard someone mutter. The brief contact with him sent a repeat tingle down her body, this one like an atom splitting in a thousand directions.

"It'll only take me a few minutes to load up my gear, if you still need that ride home. I'll be right back."

She nodded and watched him sweep up the equipment as if it were dust, even with the slight limp. She imagined him lifting sick people and their wires and tubes, maybe even forced to coerce or restrain uncooperative patients. Only someone fit could do that, someone with strong arms and a reassuring presence. Could he rescue widows with wavering self-esteem and no real sense of purpose, as well? In one night?

He was there, then, towering over her, "Ready?"

"Ready." *For what, exactly?*

He led her out to his Subaru. She told him her address,

and she willed herself to look out the window to calm the jangling in her belly. Upon arriving, he parked, and her head spun with what to do next. Expressing appreciation would be a start, she surmised.

"Thanks for the ride," she said, grasping the unmoving door handle.

He reached across her, his hair falling forward and peach-creamy skin inches away. For all his slenderness, his face was not haggard. "The lock jams, sometimes," he said, yanking at the mechanism, and she pulled his hand away and placed hers on top, tracing his fingers. She couldn't help it; she'd been mesmerized all night by the way they'd produced lovely melodies, by the intricate pattern of veins wrapping around his wrists and forearms. *Like vines on a tree*, she thought, entranced as she studied them once more.

"You have beautiful hands," she said quietly, her eyes darting up. "It probably sounds geeky, but I like to ... sketch portraits, for a hobby." She traced a ropy vein, "And I could draw this for days."

He smiled and laced his fingers around hers. "Not geeky," he said, sweeping in for a luscious, alcohol flavors-combining, tongues-barely-entwining kiss. She was the one to break off, beyond flummoxed at the turn of events.

"You should know I turn forty this summer."

"Okay," he said slowly.

"I mean, I have wrinkles. In places you can't see. And I'm getting a double chin."

He laughed, the gap in his teeth and his deliciously wide mouth causing more twinges to run straight through her. "And you're very attractive. Maybe it's the youthful freckles on your nose."

He brushed a thumb across one cheek and she felt her skin raise like braille under his touch. "They're technically sun damage. A sign of aging," she blurted foolishly. What on earth was she babbling about? She'd had the sprinkle across the bridge of her face her whole life.

"I'm turning thirty in November," he said. "Does that sound better than twenty-nine?"

She wondered if he was making fun of her, but his smile was gentle, not mocking. He leaned in as if for another kiss, "Tell me, are you purposely trying to kill the mood?"

"No, I ... I just believe in laying your cards out on the table. No games. As I said before, I'm widowed, with a grown stepdaughter. No kids. We—I mean, I—couldn't. I wanted a baby *(that time),* but it didn't happen."

"Ah. Same here. The no kid part, I mean. Which will be permanent."

There was an awkward pause and she shifted. *What? Cancer survivor? Hate children? How did this end up on the table? Because you put it there, dumbass ...*

"Not because I don't like them," he added. "I happen to firmly believe the world doesn't need a clone of myself out there."

"I beg to differ," she said, and he laughed again, this time kissing her. This time, harder, but not a plunge-down-her-throat hard. The right balance of pressure, no fish-lips, and no gross saliva smeared on her upper lip. He was insanely good, from what she could remember about kissing. Steve had been perfunctory about it; done for foreplay and not much else.

Her heart battered in her chest like a ram charging a rock wall. He backed up and caressed her cheek.

"Well." She was an aroused bundle of nerves. "Now that our confessionals are over, what happens next?"

A teasing smile, then, "What would you like to have happen next?"

"That's a loaded question ... but ... that song you did, by the Irish guy?"

"I've got his music on a CD, here. Want to listen to it?"

The battering doubled. "Yes, I do. Inside, with you. If you want to, that is. Or I could just borrow it."

"I would love to go inside."

"I have animals," she said. "I hope you like animals? Oh, my God, I sound like a rambling idiot. I'm not saying another word. I'm sorry."

He pulled the compact disc out. "My ex-girlfriend has the dog we rescued, and I have the cat," he said, taking her chin with his thumb and forefinger. "Maybe just nod, if you agree we won't be sorry for anything tonight."

She laughed, her head bobbing.

"Great," he said, and opened the car door for her, the tricky jam cooperating, for the moment.

Foy Vance wasn't the only one crooning on the CD. Song after song came on, each one a similar theme accompanying the furious make-out session in her living room.

She came up for air and said, "Wait. I've got to ask. Are we listening to a sex mix?"

He actually blushed, "I know that's what it sounds like, but, no. I make a bunch of these to practice for gigs and try to group them in themes. I feel like individual mixes should be more ... personalized. But, hey," he said, stroking her forearms, "They say if the shoe fits ..."

"It fits, all right," she breathed in sharply, then chuckled. "This sounds awful, but when we were teenagers, Summer and I made lists we called 'screwing songs.' Doesn't every girl who goes to parochial school do that? Probably not."

He laughed, "I'd like to know what was on your list."

"Trust me, nothing that original. I mostly went with the Seventies stuff my older brothers were blasting out of the basement." She gazed upward, "Let me think ... Barry White, Van Morrison's 'Mystic,' The Stones, Atlanta Rhythm Section, Rod Stewart, and, of course, Bad Company."

"Did you have a favorite out of your catalog?"

She leaned her head back, "Ahh, I don't know. Maybe 'Into the Mystic.' To be honest, I remember wishing someone would compose and dedicate a song to me. Then we would magically consummate our love to this perfect panty-dropper." She giggled, "Typical egocentric teen stuff. Even funnier, I probably would've run as fast as I could in the other direction if anyone had done such a thing."

A grin played at his lips, "Nothing unusual about that. Are you saying your lists didn't have the desired outcome?"

"Um ... no." She looked away. "They really never made it out of my head, I guess."

He lifted his glass, "Here's to their belated release."

A nervous thrill snaked through her at the certainty of what was unfolding. "Yes, cheers. This is delish. Like drinking dessert. Which beer is it?"

"Act of Contrition. It's not available to the common folk yet, according to your co-worker Zack. He heartily recommended it."

She threw her head back and laughed, "That's rich. Of all the titles."

"What's funny?"

"An Act of Contrition, if you didn't know, is also a prayer you say apologizing for your sins. I have it memorized like the Pledge of Allegiance."

"A Catholic prayer," he said.

"Yes. Are you? Catholic, I mean?"

"For a time, but I don't remember a whole lot, except for un-becoming one."

"That sounds like a story, there."

He leaned in and kissed her neck. "Not a pleasant one,

really. And I think we're exempt from any Acts of Contrition. Since we discussed apologies earlier."

"We did," she said, her voice cracking like an adolescent boy's. Feeling brazen, she took her shirt off, then her bra, and laid back on the couch. To her horror, she was shaking, but it didn't faze him. His warm nurse's hands soothed the skittish patient, his guitar-driven callouses polishing her skin to a sheen. She closed her eyes and listened to the music streaming, and the hairs on her arms stood up. Through her haze, she stopped him, "This song ... it's lovely. Is it you?"

"Yes. I've been trying to find a home for it for a while now. Maybe I just did."

She wasn't sure what that meant, but no surprise there. *This is what happens when you get naked with strangers who give you goosebumps and drink a beer called Doubting Thomas all night. Can you say 'cliché'?*

The next few lyrics meant it didn't matter.

"*... I want to do with you what lonely people do ...*"

As that lyric was sung, he laid next to her, his sweater brushing her bare chest. "Damn," she whimpered, and tears trickled out down the sides of her cheeks. "I don't know if I can do this." He wiped a drop away. His eyes brimmed with gentleness.

"Okay."

"I'm really not some head case, I swear it. It's just ... it's been years, at least three or four, since touching like this, and I've forgotten ..." she trailed off as his lips traveled downward. He moved back up and brushed her bangs away from her face.

"We can stop right now if you want."

She exhaled heavily. "Please don't."

More kissing, their heated breath mingling and ramping up to another level. He pulled his lips away and went to her throat, while his hands went to her pants and began tugging them off. "So, a refresher for your memory is in order? Possibly multiple ones?"

She shivered at the blatant suggestion. *Multiple? With me? I'd be happy for one ...*

"Yes. Past time."

He removed the sweater, and at last she could see and feel what laid underneath, the ridges of his biceps, made even more prominent due to his lack of body fat. He had soft, curly chest hair, and she buried the side of her face there, the swirls absorbing any traces of wetness from her cheek.

After several minutes, she lifted her face to his.

"Better?" he asked.

Nodding, she pressed into him, every last doubt eviscerated. She watched as he unzipped his jeans, her eyes fixated on the tantalizing, vertical line of dark hair down his belly. She tugged at his arms in expectation, but he only chuckled as he lay back down.

"All in good time," he whispered, and his hands resumed their magic work. He was the artist now, with his fingers velvet brushes and her body a willing canvas.

"Ah," she said, gripping his stationary arm and arching her back. He backed away slightly.

"Don't stop," she begged.

"I won't. But I want to see you."

His rhythm never wavered, as flawless as it had been plucking the guitar strings, and the mounting cascade in her hips descended. He was inside her then, with precious little space there from having been unoccupied for so long. He drew a sharp breath and his neck muscles strained the same way they had when he'd sung earlier that night.

The tip of his nose brushed her ear, "Are you all right?"

"Yes." This was far beyond any teenage erotica fantasy

she could've conjured up, or, for that matter, any adult ones. She gripped his back with a sudden, fierce strength.

If it was sinful, there would be no atonement offered.

At some point, they'd moved up to her bedroom, and she was glad the sheets at least were clean. The sun was making a rare appearance for February, and when her eyes opened, the light cracked a whip in the middle of her forehead. She turned to him. He was on his back, still asleep. The flowered sheet was molded tight across his chest, then gaped at his torso. He had one arm curled above his head, the muscles popping with the bend. She peered closer, her gaze traveling down the side of his body, and her belly clenched at the sight of several intertwining scars. She resisted the urge to touch the raised, white ridges staring back at her, the long, zigzagged silverfish, shiny in the morning light. How had she not seen this last night? She didn't want to think about what kind of trauma had caused such an injury. Had an unstable patient attacked him? Her insistent fingers had a mind of their own, reaching out to trace the bolts of lightning etched upon his skin, and of course his eyes flitted open.

She yanked her hand back as if burned by a stove. "Sorry. I didn't mean to wake you."

"It's okay." He moved so that the sheet dropped just above his jutting pubic bone, and a wave of want flushed through her. Not even the throb in her head nor angry scars were enough to staunch the flood. "Be right back," she said. She crept out of bed and went to the bathroom. Whatever else happened, she had to brush the cotton out of her mouth and make some attempt to not look dreadfully hung over. She put a robe on and came out, and he was perched upright on two pillows.

"The scars are from a nasty car accident as a teenager," he volunteered. "I've got so much metal in my leg and hip, my friends called me Magneto."

She smiled faintly, "By the looks of it, you're lucky to be alive."

"I didn't think of myself as lucky at the time. I have days when I still wonder." He shifted in the bed and squinted. "Could you do me a huge favor and bring me some water? And my jeans over there?"

"Of course," she said, and was back a few minutes later with a cold bottle.

"Thanks," he said, and promptly swallowed pills he'd dug out of his pants pocket.

"I didn't mean to make you wait on me so soon," he said jokingly, then saw her alarmed face and laughed.

"No worries. I hate taking pain pills, for a number of reasons. But this leg is a bitch, and I'd rather not move until it takes effect. I'm guessing this is better than filling your room up with the lovely aroma of weed."

"I actually like that smell."

He eyeballed her, skeptical, "Are you joking?"

"No. My husband used it to relieve symptoms. The difference was nothing short of miraculous."

"Good for him."

She studied him with concern. She knew well the facial expressions accompanying discomfort. "Is it like this every morning for you?"

"Not always." He reached out and caressed her cheek. "I attribute it to recent strenuous activity."

"Mmm—sorry for that."

"I'm not."

She wound her hair up into a ponytail. "Listen, I'm going

to go feed the animals and let the dog out. Lay here and rest."

He didn't answer, just closed his eyes, and when the tasks were done, she deliberately took her time going back upstairs. When she did, it was followed by a flurry of swishing tails. "Hugo and Harriet like their morning kisses," Kathleen said.

"Awe," he said, scratching their ears and getting a lick from Hugo in return. "Now, this is a nice way to wake up."

The sheet dropped away as he slowly maneuvered himself out of bed. "Do you have a spare toothbrush, by any chance?"

She said yes, to open a new one out of the drawer next to the sink. He stood up and winced. He rubbed his thigh, standing there in her bedroom gloriously naked, and she couldn't take her eyes off of him. His rippled scars glinted in the morning light, ranging in color from whitish-silver to a faded rose. The designs ran from his hip all the way down to his ankle, at certain points, puckering up like miniscule dried-up gourds.

He cast an embarrassed glance at her, "Sorry. I'm not exactly a pretty sight in broad daylight."

"No need to apologize. And I couldn't disagree more." He laughed and got moving. "There's also another robe on the back of the door, if you'd like," she called after him.

Their robes were unisex and identical, other than a slight variation in color. He came out of the bathroom, the velour hugging his neck, and she wished she was that collar.

He sat on the bed and pulled at the sleeve. "Was this your husband's?"

"I'm wearing his. I like it because it's a bit softer. You have mine on."

"Ah. That's why it smells so good."

She sat back and wound a finger through a strand of his

hair. “Isn’t this the part where you ask yourself, what were you thinking last night?”

“No. Last night was amazing.”

She blanched. She hated that word, hated how millennials threw it around to describe everything from a donut to a trip to Disney World.

“Amazing like when you take a picture of your food and wine pairing and post it on Instagram? Or when you describe bagging the old lady to your buddies?”

His expression was deadpan, “Wow. First of all, I pretty much avoid social media other than for my music. And second, I’m not an eighteen-year-old frat boy.”

She shook her head, chastened, “I’m sorry. Last night ... you ... it *was* incredible. I guess I just want to give you an out. To make this easier.”

“To make what easier?”

“You know.”

“I don’t.”

He clearly didn’t mind making her spit it out, and this piqued her. She waved her hands around. “Please. Easier for you to say, ‘Thanks. Nice knowing you. Nice hook-up. Adios.’”

He lay back and propped up on his elbow with the robe half-open, his hair mussed as if a stylist had just given his locks the beachy look, rather than a result of wild-lovemaking bedhead. His pose was that of a model, too, like the centerfold model straight from the October *Playgirl* issue her older cousin Annette had shoplifted years ago, when they’d secretly pored over the pictures in Kathleen’s closet with a flashlight. Only, she wasn’t fourteen anymore, and the flesh and blood body in front of her, perfect in its imperfections, was no airbrushed image on a glossy magazine page.

“What if I want to see you again?” he said.

"You don't." She was reluctant to look up at him, for fear he'd see the hope in her eyes. "Do you?"

He sat back up and ran a finger in-between her robe. "If I'm honest, this *would* be when I'd hit the road. I can't remember the last time I spent the entire night with someone. Not that there's a line of prospects waiting at the door or anything."

She didn't know whether to be annoyed, appalled, or complimented. And she was damned sure he could have his pick of any number of women he wanted, metal wounds or not. "What's different this time?"

His finger stopped on her breast, then dropped away. "Call it a lack of next-day dread. Of being seen moaning and groaning and not able to get out of bed in the morning." He hesitated, gazing into space. "Hey, that could be a good lyric, there. I've got to remember that one." His gaze returned to her. "I don't feel that avoidance with you. Anything but."

"That's nice, to not be avoided."

He laughed, "Listen, I like you. I think we have a real connection. Why don't you tell me what you're thinking? Maybe all this—" he pointed to his hip— "is enough for *you* to say adios."

"What? Why would you say that?"

"Seriously? You don't think some women would run as fast as they could from a gimpy pill popper?"

Not if they had the kind of night I did. "And have they?"

"I suppose I don't give them the chance. I should add manic depressive to my list of impressive qualities, as well. I mean, it's mostly under control, but when it isn't—ah, never mind."

She pushed a lock of hair behind her ear. "Help me out. Where would we go from here? Do we date? Do everything backwards? I don't even know how long you plan to be in town."

"I'm working on a new record here with my band for at least three more months, maybe longer. Our manager is working on getting us gigs after that. Probably for six months. What's wrong with taking this one day at a time, enjoying each other's company while we can?"

She was silent for a few seconds, staring at his five o'clock shadow, the whiskers dotting his dimple and the pale robe against his skin, and fought the ridiculous urge to cry. "Sounds like advice when you get a terminal disease diagnosis."

"I suppose it does."

"I apologize. I'm in a strange place right now. I don't have the faintest idea of how to navigate this—" she put both hands out in front of her— "whatever *this* might be." She glanced up at him furtively, "I admit I have desperately missed sex. But I'm sure that's obvious."

"You're human. What would it say about you if you didn't miss it?"

"That I'm a nice, chaste Catholic good-girl."

"I think Billy Joel said it best. Only the good die young ... and Catholic girls start much too late."

She laughed. "Great song, but trust me, that wasn't me back in the day." She fiddled with the edge of the bedsheet. "Here's *my* thing. I'm neurotic and I crave boundaries." *And you bulldozed through a dozen of them in one night.* "I like to know the ending of the story at the beginning. And expiration dates ... those do scare me."

"Who says there's an expiration date?"

"You just admitted you don't spend the night with people and you run before they can. I'd say the odds are good there's a use-by date."

He spread his arms out innocently. "Well, I'm here. You've already broken one pattern."

She was flustered with the direction the conversation

was taking. What was he trying to convince her to do? Why did she feel the need to argue?

"Wouldn't you say it's common knowledge that life on the road doesn't seem to be conducive to ... to relationships?"

He shrugged, sexy and unassuming wrapped up in one package. "Maybe I'm not so common. And maybe you shouldn't buy into every musical stereotype out there."

Her cheeks warmed. "You're telling me you're an exception?"

His eyes took her in like a hungry wolf, and she the wary goat. "For the right one."

"That's kind of a crappy answer. Putting the responsibility all on someone else, if they meet your expectations."

"Touché. I tried to tell you last night, I might be a horrible person. So horrible I suggest we cut to the chase. Stop talking about relationships and just make up for all that lost sex you alluded to. The amount of which appears to be extensive."

She laughed at his audacity. "My God. You really mean that, don't you?"

"I do." His nimble fingers parted her robe slightly. "What's wrong with sharing pleasure if all parties are honest? Besides, you can't deny we've got a nice head start."

"Nothing is—wrong with it. But I don't believe in *using* others. Nor do I truly believe sex and love should be separated. I know that sounds like silly church-lady nonsense."

His lips danced at the corners, so amused was he at this comment. "You don't strike me as the hypocritical type."

She stiffened. "That's not fair. I had a vulnerable window last night. This isn't normally who I am."

Now you're a liar AND a hypocrite ...

He parted her robe all the way. "Look, if this is where you want it to end, I respect that. But if you're game, I'd like to keep the window open and find out for myself. Who you normally are, that is."

She closed her eyes as his nose brushed her chest, every remaining protest flying out that hypothetical window. "Why? Do you like being disappointed?"

He shook his head, the ends of his hair tickling her skin. "What? No, I say it because the world can be a cold and lonely place, and I'm thinking we manic depressives and neurotics need to stick together."

Kathleen moaned. She was definitely game.

3

They were rarely apart for the next month, except for work and her attending church. It appeared the sky was indeed falling, at least in her world. To Kathleen, everything about her behavior with him was rife with incongruity, out of place and uncomfortable. Yet, the idea of giving him up was equally distasteful. Within weeks, she'd morphed into an unrepentant, gluttonous sponge soaking him in. When she thought she was saturated, she still wanted more. More of his half-smiles, more of his hands on her, more of his hair brushing her shoulder, more of his maleness filling spaces inside her and out. More, more, more. Like a toddler using sign language, only speaking in tongues instead of asking for cheerios. She was certain this frenzied need had to be in the same family as a chemical addiction. Then again, she didn't want to examine that possibility too much. Addiction meant eventual withdrawal, and her body would fight that surely as any waning substance.

She looked over at her alarm clock. Nine-twenty; still plenty of time to make the ten-thirty mass. She reluctantly threw the covers off and headed to the bathroom, turning the shower on as hot as she could stand. She waited, shivering. Here it was the end of March and the weather was still like February. Afterward, she put a robe on and went downstairs to let Hugo out, the chill in the air sending her scrambling back up to Thomas' side. He hadn't stirred. She stood there, the internal debate about church ping-ponging in her head, but she was lured to him like the deer in her backyard eyeing the salt licks. The does would come with their huge brown eyes searching and white tails flicking, not knowing if compromise lurked. In the end, the treat was always too much for them to resist. She sat on the bed and brushed the thick hair away from his face. She traced his nose lightly with a fingertip, marveling at its tiny but asymmetrical bend. He'd told her it was due to a break when he was young. Her fingers moved on to his mouth and his eyes twitched open.

He stretched, a momentary vision of rippling ribs and muscle. She'd been cooking many homemade meals of late, and the bit of added weight on his frame was transformative.

"Are you taking advantage of me while I sleep?"

"No. I was thinking if anyone ever tells you to get a nose job, don't listen to them." She took off her robe and climbed into bed. "Just saying."

"That's an interesting thought to voice first thing in the morning." He propped his head up with a bent elbow, the sheet crumpled under his armpit. "Someone did suggest it, once. As if I haven't had enough surgery already."

She snuggled her ear to his chest and listened to the steady beat of his heart. "I don't believe you."

"Believe it. It was my ex-fiancé. Her name was Julie."

Kathleen's head bobbed up. "You're serious. And I didn't know you had an ex- fiancé."

"Yup. But she had, shall we say, an unhealthy obsession with perfection."

"I think you just described me with you," she said, her hand going around his back.

He laughed. "I'm okay with obsession. But I'm far from perfect." He stretched over her, trying to read the time on the clock. "I thought you were going to mass."

"What's the expression? The spirit is willing but the flesh is weak?" *And missing during Lent, yet.* She touched the tiny dent in his cheek once more, her voice lowering a notch. "But I was staring at this man with a crooked nose in my warm bed and I couldn't bring myself to go."

"Hmm. Should I see if I can round up Jimmy McFarland for another game of sandlot baseball and he can aim at my nose again? Couple more breaks and I could keep you trapped here forever."

"It'd take far less than that," she said, rolling on top of him.

She added this casual disregard of mass to her mental list of sins, measuring the cost of preferring sixty minutes with him versus sixty minutes sitting in a hard pew, when listening to the word of God came down to one less hour reveling in his arms. And she knew the price was worth whatever it extracted from her.

There was one other activity that meant not one but two less hours with him, and that was Kathleen's bi-weekly meeting with the teen group she'd been bamboozled into leading. Sheila Gallagher had cornered her after church, one day, not long after Steve died. She was the catechism director at their parish, St. Joseph's, and she was skilled at cornering people.

"Since you won't do catechism, would you at least consider leading a girls' youth group? It wouldn't be that big. The teens need someone to listen to them, and a good role model."

Sheila was one of those people who appeared to be in a perpetual state of panic. She ran around like a mouse in a maze most of the time, trying to corral recalcitrant pupils, the overscheduled parish priest, Father Anthony, and apathetic parents. She was also maddeningly persuasive, a requirement for anyone trying to recruit volunteer religion teachers. She had red frizzy hair and a kind heart, and Kathleen liked her from the minute they'd met.

"I told you I'd be a terrible teacher," Kathleen said. "And I don't know why you persist in thinking I'd be this great mentor. I'm not a good person at least fifty percent of the time."

Sheila laughed. "Those are pretty impressive odds. But I'm not looking for some paragon of virtue, or even a teacher. I need a caring heart, which you do have."

"I thought Paul Johnson was the youth group leader."

"He is. But he can't take this project on right now. For some good reasons."

"What would those be, if I may ask?"

Sheila hesitated. "Well ... for one, they are girls, and two, all four of them are pregnant."

Kathleen stared. "You're joking."

"I wish."

"Well, what on earth would I be doing with them? I know next to nothing about pregnancy and babies."

Not completely accurate, but still.

Sheila knew she had her now and she wiggled with excitement. "Who cares? You're great with kids and that's all that matters. Honestly, it'd be super low-key. You could meet once a week to check in, hang out, listen to their concerns, and see what they need. Maybe open and close with a couple of prayers, talk about challenges ahead, that kind of thing."

"Super low-key? Now you *are* joking. Four hormonal girls facing the biggest hurdle of their lives? You're making it sound like we'd be sitting around eating popcorn and watching Netflix."

Sheila nodded vigorously. "Yes! You could do that!"

"Oh, I don't know about this, really ..."

Sheila's enthusiasm would not be deterred. "Kathleen, this completely ties in with what our churches should be doing. We've spent a gazillion hours and dollars on the pro-life movement. We need to support the girls, whether they opt for adoption, or not, before and after their pregnancies. And provide a safe space for all of it."

Kathleen sighed. "Where would we meet?"

"I guess it's up to you, depending on any activity you might want to do. The community hall room would be yours. For a while, anyway. I know there's a plan to remodel starting soon. Then you'd have to find a different meeting spot."

And that had been that. So far, it was going better than Kathleen anticipated. Getting to know them had been a highlight of her week. The group met every-other-Wednesday at six-thirty, and lately, she and Thomas had dinner beforehand. Today, he'd texted her he'd be at her place around five.

"Hi," he said, holding up two paper bags of take-out and setting them on the counter. "I brought Chinese."

"Mmm. That sounds good. Smells good, too."

He wrapped an arm around her waist and dove into her neck. "Not as good as you. And it definitely won't taste as good as you. The Chinese may have to wait, since I had to."

She threw her head back with a deep chuckle. "Wait ... what's it been, three days?"

He didn't answer, too busy stripping off her pants. He maneuvered her to the adjoining laundry room and lifted her on top of the washer.

"Well. This is a first," she said, a sharp intake of breath whistling through her teeth.

"It's the perfect height." He kissed the inside of her thighs. "And so are you."

The control panel dug into the small of her back, fighting against the other sensations shooting up and through her mutinous body. "I've got to get ready for my group—"

"This won't take long," he said, his head bowed, and he was infuriatingly correct. Afterward, he leaned across the washer and kissed her on the mouth. "See? And plenty of time to have dinner too." He pulled her to the floor.

She scurried about, slipping her sweatshirt on and picking up the rest of her discarded clothes. "You're a bad influence, you know that? I should've been using this time to prepare."

"What better way to get there than your current state? Satisfaction is sacred, I say." He stuck a spoon into a carton of rice.

"Good Lord," she snapped, shaking her forgotten bra in the air. "I can't be distracted. Those girls depend on me."

"I know. I'm sorry." He drew her in, plucking the garment from her hands with a sheepish grin. "But you don't really need this for reciting the Lord's Prayer, do you?"

"Technically, no. But they pay attention to things. I can hear them now: 'Let's all go braless! Who cares if we're pregnant? Ms. Kathleen does it,' they'd tell their horrified parents."

He laughed, his dimple deflating her annoyance like a popped balloon. "You could tell the horrified folks Ms.

Kathleen's boyfriend likes the freeing of the tatas look even more. On her, of course."

She grabbed the bra and sat at the counter to eat the kung pao chicken he'd dished out. "Have we crossed a line, now? Are we calling each other boyfriend and girlfriend?"

"I don't care much about labels. Does the word 'lover' sit better with you?"

"Yes. No. I don't know. That's the problem." She stared at him; at his lips and that sensuous mouth, bearer of exquisite ecstasy only minutes ago. "I don't know where to put you, or myself when I'm with you."

He leaned back and folded his arms behind his head, a stance that had proven in record time to be her Achilles' heel. "Such a quandary. Whatever will you do with me?"

A good question, one she couldn't answer, and she was puzzled by her irritation. Was it him thoughtlessly bouncing the boyfriend description around, knowing the use of this term hadn't been solidified between them? The age difference, always lurking in the back of her mind? The sex, a half-hour before Bible passages? All of it, most likely. And yet, what was *wrong* with her, acting like a whiny schoolmarm? The man had demanded nothing except her company, had only provided weeks of endless pleasure. She shook her head and proceeded to gather her notebook and materials for the evening. She made it to the community room and congratulated herself on making it there with ten minutes to spare. It was only halfway through reciting the Lord's Prayer that she bumped the table's edge, wincing, and realized in her rush to get there she was, in fact, braless.

The group mainly consisted of four girls: Francesca, Mallory, Brianne, and Amanda. The format was simple.

They began with prayer, had a small snack, then conversation and an activity, and closed with another prayer. Kathleen had an idea about introducing art as a focus. She knew it could be a middle-ground stress-reliever, not to mention it'd be a chance for her to hone her skills, but she was still mulling over the possibilities.

"I smell something," said Francesca, wrinkling her pert little nose and clutching her rounded belly. "Is it Chinese food? Is that the snack? I hope not. I'm allergic to shrimp, and this morning sickness should be called all-day sickness."

Kathleen's face flushed. "Chinese food is not tonight's snack." *No, that came after the appetizer.* "Amanda brought oranges for us. Shall we peel them?"

They did so, the refreshing citrus scent filling the air.

"I ordered these oranges from Derek," Amanda said. "It's a band fundraiser deal. They're from Florida. Pretty good, but I only bought them so I could talk to him."

"Who's Derek?" Kathleen asked.

"A band nerd," said Brianne, sucking the juice out of a slice.

"No, he's not," Amanda snapped, then appeared to reconsider. "Well, I guess Derek *is* kinda nerdy. But he's so hot anyway."

Brianne lifted a pierced eyebrow. She was the "emo" out of the group; her clothes, hair, nails and makeup all in varying shades of black. "Sure, he is. If you are into guys so skinny they look like heroin addicts."

Amanda scowled. "You'd know, wouldn't you?"

"Girls," Kathleen broke in. She tried to be firm, but she was thinking about Thomas. Did he look like a heroin addict? Black clothes, thin frame, pale skin?

"I'm sorry, but I think it's totally gross you'd say that about Derek," Brianne said. "I mean, what about Chase?

Last week you said he'd better ask you to marry him, and this week you're on about a guy who only knows you as the chick in eleventh grade who got knocked up."

Amanda's eyes filled with tears. "Screw Chase! On Monday we had a big fight and I'm not talking to him. He'd be the worst person to marry, *ever*, and a terrible dad, and I told him that, too."

The room was quiet with this admission. Kathleen said softly, "Sounds stressful."

"You're not kidding. I wanted to kill him."

"Guys just basically suck," said Brianne.

"Yeah, they do," agreed Mallory. "But it's not all their fault. I learned in science class it's kind of because their brains are underdeveloped until they turn, like, twenty-five, or something. So, until then, they do lots of crazy, dumb crap."

"God, I hope I have a girl," Francesca said, to which the other three nodded.

"Well, you might all have boys," Kathleen said briskly. "What then?"

"Pray," said Mallory, and everyone laughed.

"Speaking of praying, let's talk about Lent, what you've been doing," Kathleen said. "It's almost over. Mallory, you gave up Facebook, right?"

Mallory had a plain, sweet face and swore life as a nun had been calling her, until a seventeen-year-old guy named Brad did just that. Or had been calling her before learning of the pregnancy. "Yeah," Mallory nodded. "People just use Facebook to brag. I don't miss it."

"But you were, like, never on it," Francesca said, sounding imperious.

Francesca was the honor student, the cheerleader, and all-star athlete in the group. None of the others particularly liked her. Kathleen once overheard them refer to her as three FD, and when confronted they hemmed and hawed and gave a weak explanation about nicknames. Later, Mallory had come to Kathleen and nervously told her what the letters really stood for: "Francesca the Football Fuck Doll," she'd whispered, although she couldn't bring herself to vocalize the F-word. She'd mouthed it, instead. Kathleen was horrified. "What is that supposed to even mean?" she asked Mallory, who replied it was well known Francesca was a fan of the school's football team. Rumor had it, Francesca wasn't even sure who the father of her baby was. Kathleen had mumbled something about the toxicity of gossip and changed the subject immediately.

Francesca applied lip balm with the word POMEGRANATE in purple letters on the side of the tube. "How is giving up Facebook a sacrifice if you didn't even like it in the first place?"

Mallory sunk down in her chair and Brianne addressed Francesca, her eyes squinting with irritation. "Maybe Miss Perfect can suggest a better way to show God how pathetic we are."

"I think God knows our weaknesses already," Kathleen said quickly. "But Francesca brings up a valid point about the meaning of sacrifice."

After a few more minutes of soothing the ruffled feathers, Kathleen encouraged more discussion about the spiritual reasons behind withholding pleasures and whether they'd achieved their intentions. She swallowed her embarrassment as thoughts of Thomas flipped through her head. There had been no forgoing of pleasure on her end, that was for sure. The conversation turned to the band fruit, and there was unanimous agreement nobody had tasted better citrus since the twelfth-grade student council sponsored a grapefruit sale for a class trip to Florida.

"Maybe I'll have to give up staring at Derek for the rest

of Lent," Amanda said mournfully, and Brianne rolled her eyes. "Omigod, such a hardship. That'd be for, like, one week."

Kathleen sighed, exhaustion creeping in her voice from the effort to keep the peace. "Okay, girls. Time to clear the table and put chairs away."

The group obliged without complaint, and Kathleen turned the lights off as they trotted out. "Next week is Holy Week, so we won't meet. I hope you all have a wonderful Easter, if I don't see you."

"Do you have plans, Ms. K?" asked Mallory.

"You know, other than mass, I'm not sure. Probably have dinner at my mom's. What about you?"

She shoved her purse to her other hip. "At my dad's. I can't wait until I can decide where to go and what to do on holidays. And I think at that point, I'll just stay home."

Kathleen nodded sympathetically. "I get that," she said. They walked out and Kathleen locked the doors, thinking about her mother and whether to invite Thomas for Easter, and staying at home was looking better and better to her, too.

"It's a good thing I had a loose-fitting sweatshirt on," Kathleen complained after letting herself in. Thomas was on the couch, watching sports.

"Ah, yes. I found this after you left," he twirled the bra around his finger. "I did laugh, needless to say."

"No doubt." She stood in the living room, hands on her hips, and the prickliness of before invaded once again. "And I'm failing to see the humor."

He clicked the television off. "I can see that."

"What you don't see is how hard it is to reconcile this other person I've become. With you. Since ... you."

"I see it," he said, crossing his arms. "I think it's a mistake to believe the 'other person' wasn't always there. I'm just a happy conduit, unpeeling the layers."

She waved a hand in the air, pacing, her voice thick with sarcasm. "Great. So I've always had a hidden, insatiable *maniac* lying in wait. Good to know. There I was tonight, sitting there listening to a group of girls telling me they're using their babysitting money to give to the Lent Rice Bowl charity, and they're doing chores for their old neighbors and doing dishes for their bratty brothers, and in-between all of this, they are dealing with family stuff and worrying about their pregnancies." The pacing escalated.

"And? What's the problem? They sound like a nice bunch."

"Yes! Yes, they are, when they're not bickering. But what am I doing, amidst these charitable works? Let's see, I'm having explosive orgasms forty minutes before we wash our hands for a snack. Or how about in the shower, the bed, the floor. I'm sure I must be leaving some place out, here."

"Still not seeing the problem." His lazy amusement fueled her annoyance.

"For heaven's sake. The *problem* is that nice, widowed women who are supposed to be mentors for teenage girls don't have oral sex on top of their washing machines and then go off to church to meet with said girls."

"Says who?" he said calmly. He petted Hugo, who had trotted over, nervous at the rising emotion in the room.

"I say it, that's who."

"Wait, what year is this? 1952 or 2018? Come *on,* Kathleen. Would you judge anyone else, a girlfriend maybe, as harshly as you do yourself?"

"Okay," she said, her head bobbing. "You got me there, but I'm not talking about anyone else. I'm talking about me."

A half-smile played about his lips. "All right. Marry me, then. Problem solved."

She clamped her jaw shut, sending a shooting pain from one of her molars in the back. "Oh, yes. Let us seriously consider that option after five weeks of dating. This comment from the guy who told me to use him for sex the day after I met him, and to not worry about the future." She continued, her breath coming in huffs. "I'm starting to think I should've given *you* up for Lent."

The half-smile disappeared. "I see. Too much fucking and not enough praying, is that it? When I go away, will that get you closer to God?"

Not if, but when. Her feet ground into the carpet, all movement frozen. She cursed her stupid, shrieking self, her irritation extinguished like water on a campfire. "No."

He stood up, rigid, his slender body making him look even taller. "I'm thinking you should call me after Easter. Safer that way. You know, because I wouldn't want these multi-room orgasms to distract you from reading The Passion of Jesus or eating ham at brunch."

Her head bowed. "Don't. Don't cheapen either one like that. And I am not ready for you to go away."

There was an unbearable pause, she didn't know for how long, and he lifted her chin with a finger. "I hope you mean that, because I care about you. And any God I used to believe in, or have hope of believing in again, wants to unite people, not find ways to get in-between them."

"You're right," she said quietly. "Of course, you're right. It's like I said before. You bring out this side of me I can't ... fathom, so I'm lashing out, and I should know better. I'm acting like I'm twelve instead of almost forty. Don't go. Please." She was out of steam and close to tears now. She sat and tugged at his fingers, the long, beautiful fingers she'd begun sketching days after that first night with him. "I'm sorry."

He studied her for a few seconds. He sat, the stiffness gone, and brushed hair off her face. "You didn't think you'd get rid of me that easily, did you? There are these sides to you I need to keep discovering, after all."

"God help us," she half-laughed. "You're a patient man, that much I can see."

"Anything good is worth waiting and fighting for."

"Even if it's just for a few months?"

"I'm not the one who persists in attaching an end date to this relationship."

"That's not fair. We haven't even discussed what's going on with us, not really, and you have no reason to think this has a hope of surviving long distances and time apart."

"You're wrong. I actually do have reasons." He stroked her neck, whispering into her ear. "For someone who talks a lot about faith, you seem to be notably lacking it in the romance department."

She shivered at his breath on her and could think of no suitable reply. She was weak as a kitten under his wandering hands, and they unceremoniously went to bed, Hugo possibly the most pleased of any of them.

Kathleen still hadn't revealed what was happening with Thomas to Summer. She didn't know if he'd wake up one day (or if she would) and decide the last month had been one long bad judgment call, or if some young thing would divert his attention and she'd be history. None of the scenarios looked probable, except for maybe the "sweet young thing" one, but it didn't matter anyway. The tide pulling her to him was as strong as the threatening uncertainties. Maybe even stronger. Kathleen had been thinking of Summer ever since the argument with him, and invited her to Lucci's, a popular Italian eatery in town, for lunch.

Their waiter delivered the salads they'd ordered, and Summer pounded the table triumphantly. "I *knew* it! I knew something was up. The last Friday he was there, you walked around like a zombie with your tongue hanging out. You wanted to bang him that first night he played, didn't you?"

"That's not true."

Summer waited.

"Okay, it's true."

"See? Now, out with it. Spill. What's he like? He's pretty tall, which usually means you-know-what, in my book."

Kathleen's lips pursed. "Stop it, and, no, I won't 'spill.' What are we, comparing notes again in home ec class?"

"I'm not asking for his very short life history, for heaven's sake. You've been holding out on me."

"I'm not holding out." She lowered her voice. "Honestly, I can't even describe it. It's surreal, like I'm under some weird voodoo trance. All I want is him. With food breaks and an occasional movie. And he makes me laugh, and I feel myself falling. Hard."

"That's nothing supernatural. Nor is it satanic. It's called the first few months of dating after years of living in the Sahara Desert with an asshole."

"Aren't you subtle. Thank you for reminding me how much you loved my late husband."

"Hey. I tell it like it is. But I don't want to be the one talking this time. C'mon."

Kathleen sighed. "He's a great guy, really. But this obsession is ... it's strange, and I don't trust it. Not to mention, he'll be leaving town in a matter of months, and, you know, he's ten years younger than me. That's not exactly insignificant.

So naturally, I'll find a way to wreck the whole thing somehow."

"You'd better not, because I'll have to kill you then." Summer clasped her hand. "Listen to me. You deserve this more than anyone I know. So what if he's younger. Big deal. I think it's fantastic. He's got that scrawny body like a cross country runner. I'll bet he can go the distance and take you with him. You'd be nuts not to go with this. For as long as it lasts."

"But there are some things to consider. It's certainly not perfect."

"What is? And who the hell wants perfect at this stage of the game?" She poked a finger at Kathleen. "Let's get to the nitty-gritty, my friend. Steve was a control freak who dictated your every move, taking a big chunk out of your life before he kicked the bucket. So you, of all people, should know to make the best of every minute, try to live in the moment."

"You sound like Thomas, now."

"Then he's a wise man. And a nurse! He left that little piece out of his résumé. How divine is that? It's long past time to let someone take care of you."

"He *was* a nurse. And that's just it. I know what it's like to end up wiping your spouse's rear end. I wouldn't wish it on anyone."

"Puh-leezzee. Don't go there with the shit stories." Summer took a bite of her salad. "You know what I mean. You're overdue to let someone rub *your* back in the bath, make *you* dinner, and do all the weekend plans. You're projecting waay too far ahead. You must learn to coast."

Kathleen sighed. "Truthfully, he's the one who needs the backrubs. Remember commenting about his limp that first night?"

"Yeah."

"He was in a serious car accident as a teenager. He hasn't told me all the details, but I'm sure it was an almost-died kind of accident."

"God. Really?"

"Yes. His whole right side was a mangled mess and he had to undergo multiple surgeries. He suffers a lot of residual pain from that, and fights depression, as well."

Summer chewed thoughtfully. "Like I said, who wants perfect?"

"Then there's this part of me that's embarrassed. I feel like a fraud. Here I am this church volunteer with pregnant teenagers, of all things, who would talk about sex every session if they could, and there's me living La Vida Loca and Kama Sutra with this Adonis rocker. Pretending to be all prudent."

Summer laughed. "I love it! 'Living La Vida Loca and Kama Sutra.' It's every hot-blooded woman's dream. Except, you need to dump the guilt, girl, and stat." She shook her head. "I don't understand why in God's name you agreed to do that group in the first place. Couldn't Sheila have gotten Carolyn Biddey or Linda Moore to cook biscuits and gravy or some other home ec thing with them? Those busybodies have nothing better to do."

"Maybe, but that's not it. I'm enjoying the meetings, for the most part. It's just the old 'do what I say, not as I do' stuff that gets to me."

She stared at Kathleen, bug-eyed. "What? What is wrong with you? Those girls don't need to be privy to your sex life. And *hello,* they've already done the damned deed anyway. Go to confession if you have to, and toss the 'I'm not worthy' crap." She ate another forkful of salad, her mouth still half-full when she began talking again. "Whatever happens, you have to promise to not go batshit crazy and make Mr. Love

God end up quitting his gig with us. He pulled in some serious cash the other night. And we got major bills to pay."

"Thanks for the vote of confidence. I'll try not to."

"Excellent. And screw this water," Summer said, signaling the server. "We need some margaritas to celebrate the end of celibacy."

4

When Kathleen and Thomas weren't dining on each other, tidbits of other origins were thrown out like crumbs on a trail for each of them to sniff out and digest. They were like feral puppies circling each other, guarding their still-fragile vulnerabilities, learning each other's quirks, with the possibility that their time together was finite adding another nuanced layer.

Easter was in three days and she'd gotten the dinner invite from her mother, who'd been quite curious after learning someone might be accompanying her daughter. Kathleen had fended her off, saying she wasn't sure of his plans, yet (and she wasn't), but just in case, was it all right if he came. It turned out Thomas' sister, who lived in nearby Lewiston, was hosting an evening meal, also, so they agreed they would go separate ways for dinner.

"You could go to mass with me, though," Kathleen said tentatively, before Thomas left Wednesday morning.

He stared at her. "I could, yes. Is that an invitation?"

"I'd like it if you came with me."

He put his coffee down. "Are you sure about that?"

No. Not at all. This is probably a test to see what you'll do. "I'm sure," she said. She tried to sound nonchalant.

"I don't believe you, but, yes, I'd go."

"That's it? Just like that? I did think you'd say no."

"Let's not overanalyze this. Please."

"I'm not ... I'm surprised, is all."

He refilled his cup and added cream and sugar. "Okay. Why are you surprised?"

"For one thing, you've made your feelings about religion known."

"True." He stirred his coffee and took a few sips. "It's one day out of my life. How hard is that to manage? Especially if it's important to you."

A mixture of gratefulness and envy coursed through her. How effortless he was at decisions; no hint of backpedaling or second guessing, no worries about relentless parish gossiping.

"I wish I could be like you," she said, pouring her own coffee.

"No, you don't wish that. But tell me how, anyway."

"Everything is so clear. You don't obsess for hours about the complicated shades of gray."

"I've operated in every color there is, I think." He drained his cup. "Sometimes the black-and-white stands out and you know what you want. I want you."

Her face reddened at his bluntness.

"And speaking of colors, I love it when you blush," he said, taking her cup from her and pulling her in for a kiss. "It's like instant Viagra, I swear."

He lunged at her neck and she laughed. "I might have to learn to conjure it up when I'm seventy, or something."

"You'll be beautiful at any age," he said, shedding her robe and clothes he'd put on fifteen minutes before.

"You're going to be late for band practice."

He entered her, so sharp and swift she gasped.

"They can wait."

After he left, she went to the window. She belted her robe as she watched him walk to his car, his long gait and hair bobbing in the wind, a throb still emanating from her body. She re-heated her cold coffee and, as she curled up on the couch to sip, said a silent prayer. Perhaps she needed to consider this wild attraction as a gift from God, a gift that wasn't meant to last but to teach her something, even if it meant sorrow in the end. And He was waiting patiently to see what she would do with it.

She hoped He wouldn't be disappointed.

Easter morning came, and Thomas showed up at her door in a light-blue dress shirt, snazzy tie, navy suit pants, and expensive-looking black shoes. The entire ensemble looked expensive, in fact, and with his few acquired pounds he filled every inch of fabric like a designer's dream. She'd unknowingly picked a blue sheath dress almost the exact color of his shirt, and she knew they would draw many eyes. Even if she were not on his arm, the sight of him alone would do it.

"Hey. You clean up pretty good," she said, kissing him.

"I'd say the same," he said, eyeing her tastefully exposed cleavage. "Nice dress. Nice body in dress."

"So, I don't look like a desperate cougar with her cabana boy?"

"You do not. But I'd happily be your disfigured cabana boy."

"Don't talk like that." She looked at her watch. "All right, let's get going. My mother always goes to the 8:00 mass, so we won't be seeing her. She calls it the drive-through mass. In and out, and she likes it that way."

"Okay. What else do I need to know?"

"Nothing. Other than the tongues will be wagging, I'm telling you. Every single woman there will be staring you down today, *that* I can guarantee."

"I'm already regretting this."

She stopped, her heels skidding on the tile. "Seriously?"

"No. But maybe, as Bonnie Raitt says, we should give them something to talk about."

"Let's not. They won't need anything extra, the way you look."

St. Joseph's was resplendent with lilies, their distinctive scent overpowering. Purple and white colors adorned the altar and the cross, and the pews were packed with babies and little ones dressed head to toe in their Easter finery. Kathleen loved seeing all the satin bonnets, tights, and the squirmy boys who clearly couldn't wait to get out of their constrictive suits. Thomas put his arm around her down the aisle as the usher searched for an available spot, and, as predicted, many heads turned in their direction, but Kathleen felt only slightly self-conscious. They were seated at the end of the pew next to an old couple she didn't recognize, and she relaxed. Father Anthony, looking handsome in a white and gold vestment, was refreshing as always. He welcomed all who attended, rather than scolding the twice-a-year-attendees, and then launched into a homily reminding everyone to grab new life with both hands.

"My brothers and sisters, we must willingly carry our crosses without question, the same as Him. We can rise when life deals us death, because He shows us how. We must remember our crosses are His own; that His radiant light cancels out all darkness. My friends, let Christ be Easter in your heart today."

Thomas was bent over so his elbows were propped on his knees, his expression unreadable. She felt a stab of guilt watching him. Was it wrong of her to invite him? Wrong to bring her one-night-stand-turned-into-many-nights to mass and sashay him around for all to see? It *was* a little hard for her to grasp how they'd arrived at this point. Father Anthony proceeded with the blessings and prayers of the wine and the bread, and after the Eucharistic Ministers were in place, the organist, Sally Jorgenson, made an introduction.

"And now, St. Joseph's own Sheila Gallagher will lead our communion hymn with 'Amazing Grace,' found on page 687 in the missalette."

Sheila stepped forward. She was wearing a pretty green skirt and top, her red hair in a smooth updo.

Kathleen leaned into Thomas and whispered, "Wait until you hear her sing. She's incredible."

And she was. The entire church echoed with her clear, sweet soprano, the true voice of an angel surrounding them. She'd gotten into the second stanza when Thomas turned to Kathleen, his face tight. "I need some air. You stay." Abruptly, he was gone out the side door, like a thief in the middle of the night, and though concerned, she remained seated. Already there would be twittering about the newcomer; she didn't need to escalate the speculation with a showy exit. After communion, there were a few announcements, and the closing hymn began. People were streaming out the aisles and she, too, darted outside, the bright sun the only thing greeting her in the parking lot. She got out her phone and read a text from him.

"Sorry. I walked to HopCanon. Meet me?" HopCanon

was about a quarter-mile away; he probably was there already.

"It's ok," she texted. "Be there in a few."

Summer and Jeff had debated about whether to close for Easter. Once they got some staff onboard, they went ahead with a special brunch menu for the day. And from the looks of all the cars outside it was a good move. She parked and went in. The combined smells of sweet rolls, coffee, and yeast brewing for future beer met her nose and she inhaled deeply. There was a nice manageable crowd, lending an unexpected intimacy to the air. The hostess, Adrianna, greeted her, asking where she'd like to sit, and she spotted Thomas at the bar. She slipped in next to him.

"Is this seat taken, handsome?"

"Hey," he said. He attempted a smile. His face was drawn, his eyes red.

"Are you okay?"

"I'm fine."

She reached for a lock of his hair and put it behind his ear. "I thought only women did that."

He gave her a sideway glance. "Did what?"

"Say they're fine, when they're not."

Zack came over before Thomas could reply. "Hi, pretty lady. Happy Easter."

"Happy Easter to you, too," Kathleen said, doing a doubletake. Zack looked different today, striking, even. He was wearing all white, quite a departure from the usual denim and Bob Marley outfits, and his dreads didn't seem so horsehair-like. How was it not a spot of beer or food could be found on him? Too early in the shift, maybe.

Zack blinked, his brown eyes looking more hazel in the bright of day. "Will it be Resurrection for you? I gotta warn you, it's bitter as all get-out, but there's a refreshing mouth feel at the back end of the taste." He winked. "Like light after the tomb, right?"

"Perfect. Hit me up, then."

She pointed to Thomas' mug of stout. "No Resurrection for you?"

"No. My standby drink of doubt."

"I'm sorry if you felt any pressure to go, today. I would've been fine with—"

"It's not that." He stared straight ahead at the taps on the wall. "I've been to church exactly once since my dad died, and that was my niece's christening. So, the singing—because my father had a great voice—it brought things back I try to forget. His side is the abandoned Catholic side, as well."

They'd discussed the fact that both of their fathers had passed, but not the circumstances or much about them. "What were you thinking about? Or would you rather leave it forgotten?"

Thomas' chin dropped to his chest. "We fought bitterly about my life's direction. The arguments still circle in my head. You'd think after eleven years I'd be used to wishing I could take it all back."

She sighed. "I don't think there's any getting used to it."

He looked at her intently. "You speak with authority."

"Regret and I are closely acquainted, I'm afraid. How old were you when he died?"

"Nineteen."

"Almost the same as me. I was eighteen when my dad fell on the floor in front of me. Clutching his chest, gasping for air, the whole bit. And right up to that moment I'd been a textbook terrible teen to him. I mocked his values every chance I could by doing the exact opposite."

She remembered verbatim the battles in high school.

Her father would catch her sneaking in late, curfew broken, her clothes lopsided and stewing with the forbidden smells of weed, cigarettes, and sex. He'd banned her from seeing J.J., her boyfriend, whom he'd deemed responsible for her fall from grace. Predictably, all that did was fan the flame. "*You just hate me having any fun!*" she'd shriek. "*You live such a boring, stupid, conventional life, you can't stand to watch someone maybe enjoy themselves! No, that's a sin, to enjoy life ...*"

She'd loved his hurt reaction, his face mottled in a red rage. Victory! She'd managed to get to him. And October of her senior year, he died from a massive heart attack. In many ways, she was still living that fall night over and over, like a Groundhog's Day that never let her forget her actions.

"Isn't every teenager, though?"

His voice penetrated her thoughts, "What?"

"Terrible to their parents, going through those phases. It's just that we never got the chance to say we were sorry."

"Yes, and mine were extremely strict. *And* religious. So I rebelled. In a big way." She propped an elbow on the bar. "Sometimes I think I've spent my whole life trying to make up for it. He—well, both my parents—were only trying to protect me."

At that very moment, Zack appeared. "How are we doing, here? Need anything?"

They both politely demurred, and Thomas apologized for running out on her.

"It's fine. Believe me, I get it."

"Still. It's a holiday, and here we are."

She lifted her glass. "There's something to be said for drowning one's sorrows."

He closed his eyes, the pale lids home to blue veins that intersected like roads on a miniature map. "That's how he died. My father."

"What? Oh Lord, I'm so sorry ..."

"No, it's fine. He took a shitload of narcotics and fell off the dock at our summer home not far from here." At the word fell, he used fingers for air quotation marks. "He didn't fall. He jumped."

She was afraid to ask him how he knew this. Instead, she stroked his cheek gently. "How awful for you and your family."

"It was. Is, still. My various conditions haven't brightened my outlook either."

His lips parted slightly, and her finger fell onto the ridge of his incisor tooth, and then down. She wanted him with a sudden ferocity, feeling that sharp edge; wanted to insulate and heal him from all past ills, and he sensed the change.

"Although your magic hands have serious potential to change that," he said, spinning the barstools so they faced each other. "Enough of these sunny revelations. Let's talk about your potential side job as a massage therapist."

"I'd rather be your personal masseuse."

"Tell me more," he whispered, kissing her fingers.

"Why don't we both just hole up and stay at home, today," she said, becoming more and more animated at the idea. "We'll tell our families we're fine, but we won't be joining them." She indicated to Zack to fill a growler. "And besides, I make a mean brunch."

"Hmm. Personal therapist, chef, and masseuse. I like the way this is going."

Zack placed the full container of Resurrection down in front of them, and Thomas laid money out on the bar. "Happy Easter, Zack. I meant to tell you, earlier, you look downright celestial today."

"Thanks, man. Enjoy your celebrations."

"I will." Thomas lifted her hand up. "What more could I want, right?"

Zack smiled, a rare occurrence for him. "Amen, brother. Amen."

She made a colorful feast of eggs, candied bacon, fruit salad, and a pineapple glazed ham, all of which Thomas raved about, but mostly pushed around his place like a child. Kathleen tried to ease his restlessness with her magic hands, as he'd called them, but between drinking Resurrection and all the food, she succumbed to a solo afternoon nap. When she awakened, he was next to her.

"Hey, Sleeping Beauty."

She smiled groggily. "Who are you talking to?"

"Sure as hell not myself."

"Did you have a nap, too?" she asked, stroking his unclothed hip.

"No. I've just been staring at you for an hour."

"That's boring."

"Not at all. It's when songs form in my head. Why I keep a notebook handy at all times. Ahhh," he said, jerking back slightly when she hit a tender spot.

She tsked, immediately contrite. "Sorry. Here I am, trying to make it better and failing as usual."

"You make everything better. Along with a few other things." He reached over on top of his open notebook for a plastic baggie, and pulled out a tightly rolled joint. She refrained from partaking, since it made her loopy and unfocused, but she knew for him that was the whole idea. To distract from the relentless pain. Soon it was his turn to drift off, and she extricated herself from the bed. As she picked up a water bottle off the nightstand, her eyes were drawn to the pages he'd written. She didn't feel sneaky reading the words, since the notebook was like an extra appendage—it went everywhere he did, and he made no effort to hide his creations. Filled with crossed out phrases and black-outs, she could still make out the verses.

BACK IN THE DARK
Somewhere there in the steep divide
Between right and wrong and the other side
He thinks about the gone girl he married
A rope makes sure the pain gets carried
Into the dark, where the damage gets ferried
Into the dark, where the damage gets ferried
CHORUS
Because back in the dark it feels good to hide
Back in the dark, you let your demons hide
Back in the dark, truth becomes a lie
Back in the dark, think it's gonna be all right
Somewhere trapped behind an ancient door
Young man wonders what he's fighting for
Like father, like son, or so he's been told
Slippin' through the cracks of a well-worn floor
Back in the dark, he might sell his soul
Back in the dark, he might sell his soul
CHORUS repeat
Somewhere there in the blackened abyss
A light breaks through in the form of you
Takin' my hand you said there's more than this
But the river runs deep with that copycat bliss
It's back to the dark before I miss again
Back to the dark before I miss again
Bring me out of the dark, yeah bring me out of the dark
You're the one I didn't think He'd send
You're the one I didn't think He'd send

She put the notebook down and stood there, taking her turn to watch him sleep, and he looked even younger than usual. No pinched expressions or drawn brow, just faultless features at rest. She felt inexplicable tears well up at the tranquility that wasn't there when he was awake. *Thomas. What have you been through? Still going through?* She was overcome with the desire to sketch him and capture the moment before it was lost completely. She tiptoed into the spare room, which had subbed as a pseudo art studio, grabbed her sketch book and materials, and got settled in the big comfy chair next to her bed. He was still in the same position, and for the next thirty minutes she went into what Steve would refer to as her work trance. Harriet came in and tried to sit on her paper, soon followed by Hugo, who, seeing the vacancy in the bed, jumped up.

"Hugo!" she hissed. "Get down!"

Thomas rolled over and laughed at the face licking that ensued.

"Hugo, c'mon," Kathleen prodded, but the dog was having none of it. "He totally adores you, you know. More than he does me."

"That's because I take him to the dog park." He stretched and sat up. "Let's take him now, before the sun goes down."

They loaded him in the back of her car, and once out, he pulled terribly on his leash. It was why she couldn't take him by herself; he was too strong. Steve would be tsking her at this blatant lack of training, but she'd tried two different classes and had given up. He strained to join a pack of dogs circling the fence, and was instantly gone once Thomas closed the gate. They sat on the bench there and Thomas stared pensively into the distance. She tugged at his arm.

"Hey. You okay?"

The sun cut through the trees, casting a shadow of them on the ground. Without answering he got up. He picked up a tennis ball for an anxious golden retriever whose master was too distracted on his cellphone to notice, and hauled it far into the field. The delighted dog hesitated at first, as if disbelieving of its good fortune, then took off at top speed.

Thomas turned back to her. "I'm just kind of drained, you know?"

"Yes."

"Thank you," he said, and his voice quavered momentarily.

"For what?"

He shrugged, his hands in his pockets, and he looked like a lost ten-year-old boy. "I don't know. For being easy to be with? For not drilling me. I'm not really making sense."

The retriever appeared and dropped the ball at his feet, looking up questioningly, and for the next ten minutes, Thomas threw the ball, until the dog lay panting by his feet. She smiled at him the way only goldens seem to know how to do, and he smiled back. Hugo was far away in the distance, gallivanting with two shepherd mixes.

"Are you tired, girl?" he said, setting the ball down. He kneeled to stroke her, his hand lost in a layer of thick red-gold fur, and she splayed out onto the ground ecstatically. Her owner was across the park, still pecking away at his phone, and Thomas sat next to Kathleen on the bench. The dog immediately rose and followed him, putting her head between his legs, and a paw on his lap. He chuckled softly.

He bent over and massaged her silky ears. "I get tired, too," he said, his voice breaking off completely this time. Sadie, as her nametag read, licked the salt off his hands as he wiped his face, and Kathleen held him. They stayed this way until the sun disappeared behind the trees and Sadie was called away by her somewhat frantic person, cell phone still in hand.

Two weeks later he was feeding her Chinese food with chopsticks in bed, when he casually mentioned his brother-in-law was having a birthday party the following Saturday and would she like to come.

She clamped her mouth shut. "Oh? A family party?"

"Yes, it is that. With assorted friends, of course."

"I see."

"Is that a yes or a no, or 'I'll think about it'?"

She waved off the noodles he dangled in front of her. "I'd like to go. Maybe I'm a little unnerved."

"Why?"

"I don't know. Meeting family means new territory, compounded with my anxiety of feeling old. It could go badly on my end."

He put the chopsticks back in the carton. "You have nothing to worry about. They're pretty cool people. And you wouldn't be meeting a huge caravan. Just my brother-in-law and my twin, Courtney, their daughter Allie, and my aunt Janie."

"Wait ... I knew you had a sister, but a twin?"

"Yup. I'm older, by three minutes."

"And your mother? Would I get to meet her?"

He tensed, his back shifting against the wall. "No."

She pushed ahead. "You told me your parents split up. Is she not around?"

"You could say that. She walked out when we were sixteen and moved to Tennessee. My sister is still in touch with her."

"But not you."

"I see her at family functions that involve my niece." He said it defensively.

"I'm not judging. Trying to understand."

"Good luck. She spent years trying to get me to understand why she got tired of living with the depressed man my father had become. She failed." With that, his face shut down like a loosey-goosey storm window, the subject closed.

She said gently, "I'm sorry if I've pried. Let's talk about the party."

The storm window lifted a little. "It'll be a good time. I'm going to play a couple sets with the band, and you can meet them, too."

"Okay."

"Okay, you're in?" he asked, and she couldn't help but note his hopefulness.

"I'm in."

"Sweet," he said, his enthusiasm boyish. "You'll love Auntie Janie. She never married, and along with my Gram, basically helped raise us after my mom left. She and my dad were twins also."

"Wow. Twins run strong in your family."

"Among other things. The strong bond thing you hear about is true, though. Janie wasn't the same after my dad died. She really only got her spark back when my niece was born."

"Babies have a way of doing that," Kathleen said, putting her head on his chest.

They laid silently for a few minutes among the take-out containers, when he broke the quiet.

"What about you? Did you ever want kids?"

Her cheek lifted temporarily. "I did ... but in twenty years of marriage, it never happened."

"Did you see a doctor about it?"

"No. I knew it was me. Steve had Megan, my stepdaughter, with his first wife. I didn't need a specialist to figure out who was the likely culprit." She gestured to the box of condoms on the night table. "I keep trying to think of a way to tell you that you probably don't need those. With me, I mean."

He lifted her chin. "And who else would I be needing them with?"

"I'm just saying."

He shifted so that they were both on their sides. "Guess I'm a little risk-averse. Better safe than sorry."

"Risk-averse? Do you mean paranoid?"

He chortled. "My ex would've put it that way. It's one of the reasons I broke up with her, in case you were wondering."

"I have wondered. But you need to explain."

He hesitated, as though hedging about how much to reveal. "Julie's a teacher ... and she talked all the time about a family. Naturally. And I would say things like, 'Yeah, you'll be a great mom, someday,' or, 'Yeah, kids are great.' Both of which were true, but my stomach would be in knots picturing myself in that scenario. I knew it wasn't just pre-wedding jitters. She deserved better."

"You broke it off with her because she wanted a family and you didn't?"

His face hardened. "There was more to it than that. I was all for adoption or fostering, but she wouldn't hear of it. I feel strongly the world wouldn't be improved by one more f-ed up human walking around for most of his life trying to figure out ways to take himself out. Maybe the desire to prevent that strikes you as excessive."

She was silent for a few seconds, debating her response. "Sounds more like a copout. You're a nurse, for God's sake. You must know there's no guarantee of a child going down that path whatsoever. And you said yourself ... you're healthier, now. Doesn't that mean anything?"

"For now, I am. I'm better than I've been in a long time, and it's not a mystery why."

The afternoon sun, which had been under a cloud for most of the day, streamed light on his face. The glow made his eyes look like the caramel drops she used to get at the county fair booths, and he drew her hand to his lips and kissed her fingers. "You make me happy, in a way I've never felt, and I can't explain it. I don't say that to burden you with keeping the psycho in line. For this day and moment, it's enough."

"You're not psycho. Frankly, I'm surprised you'd use that word, as someone who used to work with a population struggling with mental illness."

He shrugged. "I'd never use it to describe a patient."

"Ah. I see. You're different."

He dropped her hand and grasped the back of his neck. "No...but, my meds could stop working tomorrow for no discernable reason, and down the rabbit hole I go. That's a common experience. You wouldn't wish it on your worst enemy, let alone an innocent child."

She propped up on an elbow. "Thomas. I don't presume to know what it's like to be in your shoes, but it seems like you're still too young to be so ... so deterministic." She leaned toward him, becoming more animated. "What if you met someone you cared for so much, that it cancelled out all those fears? What then? Break that off, too? Break another heart because of this 'biology is destiny' bullshit?"

His lips thinned. "It isn't bullshit. Not when more than half the men in your family off themselves."

"I don't mean to insult you. I'm hardly—"

He shushed her with a finger to her lips, and turned so the sun hit the back of his head. "And I think I may have found that someone. I'm hoping she doesn't break me, if you want the truth."

Their eyes met, and he was scrutinizing her for a reaction. Her ever-present flush came blooming in and she tried defusing it with humor. "Yeah? Who is this lucky young thing?" she teased, and he pulled her to him.

"She's coming to the family party, and she's going to blow them all away."

"The lucky *older* woman might," she laughed, but she only managed to coach a faint smile from him when she dove under the sheets to ensure more mutual happiness, elusive or short-lived as it might prove to be.

5

The day of the party she changed in and out of three outfits before settling on faded jeans and a simple white tee shirt, mainly because she gave up and asked Thomas what he preferred. *Old habits die hard.*

And unlike what Steve would've done, he hadn't expressed an opinion, saying she looked good in everything and she should wear what she wanted.

"Here comes Casper the ghost," she said, surveying her image in the mirror and applying red lipstick for some color. It did add some pop, at least.

"Nice," he said, coming up from behind her to kiss her neck. "Let's go."

Her belly rumbled with nerves. "Wait. Bathroom, first."

After a fifteen-minute delay, they got in his car. "I'm not leading you into a den of wolves, you know. This'll be fun. My brother-in-law is Irish and they know how to party. In fact, I think they ordered a mini-keg from HopCanon."

She smiled and put some gloss on over her lipstick. "I am looking forward to hearing you play. And as long as my churning gut cooperates, fun it will be."

The party was in Lewiston, a fifteen-minute drive from Kathleen's, in an upscale neighborhood.

"Pretty area," Kathleen said as they pulled into a cul-de-sac of well-manicured lawns and high-end homes.

"I guess. If you like robotic suburbia. Not my thing."

"And what would that be?"

He pulled into a circular drive. "I don't even know anymore, other than, the less effort at maintaining, the better. I suppose my apartment would give you a clue if it didn't scare you, first."

She laughed. "I have noticed you don't seem to want me there. Why? Typical bachelor sloth-ness?"

"Oh, I admit I'm messy. But it's not much to see. What is there, which isn't much, is all beige, which I didn't even notice until my sister pointed it out. It's somewhere to crash, eat, and practice, nothing more. Not a home."

The shadow that routinely came and went passed over his face as he parked.

"I'm starting to believe home isn't a place, anymore. It's who you're with." He smiled. "And before you overthink that one, wanna help me unload my gear?"

She said yes. She watched him slink into panther mode, helped by his solid black form, and as he skipped around, muscles protruding under the amplifier's weight, her chest swelled. For this day, for this moment, she would revel in his presence and the chemistry between them and be grateful for the changes wrought in her, and not care if anyone noticed. Doing this was about the only thing he'd asked of her, and still she'd feel herself withdraw, like a skittering crab on the ocean floor zigzagging mindlessly. Today would be different, she thought, picking up two mic stands and following him.

The party was to be outside and they'd lucked out with a beautiful May afternoon. There was even a portable stage/dance floor the rest of the band had set up on top of the lawn, under a tent, and catering servers bustled about setting up tables and getting the food ready nearby.

Kathleen grabbed Thomas elbow. "I thought you said this was gonna be simple."

"Yeah. And for the Maloneys, this is low key." He smiled, looking away. "Here they come now."

Two female versions of Thomas came up to them smiling, one arm-in-arm with a blonde-haired man wearing a black cowboy hat emblazoned with the words "Thirty Ain't Fucking Old" across the brim. The other woman was older; attractive, with little make-up and her hair up in a bun.

Thomas leaned in and kissed his sister on the cheek, then laughed, looking at the man. "Nice hat, birthday boy."

"Thanks, man. I thought it appropriate for the occasion."

Thomas put his hand behind Kathleen's back. "Everyone, this is my girl, Kathleen. Kathleen, my sister, Courtney, her husband, Jake, and my aunt, Janie."

Kathleen shook hands and exchanged greetings, still processing "this is my girl, Kathleen," knowing her skeleton-colored skin would be flaming any second. "Thomas, did you get her a drink?" Courtney prodded him.

"Uh, no. I've been busy setting up." He touched Kathleen's arm. "Would you like the HopCanon beer?"

"Sure, that'd be fine."

Thomas and Jake left, and the three women engaged in small talk. Kathleen tried not to dump her entire life story with boring, unnecessary details about Steve.

"How do you know Thomas?" Janie asked warmly. "Did you go to school with him?"

Kathleen cleared her throat, deciding the question was innocent and not an attempt to unearth her age. "No. I ... I met him at HopCanon, when he was performing. I started working there a few months ago."

"I'm so glad you came. I knew there was something different about him, lately." She put her hand on Kathleen's wrist. "He's very private, as you might know. We've been quite worried about him after all that drama with Julie, because he is sooo sensitive. Always was, too, ever since he was a little boy. In fact, this time of year always reminds me of that one weekend so long ago." Her face relaxed at the pleasant reminiscing. "We all went on a family camping trip and his dad and I took him fishing. Do you know Thomas cried at the hooks in the fish, and kept checking on them in the wire basket at the pier when we got back? Then when he realized we were going to eat them, heavens! I thought he might pass out—"

"Janie. He would die, hearing this," Courtney said.

She laughed. "Okay, okay. I'm sorry, Kathleen. I sure don't want to send you running off on account of me and my silly ramblings."

Kathleen smiled. "No danger of that happening. We're having a lot of ... fun together." The receded flame in her face came roaring back. "He's a great guy." She pointed to the band area. "And so incredibly talented."

"Isn't he, though? He's been playing and singing since he could crawl, I swear. We're so proud of him. Did he tell you he played Elvis in a school talent show when he was about ten and sang 'Love Me Tender'? I mean, how many kids would choose that song over, say, 'Jailhouse Rock'? A pure romantic, even that young ..."

"That's it," Courtney grabbed her aunt's hand. "Can you please go get Allie? She's been bugging me all morning about when is Uncle Thomas coming."

Janie rolled her eyes. "Fine. I get the message. I'll be back with the little munchkin."

After she left, Courtney turned to Kathleen. She had Thomas' same creamy skin and wide mouth, but her hair was lighter and her frame petite. "Sorry. She can be a little chatty."

"No need to apologize. I like hearing childhood stories, anyway."

"She's right about the being worried part. After Thomas quit nursing, he's been cooped up in that dreary apartment for months, with only a crabby cat for company. He told me about you and I was thrilled to hear it."

This was one of those moments in which any response felt awkward. *Ah. What would he tell you? "Hey, Sis, I'm with this cougar chick and she can't get enough of me. I never met anyone who likes to bang so much"?*

Kathleen struggled to sound casual. "Oh? What did he say?"

"Very little. "I met somebody special. I think you'd like her," stuff. But I assure you, him saying that is *huge.* He didn't tell us about Julie until months after they were dating."

Thomas appeared with the requisite solo cups. "My ears are burning," he said to Courtney. "I see you chased Auntie Janie off. What should I know about now?"

"Nothing," said Kathleen. "Your aunt and sister were telling me how concerned they are about you."

"Overprotective is more like it. Now, here's to Jake's birthday, wherever he is wandering."

"What are we drinking?" Courtney asked.

"Absolution." He looked directly at Kathleen. "A wheat ale. It must be a cousin to Act of Contrition."

He pulled her close to him and whispered in her ear. "See? This beer is a cosmic sign. Now it's official. We're forgiven of all so-called sinful acts."

Her face warmed. "You think? I don't see a priest anywhere."

"Details, details." His voice deepened and seemed to magnify. "You're blushing again—and you know what that means." He touched her cheek. "It's the same blush you get when you come. I'll bet you didn't know that."

Kathleen twisted her head like a B-movie character possessed by a demon. "Shh! Did your sister hear that?" She wriggled away before he launched more bombshells.

"No. She's off talking to her friends."

She smoothed her shirt and struggled to form a firm response. Reprimanding, even. "Oh my God, what if she heard you?"

He laughed. "She's a suburbanite stay-at-home mom with a husband gone all the time. She'd probably be jealous."

His blasé lack of concern was irritating. She frowned and took a big swig of Absolution. "You have no shame, I swear."

Their eyes met, and the look she'd come to know so well in eleven weeks, the same stubborn one that blazed through misgivings and hesitation like a wild prairie fire, was in full force. He raised his red plastic cup in a fake salute. "You are absolutely right. I'm not feeling one iota of shame. And you can pretend to be offended all you want, to avoid facing the truth."

Her embarrassed blush morphed into one of anger. "Is that so? Maybe you, in all of your many years of acquired carnal wisdom, can inform me of this truth?"

"Come on," he snapped. "I'm not being arrogant, unless it's arrogant to say what we have is ... how do I put it—uncommonly strong? It's also more than 'carnal,' and you know it. I think we both knew it from the first time we met."

"Well, Dr. Harlequin-romance-Freud, I don't know what

the hell it is, but I hardly think this is the time or the place—"

"Hey, lovebirds," Courtney sidled up to Thomas, oblivious to the tension she'd walked into. "Sorry to interrupt, but the band is asking for you."

He drained his cup, his face still pensive. "All right, then. Showtime."

Kathleen was impressed with the change in Thomas' sound with a complete band. There was no denying the fuller dimension the pulsing bass and drums added to the mix. They were all over the place with their setlist, from covering Zac Brown to U2, and the dancefloor and lawn were at capacity with zealous partygoers. After some help from Absolution, she forgot about their heated words and swayed to Buffalo Springfield's tune asking everyone to stop and look at what's going on. Somewhere in the second verse, a random younger guy reeking of weed started swaying with her.

"I love this music, don't you?" he shouted. He was stick-thin, wearing a Baja hoodie and his hair in a long ponytail. "The Sixties guys had it right, man. Not like the candy-ass wanna-be rockers today, churning out their auto-tuned garbage to stadiums filled with more robot candy-ass sheeple. Fucking posers."

She laughed. "Why don't you say what you really think?"

He spread his hands out. "You know, I just call stuff as I see it."

"The world might be a better place if we all did that."

He lifted his hand to high-five her. "I mean, right?"

They danced side by side, and she was enjoying herself.

"So, like, are you here with anyone?" Jason, as he'd introduced himself, asked.

She pointed to Thomas. "Yes. I'm with him," and then louder, proudly: "We're together."

"Damn. He's a lucky dude."

"I'd say we both are."

Jason lifted his cup. "He's really good. He belongs on a real stage, if he doesn't mind dealing with the bullshit machine the music industry has become."

"I agree, though I'm not sure how he feels about the bullshit music industry."

"Man, don't even get me started." He shook his head dejectedly. "Well, cheers to being lucky in love, and all that touchy-feely crap."

She laughed again. "Cheers," she said, and Thomas announced that the band would be taking a fifteen-minute intermission. She looked up and drew a deep breath. The stage lights illuminated the sheen of sweat on his face and neck, and the wet curling tips of his hair, and his shirt was drenched. He walked across the stage, pulled a clean tee out of a backpack and changed, his gleaming and rippled torso momentarily on display for anyone who might be watching.

Dear God. As if she needed any more ammunition to fuel her apparently bottomless state of lust. She finished the Absolution in her cup and her eyes tracked him exiting the makeshift stage.

He was mobbed with people, the majority female, and all of them in his age bracket. A girl wearing leopard print leggings plopped a goofy hat sideways on him, one of those rapper-looking types with the flat brim Kathleen hated, and they laughed at some private joke. She watched as if in a trance: their toned necks arching back like swans, crop-tops flashing flat stomachs, impossibly high heeled boots and shoes digging into the manicured grass. No time-ravaged skin, see-through locks, or lumpy bodies to be found here. One made-up doll looped an aerobicized arm around him, and he smiled his achingly sexy gap-tooth grin. Kathleen's throat and eyes swelled with unexpected tears.

You stupid, insecure fool. What did you expect or think this was going to come to? That's his tribe, one of which he's no doubt meant to hook up with and marry. You'll never fit in. Never.

She could hear them, still, the preening, and he was soaking it up. He'd deny that, but what man wouldn't be flattered by collective crushes at every turn? Every city and concert venue? If she was the least bit smart, she'd go back to her single existence, her job and her animals, and be content. Count him as a sweet memory and nothing more, before she was in any deeper. She was about to refill her cup of comfort when Janie approached with a little blonde-haired girl in hand.

"Kathleen, dear. Are you having a good time?"

She forced a smile. She could tell Janie was perceptive, but fake smiling was safer than a spoken reply, for the moment. And she *was* having fun, until the little groupie entourage made their presence known. "What a great turnout for Jake."

"Yes, isn't it? I don't know if Thomas told you, but Jake runs his own construction company. He makes a lot of friends along the way." She looked down affectionately at the child. "And I want to introduce you to our dearest one. This is Allie, Jake and Courtney's daughter. My great-niece."

"Hi there," Kathleen said, grateful for the distraction.

"Hi." Allie flashed a wide, toothless smile. "Are you Uncle Thomas' girlfriend?"

This is my girl, Kathleen. That *is* what he'd said. Then again, he wasn't going to introduce her as his Friday night fling, either.

"I suppose, yes."

"Honey, you don't ask people those things," Janie admonished her. "It's personal."

"But I was watching them before, and I saw Uncle Thomas kiss her ear."

"Allie ..." Janie started, but Kathleen chuckled and waved her off. "It's okay, really. I have nieces and nephews." She bent down to Allie's level. "Yes, he did. You're an observant young lady, aren't you?"

"You don't know the half of it," Janie said, shaking her head.

In-between several cartwheels and somersaults, Allie launched into stories about first grade, about how Uncle Thomas was the world's best sitter, and the various injustices of not having a baby sister or brother.

After several minutes of this energetic show, Janie took her hand again. "Okay, Allie. I promised that you could meet Kathleen. Now it's getting late and time for bed."

"Nooooo," she protested, crying and twisting away like a slippery fish. "Not yet!"

"Hey," Kathleen said, inspiration coming to the rescue. The groping devotees in the distance sealed her desire to retreat. "Someone told me you have a cool tent out here. Maybe we could go hide out and read some stories by flashlight?"

Allie's tear-stained face was instantly transformed. "I have a lantern! And sleeping bags!" She turned to Janie. "Auntie, can we, please?"

"Oh, I don't know. I'm sure Kathleen would like to stay out here and listen—"

"No." Kathleen said, too harshly. "It's been great, but honestly, I'm tired. Stories and a cuddle sound perfect right now."

Janie smiled. "All right, then. Go ahead."

Allie took Kathleen's hand and leaped. "C'mon. My tent

is so awesome! It's even got this hole-thingy in the top, so we can watch the stars."

"No kidding?" Kathleen said, her heart lighter already. This was a better way to end the night, and the drowse-inducing hops in the beer were hitting her hard. Damn Summer and their strong beer, anyway.

They crawled through the flap opening and Allie flipped the lantern switch on. "It's a three-person tent, my dad said. So, we can camp for real in the woods, soon. Me, Mommy, and Daddy."

Kathleen leaned back. "I love camping. I used to go with my family when I was your age. You'll have so much fun."

They read a few chapters out of a Disney Princess book, when Kathleen's phone dinged. It was Thomas messaging her, she knew, but she didn't want to interrupt.

"You can get that," Allie said, her hand under her chin. "My dad's phone never stops going off, even at dinner, and then they fight about that sometimes."

"I'll see if it's Uncle Thomas. I'll tell him I'm having some girlfriend time with his favorite niece, and I'll call him later."

"Yeah," her blonde head bobbed excitedly. "Tell him that."

"Where are you? I want you to meet some friends," he'd texted.

"I don't want to meet anyone else. I'm having some girlfriend time with your favorite niece. In her tent." She paused and debated the next part for its immaturity, then decided she didn't care. "Much preferable to watching your fan club posse paw at you. I am turning my phone off now."

How's that for truth, she thought. She pushed send and powered the phone down.

After another story, this one a bizarre take on Hansel and Gretel, the band started up. The tent was far enough away that it wasn't so loud, but close enough to hear the songs. After about four more tunes, Thomas talked.

"It's been a hell of a party. A big shout out to my sister Courtney and a happy thirtieth to Jake." Big applause, then: "We're closing out with a Van Morrison tune. Because one, what kind of Irish party would it be without a little Van, and two, what budding musician hasn't listened to this in their basement and hoped to sing it for someone special one day? Today's my day, ya'll."

The crowd shouted several variations of encouragement as the opening chords rang out.

Allie sprung up like a jack-in-the-box, her blue eyes huge. "I know this song! Uncle Thomas came every day this week to play it in his practice room! Like, over and over."

"Really? Where is his practice room?"

"Our house. My dad built one for him and the band."

Kathleen swallowed her surprise. "Wow."

"Yeah. He told me this song is called 'Into the Mythic.'"

Kathleen cocked her head as the song continued. She said quietly, "I think you mean 'Mystic.' 'Into the Mystic.'"

"Mmm-hmm, that's it."

"Know what? A little bird told me it's polite to not talk when bands play their music. So, let's turn out the light and listen now. Sound good?"

Allie laid back in her sleeping bag without protest, and she yawned. "Okay. Goodnight."

"Goodnight, honey."

Kathleen gazed up at the stars through the hole-thingy. She thought about her childish lashing out at him earlier, and as his guitar and voice soared, she knew it was *her* gypsy soul he wanted to rock, not the gaggle surrounding him that moment. She brushed an errant tear away and dozed off to the soft hiss of little girl breath exhaling into the night air.

Kathleen didn't know what time Thomas joined them. She woke to him spooned around her, fully dressed, and it was pitch black in the tent. She turned and tried to make him out in the dark, her fingers tracing his stubbly jaw. He moaned and stirred.

"Are you awake?" she whispered.

"Now I am," he said groggily, pressing into her and nuzzling her neck.

"I can't believe you remembered about 'Into the Mystic.' Are you planning on covering my entire adolescent-era sex mix?"

"It's possible. Kath, it's like three in the morning. Let's talk later."

She loved it when he called her "Kath." She'd never cared for the shortened version of her name before, but from his lips it wasn't juvenile or lazy. She rolled over and sat on top of him, casting a glance over at Allie, who snored contentedly. "I don't care what time it is. I wanted to say you're right. It's easier to make snarky comments than to face my feelings."

He sighed and moved so that the moonbeams from the tent's opening streamed in on his face, and her throat closed up as another sketch for later clicked its way into her brain. She screwed her fists into her eyes. "Oh, dear Jesus. If you could see yourself right now, in the moonlight. Sometimes I look at you and I cannot breathe. Do you know how scary that is?"

She choked back a sob, and he pulled her hands away. "Yes."

"You want truth?" She struggled to keep her voice low. "I'm afraid. I wasn't prepared for any of this. It's like I just emerged from under my safe little widow's rock, trying to find my feet, and there's this looming tower about to crash what little balance I have."

"What looming tower?"

"You know. When it's over. I mean, let's be real. I don't know whether I'm coming or going half the time. This wasn't supposed to last in the first place, and I still think I'm too old, and I don't understand why you want me at all. I'm the most uninteresting person on the planet. What have I done with my life, besides creating the perfect dinner party for 15, and then at some weird random point learning how to empty the catheter of an adult man?"

"Kathleen—"

"No. Let me finish. Here you are, this vibrant, gifted player, and you're going to be potentially reaching thousands of people, make a mark on them. Can you blame me for wondering what on earth you are doing with me? Especially when I saw those girls hanging on you, I had such a sick feeling—"

"They're friends, and bandmates' girlfriends," he interrupted.

"If tonight is any indication, they'd be up for some rollicking threesomes, then."

"Please. That's crazy."

"My sweet man, on this topic, you are clueless." She waved a hand. "Anyway. They'll be your audience, wherever you go. And when you score and make it big ..."

He scoffed. "I don't even know what that means. Maybe I just want to make a living with my craft."

She traced his damp forehead. "It matters who the talent associates with. And I'm not hip or cool in any form whatsoever. Throw in a few abandonment issues, and even your manager will tell you to dump the Plain Jane Doe dragging your image down. Still ... I can't stop. I don't want to stop."

She grabbed a pillow to muffle her oncoming tears and laid back on the sleeping bag.

He propped up on his elbow and pulled the pillow off of her. "Listen to me. You're gorgeous, in the prime of your life, for God's sake. You're smart, sexy, and funny, and I want you, every part of you, even when you talk too much, like now." He ran a hand through his hair, clearly exasperated. "I *know* firsthand what caregiving entails, and that says loads more about a person than almost anything else I can think of. Why are you selling yourself so short?"

She shrugged. "It just seems like ... anybody who's a decent person would do it for someone they cared about. It's not a special gift or anything."

"That is so not true. There's plenty of people who couldn't handle it and would walk away." He laid back down, not finished with his rebuttal. "The comments about image. You really think I care about that? All I've ever wanted is to put my music out there, use it to connect with people."

"Okay. Understood. But you're still going to be selling something," she said. "Marvin Gaye sold romantic sex. Bob Dylan sold social justice. We could think of examples all night long. Then there's you, oozing desire from every pore."

"Oh, come on. You're making this up—"

"I'm not. Onstage and off, without even trying. You're like the modern-day Caucasian version of Barry White." She lifted a finger in the air. "No! Not Barry. You were more like Tom Jones up there tonight, throwing his scarves to the audience. Only, in your case, discarding a sweaty tee shirt."

"I did not throw it out to anyone," he protested. "And I had to change. I was soaking wet!"

"So was every female watching you."

He laughed and she cupped her hand over his mouth. "Shh! We're going to wake her."

"This is absurd," he said. He leaned in and kissed her, long and slow. "There's only one woman I care about watching me like that. And as for that Barry White silliness, I blame you. You're my inspiration." He pressed into her, hard through his jeans. "See what you do to me?"

"Natural instinct," she retorted softly.

"Here's my truth," he whispered. "The unvarnished truth. I want to be with you, and only you. Tour or no tour."

She shivered, even though the air in the tent was sticky and humid. "Don't say that, tour or no tour. You're going."

"I'm gonna give it a shot. I don't even know if I can physically keep up with the demands it's going to require, and that scares me. Who am I if I can't hack the medical or entertainment field? What do I do then?"

"You're a crazy-good musician who should embark on your ventures unencumbered by a clingy, insecure muse, that's who."

His face caught the moonlight again, and a monkey wrench twisted in her chest at the sadness there.

"You're wrong," he said. "How could you believe losing you would improve my music somehow?"

"You can't argue that a relationship is a distraction to some degree. You'll need to put every ounce of your energy into making this tour a success. And keeping yourself healthy."

He was silent, and she knew she had him on that one. The group of nubile women fawning over him echoed through her head. "Plus, there's the little issue about the nightly admirers lining up to relieve you of any loneliness."

"A complete exaggeration. One-nighters are not my style."

"It was you, a few months ago. And it was me, too. Or have you forgotten?"

"That's a cheap shot, but you're also pretty transparent.

Don't shut me out because you think you know what's best for me. Or us."

"Is there an 'us?' I don't—"

He put a finger to her lips. "There *is* an us. Right here, right now, there is an us. Tomorrow, too. Now let's be quiet. Please. Listen, out there."

She did as he instructed, the serenade of soothing chirps outside quelling her anxiety, along with thoughts of groupies, tours, and uncertain futures. They were lulled to sleep by the chorus of spring peepers, all singing their own version of nature's truth bombs, the ones that ensured the world would go on if they didn't manage to get in their own way first.

6

The next week, Thomas got word his uncle William, his dad's remaining brother, died from a heart attack. They were lounging in Kathleen's hot tub when his cell rang and he clambered out like a toddler, slick and naked. He wrapped a towel around his waist and noted the number. "It's my Aunt Janie."

"Oh, no. I'll book the plane tickets. How long do you want to stay?"

There was some more discussion and he hung up. He told Kathleen the details.

She hugged him. "I'm sorry. Were you close to him?"

"We were, especially before he moved. He never married, had no kids, and lavished Courtney and I with attention. He ... worried about us a lot, I think. I found out later he was gay."

"Ah. Did he have a partner? Husband?"

"Yes, and that's the saddest part. We met him a few times. Roger. He was the reason my uncle moved away, to join him in California. There was constant interference from family, disapproval ... and Roger broke it off. And that was it. William never dated anyone again." He looked away. "Sixty- nine, and he died alone."

"How terrible."

"Yes."

"Can I do anything?" she said, stroking his wet hair.

"Come with me."

"I can't. Deirdre is off this weekend, so they'd be super shorthanded."

"Mmm." He touched her chin. "Maybe your Rastafarian friend Jason could keep you company in my absence."

"What? Who?" she asked, genuinely confused, then it dawned on her. "Oh, that guy from the birthday party. Do you know him?"

"Yes. He's a friend of Jake's. Who, if I recall, quite obviously enjoyed dancing with you."

She laughed. "He was high as a kite and on a rant about the music industry. As it turned out, *I* made it clear who I was with. He was praising you, if you want to know the truth. Said you belonged on a real stage."

"Is that so?" He kissed her hard and pulled her to the bare floor.

"I've noticed you seem to like disrobing me," she breathed.

"Truth."

Her tailbone ground into the linoleum and he held her head. "I hope I'm making something else clear."

"What's that?"

She gasped as he lunged into her. "Who I'm with, and who's with me."

He left for California, and it was a long six days filled with texts, pictures, and wish-you-were-heres. Even so, between working at HopCanon, meeting up with the Davidsons (a couple she and Steve had been close to), and giving her house a good spring cleaning, Kathleen kept busy. She was also grateful for the time and space to process how a casual liaison had moved into something so much deeper. After the pondering, she didn't have any new insights other than concluding their relationship likely never had been casual, not even from that first night. Which, ironically, is what Thomas had suggested all along. He was due back Friday and he called her from the airport that morning.

"Hey, beautiful."

How she'd missed the sound of him. "Hey. Did you just come off a bender? Your voice."

"Yeah, that wouldn't have gone well with Auntie Janie here. Chalk it up to shitty sleeping and the fact I've been up since five. It's seven-thirty, here. And we just found out there's a weather delay, so I'm literally going to be landing and heading straight to the pub."

"Ugh. You'll be exhausted."

"No, I'm disappointed. I wanted to see you before."

She laughed, giddy at the thought of seeing him within hours. "I know what you wanted."

"You have no idea."

"I think I do. Just get here safely, that's what's important. I'm working at five, so I'll see you there."

They hung up, and she was still smiling. Tonight's reunion would prove interesting, to say the least.

Fridays at HopCanon were a bustling hub from the minute the doors opened to last call, but there was a definite uptick in activity with the addition of their new singer.

"We had a whole crew who came in last Friday and

walked out because he wasn't here," Summer told Kathleen when she clocked in.

"I believe it."

"Are you behaving? You didn't break up with him, did you?"

"As it stands, we are happily coupled. But how do you know he wouldn't dump me?"

Summer tsked. "I can't see it. My God, the way he looks at you, I have to go home and pretend Jeff is goggling at me like that, just to get off."

"You're so full of it. And if that is true, I did not need to know."

"Sorry. Anyway, I'll bet you missed him this week."

Kathleen grinned. "Yes. That I did."

Summer eyed her up and down in her usual fashion. "Hey, the skirt looks cute on you. Maybe that should be the girls' new uniform."

"Thanks, but I really just got behind on my laundry and had no clean work pants. Hoping to keep bending down to a minimum."

"Yeah, good luck with that. Bending brings on the tips, ya know."

Kathleen shook her head and headed to the next table of six seated.

The evening passed in a tangled blur, as bits of her hair plastered to her neck and the perspiration beaded on her forehead. At eight o'clock Thomas walked in with his gear and started setting up, and the fluttering that accompanied every first sighting of him danced in her chest. He was staring, trying to get her attention, and her eyes darted from him to the customers in front of her. She was so flustered she mangled the couple's flight order.

"I—pardon me. Let me repeat that back to you," she

said, and after a second round finally got it straight. She dropped the order off to the bar and headed for him.

"Hey." She gave him a quick hug from behind, standing on her tiptoes to whisper into the back of his neck. "You should know your ogling is interfering with my work."

Dressed in his customary black, he whirled around. The fatigue was etched into his face even as he smiled. His five o'clock shadow was a dense dark brown, which for some men meant days of not shaving, but she knew this was him after one. He smelled like his usual pine-y self, as if he'd just stepped out of a forest shower.

"Sorry to ogle. Ah ... not sorry," he said. "I haven't seen you for six days. But you know, who's counting?" He put his arm around her waist and reeled her in close. "Nice skirt."

She laughed, her neck jerking back awkwardly. "You might want to keep your distance. It's been crazy busy, and I'm so hot, and the night's not over."

"Keep my distance? Not a chance." He picked at the damp tendrils around her ear. "As if a little sweat would keep me away. The opposite, in fact. Let me see you."

She closed her eyes as the previous flutter in her chest resurfaced and spread under his gaze. She had customers to attend to, most already happily buzzed and undemanding, but it didn't matter what they were, at the moment. Her feet were glued to the hardwood floor as she basked in his admiration, like laying on the beach as a teenager and too sun-drunk to move. She was transitioning from feeling embarrassed at his blatantly appreciative glances to reveling in them. Nobody, not from her high school romance with J.J. to her late husband, had looked at her the way he did. With J.J., it'd been the thrill of forbidden sex, and Steve was more about what she could do for him. Thomas regarded her with such undisguised yearning and acceptance that every pore in her body expanded and contracted under its warmth. She would force herself not to dismiss this as a sophomoric early lovers' reaction, and then somehow manage to blot it out of existence. She opened her eyes to find him still beaming.

"Ah," she chuckled. "This could prove to be a long evening. How about a beer to distract you? What would you like?"

"It's all good. You and Zack have a nice record of surprising me, so far."

She broke away from his embrace and went to the server station. "Zack, can you pick something for Thomas?"

Like all good bartenders, Zack was of few words and much perception, and he never lost his cool. Both of his arms sported tattoo sleeves, and he wore gauges that dragged his earlobes down and provoked many beer-fueled ignorant comments about African heritage, but he paid them no mind. His demeanor and remarkable ability to match beer styles with people earned him the taproom nickname "ZZ," short for "Zen Zack." He'd recently decided against college, opting to stay on at HopCanon, much to everyone's (except for his parents') delight.

"Hmm," Zack contemplated. "He likes stouts, so let's go with Consecration."

"That's a big one," Kathleen said. It was a Russian Imperial Stout, much higher in hops and alcohol than its fellow brethren.

"Yup." He set the pint down, his eyes studying her. "You should try it, too."

"That would knock me out in ten minutes flat. Maybe later."

The next hour flew, Thomas' music in the background, and she was so swamped with orders it never registered that suddenly he wasn't singing.

"Hey, girl." Summer poked at her with a tray. "Your man is on intermission. Take a break now."

"Let me get this out, first."

She finished her tasks and found Thomas at a crowded table, around which she recognized his bandmates and some of the same girls from the birthday gig. He spotted her, and his face lit up like she was an unexpected birthday gift placed in front of him. He jumped up, waving.

"There she is," he said, loud enough so all in the group could hear. He put his arm around her. "For those who haven't met her, this is Kathleen."

"Hello—" she began, and he went right to her ear. "God, I missed you."

She felt twelve eyes boring into her. "Me, too, but why don't we sit down."

"I have a better idea. Why don't we find a little stock-room in the back, somewhere?"

She took his hand, smiling. "C'mon."

They scooted aside for her, and the proper introductions were made. Everyone was friendly except for one with too much make-up and too much aerobics. What was her name? It was so loud she'd had trouble hearing. Lorelei or Lily, or something like that, and she was eyeballing Thomas like the evening's entrée. Kathleen stiffened in her chair.

"So, Caleb and Drew were kind enough to agree to join me for a few new tunes, tonight," Thomas said. "I owe them a thousand beers and pizzas for making them learn our set to perfection on FaceTime."

Drew nodded. "You ain't kidding, man. You're a freaking slavedriver."

Kathleen laughed. "That's a side I have yet to see. I'm sure whatever you have planned, the crowd will love it. They already do."

She stroked Thomas' hair, which was shinier than ever because of some product he'd applied. She turned his unshaven jaw to her, giving him a deep, slow kiss, delighting in the whiskers razing against her mouth. She drew away, hoping the exercise queen had been watching.

"About that backroom—" Thomas said, more than a little nonplussed at her overt show of affection.

"I think it's showtime," she said, pushing at his chest, and he reluctantly rose for the second part of their set.

He texted her before strapping on his guitar. "Are you trying to kill me?"

"Ha-ha. Why?"

"With that kiss."

"No. Just being territorial."

"No need. This entire setlist is dedicated to you."

"I'm a lucky woman."

"Not as lucky as me."

He introduced the band, then said a few words about an oldie-but-goodies night. He strummed some opening chords while he talked.

"I don't know about you all, but I'm a firm believer that a lot of music from the late-Sixties and Seventies is hard to top. And I gotta say ... there's so much awesome material from that time, when you want to express your ..." he laughed, "Affection. Yeah, that's one word for it." He played a few chords. "When you're so into someone, right?"

"Rock on, dude!" A guy who looked to be in his sixties yelled, pumping his fist. "Atlanta Rhythm Section! Yes!"

Thomas launched into the song, looking right at Kathleen.

The thump of the guitars, the suggestive lyrics, and his hungry gaze and movements were a tantalizing combination. He pulled it off without looking salacious, and she knew it was because his gestures were as natural and reflexive as breathing to him. He was as blissfully unaware as a child at Christmas, wondering where all the presents came from. And she'd been right. The crowd did love it, and him, especially the patrons of a certain age. He'd mastered the age-old musician's trick, willfully or not, of every woman out there thinking he was singing to them. The song ended and Kathleen shook her head to empty it of the images he'd conjured. Voodoo spell, indeed. She got up, her neck and face beet-red, but there was nothing to do about it. She had to get back to work.

Pint after pint flowed on, to the rocking sounds of Rod Stewart, Joe Cocker, the Stones, and she was pretty sure the taproom might be exceeding capacity by the time it was almost over.

"Hey, folks, we've had so much fun," Thomas said to the floor full of dancers. "Thanks for taking a trip back in time with us. We'll close out with a tune that might speak to how you feel about your baby on a Friday night. Or every night. Here's Bad Company."

The people went wild. The shouting increased as they sang along with the chorus, random arms flailing to the pounding bass and drums. Kathleen put her fingers in her mouth and whistled like her father had taught her eons ago. Thomas broke out a harmonica for one verse, and too soon it was over. They'd already gone over their allotted time.

"Thanks, everyone," Thomas said, breathless. "We appreciate ya'll coming out." He lifted the guitar up and off, the perspiration streaming down his face and back. The crowd finally streamed out, after realizing there'd be no encore and last-call had come and gone. Everyone, that is, except for a persistent group of punk-rocker females clamoring for Thomas' attention.

He handed out several business cards, politely smiling, the sweat still running down the sides of his cheeks.

"Thanks so much. Have a good night. And check us out on Spotify and iTunes."

Summer locked the front doors after everyone in the band, except for Thomas, got their equipment and left.

"Good Lord. I thought the little Sex Pistols tribe would never leave," Summer said, when Thomas went to the restroom. "They're all trying to score before the night is up, I guess. Here I thought it was only men who did that."

"Umm, not when there's a lead singer equivalent, in their mind, to Sid Vicious," Kathleen groaned and patted the bar. "Hey, you've been here all day. I'll stay and finish. And lock up."

"Are you sure?"

"Yup. Thomas can help me. Go."

"Thanks. I'll talk to you later, if I don't die first. This has got to be a record. Have some beers before you close shop."

Kathleen chugged a glass of water. "Goodnight."

Zack was methodically washing pint glasses and tidying behind the bar when he set two snifters of beer in front of her.

"Thanks, Zack. Consecration?"

"Yup."

She sipped, tasting a luxurious explosion of cherries, chocolate, coffee, and booze, all at once.

"Wow. This is heavenly. Packs a punch, doesn't it?"

"Yeah. In a big way."

Thomas put all the chairs on top of the tables, then came up behind the barstool and encircled her with his arms.

She twirled around. "Thank you for doing that. You must be exhausted."

"Not gonna lie, I'm motivated to get the work done. And on to other things."

"I'll toast to that," she said. They both drank the snifters dry.

The rest of the staff bid them goodnight, including Zack. She could've sworn he had a knowing expression on his face as he left.

"I can't explain it, but Zack reminds me of some type of modern-day prophet," she said.

Thomas nodded. "He's a cool guy, that's for sure."

"And you! What a performance. I'll bet anything there's some major coupling happening right this minute."

He held his empty glass up. "Hey, I'm all about serving the common good." His eyes were glazy, thick-lidded. He pressed her close and slipped his hands under her skirt, his palms squeezing her. "Thanks to you, this is what I want. Do you know what torture it was watching you zip around in this tight little number all night long?"

"Poor baby."

His breath was warm on her throat as he licked at her dried sweat, and his hair tickled her skin. She wriggled away slightly. "My, you are eager, aren't you? C'mon, let's go to my place so I can shower. I'm gross, and—"

"You're perfect just as you are. Salty and hot."

She laughed. "What am I, a pretzel?"

"Yes. My favorite thing to eat. And I want you, right now."

He picked her up as if she were the weight of a child, hoisting her into the air.

"Wait, *here?*" She grabbed the back of his neck as he carried her across the taproom, over by what was previously the confessional.

"Why not? We're on sacred ground," he said, pinning her to a wall in the partially hidden corner. He eased her panties off and kissed her navel.

"Ow," she cried. "There's something sticking out—"

She looked behind her. A holy water receptacle. And he was unbuckling his pants.

He moved her around it, proceeding to suck her earlobe. "There you go. We're purified."

"Dear God. It's empty. More like we're both going straight to hell."

"If this is hell, then sign me up," he whispered, his voice replete with exhaustion and want. His mouth found hers, and her head jerked back from the jarring impact of their front teeth clashing together. He braced her against the wall and wrapped her legs around him, and she met his every thrust with a locked-in force not even Solomon himself could've divided. She looked up when he forced her body into stillness, his brow creased as if in pain.

"Stop," he choked.

She delicately pressed a thumb on his throat, the artery throbbing like the baby bird she'd tried to rescue years ago. The sparrow had fallen out of a giant oak tree and died in her eight-year-old palm.

His breath plumed out in staccato bursts, hot on her neck. "You feel—incredible. Like moving in silk."

Kathleen gazed up at the stained-glass portholes and smelled the smoky smell of the old pews, and felt no sin at the new lines crossed here. Her back arched with the same graceful bend as the cathedral ceiling that curved above them. There was no sound except for their ragged gasps and a country duo begging for mercy on the pub's stereo in the background:

"*... I need your love, mmm, yes, I do, and you fill my cup ... with your mercy ...*"

He remained motionless, his face frozen as she shimmied herself up and down. Her lips parted. "I'm so close."

"That's what I want to hear. Because I can't take much more."

She laughed wickedly. “Yes, you can.”

“*Ahh—y*ou’re killing me, Smalls. Pretty strong for such a tiny thing, you know that?”

She ran a hand along his thigh, rigid from the effort to hold her and delay the inevitable, and she stopped moving.

“I guess years of aerobics pay off.”

She bore down and clenched her knees and pelvic muscles, creating an inescapable human vise around him. She squeezed once, twice. “I hope this isn’t hurting your hip,” she said, nibbling at his ear.

He inhaled sharply, new rivulets of sweat trickling down his forehead. “Sweet Jesus, no.” His head rolled backward and the veins in his neck raised and stretched tight. Tight across his neck, like the strings bridging the sound hole of his guitar. Her fingers resumed their path, curling under his quivering hamstring. How she did love his legs, the sinew that raised above his scars, the golden-brown furry coating that brushed her skin night after night, and as they trembled under her weight, this supreme attempt at control was her undoing. She dug her heels into his back, their hips colliding with the ancient, violent rhythm that defied time and reason.

The big, ornate space formerly known as St. John’s, host to hundreds of masses, weddings, funerals, potlucks, parish council meetings, confessions, pastoral counseling sessions and christenings, had just been unofficially consecrated under its new ownership.

7

The ten-minute drive to Kathleen's was a quiet one, spent as they were with all the evening had extracted from them. The animals were thrilled to see Thomas, a flurry of happy fur around him, while they pointedly ignored her.

"Hey guys," he said, laughing and petting them both. "What a welcoming committee."

She went to the kitchen to make some tea, and he poured a beer. Unbeknownst to them Zack, had filled a crowler and left it on the bar. Smaller than a growler, it was like a large can of beer equal to two pints.

"What did he fill it with?" Kathleen asked, sitting on the couch.

"Consecration, according to the scrawl on the cap. What is it with these names?"

Kathleen yawned. "I thought I told you Jeff, Summer, and I all went to parochial school together. He's leaning hard on every Catholic term he can come up with."

He took a swig and smacked his lips. "Ah, that is some good stuff. Little does Jeff know his establishment has earned his beer's name tonight."

She tsked, shaking her head. "We're bad, bad people."

"No, we're not." He dropped his glass to his lap. "Why would you say that?"

"I mean, sex in a church? Who *does* that?" She was trying to be light, jokey, and by the look on his face, failing miserably.

"Maybe people who feel more love than shame for each other."

It was the first time the "L" word had been mentioned between them, and Kathleen was making a mess of it. "Come on, I just meant—"

"Here's what I know." He leaned into her face and his voice was hard. "I spent a week facetiming my band so I could spend two hours singing songs to the girl I love. I booked a seven AM flight so I could get back as fast as possible to see her, to show her exactly what she means to me. I, for one, am not sorry an old church was witness to all of it."

Hugo whined and nosed Thomas. He didn't like the rising tension from his favorite person.

"I feel the same. I'm not ashamed of that." Kathleen said, her heart racing with the admission. "But it frightens me. The intensity of what we have—the strength of it—it's unnerving." She choked as the tears rushed in. "Here's the thing. I don't feel worthy. Of it. Of you. There's been no like one you."

He kissed her tenderly, all strain dissipated, and when he broke away, his eyes were the warmest buttery shade of caramel she'd seen yet. "That's a Scorpions song, you know," he smiled, brushing a tear away.

"'No one like you.' Yes."

"You may have a few years on me ..." he laughed as she cuffed him playfully on the shoulder.

"But I agree. It's very possible this is a once-in-a-lifetime thing between us. That's kinda scary, on a few different levels."

He'd barely gotten the words out before his head flopped back on the couch cushion and he was out. Kathleen kissed his damp forehead.

Once in a lifetime.

She looked up at the picture on the wall hanging right above Thomas. She'd bought it years ago in an obscure Catholic bookstore in Chicago, a scene of Jesus surrounded by adoring children, arms outstretched and welcoming.

What do you want us to do with this gift, God?

Wasting gifts is a sin.

She didn't know if that was the Holy Spirit's answer or her own jumbled thoughts, but she laid on Thomas' lap and drifted off in a deep trance herself. She dreamt that Van Morrison and Rod Stewart sang at a benefit for pregnant teens, and they threw a big baby shower for all the girls in her group, and Van started singing "Into the Mystic," when a dog's whining kept interrupting him. And woke her.

"C'mon, Hugo," Kathleen said groggily while shaking Thomas awake. "Time to get our guy to bed."

Hugo led the way up the winding staircase, looking back every few seconds to make sure everyone was following, and jumped at the end of the bed and waited anxiously for the silly humans to join him.

Kathleen unloaded her tote bag, unzipping her portfolio on the sprawling table, and spread out a cornucopia of erasers, graphite and charcoal pencils, and paper. She'd told the girls she'd provide all the drawing supplies, and they could sketch while they chatted. Amanda arrived first, followed quickly by the others. She'd had a long bout with bronchitis and had missed the last two meetings.

"Ms. B, I can't believe you didn't tell us," Amanda said, with a conspiratorial wink to the group.

"Tell you what?"

"Omigod, what a hottie your boyfriend is. We didn't even know you *had* a boyfriend."

Amanda's face was lit up with a joyous curiosity so child-like, so oddly endearing, Kathleen had to smile. It was a reminder of how close they all were to still being children themselves.

"And when did you have the pleasure of meeting Thomas?"

"I didn't. My grandma dragged me to church on Easter and I saw you guys. Of course, I told the girls all about him."

Brianne rolled her eyes. "Yeah, she did. He's, like, way tall, skinny but muscley, with tons of wavy reddish-brown hair, and also had a hoop earring. Oh, and no tats."

"No tats from what *I* could see," Amanda added. "Ya know, with his clothes on and everything. He looks kinda young, too, like in college." She stopped short, as if sensing this might be a sensitive topic. "Umm, but so do you."

"He's not in college," Kathleen sighed. "I'm not sure why we are having this discussion about my personal life, though."

"Ugh, isn't it obvious?" Brianne said. "We get so sick of talking about *this,"* she pointed dramatically to her protruding belly. "It's all we hear or think about, constantly: 'What are we going to do? How will we pay for it? Who will babysit if we keep it? How will we go to prom? Will we get big as cows?' You know, it'd be nice to just hear about someone having a normal life, for once."

The girls nodded in unison.

The irony was almost too much for Kathleen. What had

she railed on about to Thomas? "*Normal people don't go around having oral sex on top of washing machines ...*"

She closed her eyes and felt the faint beginnings of a headache coming on. "I get what you're saying. You're burned out from all the emphasis on the unknown, the pressure for decision-making. I'm afraid there's no avoiding from that now on. Maybe, though, I could talk Thomas into coming one night to meet you all. He *is* a great guy, and a distraction might be nice."

They shifted and twittered excitedly about how much they'd like that. "Yeah, because Amanda said he totally kept staring at you, like he was sooo in love," Francesca chimed in. "Also, we heard he walked out of church before the mass was over, and probably everyone gossiped about that."

"For heaven's sake, Amanda," Kathleen's face bloomed. "Did you pay any attention at all to the service?"

Amanda twirled a strand of wheat-blonde hair absent-mindedly. "Nah. It's always the same old boring blah. I swear, they pull out some manual for holidays and read it word-for-word. Every. Single. Year. God loves you, Easter means new life, Christmas means new life, go in peace with Jesus. Yada, yada, yada. It's much more fun to people-watch."

"You can do that at the mall. You should pay attention," said Mallory.

Amanda's head snapped to her right. "Who are you, my mother? Please. What earth-shaking revelations have *you* had lately, sitting in the pew?"

Mallory sunk into her chair, her plain face paling considerably. "I did have one, actually. And it's not good. I feel sick just thinking about it. About the sin."

Silence swooped in like a heavy drape as they waited for the other shoe to drop. Kathleen was grateful to steer the subject in a new direction, although it appeared art was going to be off the table for tonight.

"Would you like to tell us about it?" she asked gently.

Mallory began crying. "Only if everyone swears they won't tell."

Once Kathleen was assured Mallory wasn't in danger or a danger to others, and the girls promised their silence, Mallory looked down and said, "I think I'm gay."

Kathleen froze like a squirrel in the middle of a busy road. "Okay—"

"What do mean, okay? It's not okay!"

"Let's take a timeout. Please."

"How long did it take for you to figure this out?" Brianne asked Mallory.

"I dunno. I guess I always wondered what it'd be like to kiss a girl, which I did at Bible camp last year, actually. The guilt was awful, but the main thing I remember thinking is that touching someone else's tongue with your own was gross. When I started hanging with Brad, I think I was trying to prove something to myself, and when I slept with him ..." She crossed her arms. "Ack. I found it all so disgusting. I mean, seriously, I don't get what is the big deal. It hurt, *so bad,* and I wanted to slap his hands off me. I can tell you I am one hundred percent sure I don't ever want to have sex with a guy again."

"I bet he's just a really bad lover," Francesca offered. "I mean ... don't a lot of guys only care about getting off? Personally, Sam is the complete oppo—"

Kathleen's hand went up. "We're not getting into that now. Mallory, you're sixteen, and even without a pregnancy in the mix, means going through some major life and bodily changes. It's a really difficult time. I think you need to discuss this with the counselor at school, or someone else who's qualified, and go from there. You have our support, you know that. You and I can meet privately if you need more help, all right?"

She nodded, wiping the tears away. "I feel better already."

Amanda patted Mallory's hand. "You probably *should* be a nun. Aren't a lot of them lesbians?"

"I think so," said Brianne. "They're just not supposed to act on it."

"I wouldn't assume most nuns are gay," Kathleen said. "My guess, and it's just that, is it's the same as what would be in the general population." She rubbed her forehead. "In any event, becoming a nun is a spiritual calling, not meant to be an escape from our own fears and uncertainties." *You should know, since you thought about it, once. You're not going to tell them about that, are you?*

Mallory brightened. "Like Maria, from the 'Sound of Music.' I love that movie."

"That's one example, sure," Kathleen forced a smile. "Now. We've got time for a few comments and updates from the rest of you. What's going on, lately?"

"I thought you were going to show us some drawing techniques," Francesca said, clearly disappointed.

Kathleen's head began to pound. "Next time, I think."

"Well, since we're talking about boyfriends and girlfriends, can I say something?"

The throb increased. "Go ahead," Kathleen said. *Why not, we're on a roll, now.*

"I want to say you're all wrong about what you think. About me being this slut who doesn't know who the father of my baby is." This time, it was her own dark-brown eyes filling. "I know what everyone says about me. I'm not stupid, you know."

"People would see you coming out from under the

bleachers or the woods with different guys all the time," Amanda said.

"So?" Francesca's voice went up a few notches. "Most of them are just my friends who asked me if I wanted to smoke a joint with them. I wasn't having sex. With them, that is. I don't deserve all these vicious stories told about me."

"Fair enough," Brianne said. "But a person can't just do anything they want, especially if it looks bad, and then not expect to people to talk."

Francesca was silent at this, and they all knew it was because she was quite accustomed to doing what she wanted and getting what she wanted, without much consequence.

"Fine." Francesca's pretty lips pursed. "You want to know who my real boyfriend is, the father? I'll tell you. He's a great guy, and I'm crazy about him." She looked around nervously. "It's Sam Martin."

Kathleen nearly choked on the water she was sipping. *Jesus, Mary, and Joseph.* How had she not put it together? Sam had even talked about a Francesca to her. Did Summer and Jeff know? "Francesca ..." she broke in among the other girls' questions. "Have you told him or his family?"

"Of course, he knows. We cried like babies after I took the test."

"And your parents?"

"Mine know, but we're not telling his parents until we decide what we're doing. He says his mom will go ballistic."

"I see." *He knows her well...*

"I mean, he wants to keep it. He begged me not to go to the clinic, and I literally had an appointment to ... you know."

"Yes, because we thought about doing it too," said Amanda.

"Anyway," Francesca continued, flipping her hair off her neck, "Sam keeps talking about getting married after we graduate in the spring. I'm so confused. It's, like, goodbye college, scholarships, freedom, everything. And listen to this bomb: my mom is *so* incredibly pissed I wouldn't have an abortion that she's still not even talking to me. Can you imagine that? When it's your own grandchild?" She wiped a tear away. "My dad's different, though. He tells me he'll be there for us, and then she hears that and goes postal. She says she isn't raising another kid. Not that I'd ask her to. God help her if she misses her pedicure, massage, and personal trainer appointments."

"I'm sure part of your mom's reaction is concern for your future," Kathleen assured her.

"I highly doubt it." Suddenly, she looked at Kathleen, hard. "Wait. Didn't you tell us you *work* at the place Sam's parents own?"

Kathleen swallowed. "Yes. I do, and truly, I'm a little shocked, right now. They're very good friends of mine. But you know you have my confidentiality, as well as the rest of us. Nothing goes out of this room unless you want it to."

"Thanks. It won't be long before the dreaded 'talk,' though. I'm starting to show." She laughed and put her hands on her stomach. "Sam keeps rubbing my tummy, and we did feel a tiny kick, the other day. I gotta say ... that was pretty cool. He's been so, so sweet. He says I'm more beautiful than ever, that he wants me more than ever." She cupped her chest. "But that's probably because I actually have boobs, now. And they're gonna get even *bigger.* I won't be able to keep his hands off me by the time this baby comes!"

"Yep, same here," Amanda said. "I asked my doctor if sex could hurt the baby, and she said no."

Kathleen rubbed the nose of her bridge again. "Okay ..."

"You *are* more gorgeous than ever," Mallory said to

Francesca. "I wish I had your hair. Even your skin is glowing." This triggered a debate as to the pros of pregnancy beauty, until Kathleen intervened.

"That's it, girls, time to wrap it up. It's been quite the ... informative evening. Let's pray over it all and think of what we want to address for next time."

They said a closing prayer, and Kathleen said an extra one for herself and her friend.

It would seem Summer, who'd recently declared "grandma-hood" couldn't be in the cards for her, yet, was in for a little surprise.

"How'd it go, tonight?" Thomas was up scribbling in his songwriting notebook, guitar in his lap, when she came in.

"My God, I need a drink," was her frazzled response.

"Wow. That bad?" He looked up from his guitar and she kissed him on the head.

"Oh, it's fine," she called back, as she headed to the kitchen. "Let's just say it was a night full of revelations. One after the other." She plopped onto the couch noisily, sipped from a pint glass.

"What kind of revelations?"

"I can't say. We make a promise not to. However, I will tell you that you were one of the topics. Along with the ever-present discussion of sex."

He stopped strumming. "What? Me, paired with that topic? Unheard of."

She chuckled. "Believe it or not, they were discussed separately. Amanda saw us at church. She wanted to know why I didn't tell them I was dating such a hottie college student."

He laughed a deep belly laugh, the gap in his teeth, as

usual, inducing a twinge that ran straight through her. "What did you say?"

"I denied your college status and told them if they were so fascinated by my love life, they could meet you. They were all over it. Might be a good distraction for them."

He raised his brow in surprise. "You said that, about meeting up?"

"I did. Will you come next time? You don't have to stay. In fact, after fifteen minutes of their chatting, you'll be running for the door."

"Yes. It'd be nice to put faces with names, finally."

She laid her head back on the couch's cushion. "I really don't know if I'm the right person for these girls."

"Why?"

She shook her head, making her headache worse. "I don't know. They pipe up with this stuff that's quite intimate, which obviously they would, given what's happening to them. They're such a mixture of children on the brink of adulthood; so unprepared for what's ahead. I worry I'll respond the wrong way, or worse ... in a harmful way. I feel so responsible. Incapable. This is the fear I tried unsuccessfully to portray to Sheila Gallagher when she was first hitting me up to do this."

"You can't go wrong with true listening. You're very good at that."

"Thank you. Comforting to know I'm good at something."

He put the guitar down and sat next to her. "Don't say that. I can rattle off several excellent things about you."

"Yeah? Go."

"All right. Let's see: great organizer, cleaner, animal lover, cooking bacon so it's crispy but not burnt, cooking everything, basically ... oh, and grinding coffee the way I like it, back rubs, reading and interpreting people, waiting on annoying drunk people and not losing your cool, working hard and looking sexy all at the same time, talking about art and music, sketching and drawing, being a good friend and stepmom ... and ..." he leaned into her face to kiss her. "Will I keep going, into a whole new category, now? Starting with oral skills ...?"

"Mmm, okay," she said, giggling as youthfully as any of the girls that night.

"How about best kisser in the universe?" he murmured into her neck.

"Um—that's you, not me."

She could feel him smiling against her pulse. "It's us, together."

"Yes," she sighed. The beer, his mouth, and sweet words were quickly mellowing her. "Those are probably the nicest things anyone's ever said to me, or about me. And that's after being married."

He pulled away. "He was a fool. Call me bad, but I'm glad he's gone, or I wouldn't be here right now."

She thought about Steve, his controlling rants and the unpredictable temper as his disease progressed.

"I'm glad you're here, too," she said, drawing Thomas closer and sinking into him. She breathed in his earthy, musky smell, every perceived misstep of the evening drifting away. "More than you could know."

It was Thursday evening and relatively subdued for a June evening at HopCanon. The regulars were grumbling about the maddening tourist crush of the summer season, while others defended them for the money that poured in the little town of Mount Simon for four months. Kathleen was finishing up her shift when Summer came in, her face mottled and red. Kathleen knew, with one look at her, "the talk" with Francesca and Sam had taken place, and her stomach rolled.

"Hey. Are you okay?" she said, exiting out of the computer screen. Summer sat at the end of the bar, right next to the doors to the kitchen, her head down. She peeked up through a shock of hair.

"No, I'm not okay. Can you sit for a while?"

"Of course. Hold on."

Kathleen settled next to her, and Zack was already there with two pints. "It's St. Peter's Porter," he said, his solemn face studying them. "But we're going to call it 'Summer's Solace,' for tonight."

Summer laughed. "That's scarily accurate. Now I know why they call you Zen Zack."

He tipped his head just slightly. "I'm a noticer, as my mom used to say."

"Here's to noticing this beer disappear, then," she said, proceeding to empty half of her glass.

"Whoa, girl," Kathleen said nervously. "I think I know already, but what's going on?"

"Sam's girlfriend is pregnant, that's what's going on," Summer said, her face crinkling. She looked away.

"Ummm—"

"Yes, and they have every intention of raising the baby together. What did I tell you? I saw that one coming a mile away."

Kathleen exhaled slowly. "Promise me you won't get mad. I knew." Seeing Summer's mouth drop, she frantically added, "Only for a week, though! Francesca is part of the girls group I'm leading."

"Are you serious?"

"Yes. I didn't put it together, not until she told the whole group Sam is the father of her baby."

Summer slapped the edge of the bar. "Wonderful! Now the entire town and county will know Sam Martin is old enough to join the army, but he doesn't understand how to use birth control."

"I'm sorry, honey. How is Jeff taking the news?"

"Better than me. He keeps trying to remind me how we were at that age."

"Could be helpful to remember."

"What? *How* is that helpful?" Summer hissed. "We used condoms, for God's sake, even if it was like fucking with a goat's gut on and they broke fifty percent of the time because they didn't have Magnum-size back then for ol' jumbo Jeff."

"Shhh!" Kathleen tried unsuccessfully not to laugh. "Customers! And that was way too much information."

"Nobody can hear. I don't care if they do." Summer gulped again, finishing off the pint. "I mean, my God. It's 2018, not 1965! There is absolutely no excuse. How does this even happen? Especially with these tubes or stick versions of the pill you can shove up every conceivable body part, plus the ten thousand items people can pick from the shelves now, not to mention Planned Parenthood passing rubbers out in My Little Pony rainbow colors? What's that about, anyway? *Jesus.*"

Kathleen signaled Zack for a refill. "Did you rant like this to Sam and Francesca?"

"I'll have you know I behaved myself, for the most part. I *didn't* unload, much as I wanted to. Sam was practically bawling, which bought him major sympathy votes. I asked the usual, 'How will you manage? How do you expect to pay for this? Care for a baby?' that whole deal. You know, what reasonable people might think about when they're banging the shit out of each other without protection, thereby, scaring the guy enough to PULL OUT."

Kathleen picked up her pint and looked at Summer warily. "Ahh, such short, sweet little memories we have. Tell me, does the name Robbie Dolsen ring a bell?"

Robbie was Summer's first love in high school; the school's star basketball player who'd led the team to the state finals win and, consequently, celebrated with Summer afterward in his beat-up Jeep Wrangler.

"That's a cheap shot," Summer said irritably.

"No, it's not. As I recall, good ol' Robbie aimed for the backseat backboard and couldn't pull it off. You were a hysterical hot mess for three weeks."

She burst into laughter. "Oh, I hate you, right now."

"Listen." Kathleen's voice was stern but gentle. "You're understandably upset. It's going to take time to sort all this out. Jeff's right. Think of what it's like to be eighteen again. They're young, they're in love. You know, as well as I do, that nothing is one hundred percent. Things happen, out of our control, sometimes." Kathleen tapped a finger on the bar. "What did Sam have to say?"

"He had an answer for everything, all right. He'll work two jobs if he has to, thinks he'll go to night school or take online college classes. His buddy Andrew's parents have a vacation rental they would be willing to give them a big break on, they think."

Kathleen poked her with the pint glass. "See? That's called stepping up. He's trying to be a man, take responsibility. You should be proud of him, not ashamed."

"That's just it." Summer's cornflower-blue eyes filled. "I don't see a man when I look at him. I still see the newborn I brought home from the hospital eighteen years ago. How can *my* baby be having one?" She put her face in her hands and, after a few minutes, looked up. "It's true, what you said. He is so in love with her he can't see straight, and I'm scared to death she's gonna break his heart. I can't watch it, it'll kill me—and throw an innocent child in the mix—I don't know."

Kathleen rubbed her back. "This is tough stuff," she said soothingly, and Zack came and placed a full pint down.

"Another Summer's solace for the lady."

Summer wiped her face. "Fabulous. Forgive me and my blubbering and keep'em coming."

"He's a good kid, Sam," Zack said. "Hard worker when he's here."

"Thanks, but he has no clue what hard even is yet." She hiccupped. "Except when it's his dick talking."

Zack laughed, and Kathleen thought he was even more good-looking when he cracked a smile. "That's how it is at that age," he said, rounding up dirty glasses off the bar.

"Yeah, and when you're a twenty-, thirty-, forty-year-old guy, too," Summer said, blowing her nose.

"That's harsh." He pushed a glass down into the sink and twisted it on the wire scrubber. "I have a feeling it's all gonna be fine. He'll be a great dad."

Kathleen lifted her glass toward him. "You know, I've concluded you're some kind of psychic."

He shrugged. "Nah. You'd be surprised what you learn when you tune in to your surroundings. It's enlightening, to say the least."

"Okay, Gandhi," Summer waved a hand in the air, "Fess up and distract us. The girls working the kitchen never stop gaggling about who's doing who, but there's not a crumb about your dating world dropped around here."

"Which is just how I like it."

"Come on. Is there nobody you're interested in?"

He rubbed more glasses in the sink, his dreads falling over muscular shoulders. "There was a girl, a couple years ago. It was a painful time."

"That's it? That's all we get?"

"I'm done with that part of life. For a while."

Summer slammed forward, her abundant chest hitting the edge of the bar. "Ow. Wait, I can't even believe this. How old are you?"

"Twenty-four, soon."

"You can't be throwing in the towel permanently," Kathleen interjected.

"Probably not, but abstinence has a real freeing effect. Gives a person perspective."

Summer shook her head. "Man, whoever it is, she must've burned you *bad.*"

"It wasn't her fault. Her family didn't believe in ... interracial dating, shall we say."

"Good God. Where did you find this girl, in a time warp from 1963?"

"Nope. College. And you don't need to be in a time warp to know certain people will never accept you. Not as a son-in-law, or a father to a grandchild." He looked at both of them, his hazel eyes calm. "And I'll end my contribution to the discussion on that note."

He went into the back with an armful of plates and the two friends stared at each other.

"What do you think happened? With him and the girl?" Kathleen said.

"The hell if I know, but we won't be finding out anytime soon. He just sealed off like King Tut's tomb there." She took another big swig of Summer's Solace.

"Maybe he was in Sam's situation, once, and the lack of support broke them up." She gave Summer the fish eye, who in turn made a face.

"What are you, a writer for the National Enquirer, now? I think those gossip-mad teens are getting to you."

"No, I—"

"Don't you dare insinuate that is me in this situation. Jeff and I both said we'll be there for them through this, and that wasn't easy, let me tell you. Are we supposed to put all of our plans on the backburner, now? How do I run this place if I'm helping raise a baby? We're just getting started, here."

"I'll help you. I'll help them. It takes a village, right?"

"That's insanely oversimplified, but thank you. Truth is, I can't wrap my head around it all."

"You're still in shock. Just breathe. Baby steps."

"Yes. Breathing in-between drinking is good."

Kathleen sighed. "I grant you the timing is far from the best. But they'd hardly be the first young couple in history to face some significant obstacles right off the bat."

"I'm aware," Summer said miserably. She held up her pint. "All right, enough already. The subject of procreating is officially closed. For now."

"Okay."

"Except, I should be mad at you for not telling me about Francesca."

Kathleen's head reared back. "What? Now you're talking crazy. I can't betray those girls' confidences. They'd never trust me again."

Summer looked at her, bleary-eyed. "Of course. I'm sorry. You're a much better person than me, do you know that?"

"I'm not."

"You're the best friend a girl could ask for."

"I try. You are, too."

"Cheers to friendship," Kathleen said, and as they clinked glasses, Zack came back.

"Has Summer's Solace done its job?" he asked.

Summer drained her glass and smiled. "Yes. Thank you for ignoring possibly everything your noticer-self noticed by observing me tonight. It is what it is. I'll get by, with a little help from my friends. As Mr. Hart doing his best Joe Cocker would sing."

Zack nodded toward Kathleen as he washed another glass. "He does it well, doesn't he?"

"Yes. Yes, he does," Kathleen said, feeling loose and limber. Summer's Solace, formerly known as St. Peter's Porter, was working its magic on her, now. "Mr. Hart does lots of things profoundly well. To my benefit and eternal gratitude."

Summer rolled her eyes. "You're the only person I know who walks around sporting a post-orgasmic blush twenty-four hours a day. Must be nice."

Kathleen snorted, embarrassed and laughing, as did Zack. In fact, it was the second time in an hour Zack laughed long and deep, and with that rare occurrence, Kathleen was reassured all was going to be right in the world. She was about to order another pint when a random string in her brain unraveled, dangling from the subject of their conversation and needling its way through her beer fog. She tried to sit up straight, until the wet blanket of sobriety descended with all the weight of the killjoy it was. The threads came together. Summer glanced her way, peering closely at her.

"So much for the blush. You look like someone just pitched a bucket of water on you. What's the matter?"

"Nothing ... I ... need to use the restroom." Kathleen backed off the barstool unsteadily. The thoughts churning in her head were causing a similar uproar in her lower belly, almost like the nausea she used to get from menstrual cramps as a young teen.

The kind of cramps that came with a period she hadn't had in weeks.

Kathleen bought two pregnancy tests, as if one wouldn't be enough confirmation. Her hands shook at the drugstore register like Steve's used to do, and continued at home as she struggled with unwrapping the package and its contents. She tried to recall the date of her last period. How had this absence not been on her radar, as regular as she was? She stared at the box. Gone were the lines and symbols changing color to indicate yay or nay. She'd almost suffered a panic attack trying to decide which one to buy, and the hideous fluorescent lighting as well as the lingering clerk in the store hadn't helped her anxiety. Fluorescent lighting always had a nauseating effect on her. Hadn't it?

The little rectangle display on the white stick would simply read pregnant or not pregnant, in order to "eliminate the confusion of interpreting results at an emotional time." How about that? Some researcher had been studying neurotic knuckleheads who'd possibly incorrectly diagnosed themselves infertile, and concluded they'd have difficulty with the test. She sat on the toilet and held the thermometer-shaped object in her sweaty palm.

And waited.

She stared at the single word that appeared, and every unkind or judgmental thought she'd ever had or heard regarding unexpected life events came back to whirl through her head in a scolding teacher's voice. Not just any voice, either. Ms. Hallman's voice, her third-grade teacher with darting squirrel eyes and mousy-brown hairstyle that probably had a weekly standing appointment at the local gossip-fest salon in order to maintain. That, or she'd slept with orange juice cans in her hair every night. She'd falsely accused Kathleen of cheating on math homework, and reveled in drawing every pupil's attention to the supposed act. She was short and squat like a squirrel, too, and Kathleen remembered her stubby fingers jabbing at the corn-yellow paper in front of her, and she'd wanted to yank the pencil stuffed behind her the teacher's elfin ear and jab *her* with it.

The condemning voice, which started out as, "*I think somebody else filled in the multiplication facts for you,*" turned into a string of jabbing babble, some of which Summer herself asked: "*How does unplanned pregnancy happen in 2018? With every method known to man ... how, how, how, how? Thoughtless ... selfish ... immature ... crazy ... what did you think, to be so careless ... horrible timing ... it's not a life, not yet ... too young ... too old ... how could you do that ...*"

This did not happen to women at an age in which they are presumed to know better. To women who wanted to know the ending of the story at the beginning. This happened to fumbling, unprepared teenagers in backseats, too drunk, high, horny, or needy to care what happened.

She leaned back against her bathroom wall and rubbed her eyes.

The batik motif of her shower curtain, its cornucopia of colors she once found so appealing, mocked her now. *That's your life. You, running in circles, making the same mistakes again and again.*

She went to her bed and forced herself to take several deep breaths. The *hows* imploded: How was it possible? How? How had she just assumed it was she who had the problem when she couldn't get pregnant with Steve? To be fair, the gynecologist all those years ago was a real gem. He'd gone on about scarring, cervixes and future uterine capabilities, literally scaring the crap out of her as she'd bolted from the exam room and straight to the toilet. In any case it was pointless to ruminate now. She bit her lip to keep it from trembling. There was more to her obliviousness, as she well knew. She'd never stopped believing her inability to conceive was punishment from God for her past behavior. *Ridiculous, adolescent, Ouija-board nonsense.*

So, what's this, God? Some kind of test or ironic joke?

She looked up at the ceiling as the tears rolled down the side of her face, as the *whats* began their assault: What now? What to do? What to say to Thomas? How could she drop a bomb like this, right as he was preparing for the huge challenge of touring and putting new songs out there? It seemed unspeakably cruel.

"Hey, remember when I said you didn't need condoms? Yeah, I lied. I mean, not on purpose. I'm just a thirty-nine-year-old complete moron, is all, because it's not like you didn't tell me this was the LAST thing in the world you wanted ..."

He might say, bewildered, *"But ... I have been using them."* And then she'd say, *"Not that night you didn't, when I said never mind and rode your beautiful body like a horse with a burr under its saddle. Consecration, indeed."*

Damn.

Kathleen wasn't one to use much profanity, too many years of Catholic conditioning still ingrained, but repeating various forms of cursing was now strangely cathartic. She raved for a few minutes until Hugo came in looking anxious. She sat on the bed again and he hurried to the edge to nudge her. She scratched his ears and buried her face on his head.

"Hey, boy. You can always make me feel better, huh?"

He wagged his tail in response, and then she thought about her girls' group. If she'd deemed herself a hypocritical ninny before ... how she'd begin to explain unmarried pregnancy at almost-forty was too much to contemplate. And what would she begin to say to Sheila? She started sputtering again and Hugo's ears cocked endearingly. A smart dog, he knew his therapeutic duties weren't over, yet. He licked her hand and jumped on the bed to patiently wait out the storm.

She couldn't spill it, yet, she rationalized. No. He'd been working so hard on composing and practicing. She'd come home after a shift at HopCanon and find him with his head bowed, the well-worn notebook in front of him, and guitar in hand. Sometimes it would be more than an hour before he'd join her in bed, and when he slid in next to her, he was humming a new tune. She'd drift off to a soothing lullaby, occasionally with words, the irony of which wasn't lost on her. It was easy to see why people had sung to their babies for centuries, and these days, sleep was an elusive visitor she couldn't get enough of.

This was temporary, she assured herself. She'd tell him when it became necessary, when she'd had a chance to clear her head and figure out her next steps.

"So, what's new?" asked her stepdaughter. Megan's green eyes, so like Steve's, were bright with curiosity.

Megan was home for the weekend from college, where she was pursuing veterinary medicine, the same as her father had done. Although Steve sold his practice shortly after his diagnosis, it was Megan's hope to work there herself, someday, as a partner to the new owner. Kathleen had invited her to dinner at HopCanon to catch up, and they were seated at the bar.

"Let's see ..." Kathleen said. *What's new? How about, "Hey, Megan, what do you think about becoming the big sister*

you always dreamed about? Who cares if you're twenty-four?"
"Well, work here is great, and it's keeping me busy."

Megan gestured around the pub. "This place is sooo cool. Who would've thought, a church turned into a brewery?"

Zack approached, wearing a faded Grateful Dead tee and tight jeans. Kathleen introduced them to one another.

"Nice to meet you," he said, studying Megan in his typical manner.

She tugged at a dangling hoop earring. "And you, as well."

"What can I get you?"

Kathleen thought he might be studying Megan a little more closely than he did his usual customer, but she could be mistaken.

"I'll just have a root beer," Kathleen said, and at his quizzical expression, she added, "Maybe you can work your Zen magic on Megan and pick something for her."

"Or maybe she knows what she wants." Zack eyed her stepdaughter.

Kathleen hadn't been mistaken.

"Uh ... um, actually, I don't know," Megan said, uncharacteristically flustered and scanning the beer selection on the wall. "What the heck, I'm up for a little Zen magic. Try me."

"Got it." He disappeared to fetch a pint glass.

Megan poked at Kathleen. "Holy Moly, who *is* he?"

"Only the best bartender for miles. He's quite the mystery, too."

"He's—exotic-looking, to say the least. And what, does he live at the gym? Those arms ..."

"Shhh. The man hears and knows all. No joke."

He reappeared with "Genesis," one of their newer beers.

"Interesting name." Megan took a whiff of the head. "Smells fruity. Is this one that you drink?"

He cocked his head slightly. "It's a mango IPA, which is a nice treat on a hot day. But honestly, there's not a beer here I don't like. It's how they end up from where they began that I find fascinating. The evolution, if you will. Which, not coincidentally, leads to beers named 'Genesis.'"

"Seems an appropriate choice. And deep."

He laughed. "Beer Theology 101. Cheers."

He left to wait on another customer and Megan took a drink.

"Well?" Kathleen asked.

"Mmm. It's yummy," she said, the look in her eyes suggesting she thought as much of her server.

Kathleen laughed. "Don't get your hopes up. He declared, recently, he intends to be date-less for the remainder of his days."

"Is that so? I certainly can relate."

"What about you? How's your mom?" Kathleen asked.

"You know. Diane is Diane. Pushy and disapproving as ever."

"Oh, my. What now?"

Megan exhaled, blowing her bangs up off her forehead. She had grown into a lovely mix of spunk and pretty; a tall redhead with legs that went on forever and a mind that never quit.

"Where do I begin? First off, she keeps trying to set me up with all her socialite friends' sons. And I couldn't care less. I think she thinks I'm gay." She laughed. "Even if it were true, she refuses to wrap her head around the fact that marriage and motherhood don't interest me. She can't conceive that I want to devote myself to being the best vet I can be, like Dad."

"Maybe that's the problem. He didn't devote himself to

their marriage the same way he did to the clinic. And that stings, and she doesn't want you to fall into the same trap."

Megan threw back her head and laughed hard, her long red hair swishing. Zack's head turned.

"I think you missed your calling as a shrink. You're right, as usual. But there's nobody in my life for me to neglect, and there won't be, for quite a while. I don't have time for the drama. And I'm more than fine with that. She's no idea the shitload of things I learned *not* to want, just by watching her and Dad." She shrugged. "Sorry if that's harsh. Also, why aren't you drinking with me?"

Kathleen picked at a bar napkin. "Oh, I had enough this past weekend. A little break is good."

Megan's eyes narrowed. She'd always been an observant child, beyond her years. "You look ... different or something. Flushed. Are you alright?"

"I'm fine. Don't be worrying about me. You've got enough on your plate."

Her stepdaughter's mouth dropped. "Wait. You're dating someone, aren't you?"

"Transparent as ever, that's me. Yes, I am. Are you okay with that?"

"Are you kidding? Of course, I'm okay. Let's hear it."

"He used to be a nurse. And is now a guitar player in a band, believe it or not. He plays here, in fact."

"No way. Is it serious?"

"Yes. But, there's this little issue." *One of many, at the moment.* "He's a bit younger. Like, by ten years."

Megan let out a little howl. "How ironic, right? Considering you were younger than Dad, I mean."

"Ironic." Kathleen forced a smile. "Yes, that it is."

"Cheers to you and Mr. Younger Guy." Megan lifted her glass. "Yes!" She continued. "This beer is already making me loose-lipped, but I don't care. This is the best news I've had in forever. You know, something's crossed my mind a few times since Dad died. I even wanted to bring it up, then I didn't because I don't want to come off sounding like mummy dear. But I hope you know me well enough." She finished off the Genesis. "I was thinking, you're still young enough to marry again, even have a family of your own, if you still wanted." Again, the green eyes pinned her, like a butterfly to a science board. "Do you? Still want that?"

Kathleen strained to make her voice natural. "I suppose it could happen. What ... what makes you ask?"

Megan smiled grimly. "You don't realize what I overheard through the years, between you and Dad. The arguments. And I felt bad for you."

"Why?"

"It seemed so unfair. I was angry at him for a long time, because he wouldn't give us both the one thing we asked for."

"Those were difficult days."

Megan signaled Zack for another beer. "Remember the year when 'baby brother or sister' was the only thing I wrote on my Christmas list?"

Kathleen nodded. At the time, reading it had made her cry. Steve had been against adoption from the start with no reasonable argument as to why.

"I don't know what I was expecting Christmas morning, but I was so upset I didn't talk to Dad for days afterward."

"That was the year we got Buster, wasn't it?"

"Yes, poor Buster. I was happy to get him, no doubt about that. I'd wrap him up in a towel and pretend my guinea pig was a baby. And my patient."

Kathleen laughed. "He wasn't too cooperative, if I recall."

"Was Buster your idea?"

"Yes, but your dad was onboard."

Megan's eyes were glassy. "You know, I think I told you before, but if I didn't ... thank you."

"For what, honey?"

"Just for being you. You were, and are, a great stepmom, and I know it wasn't easy. I would've kicked me to the curb, the typical preteen nasty brat, pissed off her parents couldn't hack it together."

Kathleen waved her hand. "C'mon. You're not giving yourself enough credit. You were a normal child dealing with divorce. And whether you believe it or not, you were easy to love, sweetheart."

Zack placed a pint of Genesis in front of Megan. "I believe it," he said, a smile tugging at his lips. "I'm guessing you liked?" He pointed to her glass.

"Yes. Very much. You were spot on."

"Glad to be of service. Is there anything else I can get for you?"

"I think we're good, thanks," Megan stared at him, and he walked away.

"The guy is uncanny," Kathleen said under her breath. "But I have to say, he doesn't usually smile that much at anyone. Maybe you're the girl who could break his self-imposed monkhood."

"Hmm ... I'm always up for a challenge." Megan sipped, watching him bend over to wash glasses. "But back to what we were saying. Easy to love, my foot. I'm the most difficult person I know, and I always have been, so that means you're either lying through your teeth, which I know you can't do, or you have a gift. You do, you know. You loved me in a way even my own mom didn't. Or couldn't." She gave a rueful laugh. "Still can't."

"There wasn't any gift to it at all. You and your dad were a package deal," Kathleen said, squeezing Megan's arm, her own tears closing in. "He would be so proud of you, you know that? How independent you are, how determined. You have his drive. And his good looks, of course."

"Mom would say his bullish streak. But bullish is getting me through these hellish classes."

"I don't doubt it."

"So, when do I get to meet your man?" Megan giggled conspiratorially.

"Well ... he ... Thomas is his name ... he has a standing gig, here, every-other-Friday, until he goes on tour. You could come and listen, sometime. Or you could come for dinner, soon."

"It's a date, then." Megan's face glowed. "I'm thrilled for you. I mean it. You were so good to both me and Dad, putting up with our stubborn-ass selves, year in and out. I'll tell you something else. I think he's happy about this new development too, wherever he is." She leaned forward. "No, I *know* he is. He told me to look after you, to bug you about getting a life after him. Did you know that?"

Kathleen shook her head, unable to speak.

"He did. Looks like maybe I won't have to do that, after all."

The beer gone, they hugged goodbye, and Kathleen left feeling years lighter than when she went in, as though a burden she didn't even know she'd been carrying had lifted. She got in her car and grabbed a tissue from the glove compartment. Steve used to cluck about Megan, constantly, fuss over what a headstrong and uncooperative kid she was. She looked up, her teary vision distorted and blurry, and talked to her late husband out loud.

"I told you time and time again, and damn it, I was right. Megan's going to be fine. She's the best part of you. Maybe, even, of us."

Kathleen lunged forward and retched into the toilet, her throat screaming with the burn. She'd camped out right next to the toilet for the past few days. She told Summer and Thomas she had a bad bout with the flu, to bide some time and keep them both at bay. It wasn't easy with the former nurse, either, who kept calling and wanted to see her.

"Please," she'd said. "I don't want to be around anyone, right now. Use this time to get with the band and practice. Give me a couple days to feel good, and maybe Wednesday, if I'm better, you can come with me to my teen meeting."

"Are you sure I can't bring you anything? You sound terrible."

"No, nothing. Thank you, though. I'll talk to you soon. Don't worry."

He reluctantly agreed to keep his distance, and the minute she hung up with him, she called an Ob/Gyn office she'd googled, one with positive reviews. To her great luck, they'd had a cancellation and she landed an appointment the next day. She hadn't sat long in the understated waiting room of the Lewiston women's health center before they called her name, one in a row of three round-bellied women looking as tired as she felt.

Dr. Deirdre Love was a diminutive woman, with cropped salt-and-pepper hair, steel-framed glasses, and a brisk, refreshing manner. She had a lilt to her voice, an Irish accent if Kathleen had to guess. And the irony of her name made Kathleen smile.

"According to these dates, you're about twelve weeks along. How're you feeling?" Her hazel eyes regarded Kathleen with lively interest.

"Horrible. I'm vomiting so much my stomach muscles are sore. And my throat, too. I'm basically living in my bathroom."

"Ach, that's no fun. A good sign, but no fun at all. I can prescribe a couple of meds for that."

The tight knot in Kathleen's shoulders lessened. *Thank God.* "That'd be wonderful."

"All right, now. I'm going to measure your belly and then try to get a heartbeat. As a warning, we may not get one today, and that's nothing to worry about. It usually means the baby's positioning isn't cooperating."

She applied the gel on Kathleen's abdomen and slid the wand around, but there was nothing but a whooshing sound to be heard.

"So, that's normal?" Kathleen asked.

"Tis, yes. Your HCG levels are high, and the nausea, as I said, is a good indication all is well." She went on to emphasize the importance of eating small, bland meals throughout the day, and other nutritional points, and then said, quite abruptly: "Now, then. What about the father? Is he involved?"

"Umm—" she stammered. Did she ask all her patients this? "He's definitely in the picture. But he doesn't know. Yet." Kathleen was swept with embarrassment at this admission, at how juvenile it sounded for a father of a baby to be uninformed. "I haven't told anybody at all. For a few good reasons."

"What? That, I'm afraid, you will have to remedy. Support is crucial for successful pregnancies."

"I know. I'll talk to him soon. But ... it's complicated."

Dr. Love nodded sympathetically. "It's always that, isn't it, love? Is he married?"

Kathleen laughed at her inquisitiveness. "No. To be perfectly blunt, Doctor, this pregnancy was quite the unexpected event. I know it's hard to believe, in this day and age."

"Goodness, there's not a thing that surprises me after thirty-five years in the business, and I put square blame for these little 'gifts' on the Man above." She cackled and slapped her hands on her lap. "In any event, it'd be in your best interests to get these matters straightened round, the sooner the better. Stress isn't good for you or the baby."

"Yes, of course."

How? How do I get these matters "straightened round?" Tell me.

They discussed prenatal development, what to expect, and the doctor stood up.

"If you've no more questions, we'll see you next month. Barring any problems, such as the nausea worsening. In that case, you need to call here." She put a pen in her pocket and made for the door.

"Wait," Kathleen said, her hands twisting nervously, "You haven't mentioned my ... age. Thirty-nine, that is."

"What about it, love?"

She cleared her throat. "Doesn't that put me in some high-risk category, or the baby, too?"

She furrowed her wiry brows, which wiggled like two matching grey caterpillars above her eyes. "Nonsense. You're fit as a fiddle, as far as I can tell. Perfect weight, low blood pressure." She put her hands on her hips. "Ah, sure, where I come from, in the west of Ireland, women have healthy babies well into their fifties. Not that I particularly think having a baby at fifty is a grand idea, mind you, but, nevertheless. We'll do your usual screenings, but unless there's an indication for further testing, we'll be treating this as a normal pregnancy."

"Really? That's it?"

Dr. Love smiled, making the forked creases next to her eyes even more prominent. "That's it. Now, you go home, take the meds, and rest. And get your man onboard, if you can. You're going to need him."

8

The prescriptions helped, much to Kathleen's relief, though she still had bouts of intense wooziness. It was the fatigue she hadn't bargained on. This was an exhaustion unlike anything she'd ever experienced; as if a truck steamrolled her flat to her bed and she had to peel herself up, limb by limb, to function. She hoped this phase wouldn't last. She'd never been a decent liar. Or bluffer. She knew she was riding a time bomb, but every single scenario she dreamed up when breaking the news to Thomas ended badly. There was the distinct possibility he would reject her completely. He'd been so against the idea of having a family he'd broken off an engagement, for God's sake. What would make her any different? If anything, it was worse. Not only had she not known him as long as he had his fiancé, but she was older, not part of his circle, and pregnancy was now no longer a hypothetical situation.

She blinked back tears that were a constant presence, lately, and slowly edged up on the headboard of her bed. The only absolutes here were that she was having this baby, and ready or not, she'd change her life again. For all of his faults, Steve had left her well off financially. More than well off, as her last visit to their estate planner had revealed. Beyond this, she refused to speculate any further, other than to contemplate how to handle the other herculean task. Her family. How on earth would her mother understand? She hadn't even met Thomas, yet. She squeezed her forehead. *Think, think.*

Well, there was this: Peggy liked music, even if she wasn't a fan of HopCanon. She'd asked about Thomas numerous times, after the Easter plan hadn't materialized. She nodded. *Yes. Get her softened up with one of the ciders they'd added to the taplist.* The decision was made: she'd invite her mother to his show. Then Peggy would get to see him in his element, at the pub, so that when the story tumbled out, it would be somewhat conceivable.

See, Mom? See how your wayward, widowed daughter could end up pregnant by the splendid creature you met? Not such a stretch, is it? Oh, and by the way, the union was sanctified on the church-turned-pub property. As holy as it gets, baby, without the ring and the priest.

She'd leave that part out.

A wave of nausea erupted in her belly. Hard to predict what her mother would think, aside from massive disapproval, but Kathleen needed to make the meet-and-greet happen before Thomas left. At this thought, she was prompted to run to the bathroom, her hand over her mouth.

In less than a month, he was heading south for the first leg of the tour.

"Mmm, you smell so good." Thomas nuzzled her post-shower neck. "I'm glad you're feeling better."

"Me too," she said. "I missed you."

"Yeah?" He pulled her closer. "Show me how much, woman."

She laughed. "It's group night. And you're coming with me. How can we get into a prayerful state of mind?"

"Oh, I have ideas, if your body is up for it. What do I keep telling you? 'Satisfaction is sacred'?"

She unbuttoned his shirt. "You did say that," she said. She looked over at the bottles of water, Gatorade, and crackers he'd brought, unknowingly helping to nourish the insistent source of the upset. Helping a tiny heart to grow. She caressed his bare chest and neck, and the anxiety of the past two weeks welled up and out.

"Hey. What's this?" he brushed a tear away with his thumb.

"I love you. That's all. It's all I've got at the moment." She pressed close to his ribcage, the steady thrum of his pulse shushing her protests and telling her life would triumph. Life would find a way to flourish through the chaos, through the groundless panic that would be hard to understand years later, in the same way it had bravely persisted since the beginning of time.

"Okay, gang, I told you I'd introduce you," Kathleen said to the girls. "Thomas, meet Mallory, Brianne, Francesca, and Amanda."

He'd opted out of his usual black, wearing a maroon dress shirt for the occasion. The deep color complimented the amber in his eyes and hair for a magnificent effect. He laid his guitar case down and waved at the uncharacteristically subdued foursome. "I'm glad to put faces to names. Kathleen sure enjoys hanging out with you all."

Amanda was the first to speak. "She's awesome."

"Yeah," added Brianne. "I don't know many adults who could stand listening to our stupid crap week after week."

"The teen pregnancy diaries," said Francesca. "So much drama."

"And we don't know anything about her," Mallory said. "It's why we wanted to meet you."

Kathleen set out the art materials. "Believe me, I lead a boring life." She glanced up at Thomas, contrite. "I mean, you're not ..."

He cupped a hand around his cheek, whispering to them, "She's not boring," to which they all laughed.

Kathleen coughed. "Who would like to lead the opening prayer, this week?"

"Let Thomas do it," Amanda suggested, and the others chimed in their agreement.

"Sure," he said. "Is there a script, or am I winging it?"

"Wing it!"

"You don't have to, you know," Kathleen began, but he waved her off.

"It's fine. Let me think, a minute." He looked up at the ugly particle board ceiling, as the four waited expectantly, while Kathleen noted the curly tuft of chest hair peeking out of his shirt, unbuttoned to the second slot.

He shifted in the chair. "Okay. My grandma used to have meetings with ... people in need, you could say, in our house—"

Amanda burst in. "Your *house?*"

"Yeah, it was part of an outreach thing. Sometimes I was there, too. She'd start the gatherings with this prayer, if I can remember it."

"It doesn't matter," Brianne assured him. "Anything's a nice change from 'Our Father, who art in heaven' for the thousandth time."

"Brianne," Kathleen said. "Really?"

She smoothed her black bangs. "Sorry. Just thought I'd help a creative-type guy out."

Kathleen looked at Thomas trying not to laugh, and she took a deep breath. "Whatever you do is fine."

"All right, here we go." He bowed his head, his hair falling forward, and the group held hands. "Dear Father, thank you for your promise that where two or three are gathered in your name, you are there in the midst, a safe haven and harbor among the storms. Father, we ask that you open our minds, spirits, and hearts, so that we may receive your protection and love. Amen."

"Amen," they chorused.

"That was lovely," Kathleen said. "Thank you."

Brianne brought homemade chocolate chip cookies ("My dad's recipe," she'd said) and milk for the snack. As it was being readied, Thomas got his guitar out.

"Are you going to serenade us while we eat?" said Amanda, giggling. "Ms. K did tell us you were a musician."

"She also said you used to be a nurse," Mallory said quietly. "I haven't told anybody, but I'm interested in that, maybe someday."

"Yeah?" Thomas turned to her. "It's a great choice."

"So why aren't you still doing it, then?"

"Mallory—" Kathleen began.

"Hey," Brianne interrupted, frowning at Mallory, "Last time we met, you were headed to the nunnery. What happened to that?"

"I still like the idea," Mallory said defensively. "Who picks one career for life, anyway?"

Kathleen couldn't quite grasp what was happening. Ten minutes into meeting the man, they had him leading a prayer and were asking him things she had yet to truly delve into after three months.

"Thomas, please. Don't feel like you have to explain anything."

"No, it's okay," he said. "It's a fair question." He strummed a few practice chords. "The truth is, I loved many things about the job, but I was there for the wrong reasons. I worked in the psychiatric unit, which can be a tough gig if you don't have your own head together. So, between those issues and the physical demands—"

"What kind of issues?" interrupted Brianne.

"Honestly," Kathleen broke in again, fully annoyed, now. "That's not anybody's business."

He kept strumming, a chagrined smile on his face. "I don't mind. We're all friends, here." He stopped strumming and looked at them. "My father was a doctor who died from a suicidal drug overdose after years of suffering with depression. We both thought, at various times, that I could make a difference in the field somehow. I didn't. Not in a big-picture way."

The room was still.

"My uncle shot himself," Brianne blurted casually, as though announcing the day's weather forecast or what was for dinner that evening. "He did it in his car in the woods somewhere. The cops found him."

"Oh, Brianne—" Kathleen started to say.

Brianne held a hand up. "No. It's okay. I mean, it's *not* okay he did that, but I didn't say it to get all the cow eyes looking my way."

Francesca's left eyebrow went up. "Why did you say it, then?"

"I dunno. Maybe to say people killing themselves happens a lot. A lot more than people realize."

"You are one hundred percent right about that, Brianne," Thomas said softly. "Unfortunately." He thumped his guitar.

"But, listen. I didn't come here to bring everybody down. I wanted to play some music for you. What do you think?"

The room filled with affirmations.

"The song is from the Seventies, by a duo called Loggins and Messina. You probably don't know it—"

"We don't care," said Mallory, her mouth full of cookie bits.

"Good." His eyes met and held Kathleen's, and he began. "Here's, "*Danny's Song.*"

His pitch was perfect, as rich and melodic as the original, the lyrics about making a family equally evocative. He bobbed to the rhythm, still looking right at her with the chorus.

Then he ad-libbed an extra line, looking at all of them: "You know, everything is gonna be all right."

He leaned back, winning four more hearts simultaneously by the end of the third verse.

Kathleen's belly burbled and beads of sweat gathered on her brow. She swallowed, willing the nausea away with each beat.

He sang the chorus one last time, his head dipping down with the last note.

She'd fixed her eyes on the shapely curve of Mallory's new haircut to distract herself. Unsuccessfully.

Of all the songs.

The girls' clapping interrupted further thought and the cacophony of praise wiped out any more talk of suicides, babies, and career decisions.

"That was awesome," gushed Amanda, wiping her cheek. "Where'd you learn to play and sing like that?"

"Thanks. I think I was about eleven when I got my first guitar. And ever since, lots of wailing away in my room practicing."

"So, like, are you in a band?" Francesca asked.

"Yes. I play solo, sometimes, but a group of buddies and myself started messing around a while back. The Thomas Hart Band. How's that for original? And we're going on tour, if you can call visiting a string of dive bars touring, very soon."

"I can't believe it," Amanda went on. "I've met my first rockstar."

He flashed a wide smile. "I'd say that's premature."

"But I bet your patients missed you," Mallory said, apparently insistent on drawing the conversation back to nursing. "Anyone who would sing a song like you just did ... well, I don't believe you were a bad nurse."

"It was a bit more complicated than I made it out to be."

Mallory's doe eyes studied him. "Do you miss it? I mean, how do you *know* you made the right choice?"

The expression that fleeted across his face was somewhere between befuddlement and admiration. "I don't know that I did," he said. "I think about that almost every day."

"Oh. My. God." Amanda groaned. "Are there no guarantees in life? At all, ever? How am I going to know I will make the right move about this?" She pointed to her ever-expanding bump. "I'll just admit it right now: I don't want to be a mom, or a wife. I absolutely *hate* being pregnant, and the thought of a screaming, poopy bundle makes me cringe. I am, like, the only teenage girl on the planet who has never babysat the neighbor kid. The main reason I watch my little brother is so my grandma can get a break." Her eyes shone with tears in the florescent light. "In fact, I'm more like his mother than our own ever was. Like, I even nag better than her: '*Tyler, go brush your teeth. Tyler, it's time for bed. Tyler, it's time to get up and feed the dog. No, I don't care about your stupid light up tennis shoes' just put them ON.*' I mean, kids are so pathetically helpless, and it's not like it stops. Every day, it's the same boring routine, and I can't stand it. I'm beginning to see why my mom couldn't hack it. I can almost forgive her for checking out. Am I just a horrible person?"

"Of course not, Amanda," Kathleen replied. "The responsibility must feel overwhelming."

Amanda looked relieved to have someone confirm it. "Yeah." She picked at cookie crumbs on the table. "Truthfully, I'm leaning toward letting the father of my baby keep it. He won't stop going on about how he could manage, with his parents' help. Without me. But what mom *does* that? What if the kid grows up to be a mass murderer because I gave him up? Why does everything have to be so hard?"

"Or the kid could grow up to be a psychopath after being raised by a mother who never wanted him," Francesca offered helpfully, and Amanda put her head in her hands.

"See what I mean? Shit," she murmured, then quickly added, "Sorry."

"Okay," Kathleen said shakily. "We could debate this for hours. Nobody's holding a crystal ball, here. Every time we think we're doing the right thing, there will be doubt. I'm sorry if that sounds like a copout, but adults don't have all the answers."

"Isn't that the truth," Brianne said morosely. "I mean, my dad can't even remember to pay the electric bill on time. Forget about giving advice."

Kathleen exhaled. "Time to refocus. We're going to start drawing tonight, remember? Did everyone bring a picture or object with them?"

They all responded yes. Brianne had brought an ultrasound picture, Francesca a newborn playsuit, Amanda a baby picture of herself, and Mallory an elaborate crucifix.

"These are great, everyone. I won't spend a huge amount of time going over basics, since you've told me you've had art before. The main thing I want you to know is that sketching is a skill like any other. The more you practice, the better you'll become. I'm going to show you my piece in progress, but it's more for purposes of instruction than anything else. We will not be making comparisons to each other's work, other than to note differences or similarities in a productive manner. Got it?"

They agreed, organizing their objects while Kathleen talked a little about the importance of lighting. She set up her portable easel and her face warmed again under Thomas' constant gaze. She hadn't shown him her sketch, yet, and was apprehensive that her obsessive desire for him would scream through the canvas.

"Some artists who have been at it for quite a while don't require a picture or prop, per se. There isn't a right way or wrong way; it's whatever works for you." Kathleen unzipped her portfolio and placed the picture on the easel. "In this case, I don't need a physical picture."

Of course not, not when you're lying next to the real deal every night.

A wave of dizziness washed over her.

"Check it out! A portrait of our first rockstar," Mallory shouted, delighted.

There he was on canvas, and Kathleen tried to size it up objectively. From the first time he'd sung at HopCanon, sitting on the converted altar with the track lighting shining down on him, to the many nights she watched him hammering a tune out at home, his head bowed and eyes closed in concentration. She'd spent hours detailing his hands working the Martin's guitar strings, and the intricacy of the guitar itself, from the wood grain to the curvy body and frets underneath his fingers.

Amanda reached for another cookie. "Holy crap."

Kathleen pointed out areas of shading and what parts she was happy with, and what might need improvement.

She was immediately soothed by simply studying the sketch and touching it; the therapeutic effect of creating never failed to buoy her. "Like any art, we need to be open to feedback, not get so attached that we can't see what could be better." She looked at them reassuringly. "But that takes time, too."

"What do you think, Mr. Model?" Francesca teased. "Ya know, you *could* be one. A Calvin Klein dude, or something. Plus, a real-life Elvis *and* a nurse? Geez."

All eyes were on him and he blushed. "I think Kathleen is supremely talented. I had no idea this is what she's been working on."

"Do you have your stuff in a gallery? You should." Brianne said it with authority.

Kathleen dropped a bundle of pencils on the floor, flustered. "Oh, no. This is a hobby for me, really."

"Brianne is right," Thomas said, bending down to retrieve the pencils. "Anyone could see what you've done is way beyond hobby-level."

"For once, I agree with Brianne," Francesca said derisively, helping herself to a third cookie. "And here's what I think: you two make, like, an *amazing* couple. You should get married. Think of the gorgeous and 'supremely talented' babies you'd have. You could sing songs like the one you just did, and they'd be born knowing the song, because I just read in one of my books that babies recognize voices in the womb. I can totally see it!"

Thomas laughed. "You've got everything figured out, don't you?"

Kathleen's stomach lurched more in the last half hour than it had in the entire previous week. "Okay," she said hurriedly. "Thomas has much to do, so let's say thanks and nice meeting you."

"Wait. You're not leaving already?" Mallory said.

He got up, smiling. "Yep. I didn't plan on hanging for long. Just to say hi, get to know everyone a little."

"All right, people. Get started," Kathleen instructed. "I'll see him out and be right back."

They said their goodbyes, the group's hushed whispers trailing behind them.

"You've got yourself some new fans," she said as he put his arm around her.

"And you have one very big one right here. That's a fantastic drawing, and I don't say that because I'm in it."

They stopped and she kissed him, her thigh banging up against his guitar case. "Half the appeal lay in the subject matter. I'll see you later. Thanks for coming."

"Don't deflect." He stroked her cheek. "I mean it, Kath. You should seriously pursue getting your work out there."

"I'm not deflecting. I gotta get back."

"Okay," he winked and turned for the door. "I'll be interested in hearing what Francesca the psychic has to say next."

"Plenty, no doubt," she muttered. As she turned to go back, she saw that Amanda had followed and taken a picture of them with her cell phone. She stood there, grinning.

What, indeed, would be next?

9

"I must admit, it does look nice in here." Peggy McMillan craned her still-firm neck up at HopCanon's stained-glass windows, her dark-brown eyes taking it all in. She was nearly as well preserved as the walls surrounding her.

Kathleen watched her mother. So far, so good. "Summer and Jeff put a lot of work into trying to keep the original fixtures. To retain the integrity, so to speak."

"I don't know about *that.* But I suppose an old church not becoming a crumbling relic is a positive."

"I love it." Megan, who had accompanied her grandmother to HopCanon, winked at Kathleen. "Come on, Gram, can't you feel the cool vibes of everything that has taken place within these walls?"

Peggy smiled indulgently. "I'll leave those notions up to you young folks, my dear. The only things I feel, these days, are a sore back and shoddy knees giving me fits."

Kathleen hoped fervently the vibes Megan referred to didn't include visions of her and Thomas. She said nervously, "Mom, let me get you a cider. I think you'll like the taste. Megan, how about you?"

"Sure, I'll try one, too."

Kathleen went to the bar, where Zack promptly queried her.

"Two ciders, please."

One of his perfectly arched brows went up.

She sighed. "For my mother and Megan. God, I wish I had your eyebrows. Do you pluck them, or are they just like that?"

"Natural as a newborn's, baby. And a drink for you?"

"No. I'm still battling this stomach bug, if you can believe it." She half-expected him to respond, "*Actually, I don't,*" but of course he didn't say any such thing. She made a note to apologize to him for putting on this ruse when the truth was eventually revealed. Zack nodded and disappeared, stealthy as ever.

Momentarily he set two glasses of translucent yellow liquid down. "One pint of Judas for your mother, and one for your beautiful stepdaughter."

Kathleen made a face. "Please, whatever you do, don't tell Peggy that's the name. Why *did* they pick that?"

"I think Jeff sees cider as a concession to the non-beer drinkers. A betrayal of the craft beer trade, if I may use that play on words."

"Ah. Well, I, for one, am grateful for the choice. For her, anyway." Kathleen swept it off the bar and went back to the table where her mother sat.

"Thank you, dear," Peggy said, and took a tentative sip. "That's very refreshing."

Megan nodded. "It is. Thanks."

"You're welcome. Glad you both like it."

"Now," Peggy's voice was resolute, "You said your friend Thomas is playing, tonight?"

"Mmm-hmm. He should be here soon to set up."

Her mother's eyes kept up their perusal of the building

as they talked. "How long have you been dating?"

It was a normal question people might ask, but why did it feel like an inquisition with her? This was only the beginning. Wait until she found out what else was in store. *You're almost forty years old. Buck up, buttercup.* "Since February."

"Here it is the end of May. You must be getting along nicely, then."

You have no idea. "We are. He's a great guy. Talented, hard-working, and he treats me well."

Peggy's laser gaze focused on Kathleen. "That's good to hear. You've been through so much, it's time you were on the receiving end for a while."

Kathleen didn't know what to say. This, she hadn't expected.

"Don't look so shocked. I'm well-versed in widowhood, in case you've forgotten. I knew after your father passed nobody would ever fill his shoes. I had no desire to replace him, either." Peggy drew another sip of cider. "But your Steve was no Charles. Steve was a taker, and you're a giver." She glanced uncomfortably at Megan. "I apologize, honey. I don't mean to speak ill of your father, God rest his soul. He gave me you, my only granddaughter. Personally, I got along with him very well."

Megan laughed. "You were one of the few, then."

"I suppose what I am getting at is that I hope those roles have been reversed with this Thomas?"

What? Was the cider getting to her already? Kathleen swallowed.

"Funny you should say that, but, yes, he's extremely ... uh, generous." She didn't add, *he goes down on me ten times as much as I do him ...*

"How lovely."

"Could be because he's younger." Kathleen drank some water and waited. *Here we go.*

"Oh? How *much* younger?"

"Ten years."

Peggy gaped, making the slight lines around her mouth deeper. "Really, Kathleen, did you learn nothing from being in a relationship of age differences?"

"I think I'm gonna go talk to Zack," Megan said.

"Good idea," Kathleen met her eyes gratefully. Megan was no stranger to her grandmother's tongue, although she had never been the target. She got up, her long legs and red hair drawing many eyes, and sat at the bar. Zack was in front of her in record time. Kathleen turned back to her mother. "You were saying? How I learned nothing about age differences?"

Her mother's eyes rolled. "You're so sensitive. You know, you always were one to wilt and cry at the drop of a hat, as a child, and I thank God for your father, that he was there and could tolerate it. He wasn't all that different, is why." She took a long pull of cider. "I'm not going to elaborate about the intricacies of relationships, for heaven's sake," she said, although she proceeded to do exactly that. "But it was clear to me you married Steve for the security, and you were a lost soul after your dad died. He was a father figure to you. Not a great one, but there you have it. Consequently, you also know that marriage is hard enough without adding all the problems that come with someone of—differing maturity, shall we say? Aren't you done with that?"

"I didn't plan for this to happen," Kathleen snapped. *Along with one other thing I didn't plan on ...* "And nobody is talking about marriage."

Peggy raised her hand in concession. "All right, all right. I'm sorry. I know you're well aware of the importance of making good decisions at this point in your life. What they don't tell you when you become a parent is that you never stop worrying about your child. No matter their age."

"Hmm. I never thought of you as the fretting type." *Unless a biblical commandment was in jeopardy.* In fact, when Kathleen thought about it, her brothers and father had done more caretaking of her than anyone. Doting on her husband and the church had been front and center in her mother's life.

"Mothers hide or ignore a lot of things over the years, for one reason or another. Trust me, there's much you don't know."

Kathleen was mulling over the meaning of that comment when she spotted Thomas coming through the door, wearing a black leather jacket and carrying his guitar case. "And here's the man of the hour," she said, meeting him as he approached.

"Hi." He pulled her in and kissed her unabashedly, deeply, before she could remind him who else was in the crowd. "Sorry I had to take off so early this morning." He ran his palm down her back. "I did not want to leave, if you recall."

Her brain rewound, thinking of him waking her out of a deep sleep as he hungrily nuzzled her swelling breasts. He'd noticed the change and even commented ("They feel ... fuller?"). She'd chalked it up to PMS, which, when she used to have it, did have that effect. He'd said nothing, his body's reaction enough proof that the circumstances didn't matter.

She took his hand. "I remember. Come meet my mom and Megan."

Introductions were made and Kathleen envied his graceful ease.

"So nice to meet you," he said, hugging Peggy to him. "I appreciate you coming out."

"Ooh, I'm happy to, though I don't go out much at night. It seems I had to meet this man my daughter is so crazy about."

He grinned. "I think you've got it backward. I'm the one crazy for her." He kissed Kathleen again, thankfully, this time just a peck.

Megan returned to the table, with the introductions repeated. They chatted for a few minutes until Thomas excused himself to set up his equipment. Kathleen noted his limp was very slight tonight. Was he straining to control it? Could he? She looked over at her mother. Peggy's face was still pink, probably from the unexpected hug. She was nearly fanning herself.

"Well. He's very charming. I can see why you've fallen for him," her mother finally said, finishing the rest of her cider. "He seems quite smitten with you."

The old fashioned-descriptions of attraction softened Kathleen. "Yes."

"The question is, can it last?"

That's it. Right to my Achilles heel, in record time. "I—I don't know what the future holds, at the moment. I mean, does anyone?"

"True enough. I don't want to see you hurt, my dear. And men like him ..."

"What would that be? Men like him?"

Peggy tapped a manicured nail on the table. "Don't get defensive. Even though we just met, I wasn't born yesterday, as the saying goes." She stared at her daughter. "One can't help but wonder, with those looks and the lifestyle of a musician—doesn't he have women after him constantly?"

"I think he does. And he's choosing me. Isn't that great?"

"Yes," Megan interjected. "It is."

Peggy blinked in surprise. "Of course, it is. As long as you know what you're in for."

Kathleen was amazed at her own brevity, false as it felt. "Like I said, I don't know what I'm in for. I have to be okay with that, or I'll go nuts."

Out of nowhere, Summer swooped in with fresh ciders. "Mrs. McMillan. Megan! It's good to see you both. What do you think of the place?"

"Hello, Summer." Peggy embraced her. "You've worked hard, here, that much is clear. And how many times do I have to tell you, call me Peggy. Mrs. McMillan reminds me of my mother-in-law."

Summer shrugged. "Old habits, ya know."

"Can you join us?" Kathleen made begging eyes at her friend. "Please?"

"Yeah, but just for a while." Summer elbowed Peggy. "So glad you get to hear Thomas tonight, before he leaves for his tour. He's bringing in beaucoup crowds. I mean, for our little town, he is. I'm going to miss that."

"I can imagine." Peggy pursed her lips and drank from her refilled pint glass.

"See? Here they come," Summer said, gesturing toward the door. The place was filling with people. The band did a quick soundcheck, murmuring into microphones and giving thumbs up or thumbs down to Zack, who'd taken on the duties of manning the newly installed PA system.

The lights dimmed and Thomas spoke into his mic, "Thanks for coming out tonight, folks. Before we get started, I wanted to make sure we had a couple Springsteen fans, out there." The crowd, most of whom were forty or over, hooped it up. "I thought maybe so." Thomas smiled. "My dad had all his albums, so I grew up listening to him. One of the first songs I learned to play passably well was "Born to Run."

"Yeah, man! BRUUUCCEE!" a man shouted, among other hoots.

"... Then I met someone." His eyes sought Kathleen's. "And I remembered this." With that, he launched into "*I'm on Fire*." His face contorted in a dozen different positions, hitting notes never heard on the original.

Summer sat up straight, open-mouthed. "Oh. My. God," she whispered to Kathleen, "Even I want to bang him, now."

"Shush!" Kathleen jabbed her head toward Peggy.

Summer laughed. "Hell, she probably does, too."

Thomas went on, playing a Stones song, then some Beatles, and a rousing edition of "Some Kind of Wonderful." After the last note died down, he addressed the audience once more. "Ya'll, I'm not gonna take a break tonight. Instead, we're taking it down a notch or two with a special guest I managed to talk into joining me. I've known this girl for a long time, and she's very talented. Please welcome Miss Natalie Buchanan."

There was polite clapping as every heterosexual man's dream walked out from behind the band. She was tall, pinup-poster-curvy, with long ebony hair that bounced in loose waves with every movement. She waved, smiling, looking like one of those hometown pageant queens on a parade float. Sitting on a stool next to Thomas, Natalie flipped her hair onto her back. She picked up the mic, said thank you, her porcelain skin glimmering with sparkly makeup under the lights. Much the same as Thomas' hair did, Kathleen noted.

Summer leaned into Kathleen. "Who is *she*?"

"I have no idea." Her cheeks burned at the lack of knowledge. Thomas hadn't said a word to her about a special guest, though, looking at her, she had a good idea as to why.

Thomas pushed a lock of hair behind his ear and spoke into his mic, "Natalie's starting it off with a cover from a favorite performer of ours. Here's Grace Potter's "Things I Never Needed."

Kathleen was sure her face was crimson, now. *A favorite performer of ours.* They clearly shared some kind of past in order to have an "ours."

The song's tempo was slow, with the band's accompaniment a lush blend of harmonies, gentle drums and cymbals. Natalie sang the first verse, heartfelt and mesmerizing. She had crystal-clear pitch.

Thomas joined her for the chorus, and they looked at each other the way crooning lovers might.

Their voices complemented the other's perfectly; nary a hiccup or off-note to be found. No different than his usual skillfulness, except, this time his trademark intensity wasn't directed toward Kathleen; his eyes were locked in on Natalie's. As was that shining smile. Jealousy-fueled bile bubbled up Kathleen's already raw throat, while flashes of his swaying groupies from the birthday party stabbed at her brain. *Not your tribe ... you won't ever fit in ... why would he trade glamorous girls for boring you and a baby dragging him down?*

She swallowed a drink of water and shook the images away. It was his turn to solo now, his husky yet silky voice soothing the fire in her chest.

They came together for one more round of the chorus, with the same adoring expressions on their dewy faces. Kathleen's entire body tensed. Was she imagining this intimacy playing out in front of her? It was like an accident scene she didn't want to see but couldn't look away from. Amidst copious applause, the duo moved on to James Taylor's "Fire and Rain," and Thomas' voice lamented about sunny days and never seeing a friend again.

Kathleen closed her eyes and practiced yoga breaths. *Get it together, Brooks. You won't last a hot minute if this is how you deal with someone who's just a singing partner. If there is a future ...*

Was that all this girl was, though? *Why* had Thomas not talked about her? Perhaps she was simply overreacting. She hadn't felt well for days on end, bloated and emotional, undoubtedly due to the rush of hormones and endless fretting. Or maybe her reaction was an undeniable confirmation she and Thomas were ill-matched. Baby or no baby.

She opened her eyes to her mother staring in her direction, her brows arching at her as if to say, *"See? What did I tell you?"*

She took a few more deep inhales, and then the cozy duet was done. Natalie nodded in acknowledgement, rising and waving, as she was swooped into the crowd. Kathleen tried to make out where she disappeared to, but there were too many people blocking her view. Thomas and the band continued, finishing out with a cover of Tom Petty's "Free Fallin'."

Peggy excused herself to the restroom. Summer said carefully, "Jeez. That was ... something,"

"That's one word for it."

"You're annoyed."

"Okay, you tell me. Did it look to you like she was more than just a CoverGirl sidekick to him? And why didn't he mention about her coming tonight?"

"I'm thinking people who sing duets have to seem as if they're ... I don't know, into each other?" Megan diplomatically suggested. "And it's anyone's guess why he didn't say anything to you. Guys can be so clueless. I mean, *some* of them, anyway." She cocked her head toward the bar, where Zack appeared to be busy estimating a new customer's beer palate. "Excluding him."

"Truth spoken from the lips of a mere babe," Summer smiled at Megan, then addressed Kathleen. "Just ask Thomas about her."

"Believe me, I will."

Summer laughed. "The green-eyed monster has struck. I've literally never seen you act jealous."

"Somehow, I think it might be a permanent state while dating him. That hardly seems healthy."

"Relax, my friend. He is so head-over-heels with you, even a blind man could sense it. And here he comes, with her."

"Yes. Hand-in-hand, I might add."

Peggy came back, too, and Thomas made the introductions.

"Such a pleasure," Natalie said to Kathleen, who in turn stared at her burgundy-rimmed lips. "Thomas has told me a lot about you."

They shook hands and Kathleen struggled to be polite. "Oh?" She choked off the rest of her response, which was, "*I can't say the same, unfortunately ...*"

"Yes. I couldn't wait to meet the one who stole his heart after all this time."

"I'd say that remains to be seen," Kathleen said crisply, avoiding Thomas steely gaze. "Please, won't you sit down?"

Natalie shook her shiny head. "Thanks, but I can't. I've got a lot to do, the next few days, to get ready for the tour."

"Tour?" Peggy's eyes widened.

"Yeah, Natalie's joining us for four different dates," Thomas said, almost guiltily.

"I can't wait," Natalie shimmied with the excitement, exposing even more of her considerable cleavage. "I haven't performed in over two years, so I'm nervous, too. But Thomas is incredibly easy to be with. And so good he'd make a broken record sound like Barbra Streisand. Or Adele!" She actually squealed a little bit. "I feel excited more than anything."

I'll bet you do. Kathleen sat unmoving, a mannequin with a fake, frozen smile.

"I'm sure it'll be great," Summer said. "You two sound fantastic."

Natalie's black eyelashes batted. "Thank you! It's from all that strumming around, back in the day." She was practically glowing at the memory. "Well, that's it for me. Got a lot to do! So nice to meet you all."

They said their goodbyes and Thomas said, "I'll walk her out. Be right back."

The four wordlessly watched him leave. Kathleen drank some more water and jammed her glass down. "Don't say it, Mother."

Peggy turned. "What? All I did was ask about the tour. I'm gathering, by the look on your face, you didn't know about her going along."

"No. I didn't. Just, please don't judge him by that, or *her.* All right?" *Give him what I can't,* Kathleen pleaded silently. *The benefit of the doubt.*

Peggy swallowed the last of her cider. "My dear, it's your life. He's a captivating man who appears to be madly in love with you. And you him. Far be it from me to dictate or presuppose anything."

"Thank you." Kathleen was flush again, this time with relief, although she was thinking it was not far at all for her mother to dictate or presuppose. That or she really had mellowed and Kathleen couldn't see it.

"However, you are my daughter, and as I said before, I don't want to see you hurt."

"I'll be fine."

Her mother clutched her purse. "Yes, yes, well, it's time for this old lady to go. If my ride doesn't mind calling it a night, that is." She looked at Megan.

"That's fine with me, Gram. I've got studying to do anyway."

"All right, then. It's been grand, but way past my bedtime. Do tell Thomas I had an enjoyable evening and I look forward to hearing him again."

“I will. Thanks for coming.” She hugged her mother and Megan, and Summer did the same.

Kathleen was suddenly swamped with fatigue and wanted nothing more than to go home and crawl into bed. She rubbed her forehead wearily.

“I’m gonna get going too,” Summer said. “Are you okay?”

“No.” Tears filled her eyes and she blinked them away. “But it doesn’t have anything to do with the glittering starlet. We need to talk. Soon.”

“All right. Call me tomorrow? We’re both off, so maybe we can go to Ching Chang’s and get our nails done.”

Kathleen laughed in spite of herself. “Don’t call it that. It’s Nail Express.”

“Whatever.” Summer leaned over and kissed her on the head. “Try not to make too much out of Miss Streisand wanna-be. Promise?”

“You know I can’t promise that. See you later.”

Kathleen took the dirty glasses up to the bar, and Zack thanked her. “Have a good time tonight?” he asked. Gently, she thought.

“It was fine. And it looks like you mastered the new PA system. Mr. Hart never sounded better.”

“You inspire him.”

“Or an old friend does.”

Zack wiped a glass. “C’mon. He’s a pro, through and through. Give him some credit.”

He was right, of course, which irritated her further. “Listen, I’m tired, so I’m taking off. Oh, and my mom really liked Judas.”

He nodded. “Did you try it?”

“No. Maybe ask Thomas what he thinks,” she said, despair flooding over her as she recalled him holding Natalie’s hand. “Have a good night.”

Kathleen texted Thomas she was leaving and didn't wait for a reply. She unlocked her front door. She was greeted gaily by Hugo, followed by Harriet, who hissed at the dog for stepping on her paw. She took Hugo out for a quick pee and then made herself a cup of chamomile tea. Within minutes, Thomas called her, and she picked up.

"Why did you leave in such a rush?"

"I wanted to get home. Simple as that."

"I don't think it's that simple. I'm coming over."

She sighed. She so did not want to get into it now, but she didn't have the strength to protest.

"All right, then."

He was there faster than usual after a gig, and she let him in. Hugo nearly tripped her trying to get to Thomas first.

"Hi," he said. His black shirt had rings of perspiration around the armpits, and she could smell deodorant mixed with his body's sweat. She inhaled, intoxicated and weakening already.

"Hi." She sat on the couch with her tea, patting the cushion. "Come, sit."

He complied, studying her. "You're upset."

"I don't want to argue. Please."

"Neither do I. May I assume it's because I didn't tell you about Natalie?"

"You assume correctly."

"It wasn't purposeful. She called me up a couple of weeks ago, out of the blue, and we got together to catch up and jam a little. I hadn't heard from her in years. I was actually worried about her for a long time."

"Is that so? Worried, in the way former lovers worry?"

He scowled. "I knew this was coming."

"I wonder why! Out walks this Elizabeth Taylor looka-like, whom I know nothing about, and you're staring like a couple of cow-eyed newlyweds for all the world to see. Singing mournfully about regret and lost chances and lost friends."

"It was nice to see her and perform. It doesn't mean I want to sleep with her again. Or she me. Far from it."

Kathleen's mouth dropped. *"Again?* Well, you get bonus points for honesty, I'll grant you that. What is she, a high school or college sweetheart?"

"Neither. She's somebody from the troubled past. For a short time, we met a need for each other, but that's all it was. Tonight, she sat in on a couple of songs. That's it."

"That's not it! She's going on tour with you! Another little fact you neglected to mention."

His jaw twitched, and he clasped his hands together. "You know what? If I'd been able to spend more than one day for the past two weeks with you, maybe we could've talked about it. But that didn't happen. You haven't just been sick with the flu. You've been distracted and not yourself. I'd even say you're avoiding me. And you need to tell me why. Right now."

Kathleen's head pounded. "Why don't you tell me more about this troubled past part?"

"You're changing the subject."

"Explain what the history is. Since we are all aware, now, that you both share at least one favorite tune from 'back in the day.' Did you make up a sex-mix song list for her, too?"

"Jesus. Stop it."

Her face was red-hot and she couldn't stem the uncharacteristic sarcasm biting at her tongue. "Oh, and let's not forget, you're so easy to be with! How exactly has she gotten accustomed to that endearing trait?"

"I don't feel like I have the right to tell you about her

circumstances."

"What the hell does that mean?"

He leapt off the couch. It never failed to impress her how agile he was, even with his limitations. "I met Natalie when we were both part of a therapy group for suicidal teenagers. How's that, for starters?"

She kept her face expressionless. "Okay. What was that like?"

"Barrels of fun, let me tell you. It was at a four-week summer camp—minus the canoeing and scavenger hunts. Natalie and I used to pass leisure time by comparing who had the biggest scars ... me from my accident, or hers, from three years of cutting herself."

"I'm sorry."

He didn't appear to hear, or was ignoring her. "A bunch of us would sneak away at night and get high as fuck and debate all the world's societal ills, and Natalie and I would laugh and laugh because we were the only ones who didn't want to fall in love with anyone or get married. We were hurting, damaged, stupid kids."

He stared. "There. Do you feel better now, having that information? Because there's more where that came from."

She bowed her head. The room was quiet, with the exception of Hugo's anxious panting in the background.

"Go on," she said, and looked up at him. His eyes fiery and his bottom lip trembling, Kathleen thought he was never as beautiful; so close to how he looked when locked in the throes of passion on that fateful night at HopCanon.

"Here's what you don't know. My father was driving the car when I had my accident, and he shouldn't have been. He'd lost his medical license because of drug abuse, and that night when he got behind the wheel, he was all jacked up or spaced out on something. I found that out later, of course. I was asleep, at the time."

He was pacing like a caged lion now.

"He wrapped the car around a tree. The only good thing to come of it was he didn't take anyone else out." He scoffed, bitterly. "Except for me, almost."

Kathleen felt tiny and afraid to move, like a paralyzed mouse Harriet was stalking. "What happened then?"

"He did get clean, and stayed that way right up to the day he died. But he never got over the guilt of essentially destroying my soccer scholarship. Not to mention witnessing my months of grueling rehab and constant pain. I think during that time he cried more than I did. I'd tell him, 'Dad, I forgive you. Let's move on. Shit happens.' And then ..." He stopped, mid-pace. "One night, we argued about college and he broke. I could see it in his eyes. He shot up a load of heroin, a dose he knew would kill him, then went for a swim and never came back."

"I can't imagine," Kathleen said, although she could.

"Yeah, so, there I was, about as rock-bottom as it gets, Courtney and I living with my grandma and all of us grieving ... and the following summer, I met someone who understood, who'd been through even worse."

She knew she should've been more sympathetic, given the burden he'd revealed. Still, she couldn't erase the picture of the two of them gazing at each other with such obvious affection. "Trauma can create some strong bonds. Ripe ground for a romantic connection."

Even if true, it was the wrong thing to say at that moment.

"No!" He roared, and she physically pulled back at the force of it. "It wasn't like that. I'm trying to tell you we were *fucked-up* eighteen-year-olds, helping each other through a very dark time in our lives. It was anything but roses and sunshine and Harlequin endings."

Kathleen counted to five in her head. "I'm sorry. So sorry

for all you went through. I can relate to the pain and regret with your father on many levels, which I've told you a little about. Please forgive me if I feel slightly threatened at the idea of you going on the road with a previous lover. Not just any lover, but one that you have a tortured history with. A drop dead gorgeous one, on top of that. I didn't mean to churn up difficult memories."

"Too late." His voice was still tight. "I'm sorry, too, for hoping you'd be cool about it, about her."

"How could I be cool about being left in the dark? Does that seem fair?" She cringed at the cruel irony of her own words.

Silence filled the air. She got up and put her cup in the sink. "Let's not do this. Please. We're both tired and need to go to bed."

He was looking out the bay window, his back to her, with Hugo sitting at his feet. "Maybe I should go."

"Maybe you should," she said, more sharply than intended. "It's not a secret we should start getting used to being apart."

He turned around and said nothing for a few minutes. "You can't fool me, you know."

A snake of fear curled through her. He was a sensitive, observant, intelligent man, and a nurse on top of that. He was right. How long could she keep up this insane charade? And to what end? What was she hoping would happen?

"You're pushing me away in preparation," he said. "Of what? Breaking it off? How convenient that Natalie happens to be a catalyst to help your plan along. So, okay. I'll bite, for tonight." He went to her and roughly pulled her to him. "It won't work," he whispered against her ear.

Then he slowly backed up, gave a disappointed Hugo one last scratch, and walked out the door.

10

Kathleen had a restless night and woke up in the morning feeling no better. She fed both the animals, let Hugo out, and promptly vomited in the half-bath off the kitchen. She wiped her face with a cold rag and sat at her kitchen island. *Dammit.* She'd need to call Dr. Love, if this was starting again. Dr. Love, who'd advised her to get her baby's father "onboard, as soon as possible." She gritted her teeth. *You could've told him last night and you chickened out. Why?* Why, indeed. She openly bragged about what a "wonderful man" Thomas was. How wonderful could he be, if she thought he'd walk away and abandon her?

He's not capable of that and deep down you know it. You're afraid for other reasons. Other reasons you can't face, and you're going to use the excuses of age, insecurity, centerfold ex-flames, and his own casual admissions, to avoid the pain ...

She kneaded her forehead and remembered about the anti-nausea wristbands she'd bought and hadn't used. It was worth a shot. She got them out of the cabinet and put them on, and thought about her nail date with Summer. She desperately needed to talk to her, but that, too, seemed wrong and self-indulgent. Tell her best friend, but not her lover? She texted her, knowing it would probably not go well.

"Hey. How about a raincheck for hanging out today? I just need to relax here by myself for a bit."

"What's going on? I'm worried about you."

"Please don't. And no fifth-degree. I promise it's ok. We'll talk after."

"Okay. But I don't like it."

"LOL. Love you."

"You, too. See you soon."

She sighed with relief. That was easier than anticipated. She gazed out the kitchen window to the cardinals on her birdfeeder and smiled. A brilliant blood-red male was feeding his dull, olive-colored mate sunflower seeds. She'd read somewhere that cardinals were signs from loved ones in Heaven. *Is that you, dad? You always loved feeding the birds.* Tears welled up and over, and she used the terrycloth wristband to wipe them away. All at once, she was overwhelmed with the idea of getting out of town for a few days. Running away was easy; she was good at that. She impulsively called her mother, and after hanging up, she called Summer.

"Hey, girl. You change your mind about meeting up?"

"No. I'm calling because I wonder if you can get one of the girls to cover my shift, this week. I know I missed a lot, recently, and I'm sorry. Here you thought having your buddy working for you would mean reliability."

"It should be fine. But you do have me seriously wondering what is going on with you."

"I know. I'm—it's a confusing time, right now, with Thomas getting ready to leave, and I don't know what's going to happen. We had a fight, last night, big surprise, and I feel the need to clear my head, ya know?"

"Yes. Go on."

"I decided to go up to the family cabin at Bear Lake. For a few days, if you can spare me."

"That's it? You sure?"

"I need some quiet, and that's the place to do it."

"That's true enough. All right, honey. You take care. And we'll have that nail date, because you forget it's *me* you're talking to. I know something's up, but I won't grill you."

"Thank you."

They hung up and Kathleen felt a huge weight lifted. Even thinking about Bear Lake brought her peace. She'd have to explain to Thomas, now, and hope he'd understand. She called him, hoping it wasn't too early.

"Hi." His voice was ruffled from sleep.

"Sorry if I woke you."

"It's fine. It wasn't a good night, anyway."

"Same."

She could hear a sheet crackling. "Hey, listen. I'm sorry. I shouldn't have sprung Natalie like that on you. It wasn't fair."

"I'm sorry too, for being snipy. I guess as long as she's not springing herself on you, or vice-versa, we're good."

He laughed. "No. That won't happen. But I gotta admit, you're even more sexy when jealous. It was strangely arousing."

"I thought the same of you. You were just like—oh, God. Never mind."

He laughed again. "Hang on to that thought."

"I will." She was quiet for a few seconds, then said, "On another note, I'm going out of town for a couple days. I'm not running away (a white lie?), I just want to go to our family cabin and chill."

"By yourself?" He sounded disappointed.

"Hugo, too. You told me this week is jampacked for you, right?"

"I did, but—"

"I promise this isn't about avoidance. I'll be back for my group on Wednesday."

An audible sigh. "You know we need to talk."

"Yes. We do, and we will."

"Okay. Well, have fun. I'd love to see the family cabin, sometime."

Her chest squeezed painfully. "I'd like that, too."

"I love you," he said, so sadly a part of her wanted to abandon the whole plan and run to his apartment, lie down with him for hours and just touch and smell him while she could. As appealing as that sounded, the fresh air and pine trees of Bear Lake were calling her even more strongly. The mere visualization also helped bring the roil in her belly to a simmer.

"I love you, too."

They hung up and she texted Sam to see if he could look in on Harriet. Once that was confirmed, she made another cup of tea, ate some crackers, and happily began to pack.

Bear Lake was an hour-and-a-half north of Mount Simon, the perfect distance for a quick getaway. Though living near Lake Michigan was itself beautiful and a destination for many, locals needed their escape, as well. She loaded up Steve's convertible, an older model BMW, strapped Hugo's dog crate into the backseat, and off they went. It was that rare and spectacular Michigan late-spring day: sunny and warm, no humidity or rain, no bugs, the iridescent sky free of clouds. It was the kind of day Northerners lived for, as they sat outside on decks with uplifted faces, soaking up the justification for tolerating frosty, grey, and schizophrenic winter weather eight months out of a year. The glowing, if unreliable, rays of the sun filled a faltering soul with hope, providing sustenance like no substance ever could.

Kathleen had the car's top down, of course, her hair up in a bun so the wind wouldn't whip it into a frenzy, and she had the smallest grin on her face for the entire drive. She was remembering the many comedic family moments that the cabin was at the center of, over the years, and she was grateful her mother had held onto the property. She gassed up at a small convenience store ten minutes from the place, where a young girl with a nametag that read "Arnica" waited on her. Arnica? Wasn't that, like, a pain-relieving gel she'd bought a couple of months ago? She smiled at the pimply-faced teenager and said thank you. Hadn't people had been breaking baby name rules for some time, now? Arnica was probably better than naming kids after fruits and vegetables, like some celebrities did.

She pulled into the drive lined with pine trees.

"Here we are, Hugo. One of our favorite places."

She let him out of his crate and he jumped out, his hind end wiggling with joy. The place was all that came with a traditional vacation cabin, meaning, not fancy. The décor was dated and rustic; there was a television and VCR. No internet. But it was well-stocked, and Peggy had replaced all the beds, recently. She'd also conceded to installing air conditioning, which was a plus in July and August. Best of all, it boasted a view of Bear Lake, an inland body of water popular with kayakers and swimmers all summer long. The town had outlawed jet-skis years ago. Kathleen opened all the windows to air the rooms out, and put her things away in the main bedroom.

She took Hugo for a walk and made a note of everything around that was the same or different. Nothing changed that much at Bear Lake, which was a big part of its charm. Her stomach rumbled. It was hunger arguing with nausea, so she'd need to eat an early dinner in town. She changed her clothes, freshened her make-up, and bid a doleful-looking Hugo goodbye. The town of Bear Lake wasn't big, so her food choices were "Viola's Café," a quaint diner, or the sports bar, "The Dive."

She chose The Dive, mostly because she was craving one of their famous hamburgers. She went in and sat at the bar. There was a spattering of customers about, and as she glanced around, she observed nothing changed much over the years here, either. Multiple mirrors with Coors and Bud Light emblems, Michigan college football flags, and the faint smell of grease and stale beer in the air. She smiled. Perfect. The bartender was an older man, bald with a goatee, and he took her order. He filled a yellow plastic tumbler with Coke, put it down and disappeared into the back. She fixed her gaze on the television anchors predicting more weather loveliness, when someone called her name.

"Kathleen? Is that you?"

She turned, lurching on the edge of the barstool in disbelief.

"J.J.?"

Short for Jeremy Johnson, her last serious high school boyfriend. The relationship her father had tried to put the kibosh on, and didn't. Kathleen used to wonder how things would've turned out if he'd been successful.

"Yes!" J.J.'s face split into a huge grin. He walked over and sat on the stool next to hers. "My God, how are you? I haven't seen you since ... well, forever!"

"Yes, that's about right." They sized each other up. She tried to take in details without being obvious. There was the predictable hair loss and more belly, his blue eyes still bright. The cute baby face had squared out, a few more etches here and there. He'd matured, and it suited him.

He stood there, his elbow on the bar, with nothing less than an enchanted look on his face as they caught up. Turned out J.J. owned The Dive, now, had bought it when his recent divorce was finalized. He'd lived in Chicago for years. When he and his wife Andrea split up, she got the cars and house, and he got the getaway condo they'd bought in Bear Lake, long ago.

The Dive's bartender, whose name was Eddie, brought her food, but she only picked at the burger she'd been so looking forward to. She'd take it back with her for later.

"I'm sorry," J.J. said, not looking very sorry. "I know I'm staring. I can't help it. I mean, you were always beautiful—"

"No, I wasn't," she laughed. "Nobody was then, except maybe for Kimberly Swanson and her posse."

"You were. Every guy talked about trying to date the hottest Catholic chick. The untouchable Kathleen McMillan."

She twirled her fork in the coleslaw, the kind made with oil and vinegar. The kind she liked, but the more he talked, the more she couldn't eat.

"Well. You'd know firsthand I wasn't untouchable at all. Was I?"

His joyous grin faded. "Why haven't you gone to any of the school reunions?"

"I pretty much still see everyone I want to see." She put the fork down and looked at him. "That's not a time in my life I wish to re-visit."

He finally broke his scrutiny of her, his head down. She asked Eddie for a to-go box.

"Kathleen, stay for a minute." His eyes pleaded with her. "Can we go over to a table and talk? I'm not exaggerating when I say that I've hoped, prayed, even, for this moment, many times. To run into you again."

She exhaled, heavily. This was definitely not part of her

peaceful, restorative plan, but he always was a persuasive one. "Okay. For a little bit. I've got to get back to the cabin and walk my dog, soon." A lie, as she'd already done that, but she needed an out.

He led her to a corner table where there were no nearby guests. "I'm going to get a beer. Can I bring you something?"

She declined. She doubted chamomile tea would be available.

He came back with two bottles of Coors Light. She smiled, thinking of something Thomas had said. "*How is there even a market for that? Coors by itself is like drinking filtered piss water.*"

Perhaps there was a niche in Bear Lake for HopCanon's delights.

"What are you thinking about? How much of this we used to put back?" He cracked one open and drank.

"No. We certainly did our share, though."

"Are you sure you don't want this one?" He tapped the bottle with his own. "For old time's sake?"

"I'm sure." Her next words were as if someone else had taken control of her mouth. "Because just like old times, guess what? I'm pregnant."

His expression was priceless.

"I never dreamed I'd be saying those words to you twice." She laughed mirthlessly. "And your reaction isn't much different than before."

He looked to the side, out a little octagon window, and she could see his eyes were full, shiny. She almost felt sorry for him. His Adam's apple bobbed as he swallowed.

"You don't know how much I've thought about ... that ... over the years. How I wish I could take it all back."

"Yeah? How so?"

"I mean, not you, or us. My actions, and, yes, my reaction to that news. It was unforgivable."

What to follow up with? Oh, ya think?

She allowed her mind to go back there, ever so briefly. They'd been foolishly careless, sometimes using protection, other times not, depending on how stoned they were. Caution was thrown to the wind when all you wanted was to learn more about what you weren't supposed to be doing, and experience more breathless moments of, *"Oh, God, how can feeling this incredible be wrong? Every do-gooder adult can take their warnings and shove it up their jealous asses. They just wish they could do this, instead of having to take little blue pills to get it up for even one time."* That's what she and Jeremy would say to each other afterward, lost in a weed-induced stupor and giggling uncontrollably. But weeks later, when she told him the party was over, it was more awful than she could've envisioned. He was driving and came close to putting the car in a ditch.

"You're what?" He parked to the side of the road and stared at her, open-mouthed, as if the impossible had occurred.

"You heard me."

"Jesus Christ."

"Yes, Jesus. Help me," she remembered thinking. She'd prayed the rosary for weeks, begging for intervention from the Holy Mother, and with every second that passed, help seemed ever more out of reach.

His hands slammed onto the steering wheel. "What the fuck! We can't have a ... a baby. There's no way in hell this could work. Last week, I signed to play baseball for Central!"

She was silent. Any flicker of hope that this situation might have a bright light was snuffed out, like a dying star in the night sky.

"I've got money," he said, panicky. "For you to get ... you know."

She made him say the word, *abortion.* His family was

almost as Catholic as hers. They'd met in catechism class, for God's sake.

"Okay, okay, abortion!" He'd screamed it in the car so loud she'd plugged her ears, even after provoking him to spit it out.

"You have to do it, Kathleen. There's no other choice. Your parents would kill us both, at you getting knocked up! And mine, too!"

"At "me getting knocked up?" You *jerk*. As if you had no part in it!"

She'd jumped out of the car, at that point, and refused to get back in. He drove beside her, rolled the window down, begged her to stop.

"Come on, Kathleen, get in the car. I'll take you home—"

"Go to hell!" she snarled.

He kept up with the apologies until she stopped abruptly and grabbed the edge of the car door's window. "You'll get what you want, the same way you wanted me and got me. So, here's the deal. Don't call me, don't ever try to see me, or I swear to God I'll call the cops."

She ignored his protests, walking the two miles almost as fast as if she'd jogged.

The irony about her parents finding out was that Kathleen knew her father suspected, and she was equally sure he hadn't breathed a word to her mother. He'd heard her more than once in the bathroom gagging and heaving. One time he stood outside and waited until she came out, and he didn't ask her dumb questions like did she have a stomach bug. Instead, he asked he if she'd seen a doctor, yet, and, shaking uncontrollably, she'd said no, she was fine. Another lie, in a string of them. Two months later, her father was dead, and she'd convinced herself his disappointment in her had helped it happen.

She blotted it all out, forced herself back to the present. What had Jeremy said? Unforgivable actions?

"You were a scared kid thinking of your future," she said, trying to be charitable.

"True, but after that argument in the car, I knew I was wrong. Kathleen, I tried to tell you I was sorry, that we'd work it out somehow. Then it was summer and you completely cut me off. I was heartbroken, in case you didn't know."

"Yes." Twice, he'd come to her house in the middle of the night, and her father had called the police. "So was I."

"You went and *did* it, before hearing me out." He had the gall to be accusatory.

"I'd heard enough, if I recall. Truthfully, sitting here reliving that nightmare is too much. I can't do this, Jeremy."

He put his hand on her wrist. "Ah, shit, don't. Don't go. I'm sorry. We can talk about other things. I want to hear more about you, your life. Tell me about ... this baby. I want to know, please."

He was so earnest, so much like how she remembered falling for him, she capitulated. She laid it all out, not identifying Thomas, but everything else, and it felt strangely cathartic. He was an attentive listener, letting her talk and not interrupting.

"He cares about you, then. The father." He said it plaintively.

"Yes."

"I'm happy for you. This is a second chance. A new beginning?"

"That's how I'm seeing it, too."

"I'm not trying to change the subject, but my only child, Sophia, got brain cancer when she was three. She died a year later."

"No—"

He shook his head. "I can talk about it now. Not gonna lie, I spent many an hour asking God why, and it wasn't too hard to imagine why. It was my punishment."

"I've thought that, too," she whispered. "Even though I don't believe that's how God works, I couldn't, *can't* seem to apply it to myself."

They wiped at their faces with bar napkins, and he took her hand. "Forgive me, please. For everything."

She squeezed it back and it felt surprisingly good. "We were both to blame."

"And—just for the record, I really loved you. In-between acting like the world's biggest ass, I did. I even bought a ring. Then after everything ... I pawned it off somewhere."

Her breath caught in her throat at this. She'd never known. His expression longed for a sign of empathy from her, and she gave it willingly.

"We were kids still learning about relationships. Stumbling, making mistakes."

"Sometimes I think I never stopped. Loving you, that is. After Andrea left, I tried to find you on Facebook."

"Yeah, I don't participate," she said lightly. She had to steer the conversation away from the uncomfortable rabbit hole it was going toward. "Listen, it's been good seeing you again. I mean that. I've got to go, before my dog pees everywhere."

"Okay. One piece of advice, if I may be so bold."

It was a little bold, but what did she have to lose, at this point? "Sure," she said.

"Give this guy a chance. And another one, if he doesn't ... if he doesn't react well, let's say. Don't give up on him."

She stood up. "That's the part I'm afraid of. What he'll do, think. This time, I'm forging ahead, on my own, if I have to."

"You don't have to be alone. I want to stay in touch. I'm just putting that out there, if you need a friend."

He hugged her, so tightly her nausea resurfaced. "Thank you, old friend," she said. She took her box of food, gave his tear-stained cheek a peck, and walked out to the car. She breathed in the tangy scent of the pine trees hugging the parking lot. A hundred emotions raced through her, but the prevalent one was that of peace. She smiled. Going to The Dive had proven to be more restorative than she would've ever thought, and she knew it wasn't chance that had led her there. There were other powers at work, forces with the power to heal festering wounds, and as she glanced at the azure skyline, she was grateful the process finally seemed to be in motion.

Kathleen's wristbands seemed to work for those few days, until they didn't. She'd left the cabin Wednesday morning and had to pull over twice to throw up. She called Dr. Love's office on her cell and arranged for new prescriptions to be sent to the drugstore in Mount Simon.

Thomas called on her way home, in-between the vomit stops. They'd see each other after her group that night, and the spark of excitement that lit up at the thought of seeing him spread through her. She drove the last half-hour home with thoughts of him whirling. Would it always be this way? Hot adrenaline shooting in her veins like a drug? Of course not. Everyone knows it's the honeymoon phase, even if you're not married, and that kind of heat cannot be sustained over time. Still, she thought of her parents. How they'd arrange for "alone" time, the way her father was always touching her mother, and the private jokes that had confused her as a child but made sense much later. For all her battling with them in her teen years, their marriage was a good example of what love could be. It was probably one reason why life with Steve was that much harder; so many gaps she was always trying to fill, and all of them too wide.

Once home, she was busy unpacking, tidying, and doing laundry, and before she knew it, it was time to go to the meeting with the girls. She unlocked the door to their room in the community center and set out the drawing tools. She'd told the girls to keep practicing at home. Hopefully, they'd listened. Brianne was the first to arrive, and she came in smiling. Unusual, for her.

"Hi, Brianne," Kathleen said, taking a tray of muffins from her. "Don't you look radiant tonight."

"Hi. And thanks."

"Things going well, then?"

Brianne nodded shyly. "I was excited to come tonight to show everyone." She held her left hand out.

Kathleen grasped her palm, whistling. "Look at that! An engagement ring!"

Brianne pulled her hand back, admiring the sparkle with her fingers splayed. "Yeah. It's small, I know, but it's still pretty, isn't it?"

"It's beautiful, honey. Congratulations."

"Thanks. Nobody else is excited, of course. I mean, I guess my dad is relieved, so there's that. Matt's parents—um, nope. Then again, they never liked their track star son going for the weird chick, either." She laughed a little, but when she looked at Kathleen her eyes were watery. "We love each other. I mean, I'm not kidding. A *lot.*"

"I believe it," Kathleen said softly.

"See, that's why I like you. You don't treat us girls like clueless little kids. You respect us, as people, and not as disappointing freaks." She tugged at one of her many earrings. "Tell me the truth, Ms. K. Do you think me and Matt stand a chance? To make it, I mean?"

Kathleen edged around the table and hugged her. She backed up and said firmly, "Relationships are challenging. Heck, *life* is challenging. My dear, anything is possible with a strong commitment to each other."

Brianne smiled again, and the other three came in chittering. After opening prayer, Brianne passed out the muffins.

Kathleen poured milk. "These look delicious. What kind are they?"

"Sour cream and chocolate chip. I found it on Pinterest."

"I love Pinterest!" Francesca said. "All the baby ideas are so much fun!"

"I only look at recipes," Brianne said. "I love to bake. Like, so much that I might want to have my own bake shop. Someday."

Everyone agreed the muffins were scrumptious, and Kathleen said, "I'm not sure if you all already knew, but Brianne has something exciting to share."

The ring turned out to be news for everyone, and they oohed and aahed appropriately. Of all of the group, Brianne was the farthest along in her pregnancy, and she and Matt weren't waiting to get married until after the baby was born.

"Matt's been working at the golf club constantly, saving," Brianne said. "Ya know, caddies can make excellent money, if they're good. And he is." It also helped that Hidden Dunes, Matt's employer, enlisted millionaire members who tipped handsomely.

"You've said before traditional college isn't for you, but does Matt want to go?" Kathleen asked.

"He used to talk about a physical therapy program. Not now, though. Which kinda worries me, that he'll be resentful, someday. Of me, or the baby. Ya know what I'm saying?"

Kathleen swallowed the creeping bile sneaking up her throat. *Oh, I know.* "Uh, excuse me, girls, while I run to the restroom. You finish the snack and chat."

She barely made it on time, and even worse, they'd probably heard it all. Four faces looked at her questioningly when she came back.

"Are you okay?" Mallory asked.

"I—I seem to be having a time of it, lately, with my stomach." Kathleen swept her hair up into a ponytail. "Don't worry. I'm fine."

They refocused and brought out their pictures in progress. To Kathleen's surprise, they'd each been working independently on them. Amanda was coyly hiding hers, until Kathleen said, "What's up, Amanda? Do you not like the ways yours is going?"

Amanda couldn't contain herself. "No! I love it. In fact, I changed my subject. Remember when I took a picture of you and Thomas? Well, after I developed a copy ... omigod, I *had* to try to draw it."

She threw the two pictures down on the table dramatically.

"Wow," said Francesca. "I had no idea you were that good."

Neither did anyone else. Kathleen blinked, staring at Amanda's work. There they were, in pencil, her arms locked around Thomas' neck, with one of his around her waist and the other holding his guitar case. It was beautifully captured, especially their facial expressions.

"Well?" Amanda said excitedly, wiggling like a kid on Santa's lap. "What do you think?"

"I—I'm speechless. You told me you'd had art, but this, this is fantastic. Your shading, the contrast, all of it."

"It's not done, obviously," Amanda said, pulling the

pictures back to her. "I've got a good head start, don't you think?"

"Yes, for sure."

"I've already given it a title. I'm calling it 'Real Love.' You and Thomas ... well, it's so not like anything I've ever had, and what I wish I had." She looked at Kathleen expectantly, who knew, at that very second, she had to leave again for the toilet.

"Be back in a minute," she managed, before bolting.

After Kathleen left, the four girls looked at each other anxiously.

"What's going on with her?" Brianne said, almost in a whisper.

Mallory whispered back, "I dunno, but it's weird. She looked kinda green before, when Thomas was here, now that I think of it." Her pale face paled even more. "I hope she isn't, like, sick with something *bad*. What if she's got Crohn's disease? I read about that, the other day, in my mom's Reader's Digest."

"What's that?" Amanda asked.

"It's this little square magazine that looks like ... a tiny book. With articles and stuff."

"Guys," Francesca leaned in, and the others did, too. "I bet it isn't anything like that at all."

The three waited for her to elaborate. "You know," Francesca waggled her hand, keeping an eye on the door and lowering her voice to a deeper hush, "Last time we met, she had these nasty chips and Gatorade with her. I remember, because she didn't eat the cookies Brianne brought."

"Yeah? So what?" Amanda said dismissively.

"So? So, who the hell eats cardboard communion-like crackers over chunky chocolate chip cookies?"

Mallory frowned. "Well, I might."

Francesca sighed impatiently. "You're not the norm. What I'm saying is, she's acting like ..."

"Like what?" the three said it all together.

"Like, someone who's *pregnant.*"

There was a four-second delay as they digested this possibility.

"No way," Mallory shook her head as if bees had invaded her ear. "Isn't she a little old? And she's not that dumb."

"You morons!" Brianne hissed. "She's definitely not too old, and she's anything but dumb. Why do people always think when a woman pukes it means she's pregnant? There could be other reasons too."

"Such as?"

"Such as, I don't know ... Crohn's is actually one possibility. Or cancer. Maybe chemo side effects?"

Mallory recoiled. "Oh, God. Don't even say that."

Brianne's tattooed arms cradled her belly. "Sorry. Anyway, if it is a baby, people make mistakes in the sex department. We should know."

"Yup," Amanda pointed to her illustration. "Imagine going to bed with that rockstar gorgeousness every night. Jesus God, who *wouldn't* end up pregnant?" They all laughed at this, even Mallory, and then they heard the toilet flush.

"She's gonna be back in a second," Francesca looked around the group, as if taking a vote. "Do we ask her?"

They agreed this was not the best idea, that she might become upset with that invasive of an inquiry, but they also agreed to keep a close eye on their beloved Ms. K. There was something up with her, no doubt, and they would find out what, one way or another.

Thomas kissed the side of Kathleen's head and buried his nose there. "You smell like fresh air."

"The benefits of driving with the top down."

"Top down." I like the sound of that. Or top off, specifically," he said, running his warm hands under her shirt.

"Mmm-hmm. How's the practicing? Got your setlists nailed down?"

"We do. I think we're as ready as we're gonna be. I'm tired, to be honest."

He did have an ashy look about him, which was worrisome. "Are you eating?"

"Yes, if fast-food counts."

She groaned. "Is that how it will be on the road, too? Constant fast-food?"

"Probably, unless you agree to come and be our personal chef."

"Don't forget masseuse, too."

His face became serious. "What would it take for that to happen? For you to come with?"

"It would take me cloning myself. I can't just walk out on Summer and Jeff, and my girls."

He sat up, crossed his ankle over a thigh. "You know what? I'm not looking forward to doing this, anymore. Not without you next to me every night. That's not a good sign before even hitting it."

She flinched as if he'd struck her. This was what she'd feared as much as his reaction to a baby; that his preoccupation with her would bring him down, his ambition screeching to a halt before even launching.

"Please. Please don't put that pressure on us. I am begging you, do not."

"It's not pressure. It's what it is. I can't change how I feel."

"No, but if you take a different perspective—"

"What perspective would that be?" His voice went up a

notch. *"Oh, you can do this alone, dude. No matter that your whole world for four months has been this woman. Every song you write and sing is all about her, but it's gonna be a rockin'-ass show, night after night, without her in your life anyway!"*

Quietly, she said, "You can do it, and just as importantly, I want you to."

He stared at her, stricken. His eyes swelled with water, the irises expanding like two golden brown chocolate candies held in a palm for a few seconds too long. She felt herself dissolving too, in those depths.

"I know you do. Why, though? I don't—" he stopped, turning his head away to gain control, and she squeezed his shoulder.

"Thomas. I said it at the very beginning and I'll say it again: I think you need to give this tour and your music one hundred and ten percent, with no distractions. No tortured texts and three-hour conversations that leave you exhausted and split in two." She inhaled. "Then, let's say in a couple months, or whenever the time is right, we re-group and see how it goes."

His face was in his hands. "Nice. That's coming back to bite me in the ass. The same thing I said, too, when we first met. "Why not see how it goes?" I feel like that's the biggest copout phrase ever invented, right now. It means nothing."

"It can mean something." She pulled his hands away from his head, and clasped them. "We can use this time ... this time apart, to our advantage. We can use it to clarify what we want." She stroked his face, and for once, it was her turn to brush a tear away.

He wiped his nose roughly with a sleeve. "This is one string of euphemisms after another. 'Let's see how it goes,' and, 'Oh, we're taking a break to go find ourselves,' just seem like code for, 'Adios, buddy, and don't let the door kick you in the ass.'"

She couldn't help but laugh at the utter untruthfulness of his words. "No. Not this time."

"I already *know* it's you I want. I've told you that a dozen times. I don't—I don't need any clarification." His lip trembled like a distraught little boy's. "Do you?"

No. But you will, once you know about the package deal.

She cupped his face, hot and wet, and brushed his auburn sideburns with her thumbs. "Listen to me. I'm not going anywhere. I'll be watching you become the next 'Star is Born.' Waiting for you."

"Please. Everyone knows how that dumbass story ended. I don't—"

"Shh." She put a finger to his mouth. "Shh."

She kissed him on his lips, his salty cheeks, his forehead, all of it, with the pressure of a bumblebee on a flower. "We love each other," she whispered into his ear. "Let's have this time together tonight to show how much, and let that be enough."

She unfastened the buttons on his shirt slowly, all the while nibbling his chest as it was exposed. He lay back, his red-brown hair splayed out in glorious contrast to the cream-colored couch. She undressed them both, in pieces, nuzzling his midriff as she teased off her bra and panties. He arched his back as her lips and tongue circled down and down, as delicately and quickly as licking an ice-cream cone before it melted.

"Ahh." He shuddered, pulling her by her elbows up to him. "That feels incredible."

She smiled. "So, I'm getting better, then?"

"What? What are you talking about?"

"You know, at *that*. I didn't ever ... well, Steve didn't want us to. He was kind of a prude."

"A prude and an idiot," he muttered, pressing her hand

onto him. “I was seconds away from coming like a thirteen-year-old schoolboy, there. Does that answer your question?”

“Mm-hm. And it really—” She licked at his pulsing neck. “Really turns me on.”

In one fluid movement she straddled him and lowered down. She thrust forward briefly, then lifted herself off and went back to her ministrations below, stopping when she sensed he was close. She stroked a strategic spot, delighting in the visceral display of euphoria in front of her; his mouth slightly open, his brow drawn tight like a bow, his skin throbbing everywhere she touched.

“Omigod, what are you doing to me?” he moaned when she withdrew.

She laughed mischievously, resuming the delicious dance on top of him. She went back and forth on his body until, finally, he gripped the sides of her face and pushed her shoulders down.

“Stay. There,” he rasped, somewhere between a plea and a command. “Your schoolboy—is all—tapped out.”

She looked up for a split second, searing this picture into her mind for safekeeping, his perfect face awash with ecstatic pleasure and love. A picture that, this time, would remain in the canvas of her mind for as long as she could hold it there.

The sunrise the next morning was jaw-droppingly radiant. Ribbons of flaxen gold and scarlet streaked across the sky as Kathleen opened the French doors that adjoined a deck off her bedroom. She took her cup of ginger tea and tiptoed out. Thomas was still sleeping. She’d tried to beckon Hugo, who was curled at Thomas’ feet, but he was having none of it. The dog was going to miss Thomas as much as she would, she thought sadly, watching them.

Harriet had other ideas and hopped up on Kathleen's lap the second she sat on the chaise lounge outside. "Hi, baby," she said, scratching under the cat's black-and-white chin. Kathleen bit into the bagel she'd toasted, which Harriet nosed with interest. She let her lick the rest of the cream cheese off. Kathleen didn't want it anyway, but she had to try to keep something in her stomach. So far, the new prescription regime seemed more effective. The nurse on the phone had said it was a combination of a sleep aid and Vitamin B6. She might experience some drowsiness, but the trade-off would be worth it. She leaned back and smiled, thinking about the night before.

"Hey, pretty woman. What are you smiling about?" He leaned against the door frame, arms crossed against his bare torso and wearing pajama bottoms that sat as low on his hips as they could go without revealing all. She wondered if the mere sight of him would always cause her breath to catch in her throat, even an aging, balding version, with saggy jowls, speckled skin and trifocal glasses.

"I'm thinking about you. How if, when you're an ancient old man and I'm even more ancient, would I still look at you and feel my heart stop."

He limped over and swooped down, kissing her neck. "It's a good sign you're thinking that far ahead."

"I think the answer is yes," she said. "Even better, I think I've managed to capture why, in that portrait of you."

"That's all you, there."

"Oh!" she said, sitting up so suddenly she startled Harriet. "I almost forgot. Wait until you see what Amanda's drawing. It's a sketch of you and me."

"Yeah? Is it good?"

"Is it ever. She is quite the artist, which I had no idea."

"Why did she pick us to draw?"

Kathleen waved a hand. "Who knows, other than they are all half in love with you."

"Too bad I'm taken. Aren't I." He kissed her neck again. "And if you were hoping for a memorable send-off last night, you succeeded."

It was exactly what she'd hoped for. "About that taken part."

He sat across from her in the other chaise. "Yes?" he said warily.

"If ... and I do mean if, you end up succumbing to or hooking up with, whatever it's called now, with one of your besotted fans ..."

He got up. "Jesus, Kathleen. Really?"

She twisted toward him and Harriet jumped off, disgusted with the excess movement. "Hear me out. Will you please not say anything and listen?"

He looked at the sunrise in response.

"Don't tell me." Her voice broke as she thought of Natalie. "That's all. I don't ... I don't want to know."

"It won't happen," he said tightly. "Do you think I'm so incapable of commitment that I can't keep my dick in my pants for a few months?"

"No. I don't think that. But I know human nature. I'm talking about some semblance of a loose reign, here. You know that old cliché about if you love something, set it free; if it was yours, it'll come back to you thing? There's a lot of truth to that."

"Are you wanting to see other people? Is that what this is about?"

She would've laughed if he weren't so serious. "No. God, no."

He turned back toward her. "I guess I don't get it. You

went ballistic about Natalie, and now I'm getting the greenlight for groupies coming around?"

She reddened. "First of all, Natalie's in another category altogether. That was unexpected, and in my face. I still hate the idea of you being around with an ex-lover, but it is what it is. Secondly, this isn't a greenlight for anything. I'm *trying* to give you permission, or room, for mistakes. Not that you need it, of course—"

"I looked at rings when you were at Bear Lake."

The adage about time standing still was never more apt than at that moment. She didn't trust herself to speak, so she didn't, could only stare at his broad shoulders in the sunlight and his hands in his pajama pockets.

After a few moments, he said, "I have to admit, I figured you'd be surprised to hear that, but I didn't expect dead silence. Plus, I said looking. That's all I did."

"It's ... well ... my hesitance is nothing new, but the speed, the strength of it all, is overwhelming. And it doesn't help what I heard on the radio coming home, that a study showed it takes couples three years to truly know each other well."

He made a face and she laughed. "Okay, so maybe giving credibility to a five-minute soundbite is dumb, but it made me think."

"No, it made you doubt." He kneeled down and took her face in his hands. "Look. We can talk all day about clickbait pseudoscience, questionable liberties, remorseful fucking, whatever. I know that now and at the end of the tour, it will still be you I need and want. Do you understand me?"

"Yes."

He got off his knees, grunting with discomfort, and sat across from her again. "We have that *'it,'* that thing people spend their whole lives searching for, writing about, singing about, whether it's after three days of meeting or three years.

You know it, too. So, I can go along with this silly hold-on-loosely concept, because what we have is stronger than anything we can throw in its way."

Kathleen looked down. *Praise God, that was some speech, and I hope you're right. How I hope.*

"I agree with you. But you also thought Julie was the one, too."

"No." His voice was loud, firm. "I gave into the pressure, and used excuses to get out of it. Which I know was shitty."

"I don't know if it was that. You seemed pretty steadfast in your reasoning to me, about you two wanting different things out of life." She held her breath. *This could be it. The moment of truth. The time to reveal.*

It wasn't. He was agitated, now, and in pain. "Why do I feel like you're arguing with me? Testing me, even? I don't want to talk about Julie. I screwed up and I was wrong to lead her on. End of story." He laid back in the chaise and rubbed his hip, his face pinched.

She sat next to him. "I'm sorry. I'm not trying to be disagreeable or play devil's advocate, I swear." She rubbed his side gently. "Is it worse than usual, today?"

"I took some pills. I just need to eat."

"All right. How about some French toast?" She leaned down and kissed his belly. "With a side of something else?"

"Mm," he raised his head. "The day is getting better already. Still think you need to hone your skills?"

"Practice makes perfect, as they say."

She got up, feeling the cream cheese curdling in her gut. "You stay here and enjoy the view. I'll bring you breakfast in bed. Like you've never had."

"I'll take it. The side dish special."

She laughed. "One side dish special coming right up."

The next six weeks passed in a blurry mix of missing Thomas, hoping he was doing well, and then wondering what the hell she was doing. They'd agreed to communicate monthly. A trial basis, she'd said. So far, the crowds the Thomas Hart Band had been playing to were sizable, and Kathleen could hear the surprise and pleasure in his voice when he'd relayed the fact. She was genuinely happy for him. Happy, that is, when she wasn't heaving in every corner of her house.

She was at the point where she was afraid to go out much at all. She put Summer and her suspicious questioning off easily, due to the preoccupation with Sam, Francesca, and the upcoming baby. Kathleen told her she needed to cut her work hours temporarily, and that had been the end of it. For now, anyway. She knew the reprieve was temporary.

"Kathleen Brooks?" A young nurse called out her name into Dr. Love's waiting room. She was wearing scrubs with a baby zoo animal design, and matching eyeglasses with zebra stripes. Her nametag read "Madi."

"Good morning!" Madi squeaked cheerily. "This way, please."

Kathleen followed her down the hallway where the obligatory scale waited.

"Let's get your weight."

Kathleen stepped on and Madi tsked. "How are you feeling, Kathleen?"

"Terrible, to be honest."

They went into Room 2, where she took Kathleen's vitals. "Still repeated vomiting?"

"Yes. It comes and goes, but it does seem to be getting worse instead of better. At least five or six times a day."

"Yikes!" Madi's button nose scrunched up. "You poor thing." She swiped a card on a computer and typed some notes on the keyboard. After a couple of minutes, she swiped it again and then pointed to a gown on the examining table. "Everything off, please. Dr. Love will be in momentarily." She pumped hand sanitizer from a container on the wall and left.

After a few minutes, Dr. Love swept in.

"Good morning, good morning," she said, extending her hand. "How are we today?"

"Not so good, Doc."

Dr. Love swiped her card through the slot and got on the computer. "You're taking the Vitamin B and Unisom?"

"Yes. It seemed to work at first, but now I feel sick constantly. And I do mean constantly."

"Ach, and you're down four pounds from last time. That's not good. Are you trying to eat?"

"Yes. The only thing that stays down is cream of wheat. And oranges. And orange Gatorade." She held up a jug of it she'd been toting around.

"Good. Keep up with the Gatorade, especially." She examined Kathleen's skin and said, "I'm afraid what you're experiencing is beyond average. It's what we call hyperemesis gravidarum, or HG. Just a fancy phrase for excessive nausea and vomiting."

"I did see that come up when I googled all this. I'm worried, truthfully."

Dr. Love nodded. "It could ease up in a few weeks, or you might have it like this until the day you deliver. I don't want you to worry, though. I'll test your blood for electrolytes and potassium, make sure you're not getting dehydrated. We'll keep a close eye on this and keep trying different meds."

Kathleen sighed in relief and hoped the subject of getting the father on board would not surface. "Great," she said.

"You're at eighteen weeks. Any movement?"

"Uh—no, I don't think so."

"You should be feeling it anytime, now. A flutter you might even mistake for gas or indigestion. We're going to do an ultrasound in a few minutes, so we'll get a peek at how things are progressing." Dr. Love peered at Kathleen above her glasses. "I see you came alone today."

Crap. There it is. Kathleen cleared her throat. "Yes, Thomas will hopefully be able to come soon. He's travelling right now."

It wasn't a complete lie.

"Excellent." Dr. Love smiled and Kathleen noticed a dimple among the creases. Which brought to mind someone else's, and she felt her sinuses tweak and her eyes fill. Everything was a reminder of him. She forced it all away, to be dealt with later.

"Yes, excellent," she agreed.

"Sure, now we'll have our sonogram girl, Rachel, in here and get a look-see at the wee rascal causing all this fuss."

They got Kathleen prepped and Rachel applied the cold gel on her belly. "You've popped out quite a bit there already," she said. "Then again, you're a tiny thing." She waved the wand around. After what seemed an interminable amount of time, Rachel grinned. "Congratulations, mama. Are you ready for this?"

No. Not in the least. Could you tell? She lifted her head up. "Is everything okay?"

The technician said giddily, "You're having twins!" She turned the monitor around.

"Wh—what?" Kathleen gripped the edges of the table, feeling the blood drain from her face.

"They're facing each other. Don't see that very often. I'll be able to get you a print of that."

Dr. Love's excitement was palpable. "Ach! There you

have it, love. I had my suspicions! Little wonder you've been so peaky!"

"I think I'm going to pass out," Kathleen said. She closed her eyes, but she didn't faint.

"It's quite a shock. Just breathe and relax for a minute."

Kathleen blinked rapidly, trying to focus, trying to listen as Rachel talked. "I think fraternal twins, and from what I see so far, they look perfect."

Rachel pointed out various body parts on the two images, temporarily christened Baby A and Baby B, as they squirmed about on the fuzzy screen. They were fully formed, miniature miracles in action, with silvery bones and zipperlike spines bending in the murky shadows of her depths.

"Look!" Rachel said, "Baby A is sucking his thumb!"

Kathleen was mesmerized as she watched their acrobatics. *She* was growing these babies, providing shelter and protection, and a sense of fresh resolve took root, as strongly as they had within her. She'd plow ahead through the unrelenting sickness, and every time she wanted to complain, she'd remember the picture in front of her. People had been giving birth for centuries in circumstances far worse than this. She squinted at the monitor. Her eyes were drawn to what looked like a tiny pebble throbbing with light.

"Is that—" her voice broke off "—a heartbeat I'm seeing?"

The technician's grin got even bigger. "Yes, two strong heartbeats, and even after fifteen years on the job, it never gets old."

"Twins," Kathleen said. *Thank you, thank you. Twins. Twins. Twins. Unbelievable. Twins.* The words went on a loop in her head, and Thomas' absence was keener than ever. *He should be here. Yes, here with me. To find out he'll be a father to not just one baby he didn't want, but two.*

She'd cried more in the last two months than in the past two years, she thought, as another onslaught slid down the side of her cheeks and wet the papery pillow. How pathetic and lonely to not have anyone but two medical professionals to share this moment with. Adding to that, a vicious voice piped in to suggest this was her price to pay for another lost life so long ago. To be sick as a typhoid patient for nine months and suffer every minute in sad isolation.

Did you think you could have it all, Kathleen? That there would be no consequences?

"I never thought that," she said, starting to sob into her hand.

"Thought what, dear?" the doctor asked softly, squeezing her other hand. "Ah, never mind. It's an emotional time, isn't it?"

Through a blurry haze, Kathleen looked again at the figures floating in her womb.

We did this, Thomas. We made these beautiful creations, with God's hand, and though I don't deserve it, He's giving me my second chance. You have to see that.

Dr. Love added another prescription to Kathleen's regime, and she found that while mornings and evenings were still horrible, she could function in the day for a few hours. She asked Summer to schedule her for afternoon shifts at HopCanon, in the hopes she could pull that off. Peak tourist season, and she wasn't proving to be much help. She got in her car and headed there, praying it wouldn't be too crazy-busy. She knew she was early, but that would give her time to ease back in.

Zack was behind the bar doing prep work. His stern face brightened upon seeing her. "Hey, stranger."

"Hi, Zack. How've you been?"

"I'm good." He pinned her with one of his stares. "And you?"

"Back in the saddle, as they say." She tied a bar apron on.

"Those working for you?" He tipped his head toward her wristbands. She'd put them on for additional support. Just in case.

She bit her lip. "Yes, somewhat."

He folded his muscular arms and leaned against the back counter. "So, pretty mama. Tell me. When's the due date?"

Her eyes flew up to his and panic streaked through her, red-hot. Was he joking? He wasn't much of a kidder, that she knew.

"Umm—due date?"

"Look, you don't need to pretend. I've suspected for a while. You can trust me."

She edged over to him, her voice a breathy hiss. "B ... but, *how?* Nobody here knows, not even—"

Her throat closed up.

"Thomas?" Zack filled in gently.

"Yes. I'll talk with him soon, when the time is right. Which is not now. It's too early in his tour and he can't afford to be off his game with—well, *this.* Oh Lord, listen to me babbling." She grabbed Zack's hand. "Please, keep this to yourself. For now."

"I don't talk. You know that."

She gawked at him. "Seriously. I managed to hide it from a freaking nurse, from my best friend, my mother, and you nailed it *weeks* ago? How? The bolting for the bathroom and no drinking gave it away?"

"I've seen that certain look before. You're ... more filled out. I don't mean that in a creepy way. It's a compliment."

"I know."

"Or maybe I'm just not as distracted as the average Joe."

"God. I'll second that." She got herself a glass of water and sipped it.

"Are you okay, though? All the vomiting can't be good."

"I'm on some meds to help with it. It's rough, I'll be honest. There's a good chance it'll be like this until the end. I'm not even sure if I can handle work."

He nodded. "I'll try to help you as much as I can. Also, if you need anything else, outside of work."

She swallowed hard to fend off the faucet she'd turned into. "I can't tell you how much that means to me. And what a relief it is to actually talk to someone about it. I feel so alone."

He came out from behind the bar and hugged her, and she gasped.

"What? Did I hurt you? What is it?"

"No, it's—" She put both hands on her belly, thrilled to the core. "I felt one of them move, I think!"

Zack raised a pierced brow. "One of them?"

"Yes! I'm having twins, if you can believe it." She giggled joyfully. "That was definitely a kick."

She told him all about the ultrasound, all that she hadn't been able to share as it was happening before, and he smiled and told her how wonderful it was. She paused in her play-by-play to look at him gratefully. "I needed this talk, Zack. To hear that what's happening is an incredible, awesome thing. Not, 'What? At your age?' or, 'Oh, no, how will you manage?' Because I'm sure those comments are coming."

"Undoubtedly."

"About Thomas ..." she began, then faltered. "I've kept this to myself because I didn't want everyone but him knowing. There's so much to consider, and I'm such a *chickenshit.*"

"I'm not so sure about that. Months of upchucking to push out two humans sounds pretty brave to me."

She laughed. "Spoken like a true man. A true friend." She helped him fill some salt and pepper shakers. "You know, it seems like you're always witness to somebody's drama around here. People having surprise babies and becoming surprise grandparents. What about you? Any life traumas I can assist you with? Not that I'm such a shining example of how to cope."

Zack took the shakers from her. "It's no trauma, but there is something."

"What? What is it?"

"Bring your stepdaughter back in for a drink. Then we're even."

"It's a deal. She's given up on dating, too, so you two could discuss the many benefits of chastity."

He set the shakers down at a nearby table. "Or ... not."

She laughed again as he walked away. Talking excessively would not be on the agenda for a future meet-up with Megan.

Especially not for a man of much insight, few words, and the possibility of crumbling celibacy in the air.

Kathleen flushed the toilet into which her lunch had been emptied and washed her face. She fretted that her cargo was not receiving the nourishment they needed, but Dr. Love assured her they'd be fine. The doctor was more worried about the toll it would take on Kathleen, aspects she was monitoring with blood tests. All was well with results so far, thank God, but the last couple of days had been like the beginning again. She went into the living room with her Gatorade and debated cancelling the group meeting that night. She hated to call it off; she knew the girls looked forward to it as much as she did. Maybe she'd make a fruit smoothie for dinner, one of the few things that didn't come back up, and rest until then.

She dozed off and dreamed of Thomas. A regular occurrence, some of the dreams were lovely, and some not so much. This particular one had him leaving her in the middle of the night, after one baby and then the other screamed for hours. On the kitchen table was a note he'd written: "I didn't sign up for this," and when she looked outside, he was getting in Natalie's car *with Hugo,* and was gone before she could do anything. She woke up in a cold sweat, already nauseated, and sat on the couch for a few minutes to let it sink in that it wasn't real. Hugo whined. He'd been staring out the bow window often, apparently still hoping his guy would come back.

"C'mere, boy," she called, and he trotted over. Even his starting- to-grey muzzle seemed sad and whiter, of late. She scratched his neck. "I know, baby. I miss him, too."

Her phone dinged with a text and she picked it up.

"Have a good meeting. Hi to the girls from their favorite rockstar playing in East Lansing tonight."

She smiled and sent a heart emoji back.

She got up, feeling slightly dizzy, so she took her time padding into the kitchen. She'd drink her smoothie on the way to church and hope it stayed down.

Kathleen knew, within minutes of arriving, she'd made a mistake in coming. She threw up on the grass next to the door, felt bad about that, and stood by the entrance for a few minutes to gather herself. She went in reluctantly. She was running late, so everyone was there waiting.

"Hi, girls. I'm sorry, but I think we all have to go home. I should've cancelled earlier." She took a few steps, her dizziness increasing with each footfall, and stopped in the rec room. Somebody had donated an old couch for the kids and she sat on its burnt-orange, threadbare arm. "I ... I haven't been feeling well, today ..." Her neck rolled to the side, and in one swift movement, she collapsed like an accordion and sank back into the cushions.

There were a few seconds of silence as the girls processed that she wasn't getting up.

"Shit! Did she just pass out?" Amanda's eyes, which protruded just a bit normally, now bugged out like a pug rescue dog.

They scrambled to Kathleen, their voices colliding in a frightened tumble.

"What just happened?"

"Is she drunk?"

"Don't be ridiculous. She is not drunk."

"Well, what the hell? Is it a seizure? Who keels over like that?"

"Omigod!" Mallory cried. "I've never seen anyone faint, before! She looks horrible. What do we do, what do we do?"

"First, we stay calm," Francesca said.

Amanda rolled her eyes. "As if saying 'stay calm' to freaking-out people *ever* worked."

It certainly wasn't working now. Mallory was beside herself.

"Should we take her to the hospital? I have the biggest car, but we can't take that. It's my dad's, and if she puked on the seat, I'd get in so much trouble. Oh, this is just awful!"

"Jesus, Mallory! Some nurse you're gonna make," Brianne snapped. She went to the kitchen and wet a dish towel, then rolled it up and put it on Kathleen's forehead. "We'll get an ambulance to come. Now, make yourself useful and see if there's a bottle of water somewhere for her. Francesca, call 911."

Francesca did as she was directed. "The EMTs will be here in less than ten minutes."

"Thank you, God," Mallory said, crossing herself. "Is she breathing?"

"Yes, she's breathing."

"Still. She looks like my gram right before she died, all chalky and white. Even her lips. This is bad." Mallory gave Brianne a water bottle and started crying.

"Are you for real? Bawling is not helpful, and she's not gonna die. Get it together!" Brianne unscrewed the cap off the bottle and sat next to Kathleen.

"Ms. K, can you hear us? Are you okay?" Amanda shouted.

That may have done the trick. Kathleen shifted. Her eyes were slits, but she managed to mutter, "What happened?"

"You fainted," Brianne said. "We called 911."

"I need to get to the bathroom ... I feel sick—" Kathleen said, to which Brianne barked at Amanda, "Get the bowl off the table! Hurry!"

"But it's got fruit in it."

"Then dump it on the damned table!"

The bowl was placed under Kathleen right in time.

"Eww," Amanda moaned. "I'm not good with vomit. I mean, I gag for ten minutes straight when I have to clean up the cat puke."

Brianne stood up ungracefully, due to the front load of weight in her belly. "You two are hopeless. I'll go rinse the bowl out. Francesca, put this on her forehead."

By the time Brianne returned, Kathleen was more alert. "You called 911?" she asked groggily.

"Yes. They'll be here soon."

"The responders will need to know," Kathleen inhaled. "So, I might as well tell you all. I'd have to, eventually."

She couldn't help but laugh, albeit weakly, at the four of them waiting for her confession.

"I passed out because I'm pregnant. And, I suspect ... dehydrated."

Francesca pumped a fist in the air. "I called it! I *told* you guys!"

"She totally did," Mallory said. "I didn't believe it."

Kathleen sighed. "I'm sorry. I'm a terrible role model, I know. Just what expectant teens need. An unmarried, sickly, equally pregnant leader."

"Shh. Stop that silly talk and rest," Brianne commanded.

Amanda picked up an apple from the overturned fruit bowl. "Geez, since when did you get so bossy, Brianne? Maybe you're the one who should be a nurse."

A siren wailed in the near distance.

The medical team arrived, no doubt causing a stir in the neighborhood. They introduced themselves as Patrick and Theresa, and Brianne led them over to Kathleen. Patrick was short and burly, bald, and had a kind face. He sat down and opened a laptop. "Theresa's going to take your vitals and ask you some questions as I type." He patted Kathleen's hand. "We're going to take good care of you."

Kathleen tried to focus on Theresa's questions, but the exhaustion was making it difficult to concentrate. She stared at Theresa's dishwater-blonde hair up in a bun and her tired eyes, and realized the technician was waiting for an answer to something.

"I'm sorry, what was that?"

"I was saying that, as you suspected, the vomiting is causing some dehydration. We're going to get an IV line in and take you to Mercy, in Mount Simon. Is that hospital all right with you?"

Kathleen agreed, and there was debate among the group as to who should accompany her.

"Girls," Kathleen said, "You've had enough excitement for one evening. All of you, go home. I'll text you to let you know what's happening, I promise. Thank you for taking care of me."

"Wait!" Mallory was still distressed. "Shouldn't we call somebody for you? Like Thomas?"

"No," she said sharply. "You know he's not available, anyway. And—he doesn't—oh, never mind. Just everyone ... keep this to yourselves, as if we had a regular meeting."

Her energy spent, she closed her eyes, and the last thing she remembered was Patrick and Theresa wheeling her out to the waiting ambulance.

11

"This sucks balls," Amanda said, rubbing her belly and tossing back two Tums in-between licking her ice-cream cone. "Nobody can listen like Ms. K."

Amanda was referring to the fact that Kathleen postponed the next meeting until August. Though the four of them were not particularly friends outside of the church group format, Amanda had taken the initiative and decided they should get together (at The Deep Freeze, Mount Simon's Dairy Queen equivalent), to discuss concerns regarding their fearless leader. All of them agreed, and sat outside on the stiff wire benches trying to eat their treats before they melted. It was a hot, sultry day, and ice-cream was just the ticket for four moody, pregnant females.

Francesca used a spoon to dig out some of her vanilla shake. "I could be dead wrong, but I have a feeling she hasn't told our hot crush he's gonna be a daddy."

"Yeah, I know," Mallory said. "Did you see her face before the ambulance took her away? I mean, other than she looked like a corpse, she almost admitted it."

"C'mon, guys, cut her some slack," Brianne groaned. She

was growing more uncomfortable by the day, weeks away from her due date.

"What do you mean?" Amanda said.

"We don't know what's going on with the two of them. You know how she says we shouldn't gossip."

"True. But it's not gossiping if we're worried about her," Amanda said. "We are legit worried, am I right?"

Francesca shifted on the bench. "Shouldn't we be? She's been in the hospital, and what? He's rocking it out every night? That doesn't sound right to me. So, I think he doesn't know."

"Geez, Francesca," Mallory said, taking a bite of chocolate shell encasing her vanilla cone, "you were right about her being pregnant in the first place. I believe you this time."

"Let's say Thomas is clueless," Brianne said. "How is it any of our business? We have no idea about anything, either. Maybe he's a real jerk. Maybe he's not. Maybe they broke up. They're adults. Most adults I know fuck up and do dumb shit all the time. They just get better at hiding it so they can pretend to be 'good examples.'"

They were all quiet, then, knowing she was right.

"Why *wouldn't* she tell him what's going on?" Mallory finally said. "Because he is most definitely not a jerk."

"Who the hell knows? Like I said, adults."

"You know what we should do?" Amanda chucked the last bit of her cone into the trash receptacle.

"Uh-oh. I already don't like the sound of this," Brianne said.

Amanda grinned. "What if we actually went to one of his shows? I looked it up and he's playing in Chicago this Saturday. I could drive us; it's only two hours away. Even better, it's an all-ages show, so we can get in with no problem. Then afterward, we can surprise him, talk to him."

"About what, exactly?" Mallory unwrapped the napkin from her cone.

"We'll say she's been sick, but didn't want to worry him. We won't give specifics."

Francesca shook her head, her black ponytail swinging. "He won't buy it. He'll want to know more."

"We *can't* say more. That's interfering," Brianne rubbed the small of her back. "This whole plan is crazy."

"It's not crazy. We plant the seed, that's all we'd be doing. I'll bet you dollars to donuts he comes back to see her. And then love will conquer all."

Brianne laughed. "Dollars to donuts?"

"My grandma always says it." Amanda got up and crossed her arms. "C'mon, you guys. She *needs* him, even if she's too stubborn to see it. We can see it. Mallory and I know how crappy it is to be pregnant without a good partner. I mean, Chase wants the baby, but he doesn't want me. And I don't want either one of them. I guess what I'm saying is, the chances for me having a happy ending in my situation are pretty much zero. I think they have a good shot, if they don't screw it up."

"Let's do it," Francesca said, her voice lowering as if they were discussing a top-secret mission. "Let's go, tell Thomas we wanted to see him perform, he'll ask about her, and we'll say she's really not doing well. Which is the truth. We'll make it clear she had nothing to do with us being there, too."

Brianne was the only one left who hadn't agreed with the strategy.

"Well, Brianne?" Amanda said.

"Yeah, yeah, okay, but I've got reservations. There's a hundred ways this could go off the rails. And thinking love conquers all is one of them."

Amanda sighed dramatically. "I just *meant* that they'd be

forced to work it out, once he gets with her, sees she's pregnant. 'Cuz she is super big already, ya know, since she's so little. I feel like we owe it to the universe to ... to help bring them together. I know, lame, but I don't care."

Brianne squinted at her. "Owe it to the universe? Are you high or something?"

"Ha! I wish. What I am is a hopeless, stupid romantic. Now, are you in?"

"I'm in, although I still have my doubts. This reminds me of a reality show with serious going-bad potential." Brianne got up slowly. "Now I owe it to the universe to get some more chocolate, before I lose my mind from this back pain and, like, go postal."

With that, they all decided a second helping was in order to maintain their sanity, and wobbled back into The Deep Freeze for more frozen stress relief.

Saturday came and the girls met at Amanda's before leaving for Chicago. She surveyed everyone standing in the cluttered living room and laughed. "Aren't we a sight for concertgoers. Probably not too many fans like us out in the crowds. Did everyone bring a camp chair and ten bucks to get in?"

"And money for food or drinks?" added Francesca.

They hadn't thought of that last part.

"No worries. I've got plenty from my dad to cover anything. I think he was disappointed I told him he couldn't come with. He saw Thomas play at that bar where Ms. K works, and said he's great."

"It's a brewpub that used to be a church, not a bar," Mallory corrected her. "And I'm so excited! I've never been to any kind of concert before."

"Don't be surprised at what you see," Brianne cautioned her. "Or smell."

Mallory's face scrunched up. "What, like B.O.?"

The other three laughed and Brianne said, "No, you goof. Weed!"

Mallory waved a hand. "Oh. That. I smell it every day coming from my brother's room. He tries to cover it up with some other bad-smelling stuff, but I know what he's doing."

Amanda's grandmother, whose name was June, came in from the kitchen. Amanda introduced the group.

June had long hair whose original color had been blonde, but was now grey with leftover yellowy streaks. She was still maintaining her original hairstyle from the seventies, too, of no bangs, and she was as thin now as then.

"You girls have a nice time, tonight," June said, lighting a cigarette. "Nothin' better, when I was your age, than goin' to see some summertime music." She sat down on a couch that, much like her, had seen better days. "That was when entertainment was good. Like the Beatles or Johnny Cash. None of this rap an' hip-hop crap you all are listening to now."

"Gram, don't start. Some of it's awesome."

"Naw, it ain't either. But that's how it is with the generations, always arguing. My dad hated rock 'n' roll, especially Elvis. Called it devil's music. Talk about nuts! Elvis Aaron Presley was as Christian as the day is long, and sang the most beautiful gospel music you ever heard." She pulled on her cigarette and exhaled. Amanda turned the ceiling fan on, waving her arms around.

"Ugh! What did I tell you about smoking in the house? It's bad for the baby."

"I'm sorry, darlin'." June said, stubbing the end out in an empty Miller Lite beer can. "I forget. You know that."

"Never mind. We gotta go. Remember, Riley's going to

his friend Joshua's to spend the night, tonight. They'll come and get him at six, his mom said. So, you get a night to relax, too." Amanda leaned over and kissed June on the cheek. "It'll be late when I get in. Don't wait up."

They piled into Amanda's Honda Accord and strapped seatbelts on. The car was the one item of value Amanda's mother Tammy had left behind when she'd taken off to be with Ted, a man she'd met online. He was the owner of a honkytonk in Alabama, and every now and then, Tammy would call home after a night of drinking to have a beer-laced conversation with Amanda.

"Ted and Tammy. Has such a nice ring to it, don't you think, Amanda? He's The One, this time, honey. You need to find yourself a nice man like Ted, instead of these boys you're sleepin' around with, and now one of them gettin' you knocked up. Just like your no-good, loser father done."

Amanda had hung up on her.

Francesca punched in the address of the venue on her smartphone, and within minutes, they were on the road.

Mallory wiggled in her seat. "This is going to be an adventure!" she announced.

"Let's hope in a good way," Brianne said.

"Don't be such a Debbie Downer. What could go wrong?"

Francesca laughed. "Every time someone asks that, you know it's gonna be a shitshow."

"Yeah, so everyone, stop talking," Amanda said. "Let's listen to Ed Sheeran sing about loving someone until they're eighty, like Thomas and Ms. K are gonna do."

"It's seventy. Loving until they're seventy, not eighty," Mallory said.

"*Whatever.*" Amanda turned the volume up, and not wanting to tempt fate any further, her passengers were quiet for the rest of the drive.

The festival was on the outskirts of Chicago and the event was called “Lake Street Jam,” presumably due to the fact the stages were set up on a street of the same name. Francesca had to pony up twenty for parking, another unexpected expense, but they didn’t have much choice. And except for Francesca who had family in the area, the group hadn’t been to Chicago outside of the school fieldtrip museum circuit.

“There’s so many ... people,” Mallory commented.

Brianne laughed. “It is a major city, ya know.”

“I know, but still. Now I see why so many of them come to our town to relax.”

They had a bit of a walk from parking to the venue, and the air was sticky and stagnant.

“Omigod, I am roasting,” Amanda said, pulling her thick hair up into a bun. “I hope we can sit in some shade.”

“I just hope I don’t go into labor,” Brianne stopped to catch her breath, and Francesca looked at her.

“You’re joking, right? You’re not having pains or anything, are you?”

“No pains, but, no, I’m not joking. I think we can all agree that going into labor right now would be disastrous.”

They followed the signs posted amidst the temporary orange fencing. Since the event was in a park-like setting, there were large trees to provide respite from the waning sun. The four stepped over clusters of people making out, smoking, or eating, and found some cool space in the shadows of oak leaves waving in the slight wind. As they set up their chairs, another act was finishing up. The female singer was wearing a black leather dress and had metal bracelets all the way up both arms, and her chartreuse tipped hair was damp with sweat. She was breathless talking into the mic.

"Thanks, everyone. We are Dominatrix, from Indianapolis! Hope you liked what you heard. Next on deck is the Thomas Hart Band, so make sure you stick around for that."

The girls hooted and clapped at this, and continued people-watching. The vast lawn was liberally sprinkled with all kinds of colors, clothes, and bodies, the likes of which this group had only been exposed to on screens or in magazines, and they were soaking it up. Mallory gawked as two teens with matching rainbow mohawks walked by holding hands.

"Wow. You don't see that every day in boring old Mount Simon."

"Boring is right," Amanda agreed. "I can't wait to get the hell out of that town."

"Does anyone want anything to eat? I'm starving. Looks like they got a ton of food trucks, over there." Francesca stood up.

"What's a food truck?" Mallory asked earnestly.

"God, you're a sheltered child. It's like a restaurant on wheels. What you'd see at the county fair."

"Oh. Well, I hate fair food, so I'm fine."

Brianne went with the worldly Francesca to see if they could find tacos.

In the meantime, Dominatrix was rapidly tearing down their equipment to make room for Thomas and his band. Mallory and Amanda could see Thomas hauling big black boxes and jumping on and off the stage like a nimble Billy goat. His hair was so long now, he'd pulled it back into a ponytail.

"Didn't Thomas have some kind of limp before?" Mallory asked Amanda.

"Yeah, from a car accident, he said. Why?"

"You'd never know it, watching him leap around up there."

Amanda laughed. "Are you enjoying the show already?"

"That's not it. I was wondering what happened from a medical perspective."

"You think he should still be a nurse, don't you?"

Mallory shrugged. "I guess I can so easily picture him doing it. I don't know why."

The other two came back then with food in hand. "Thirty bucks for two orders of tacos!" Francesca complained. "They'd better be good."

Mallory watched the stage set-up. "Duh. Everything is more expensive in a city. *Some* of us managed to ace geography in eighth grade and remember those little factoids."

"Lucky you. But we all must have flunked the part in health class where they went over birth control."

They laughed, as the point couldn't be argued.

The sun continued to recede, and with it, as predicted earlier, the pungent odor of marijuana wafting through the air. Amanda sniffed.

"Do you smell that? Ahh. There really *is* a God. We actually might get high just sitting here, and then get the munchies. Do you have any more money, Francesca? I can pay you back after my gram gets her check in the mail."

"Yes. Don't worry about it, since you drove. Look, I think they're getting ready to start."

She was right. Within seconds, the guitars and drums blasted out in what appeared to be an original tune, and a minute later, Thomas stepped up to the mic.

"Hey, everyone! We're the Thomas Hart Band, and we are so pumped to be in the Windy City, tonight! Thank you to Summer Jam Productions for having us. We've got a couple new ones, tonight. Here's 'Travelin' On.'"

It was a straight-up rock number, heavy on guitars, and the crowd loved it. As did the girls. Thomas pumped his fist, weaving around the stage like a figure skater, smiling and trading cues with the rest of the band. The drummer and keyboard player did killer solos, and Thomas went to the mic. "Everyone, give it up for Eli Clark on the keys, and his brother, Drew, on drums!"

The next two songs were more originals in which the bass player was featured and introduced. After his solo, Thomas gestured to him. "And there's Mr. Caleb Swanson on bass. I know you ladies like a hot bass player!"

"No kidding," Francesca said, clapping and cupping her hands around her mouth to shout, "YAAASSS!"

"They're ALL hot, aren't they?" Amanda said. "Literally, they should be called 'The Female Fantasy Foursome!'"

"I don't know." Mallory's face pinched in displeasure. "I'm not into that long hair. And except for the drummer with dreads, it looks so greasy, even from here. Don't they shower much?"

Brianne sipped water from her bottle. "Mallory, it's like eighty-five degrees out. They're *sweating.* I'd take a perspiring, long-haired rocker any day over some nerdy bookworm."

"Ugh. Not me. But it doesn't help they're the wrong gender, too."

Amanda stared at her. "Do you still think you're gay?"

"Yes. But it's not like I have this uncontrollable need to act on it. It's just ... there."

Francesca snapped her fingers at them. "Excuse-moi! Can we not talk about sexual orientation, now? Let's listen and enjoy the show!"

For the next hour, they did, until Thomas got their attention another way.

"Folks, we're going to end our set by introducing a special friend who's coming along for a few of our shows. Please welcome Miss Natalie Buchanan."

Natalie came out wearing a denim miniskirt, a tight-fitting white tee, and thigh-high boots. Her hair flowed loosely about and she tossed her head like Cher at the end of her old Seventies-era variety show, flipping one side of hair back. She waved to the crowd and stepped up to the mic.

"Thanks for that welcome! I'm having a blast on this tour and am so glad to be here. We're gonna do a tune I think you all might know. There's this incredible rocker named Tina Turner ... ever heard of her?"

The crowd roared in response and Natalie smiled. "Well, she likes to take the beginning of this song nice ... and ... easy. And the finish, nice and rough."

Thomas backed her up with a mellow, deep bass Ike Turner would've been envious of.

Someone yelled out, "PROUD MARY!" and a small band of dancers gathered in the front.

The song's tempo racked up, and with it, both the dancers and Natalie shook and shimmied for all they were worth.

Francesca whistled in admiration. "That Natalie looks like Beyonce, up there. Who *is* she? I mean, to him?"

Nobody had an answer, other than to observe silently that the two were obviously enjoying themselves onstage. Proud Mary segued into another high-energy song that appeared to be an original, and after that, Natalie spoke again into the mic.

"Here's a song we wrote together a long time ago, called 'Second Chances.' Hope you enjoy."

The song was slower and the dancers scattered. Natalie and Thomas sat close on stools, gazing at each other in-between every stanza, and singing harmony to rival the Beach Boys.

"One more day, one more chance, it's all I ask, Lord, it's all I ask..."

After the song, there was no encore. "C'mon, you guys," Amanda said when the last of the applause died down. She stood up and folded her chair. "We need to get up there before he takes off and we miss him completely."

They gathered up their things and navigated the patches of grass poking up between the sea of blankets and overheated bodies, finally making it to within yelling distance of the stage.

They shrieked his name out with all the breath they could muster.

His head jerked up immediately from cables he was looping together. Shading his eyes from the bright stage lights, he saw eight hands waving at him frantically. He jumped down and ran over to them, laughing. "Wow! I can't believe it! Did you guys come alone?"

Amanda hugged him first, followed by the rest, amid profuse apologies for dank, clammy skin.

"Yeah, it's just us. I drove. My first time in this crazy traffic, too!"

He stood back. "Geez, I can't get over this. Look at you guys! You're all—"

"Huge? We are. Some of us more than others, but you can say it."

"That's not what I was going to say, either." He glanced back at the stage. "Hey, can you all stick around for a while? I gotta help deconstruct, and then we can hang out and catch up?"

"Of course! We definitely need to fill you in on stuff. We'll be right here."

"Great."

The girls put their chairs back down to sit while they waited, resuming their enjoyable people-watching.

Mallory leaned over. "Okay. Who else thinks Thomas looks terrible?"

"What do you mean?"

"I mean, hello? I know he was skinny before, but now he's practically anorexic looking! And those big gray circles under his eyes. He is not well, if you ask me."

Brianne wiped her brow. "I agree. Kinda rundown-looking."

"I think he's high on something."

"Says Amanda the expert."

"Well, if checking your mom's pupils every night makes me an expert, then I guess I am."

"Shit. Sorry."

Amanda fanned herself with the festival guide they'd received at the entrance gate. "It's okay. But let's wait until we can talk to him before jumping to any conclusions."

"Here's another question," Francesca said. "Who else thinks he might have a thing going with Tina Turner up there?"

They began arguing over the likelihood of this scenario, with Amanda, unsurprisingly, voicing the loudest objections.

"Yes, she's obviously hot, but I don't believe it. No way."

Francesca shrugged. "I don't know. They were looking pretty cozy. If *I* were Ms. K and saw them like that, I'd totally flip out."

"Maybe that's because you're a hormonal, insecure, pregnant eighteen-year-old," Brianne said.

"Oh, and you're not?"

"I'm not saying that. I'm saying that's not what Ms. K is."

"Shh. Here he comes now."

He walked over, wiping his face with a towel from his back pocket.

"Dang, it's a scorcher," he said. "Are you guys okay? Can I bring you some water or anything?"

They assured him they were fine, and Brianne was the first to comment about what a great show it was.

"Thanks. I still can't believe you're all here. It means a lot that you took the time, made the effort. It's been a crazy couple of months, let me tell you."

Francesca's dark eyes were wide. "We're so excited to see our first rockstar in action. What's it like?"

"Truthfully? It's a lot of things. Exhausting and exhilarating, all at once. I'm lucky that the band are all good friends of mine, and we get along and help each other out when it gets rough."

"What about that Natalie?" Amanda blurted. "Is she 'helping' out, too?"

He laughed. His tired face was transformed with that charismatic smile. "You sound exactly like someone else, right now. And the only help Natalie is giving is on stage. You can report back with that, I promise."

"Uh—um, no," Amanda stumbled. "We're not here to, umm, spy. Ms. K doesn't even know we came."

He guzzled water from a bottle. "I see. How is Kathleen?"

Before anyone could reply, Natalie sidled up to him. Natalie, whose makeup was remarkably un-melted, whose cascading hair was still formed in smooth ringlets despite the soaring humidity. "Hey!" she chirped to the group, putting her arm around Thomas' waist. He introduced the girls.

"Yes, Thomas told me about ya'll. Don't you have some adventures ahead! When is everybody due?"

Baby talk ensued for a few minutes, and she nodded politely. It was obvious she was quickly bored with the topic. "We are about wrapped up," she said to Thomas, squeezing his arm. "Meet me in the van in ten?"

"Sure."

She walked away and Mallory stepped toward Thomas. "To answer your question, our meetings have kind of stopped. Ms. K has been super sick." Miffed at the familiar arm squeeze display and the time limit given, Mallory added, "Which you wouldn't know, of course."

He frowned. "Sick? Sick, how? The flu-like stuff again?"

Brianne intervened. "Not the flu. Listen, we gotta go—"

"She's been in the hospital twice since you left." Amanda's eyes were buggy.

"*What?* What's going on? She hasn't said a word!"

The four girls looked at each other, and what they suspected was confirmed. He didn't know.

"She ... she ..." Amanda stammered nervously, "She thinks you're busy and she doesn't want to worry you. But I —we—think it'd be a good idea for you to go back and see her."

He studied her for a few seconds. "We agreed not to do that, for now."

Francesca made an audible huffing sound. "Forget about any so-called agreements. She needs you. Like, seriously. Trust us, we know what we're talking about."

"Okay, but it's not exactly easy to take off in the middle of a tour, especially when I don't know what's happening—"

"Thomas!" Natalie called from a distance. "I've got a question about tonight for you!"

"I'll be right there," he yelled back.

"Never mind about *her*," Mallory jerked her head in Natalie's direction, her face flushing a deep shade of pink. "You want to know what's happening? Listen up."

"Mallory," Brianne warned.

"No, I don't care. This is insanity. Everyone can hate me, big deal. I'm used to that." She got in Thomas' face. "Ms. K is *pregnant*, with your baby, and she's been puking her guts out for weeks now. She literally fainted at one of our meetings, and I was scared out of my mind. I thought she was dying."

"*Wh*...?"

"We had to call an ambulance. That's when she told us, although Francesca suspected it already."

This time it was Thomas who appeared as if he would pass out. What little color he'd had before dissipated and he was even swaying slightly. "Is this ... some kind of joke?"

Mallory was more emotional than the others had ever seen her. "Uh, no. We are very serious."

"Jesus," he whispered, and his handsome face turned up to the almost-night sky. He walked a few steps away, as if trying to compose himself, his hands in his pockets.

"*What do we do now?*" Amanda mouthed to the others.

Brianne scowled, hissing, "We *apologize.*"

He circled back to them, still ashen, and Brianne touched his shoulder. "Thomas. We're so sorry. We came here tonight to, yes, hear you sing, but also just to try to convince you to come back for a visit. This was *not* the plan. You shouldn't have found out this way," she glared at Mallory. "We know Kathleen's been really sad since you left, for what it's worth."

"No, it's okay," he said quietly. "Although you're right that it shouldn't have been like this. A lot of things make sense now. We have a break in the schedule coming up. I'll find a way to get back there. How far along ... never mind. I'll find out soon enough."

"I think, like, 20 weeks," Mallory informed him anyway. "She's starting to show, but she looks awful because she's *lost* weight, instead of gaining."

"That's not good," he said, his brow growing stormy. "Twenty weeks! Unbelievable. If I'd have known..."

"We won't tell her you're coming," Amanda fretted. "Oh, she's gonna be really mad at us, now."

"Hey." His anger evaporated, he tipped Amanda's chin up. "Don't worry about that. None of you should feel bad. In fact, she's lucky to have you all looking out for her. But you've each got enough to deal with. The last thing you should be doing is running around like this, trying to make adults act like ... adults." He shook his head, all the energetic glow onstage now sapped out of him. "I feel like such a fool. You guys must think I'm a real asshole."

"Don't say that. We never thought that for a second. You've been distracted and, well ... as they say, love can make a person blind. In her case, a little nutty."

He smiled sadly. "I suppose. Listen, I want you to be careful going home. Are you driving back tonight?"

"Yes. We'll stay awake, though." There was little doubt of that, thanks to the turn of events.

He looked at all of them. "Thanks again for making the trip. One of you message me when you're back safely, okay? I'll be in Mount Simon in a couple of days. And thanks for —" he hesitated, "For caring. You guys rock."

Everyone got another hug and he walked back to the waiting van, this time his limp much more pronounced.

Brianne whirled around to Mallory. "Way to go, big mouth!" she snarled. "Look what you started! This is gonna turn into a damned soap opera, thanks to you. And you still couldn't shut it, even when he said he'd find out himself about her. Now he'll be worried out of his mind and probably not be able to perform. He might even cancel the whole tour! Which, if I'm right, is exactly what Ms. K doesn't want to have happen. I *knew* something like this would go down!"

Amanda and Francesca turned toward Mallory, certain she'd be crushed under this tirade and dissolve into tears, but they were wrong.

Mallory's eyes flashed defiantly. "First of all, coming here was Amanda's idea, so you should blame her before me.

Second, his girlfriend is sick AF, remember? The last straw was that Natalie chick pawing at him and then interrupting with her, 'Oh, Thomas, I need to ask you something,' when he was obviously still talking to us. All I could think about was Ms. K passing out, and there's glamour girl acting like she's ready to jump his bones any second. On top of all that, he looks like crap, too. I'm guessing he needs Ms. K as much as the other way around." She crossed her arms. "Yell at me all you want. Like I said, I'm used to it. I'm not one bit sorry I told him."

Amanda laughed. "Wait, did *you* just say, 'sick as fuck'?"

"I didn't say it, I abbreviated."

"Also, 'jump his bones'?" Francesca piped in. "Where did you hear that, from some bad Eighties movie?"

They all laughed then, even Brianne, which broke the tension. "I'm sorry for yelling, Mallory. I just don't want us to make the situation worse, you know?"

"They're grownups, for heaven's sake. They'll have to put their big panties on, like we're always being told to do, and figure it the hell out."

Francesca howled. "Omigod, Mallory. Your second swear word in one night. You're just full of surprises, aren't you?"

She smiled slyly. "Maybe I am. Now, where's the bathroom, because we should all go pee before the ride home."

They made their way through the throngs, found the port-a-potties, and once there, Mallory pushed her way through the line shouting, "Make way for pregnant women!"

Like the miraculous parting of the Red Sea, the festival crowd obediently and amazingly did just that.

12

Kathleen stood back and tilted her head for a better perspective of the finished portrait of Thomas. On the whole, she was pleased with how it had turned out. She twisted a piece of Kleenex to blend a spot around his hairline a little more.

"I think I'm done, Hugo. What do you say?"

Hugo lifted his head up at his name, looked at her and the picture, then put his chin back down on his paws.

She laughed. "Not quite the same as in the flesh, is it?"

Her phone dinged and it was a message from Megan. In the middle of her response, Hugo ran up to the door, barking and tail wagging wildly. The bell rang and she stared at the door stupidly. It was nine-thirty at night. *What on earth ...?*

She looked through the peephole to see the distorted profile picture of her love. Her knees threatened to buckle and she braced a wrist on the wall.

Thomas rang the bell rang again. There was no hiding or excuses to give now. *What is he doing here?* She inhaled deeply and opened the door.

"Thomas—"

He took two steps and she was enfolded by him without a word. She was still so shocked she could do nothing but wonder if the babies inside her knew who was pressing against them. Hugo jumped and put two paws on the side of his leg, and breaking away from her, Thomas knelt. "Hello to you, too, sweet boy." He rubbed the dog's ears and laughed at the ecstatic face washing that followed, and, of course, Harriet had to get in on the commotion.

"What ... what's happening? Aren't you supposed to be heading to Cincinnati?"

He stood, his gaze going right to her belly. She'd bought some loose-fitting athletic wear and a couple of tunic-looking tops, but not any maternity wear. Yet.

"Yes, in a few days." He picked Harriet up, holding her in her preferred infant-cradling position. She stretched out a paw up to his chin. "This is where I'm supposed to be, right now."

Kathleen teetered, as if she were walking on heels, to the kitchen. "Can I get you something? Beer? Water?" She glanced back.

"Sure. A beer would be good." He went to the couch, which was draped with a beautiful quilt. Even though it was July, he pulled it onto his lap, because that was what Harriet liked to sit on. Kathleen's glance lingered on the patchwork squares for a few seconds. She remembered, as a little girl, handing her grandmother fabric pieces as she labored away.

"*Tell me again about when you met grandpa,*" Kathleen used to beg her, as she would sit sewing with her reading glasses on the end of her nose. And Grandma Mary would laugh and repeat the same story again.

Kathleen went to the kitchen and gripped the edges of the sink, trying to calm the nerves zapping under her skin like tiny currents. She looked out the window. Even in the dark purple of dusk, she could see the cardinal couple from weeks ago were back at the feeder. She knew it was the same pair, because the female had strange, mottled markings Kathleen had never seen before. The fire-engine-red male offered his mate a seed, who took it from his beak.

"Is that you again, Daddy?" Kathleen wiped the sink absent-mindedly as the female spit out the sunflower's shell. *"Maybe it's you and Gram. Help me. Please. You both always knew the right thing to say. Especially you, Gram ..."*

The male cardinal moved over as another bird joined in the feast.

"Get him the beer," went the dialogue in her head, and she laughed. Her father and grandmother had known how make guests feel welcome, always breaking out Chex Mix or other snacks, and offering an array of drink options to weary travelers. She took a can out and poured it into a pint glass.

She set the glass on the coffee table and sat, perusing him as he stroked Harriet. His face was wan with exhaustion, or pain, or maybe both, and he'd lost the weight he'd gained since they'd first met.

"Thanks," he said, avoiding her gaze. "HopCanon?"

"Yes. Consecration."

"Ah, yes. How could I forget?" His lips sealed around the edge of the glass, and desire curled up her belly as she watched his throat bob up and down rhythmically.

He'd swallowed the whole pint in less than a minute.

"Would you like another?"

His eyes finally met hers, glinting like copper rocks in the hot desert sun. "Hmm. How about you look and see if you can rustle up the one they called 'Betrayal.' That might be more fitting for the moment."

Oh, God. Here we go. "Meaning?"

"It means you didn't trust me enough to inform me of a life event that affects me as much as you. But. You haven't had faith in us, not even from the beginning, so I shouldn't be shocked."

"That's not true," she cried. "That's not true at all—"

You sure about that, Kathleen?

He jerked forward, prompting Harriet to jump down. "You're pregnant. Have been, for months, and couldn't find an opportunity to inform me, the presumed father? What do you call that, then?"

She bristled. "Not 'presumed.' You *are* the father. And I can say I'm sorry a million times, but I had some good reasons to keep it quiet until we met up again."

He sprang off the couch much like the cat had moments earlier. "I'm ready to hear them. I'm ready to hear why it took four girls to tell me something my lover should've told me long ago." The shock on her face amped him up even further, and he paced in a circle in front of the couch. "Yes, that's how I know. The girls actually drove to Chicago to one of my shows, they were so worried about you. Whatever you think, *do not* be angry with them. You're damned lucky to have kids who care about you like that."

"I'm not angry. Just surprised, is all. And I don't need you to tell me how to feel, or remind me what good girls they are."

His pace increased without a wrinkle in his step, and she wondered how he was managing it. "No, because that's your job, isn't it? Assuming what people feel or think."

"I wouldn't say that."

"Really?"

She started to protest, but he stopped her. "Speaking of surprised, let's talk about that. Let's talk about humiliation, too, while we're at it." He swooped down, inches from her face. "Do you have any idea how utterly stupid I felt, listening to Mallory detail everything? How sick you've been, calling an *ambulance,* for fuck's sake, and there I was, my ears still ringing from the night, dog-ass tired, hungry, and, hey, guess what, Thomas? The rabbit done died."

"That's a horrible expression," she snapped.

"I'll tell you what's horrible. To think that someone you love isn't who you thought. Isn't being honest with you."

"This isn't about honesty!"

His pace and his voice picked up even more. "I seem to recall that expression, 'lying by omission.' What makes this situation any different?"

"I never meant to deceive you. You have to believe me."

The wan color of his cheeks morphed into two matching flames, and as he ran his hands through his thick, uncut hair, waving his angry, flawlessly-shaped hands, his shirt raised to show his muscled midriff. Despite her weeks of sickness and anxiety, he could've had her then and there. She closed her eyes to concentrate on his heated words.

"Why, then? Why in the hell would you keep silent about this?"

"It's complicated. I did think it was best, but only temporarily—"

"*Best?* For who?"

Her own frustration grew. "For you! To keep your plans from getting derailed. Is that so bad, that I was trying to think of you? That I felt a need to protect a dream?"

"You weren't!" He bellowed so loudly she shirked. "You were making decisions for me! Do you not understand I'm the captain of my own ship, perfectly capable of navigating my life and coping with any perceived 'obstacle' along the way?"

"Of course, I think you're capable. I never doubted your abilities! Not for a second."

"Then why are you treating me as if I'm this helpless kid and you're my mother?"

At this, she broke. "Maybe that *would* be apropos. Since

people will undoubtedly be mistaking me for her at some point."

"Don't start with that bullshit, goddam it. There's more you're not telling me."

She whipped her neck around and spit her words out as if coated in poison. "Yes! All right! There is more, and you know what? It has to do with the most painful period in my life, a time I'm not proud of. So, if you want to hear it, you'd better take it down a couple notches and listen to me like never before. Otherwise, you might as well leave."

He stopped mid-pace. "Okay. I'm sorry. I seriously feel like I'm losing it. I'm torn between wanting to rip that loungewear off your body and staying here arguing all night."

She stood up. "Do it," she seethed. "I wish to God you would, and I don't mean arguing all night."

He grabbed her around the waist and kissed her with no hint of gentleness. He broke off, his breath hot on her ear. "Believe me, I am sorely tempted. I've had this hard-on for how many weeks, thinking about you. Too bad it feels like we're Adam and Eve in the garden."

"There are some things that need to be said first anyway."

"I know why he bit into that apple." His hands were under her new, oversized bra, and she moaned.

"Why?"

"Because as pissed off as I am, I want you more than ever. I want this body next to mine, to be inside you and go to sleep inside you, and keep doing it over and over. Whatever the cost."

She could barely breathe. His words were so close to what she'd told herself about him, it was uncanny. "Maybe just once there doesn't have to be a cost. We can find a middle ground somewhere."

"Yeah. Middle ground is not my forte."

She took his hands off her breasts and kissed his knuckles. "There's time. When our minds are clearer and some healing happens. After you hear me out."

He said nothing, just nodded, and she tried to think where to even begin. She'd imagined this scene so many times it was comical. The quilt caught her eye again and her racing heartbeat calmed. "I was afraid," she said quietly. "Of many things, but we'll start with being afraid of looking like I trapped you. Of your resentment, especially."

"Resentment? How do you figure that?"

She almost laughed at his genuinely confused expression. "Have you forgotten you told me you broke off your *engagement* because Julie wanted a family and you didn't? All the times you told me the world would be better off without another version of a screwed-up you walking around?"

"That last part is still probably true, but you left out the most important piece of the equation. The one that has the potential to change everything."

His arms encircled her, pulling them both back to the couch. "You. You're the reason whatever came before feels meaningless. Moot points."

She looked up. "I don't see how that's possible. You think I'm some magical being? That with a wave of my hand, these very significant concerns will *poof,* disappear? I have no superpowers. I'm boring, unaccomplished, cafeteria-Catholic Kathleen Brooks, without a single accolade to my name. The worst kind of sinner there is. A hypocrite." A single tear rolled down her cheek.

"You're none of those things—"

He tried to brush the tear off her face, but she wriggled away.

"I can say with conviction that taking this pregnancy to

term will be the most noteworthy thing I've ever done. Or will do, I'll bet." She smiled faintly. "Maybe I set the bar pretty low, I don't know. The reason I didn't think it could happen, why I was reluctant to tell you right away, is because I—" she stalled, her voice warbling as she fought for composure. "I'm sorry ... I've never told a soul what I'm about to tell you."

"I'm listening."

A visceral voice not her own surfaced within her. Whether it was one of her grandparents' or someone else's wasn't clear, but she heard it as if an urgent lifesaving directive was guiding her, guiding her through the tangled weeds of the past that had kept her mired in guilt for so long. *You can do this, Kathleen. You're safe with him.* She gulped at the air, willing the mysterious voice to spread its strength to her throat and tongue and form the words.

"I was a senior in high school and I had my first serious relationship with a guy. J.J. We were in love, or so we thought. Let's just say we were hideously irresponsible." Her head drooped down until her chin almost touched her chest. "Lo and behold, I got pregnant, and long story short, J.J. went nuts. A long, knock-down, drag-out screaming match. He insisted I have an abortion. It was the only way, he said. It wasn't 'in the plan.' Looking back, he was no more than a scared kid who didn't want his college sports scholarship jeopardized. Didn't want the shame and embarrassment. Frankly, neither did I, but there was a part of me that hoped it could be worked out."

Her limbs felt numb with cold, and she reached for the quilt and wrapped it around herself. "So, I gave in. I could've fought him, but I felt so completely alone. I can make these excuses, but in the end, I was a spineless coward. I did it, and it was every bit as hellish as you can imagine. I was so torn up about making the decision that I

—I waited too long. There were complications. Then, when I couldn't conceive with Steve, I was certain it was permanent. And my fault."

Thomas fondled a lock of her hair. "What a terrible thing for a young girl to endure."

Her shoulders went up and down a notch. "It was my own doing."

"You didn't get in that position by yourself."

"No, but ... when I found out this time, once I got over the shock, I saw it as my second chance. My—our—miracle. And like I said, you'd voiced your feelings about fatherhood before, and every traumatic memory of J.J. came crashing back. It literally paralyzed me."

"I understand, to a degree. Now."

She shook her head adamantly. "I don't think you can. I didn't even realize myself how deeply I had shoved it all under the rug, until I held that test in my hand."

"This makes me sick, that you went through this alone. Where was I? Off practicing, I suppose?"

"It doesn't matter. The truth is, I didn't want you to know until it was too late to do anything about it. I wanted to feel what it was like to be *happy* to share the news. I dreaded your anger, and I didn't want to face you trying to convince me to—" she broke off, tears engulfing her. "To do what I did before—"

Her chest ramped up and down as she let go, and he gathered her in his arms again.

"It's all right. I'm not angry. I'm hurt, more than anything, and confused." He tilted her face up. "I'm here, and I love you. That's as far as I've gotten with processing it all."

She buried her head into his chest, so happy to smell him once more. Relief washed over her, the grateful sigh akin to waking up from a nightmare and realizing it was all nighttime fiction. “I was so scared you’d think less of me once you knew ...”

“No. How could I, given the circumstances? Especially when I have my own demons to wrestle with?” He squeezed her shoulder. “I think it’s *you* who thinks less of herself. Who needs to forgive that frightened young lady.”

“You should add therapist to your impressive resume. And take your own advice.”

“Ha,” he said, not laughing. “I’m no therapist, but I might need one now.”

Her heart skipped a beat. This was it. This was the reckoning she’d so feared, his resistance and distaste to a life change he’d never wanted.

“I’m almost scared to ask, but why? Why now?”

“For two days I’ve been thinking of what I learned growing up. About fatherhood, about trying to balance a demanding career with family. I mean, my dad tried. He did his best, when he wasn’t all strung out on shit. Do you know how many patients came to his funeral? It was unbelievable. But I lost count of all the soccer games he missed, school events, boy scout meetings. Amazingly, I wasn’t resentful. I’d make excuses for him, even, which drove my mom nuts.” He laughed, mirthless, and looked at Kathleen. “I could *see* how hard it was for him, though. It’s why I stayed with him when she left. I could see how powerless he was in the grip of it all, and the way to feel better was through these drugs at his fingertips. He was a good role model in a lot of ways ... until he wasn’t.”

He sank into the cushions, looking small and helpless, more vulnerable than she’d ever seen him. She brushed his cheek, rough with whisker stubble, wishing she could erase all the doubt and uncertainty plaguing them both. “You’re worried you’ll be like him.”

“Hell, yes, I am. Afraid of what it means to be a dad, a

husband. Because believe me, the apple doesn't fall far from the tree." He leaned back, gazing at the ceiling. "The demands of the last couple of months have me spinning."

"You do look—spent. I want to hear all about the tour, when you're ready."

He sighed. "Right."

For several minutes they sat together, silent and entwined, and both animals jumped up next to them. Hugo pushed his snout under Thomas' arm. She laughed, blowing her nose. "Do I need to tell you who else missed you terribly?"

He scratched under Hugo's chin. "It's nice to be loved."

"You are, you know." She stroked his bushy sideburns, curly with overgrowth, then looked down at her lap. "There's something else I found out about a few days ago. You might even feel less equipped for what's ahead after you see this."

"Oh?" He said it apprehensively.

She reached for a folder on the coffee table. "Take a look." Her pulse surged with anxiety as she gave him the ultrasound prints.

His eyes were tired slits, his lush eyelashes like half-moons fringed in black. They flew open upon registering what lay in his hand. "My God. *Twins?*"

"Yes."

He stiffened and bent an elbow on his knee, holding his forehead as he studied the images. Even Hugo sensed a change and whined, pawing at Thomas' leg. "You're right," he whispered.

"About what?"

He tossed the pictures on the table roughly. "I feel even less adequate, if that's possible."

"Thomas ..."

"I can't do this now. I really can't, my head's gonna

explode. I'm going to Courtney's. I told her I might be coming by tonight."

Flooded with disappointment, she groped for a rational response. "It's ten o'clock! You don't want to stay here?"

"It's not that. It's ...I'm teetering on the edge. Whipped, coming off the performing high, and at the same time, overwhelmed and unbelievably horny. I'm all kinds of messed-up, right now."

He rose slowly and winced, rubbing his hipbone as she'd seen him do so many times.

She thought she'd faced desperation before, but it was nothing like watching him now about to leave. Her response tumbled out like a toddler's high-pitched cries as they clung to a departing parent. "We can just—sleep! No more, no less. No expectations." *Shut up, Kathleen. You sound like an old hag clawing at her last chance lover ...*

He laughed bitterly. "Right. You know that's impossible. I'm looking at you, touching your body that I thought was perfect before, and now you're filled out like a goddam Renaissance painting and I want you so much I think I'd hurt you. Or them."

"Please. That's not you. You could never hurt me—"

"It *is* me!" he shouted. "There are sides to me you've never seen. Let me assure you, I don't paint a picture nearly as pretty as the one you made of me."

"You've said that so much. I can't imagine it."

"No. You can't." He traced a finger over her cheek and became quiet. "I've never felt about anyone how I feel for you. And I'm mad as hell on top of the fifteen thousand other things racing through my brain. That you actually thought I'd ask you to ... God, I can't even say it." His face crumpled and the tears fell. "Let alone, two babies! I'm a *nurse,* for Christ's sake! In the business of saving lives, not snuffing them out—"

"Like I did." She made a mental note he was using present tense with the reference about nursing.

He crossed his hands in front of him like an umpire calling an out. "No. That was totally different. What happened to you was nothing short of abusive. I'm talking about myself, here." He wiped his face and snorted. "You wanna know what's ironic? I even—I even dreamed about this on the road, having a family with you."

"Fair enough," she said, her voice pleading. "You have to understand. My actions—or lack of them—were always about my hang-ups, not about what kind of man you are. I swear on all that is holy, this is true."

He rubbed his temple on both sides and gained composure. "We're both dealing with a lot. I need time to decompress and, as crazy as it sounds after months apart, a little space to think." He dug in his pocket and threw back whatever he'd retrieved there into his mouth, then swallowed the rest of the beer. "Later, that is. What I also need is to sleep for about three days. I have to go, before these little helpers start taking effect and I crash at the wheel. Been there once, don't need to relive it again."

He kissed her perfunctorily on the forehead and gave the dog one last pat. "We'll talk tomorrow. I'm not going anywhere, I promise."

She choked back words begging him to stay and simply nodded. Hugo sat with his snout pressed up against the bay window, whining softly as Thomas got into a car and drove away much too soon for his liking.

Kathleen wrapped the quilt even tighter around her shoulders to dispel the chill that had settled into her bones. Midsummer, and here she was shivering. She patted the couch. "C'mere, buddy." The dog circled back to her and jumped up. "He'll be back," she whimpered into his fur. Then, as if to convince them both, she added, "He will."

13

"I'm glad we made this happen," Summer said, pulling up the handle of the cushy massage chair and switching the programming to NECK/SHOULDER.

"Ouch!"

Tiffany, the salon's co-owner and pedicurist, looked up questioningly after digging into Summer's toe with a sharp tool. "Yoo okay?"

"Ahh, it's fine. Reflexive reaction."

Kathleen took a drink from her water bottle. "I'm glad, too."

"And I'm sorry I've been so taken up by all this stuff with Sam. How're you doing? Are you finally over that flu crap?"

Kathleen laughed. "Don't apologize. Plus, I think you're gonna be 'taken up with stuff' for quite a while."

"Still. It's no excuse for neglecting my best friend."

"You haven't. I've been purposely trying to keep a low profile."

Summer peered at her. "I did notice that, believe it or not. Why?"

"A few reasons." Kathleen shifted uncomfortably and switched her chair's controls to, "TOTAL BODY FATIGUE." "I need to come clean with you. I probably should've told you right away. Go ahead and add it to my growing list of sins."

"What the hell are you talking about?"

"I—I never had the flu. I've been sick, that's for sure. But not from that."

Summer's face fell. "You're scaring me."

"Don't be. I'm not dying."

"What on earth, then? Spit it out, Brooks."

"Oh, God. Here goes nothing." Kathleen exhaled. "I'm pregnant. Almost five months."

Summer wrenched forward, prompting protests and waving hands from Tiffany.

"You no move! I do ovah now!"

"W*hat?* You are *what?*"

Lisa, the technician working on Kathleen, looked up at her as if waiting on an explanation, too.

"I know, I know, it's crazy. I was in complete shock for days. In some ways, I still am."

"Jeezus. I thought you looked a little, I don't know, *rounder,* but I figured it was from all that Chinese food he kept feeding you in bed." She sat up straighter. "I don't understand. All those years, it was Steve who had the issue?"

Kathleen shrugged. "Could've been both of us. I've stopped trying to figure it out. Thomas even insisted on protection—until—um, once. As the old guidebook goes, that's all it takes. At HopCanon, of all places."

"Lord help me. That I didn't need to know."

"Sorry."

Summer leaned back in the chair and stared straight

ahead. “I cannot believe it. Literally. You’re forty years old, and pregnant with your boy-toy’s baby.”

“Almost forty,” Kathleen snapped. “And Thomas is no *boy-toy.* I’m in love with him. Honestly, can you please say something I don’t know, that might be slightly reassuring?”

She ignored the plea. “I knew he couldn’t keep his hands off of you, but really? Sex in an old church? Which is now my business?”

At this, both technicians stopped their work and cocked their heads. Summer always insisted they knew more English than they let on.

“It wasn’t planned, for God’s sake! Nobody saw us and it wasn’t by food or anything.”

Summer was still miffed. “I’ll make sure the health department gets that memo. Why am I just learning of this pregnancy now?”

“I—I didn’t feel right having people know without telling Thomas, too. It was bad enough that Zack totally knew without me saying a word—”

“What?? Zack knows?”

“Yes, well, he basically cornered me a few weeks ago and I couldn’t deny it. It’s as if he can see through to one’s *soul.* I mean, seriously. You should start a side business featuring him doing fortune telling or psychic readings. For HopCanon patrons.”

Summer tilted her head as if she was considering it. “There are goofballs out there who go for that nonsense.”

“Um, like me?”

Summer laughed.

“Anyway,” Kathleen continued. “Thomas only recently learned what’s going on. I tried to keep it from him, so as to not interfere with his music plans, the tour, all that. Temporarily, of course.”

"You know how crazy that sounds, right? Your martyr streak is in action mode again."

"Possibly," Kathleen said tersely. "But can you give me a little credit? I'm trying to do the right thing. Whatever that is. Unfortunately, Thomas doesn't see it, either. He's quite frustrated with me, at the moment, and that's putting it mildly."

"He's probably in shock, too."

"Don't defend him. Even if you are right." Her voice broke. "I desperately need you in my corner."

Summer grabbed her hand and squeezed it. "Come on, Kath. You know I am. Start from the beginning. Let me have it."

As Lisa rubbed her tired calves and polished her nails, Kathleen spilled out all the details of the past weeks, with the exception of the interaction with J.J. And the same as she'd felt with Zack, it was liberating to be able to openly talk about it all, at last.

Summer sighed. "I gotta hand it to you, you certainly know how to make a pedicure memorable. And twins? Where the hell does that gene come from?"

"He is one, if that means anything. He has a twin sister, Courtney. I thought I told you before."

"Oh, you could've. I can't trust my brain, these days."

Tiffany frowned, folding a tiny piece of tissue and blotting a corner on Summer's pinky toe. "Stay. Let dry ten minute." She turned and shouted at the new customer who'd walked in the salon minutes ago, "Pick ya culla!"

"I've given them new stories to talk about today," Kathleen said. "Wonder how it will be translated."

Summer laughed. "Well, they might come to HopCanon just to see if it's a brothel in disguise or something. Or maybe a fountain of fertility, since people who work there appear to be getting pregnant at an alarming rate."

"What? Who else are you talking about?"

"Liz and Micah," she said, referring to Hop Canon's head cook and her husband. "Wait. Is there some secret taproom copulating spot I have yet to discover, that everyone else is in on?"

Kathleen reddened. "Don't be silly. No. But didn't Liz have a baby last year?"

"Yes. This will be their third, and she's none too thrilled about it. Micah, on the other hand, is over the moon. He wants a little girl so bad." She pointed to Kathleen's belly. "Speaking of, do you know the sexes yet?"

"No. Not sure I want to. My current obsession has been how to break the news to my family. Maybe I'll have them all over for dinner and get it over with in one big swoop."

"You know, it doesn't have to be like that. I can help you. We can make it a party, a happy thing. I could throw you a shower, too!"

Kathleen's eyes swelled. "Thank you for saying that. And you're right. It is a happy thing, isn't it?"

Summer leaned over and hugged her, taking care not to move her toes and risk the wrath of Tiffany. "It is, my friend. It certainly is."

"Allie, I've got a surprise for you." Courtney set out a box of Honey Nut Cheerios and milk on the granite counter.

Allie jumped up on the stool next to the kitchen island with an excited squeak. "I know what it is! You're gonna have a baby so I can be a big sister?"

Her mother's grin faded. "No. Honey, we've talked about this. We would love it, right?"

Allie nodded, looking down into her bowl. "Yeah. But

what if God doesn't bring us a baby ever? Does that mean He doesn't think I'd be a good sister?"

"You'd be a wonderful sister." Courtney poured the milk on Allie's cereal, and some into her coffee mug. It was too early for philosophical discussions with an egocentric six-year-old, especially when that same conversation took place on a weekly basis. "Sometimes there isn't a reason why things happen or don't happen. That's really hard to understand, even for big people, but we have to accept it. Okay?"

Allie swallowed a spoonful of cereal. "You always say that."

"I'll keep telling you until you believe me."

"What's the surprise?"

Courtney bent her forearms on the counter, her chin in her palms. "Guess who came in late and is staying in the guest room? Who loves you to the moon and back?"

Allie's face split into a wide smile, complete with a milk moustache. "Uncle Thomas!" she shrieked, forgetting all about breakfast and jumping off the stool. She took off down the hallway at top speed, her mother's voice trailing after her that he was still sleeping.

"Knock, Allie!"

She did as she was told, rapping on the door amid cries to wake up.

"I'm awake," came a muffled reply.

Allie burst in the room and leaped on the bed. "You're here, Uncle Thomas! You're here!"

"I am." Thomas sat up, yawning. "I had to come see my Allie-Oop buttercup."

He pulled her in for a bear hug as she giggled. "You're so silly! Why do you have a different name for me all the time?"

"Cuz it's fun, that's why." He leaned back and made a face. "You grew, like, into a giraffe while I've been gone."

"I didn't!"

"You did. I don't even recognize you."

"I'm not a giraffe!"

He swiped her cheek with a thumb. "Okay, more like a baby cow, then. Because you've got milk all over your face."

"No, I'm not. I'm just me. Allie."

He kissed her forehead. "Yes, you are. And I love just you."

"I missed you soooo much," she said, collapsing onto his chest. "Why did you leave for so long?"

"C'mon. You knew what I was doing. Playing my music for people."

"It felt like forever." She cried, her blonde head lost in his faded Stones tee shirt.

He didn't shush her or tell her she was overreacting. He held her tightly until she was done, and because he didn't try to circumvent her, the sobbing lasted less than a minute.

"It *was* a long time," he said gently, holding her shoulders and looking her straight in the eye. "But I'm here now, for a little while. Why don't we think about what we can do together."

She immediately brightened. "Play in the pool? You can throw me in like before, really high! Remember? When mommy yelled at you? Then later we can roast hot dogs by the fire pit, like last time, and you can drink beer and play that song, 'Into the Mythic.'"

He laughed long and hard. "You've got it all planned and I'm still half-asleep. That's impressive."

"What does impressive mean?"

"It means you made me think you're super-smart. But I already knew that, didn't I?"

She giggled, and there was a soft rap on the door. "Knock, knock. Can I come in?"

"It's Mommy."

"Should we let her in?" he whispered.

"Yeah, I guess so."

"Come in!" Allie yelled.

Courtney peeked around the door with a hot mug of coffee for Thomas. "Good morning."

"Good morning. Llook at this service, will you? Thanks, sis!"

"Okay, Allie. Go finish your cereal and play for a while. My turn to talk to Uncle Thomas now."

She fussed a little and Thomas took the opportunity to go to the bathroom. When he came out, Allie was gone.

He stretched. "To what do I owe this pleasure?"

Courtney pulled up a chair next to the bed. "I think I can spoil my brother a little, can't I? Before he gets famous and leaves us all behind."

"Ha! No to both counts."

Courtney studied him. "Why are you here? You look like shit, by the way."

He laughed. "Cut To the Chase Courtney, isn't that what Auntie Janie used to call you?"

"Did she? I don't remember that, but I'll own up to it."

"I'll reciprocate by doing the same." He took a sip of coffee and looked at her. "I'm here because I needed to see Kathleen."

"That's nice—"

"She's pregnant."

Courtney nearly spilled her own coffee. "Are you freaking serious?" she gasped.

"Yes. Do me a favor and don't ask how it happened. Trust me when I say it hit us both out of left field."

"Okaaay—"

"I'll tell you this much. She didn't think she was able to conceive. Turns out not only is that not true, but she is carrying ... wait for it ... twins."

Courtney burst into laughter. "I'm sorry, I know it's not funny-funny, but—Oh. My. God. For how long have I been nagging at you on this topic?"

"Too long."

"Thomas. I can't even. You—" she couldn't continue, her laughter having turned to tears. She put her mug on the nightstand and hugged him. "You'll be the *world's* best dad, ever."

He hooted loudly. "That's one hundred percent something Allie would say."

"Because she's one smart cookie who's been loved by an amazing uncle."

"I don't know, Court," he said morosely. "I'm not feeling too confident."

"Don't be ridiculous. You have every single quality that matters. Hardworking, loving, fun, stable—"

"Stop right there. You know damned well that stable is not the word to describe me. I'm a fucking train wreck and have been for years."

"You are stable! You're the rock I could always depend on!"

He tsked. "You mean, when I wasn't threatening to off myself? C'mon."

"Don't talk like that. Nobody has a life without bumps."

"It hasn't been bumps. More like volcanic craters."

"Even so. Everything that went down with dad ... will only serve you better in this new role." She looked at him, reluctant. "Can I tell mom? I mean, unless you were going to."

He yawned and shrugged at the same time. "That's the last of my concerns. Go for it."

"She'll be so excited! You know she's coming for Christmas, right?"

"I know."

"And Allie! She's gonna absolutely flip out."

Thomas rubbed his eyes and didn't respond. Courtney continued to stare at him in disbelief.

"What?" he said warily.

"I guess I'm wondering if you're considering, you know—"

"Getting married?" He leaned against the headboard. "I have, and I am. I was thinking about it even before this happened. I don't know if she is, though."

Courtney slapped the sheet. "Get real, brother. I can guarantee she is. Hoping for it, if watching you two together is any indication."

"Maybe."

"Mommeee!" Allie's voice drifted down the hallway. "Are you done talking, yet?"

"I guess my allotted time is up," Courtney laughed.

She opened the door and her daughter ran in a blur past her. "Can we go swimming, Uncle Thomas?"

"No. Not yet," Courtney said firmly. "We're letting Thomas go back to sleep now. He came in very late and needs some rest. You can help me get ready for the party we're gonna have later this afternoon."

Thomas raised an eyebrow. "Party?"

"Just a chill pool party to which you will invite Kathleen. It looks to be a perfect day for it."

Allie leaped into the air, clapping her hands. "Kathleen, your girlfriend! She's the best!"

"Alrighty, you," Courtney said, steering Allie around. "Out we go."

After confirming Kathleen could come by later, Thomas slept for four more hours. He woke up at noon and jumped in the shower, feeling refreshed, and when he went out to the kitchen, the smell of breakfast greeted him. Sure enough, there was a plate covered with wrap, and a sticky note on top that said, "FOR THOMAS ONLY. Mom and me ar shopng. Love, Allie." He took off the wrap and his stomach growled. There was a big stack of pancakes, scrambled eggs, sausage links, and a bundle of bacon. He popped the plate in the microwave, poured some more coffee, and ate like he hadn't in weeks. It felt good to be back here and not in his depressing apartment. Better than he'd expected. He looked around the kitchen, at its variety of indications that a family lived and loved there. Magnetized pictures of Allie on the fridge, as well as an assortment of watercolor artwork; the chalkboard on the wall with daily quotes Courtney sketched in. Today's quote said, 'Wag more. Bark Less.'"

He read the quote again and smiled. Today, he would wag more, for Allie and Kathleen. He'd start it out clear-headed and med-free, a plan that was immediately challenged as soon as he bent down to put his plate in the dishwasher.

The bite began in his midsection and forked like a divided highway down his side, lighting miniature fires the whole way to his knee.

"Fuck."

He leaned on the granite counter, squeezing his eyes shut. Sometimes, if he didn't move for a few seconds, the fire could be momentarily extinguished. Sometimes not. This round was successful. He slowly maneuvered to the stool at the kitchen island and put his head in his hand, thinking about Kathleen. How would he do it? How would he chase after two toddlers when he couldn't even put a plate in the *fucking dishwasher* without doubling up?

He took a deep breath and meditated for at least five

minutes, then opened his eyes and stared at the chalkboard again. He'd headed off the gunpowder path within him that was forever trying to connect with flammable nerve endings. Of course, he told himself, he'd been putting his body through hell the last few months, so he wasn't exactly at peak form physically. Between the endless hauling of equipment, the mental strain, and performing itself, he'd been surviving on adrenaline. That and a few doses of what he'd termed "helpers" were getting him through. He was smart enough to know he was treading on dangerous ground and the pace was unsustainable. The seductive part was that the crowds had been getting bigger and bigger, along with his social media presence. Wasn't this what he'd wanted?

No, it wasn't, not completely. Though it was a thrill, what he really thrived on was the intimate connection. When a song he'd written resonated with someone in the smaller venues, like at HopCanon.

He looked down to find Allie's cat, Jasper, brushing up against his leg, and he thought of his own cat, Nala. His widowed neighbor, Helen, whom he'd gotten to know at the complex, had taken the cat "temporarily." Helen and Nala were suited to each other. Both disagreeable, judgmental, and picky about who they liked. Helen kept hinting the cat was better off with her, and maybe she was right. He'd have to call her today to check in.

"Hey, Jasper."

Jasper promptly jumped up to his lap, a feat that wasn't easy given his enormous size. He began nudging Thomas, then nudging a nugget of leftover bacon on another platter Courtney had left. Thomas laughed and moved the plate. "Ah, you can't have that, buddy. The eternal paradox, I know. We can't always get what we want."

In true cat fashion, Jasper cast a dismissive look his way,

leaped to the floor, and paraded to the nearest block of sun to sprawl. Thomas stood hesitantly, waiting for the streak scissoring down his side to resurface, but apparently it meant to stay in hiding.

He exhaled gratefully. Whenever that rare occasion happened, it was going to be a good day.

14

"Higher! Throw me higher! Please?"

Allie bounded up the inground pool's stairs to repeat the routine of Thomas pitching her into the water as far as he could manage.

"No," Courtney said loudly. "Let him rest now. He's our guest, remember?"

"A few more times," Thomas conceded. In two hours, the sun had darkened his skin considerably, even with sunscreen. Kathleen leaned up against the pool's side and smiled, watching them frolic. He was so good with Allie, as she knew he'd be. He was still acting very guarded toward her, but she expected it after last night, and she wasn't bothered by it.

She was reveling in being near him after having been denied it for weeks. She stretched out her arms and the suit pinched her armpit. It was a modest one-piece black tank from last summer that still fit by a thread. She felt as if her chest was spilling out, and her belly strained at the seams. When she'd gone shopping, she hadn't been impressed with the maternity swimsuits. Either you looked matronly, with the billowy blouson top in front, or like a teenager, with the overly-revealing two pieces. In any event, she needed to use the bathroom, so she took one last look at Thomas' shoulders rippling in the sun as he hoisted Allie into the air, and went to the stairs to climb out.

When she came back, Courtney was sitting by a firepit far too elegant to be called that. The round drum was encased by brick and the top brandished by black wrought-iron grates designed for grilling. Kathleen joined her.

"Kathleen, how about a strawberry slushie? Alcohol-free, for minors and mamas-to-be."

She smiled. Thomas had told her that Courtney knew. "That sounds perfect."

Courtney went to the poolside bar, which was outfitted as efficiently as an inside one, and came back with two frozen concoctions.

"A virgin, for you, and one not-virgin, for me."

Kathleen laughed and sipped. "Thank you. This hits the spot like nothing else has. And I'm not kidding."

"Thomas said you've been struggling with terrible vomiting."

"Yes. It's somewhat better, of late."

Courtney beamed at Kathleen. "I can't begin to tell you how excited I am about this news. I know it was unexpected, and that's always hard, but Thomas will come around."

Allie squealed in delight, and they both looked over at them. She was on his shoulders now, her tiny wrists and legs enveloped by his graceful hands.

"I know him," Courtney said, looking very much like her brother at that moment. "Not that you don't, I don't mean that—"

"It's okay."

"Deep inside, he is thrilled. Even if he isn't exactly showing it."

Kathleen sighed. "It's all very fresh and raw. Right now,

he's angry at me for not telling him about it earlier. Which is another convoluted story. Time will help us both, I think."

"Yes, for sure."

Courtney dipped a chip into some salsa. "Jake and I've been trying for another baby, pretty much since Allie was born."

"Oh?" Kathleen had suspected as much, from various comments Thomas had made.

"I don't know why it's not happening. The doctors can't find any reason. You've probably heard that whole depressing spiel: 'Just relax.' As if that ever helped anyone."

"I do know, actually. I underwent some of that in my first marriage. It's awful."

"We're at the point of acceptance, now. Except for Allie, that is." Courtney looked at Kathleen with glassy eyes. "She will be so over the moon when she hears about not one but *two* cousins."

Kathleen fumbled nervously with the edge of her beach towel. "This is embarrassing, but are you sure it's ... okay? I mean, to tell her, when we are obviously not married?"

"No need to be embarrassed. We'll explain it to her the same way we've explained the lack of a sibling. As in, sometimes, God has a different plan."

Kathleen smiled. "That's certainly the truth."

"Mommy, we're getting out," Allie yelled. "We're hungry!"

"Alrighty, then!" Courtney encased Allie with a Dora the Explorer towel and steered her toward the house. "Back with dinner after we change."

Thomas walked over to Kathleen, dripping water all over. "I see you're not waiting with a towel to wrap me in," he said, half-joking.

"I would've, if I thought you wanted that." She stood up and untied her own oversized one, dotted with a bright-red hibiscus flower pattern. "Here you go, handsome," and she spread it around his shoulders. He pulled her toward him, encasing them both in the towel, and kissed her.

"I'd tell you what I want," he breathed into her wet hair. "But I think you already know."

"Do I? You've hardly looked at me since I got here."

"When I do ... I can't very well let my sister and niece see me like this." He pressed against her side.

"Uh-oh. Now what?"

"We're going skinny-dipping later, that's what."

"Is that so?"

"Yes, it is so. This thing—" he snapped at her suit's strap "—needs to come off."

"I do agree with that part. It's horribly small."

He hid his head with the towel and dove for her overflowing breasts. "Gee, I didn't notice."

"I thought I'd go home after we eat."

He looked up, heavy-lidded. "What? Why?"

"Why? You seemed pretty sure we needed space last night."

"That was last night."

She backed up and folded her arms. "You're going to tell me everything between us is peachy-keen, now?"

"Well, no, but—"

"But?"

"You can't exactly expect me to let you walk away, after being next to you all afternoon, so tan and gorgeous—I mean, your skin, your hair, everything about you is—"

She stepped back to him, kissing his still-wet, sun-warmed neck. "Is what?"

"*Lush* comes to mind."

"Is lush another word for rapidly expanding?"

He cupped her rounded belly. "You've never looked sexier."

"I can't stay here overnight. What would that look like, to a six-year-old?"

"Like playing house."

She laughed. "Is that what we're doing?"

Their eyes met, both of them suddenly serious. "I think we're both too old for that," he said. He drew her to him, the swimsuits the only barriers between them as they kissed almost as fervently as the first night they'd met.

He broke away and lifted her chin. "Don't you think? Too old for playing house?"

"That depends."

"On?"

She shrugged. "On whether it's with a child or a grown man."

"I'm no child."

"No, you definitely are not." She raised on her tiptoes to whisper. "Maybe I could leave before she gets up."

"Or maybe not."

"Look, I'm not going to debate this with you—"

"Who's ready to eat?" Courtney's voice interrupted as she came out with a trayful of sausages.

"Me!" Allie came running up behind her mother, carrying buns.

Everyone got a roasting stick and proceeded to cook over the fire, with Thomas providing Allie assistance in the turning of her hot dog. Afterward, Allie snuggled in-between Thomas and Kathleen on the big outdoor couch that invited slumber with its fluffy cushions. She yawned and said groggily, "Mommy, can we have s'mores?"

"It's kind of late, honey, but I suppose this is a special occasion. I'll go in the kitchen and see if I have everything."

By the time she'd come out again, the little girl was sound asleep, her head resting on Thomas' shoulder. Courtney smiled. "Well, does anyone else want s'mores?"

They declined, talking quietly amongst the three of them about the construction company. Jake was out of town dealing with a potential business opportunity, and would be back in two days.

"He seems to be gone a lot more now," Thomas commented. "How's that working out?"

"We miss him, of course, especially Allie. He feels a lot of guilt."

"I'm sure."

"But ya gotta do what ya gotta do. A business can't run itself. And we're in it together, for the long haul. For everything I rail against when it comes to the Catholic church, they do get one thing right about marriage."

"What's that?" Kathleen asked.

"You don't get to walk away easily when it gets tough. I think that's how it should be. In most cases."

"I agree," Thomas and Kathleen said at almost the exact same time.

Thomas slapped his knees. "On that note, before we jinx ourselves into any more deep-seated theology, I should take her to bed."

He got up and carefully gathered Allie in his arms.

"Thanks, that's a big help. I'll be following you," Courtney said. "I'm beat."

Kathleen rose, as well. "I'll be going too, Courtney. Thanks so much for a wonderful day."

"It was, wasn't it? Listen, you're more than welcome to stay the night."

Thomas looked at her expectantly.

"Thank you, I can't. I've got animals to go take care of, for one thing."

"Okay, then. But stay for a little evening swim." She gave her brother a look and started back for the house. "See you soon."

"Yes, see you soon."

Thomas regarded Kathleen, almost triumphantly. "You heard the lady of the house. A little evening swim is in order."

"All right. I'll wait here for you."

"And be naked."

"Shhh!" She pointed to Allie's sleeping head on his shoulder.

"She's out for the count," he said, laughing. "Back in five."

Kathleen finished her completely melted slushie, and then took advantage of the convenient changing hut by the pool. She peeled the suit off and put her loose cotton cover-up on. The lack of constriction felt wonderful. When she came out, Thomas was already in the water, his face and bare upper-body illuminated by the pool lights.

"What's that you're wearing now?" he frowned.

"It's a cover-up."

"That's the opposite of what we want," he said. "Take it off."

"My, aren't you bossy today." She looked around a little apprehensively. "Not to mention, it feels quite—open, here."

"That's a high fence around us. No one can see. Too bad for them." He waved at the dress impatiently.

She lifted the sheath over her head. "What's your next command, master?"

"Turn around."

She giggled, embarrassed. "I feel ridiculous. Are you secretly filming this? I don't think there's a market for pregnant porn shows—"

"Stop talking and do it."

She reluctantly twirled around, and he let out a low whistle. He swam up to the pool's side, his index finger motioning for her to approach. She sat down slowly on the hard concrete in front of him, her legs dangling in the water, and his hands went up the sides of her body.

"You. Are like something out of a wet dream, I swear to God. If there *is* a market for pregnant porn, you could be the lead star."

"That's disgusting. And I highly doubt these stretch marks and ass padding would do much for my big-screen desirability."

He threw back his head, laughing. "You are so wrong."

"Am I?"

"Yes." He kissed the inside of her thigh. "You want a command? I've got one for you."

"Fire away."

"Don't doubt me. Even when I can't believe in myself, I need you to."

She brushed a water droplet off the end of his long eyelashes. "I could ask the same of you."

He reached up under her arms and pulled her in, creating a minor splash. The water was perfect, like silk rivulets running over her.

"It's mutual, then." She laced herself around him, weightless.

"Yes. Shall we seal the agreement here and now?"

"Not the way you're thinking. As I recall, the release of bodily fluids in pools is highly discouraged."

"There are other ways," he said. He grabbed a pool raft, a sturdy one with sides, and effortlessly picked her up.

"What are you doing?"

"Just lay back."

She did so, surprised at how comfortable the raft was, when his head disappeared between her legs. She drew a sharp breath and sat up halfway, knowing the words she was about to say were the same as that night at HopCanon. "Oh, God. Here?"

"Yes."

His hands were on her belly, massaging her gently, and she felt the ripple of a kick. She gasped. "Did you feel that?"

He grinned. "I did. See, they like it too, when Mama's happy." He lifted himself on the raft, causing it to tilt and their faces to meet. "Now, relax," he said, his voice a low growl. "Let me do my thing, because when I finally get inside you, I'm gonna last approximately sixty seconds. That's nowhere enough time for you to fully ... experience ... a proper reunion, shall we say."

His head dipped back down, and she leaned back, saying no more. Her eyes gazed at the charcoal sky as the lapping of the water matched the waves building inside her, and her hips rocked forward with a will of their own.

"Thomas." She gripped his head with both hands as the final curl of pleasure crested, dizzying in its speed and force.

When she relaxed her hold, he raised up. His face was glowing with the help of the nearby tiki lamps, and his eyes reflected the embers in the waning fire.

"You're the one who's beautiful," she said.

He slid his hands under her back and pulled her off the raft.

He was nuzzling her chest when her phone went off to the notes of the singer Madonna.

She lurched away, her hazy dream-state evaporating. "How's that for timing? I have to get it. It's one of the girls."

"That's a pretty ingenious ringtone. 'Papa Don't Preach?'"

"I thought it was fitting."

She clambered out of the water faster than a seal, and answered it in time.

"So wonderful, honey," Kathleen was grinning ear to ear. "I'll meet you at the hospital as soon as I can."

She hung up and Thomas got out and wrapped the same towel they'd used before around her.

"Well?" he said questioningly.

"As of an hour ago, Brianne and her husband Matt are the proud parents of a baby girl."

"That's awesome," Thomas said, then added, "Wait. She got married?"

"Yes, just a few days ago, at the courthouse."

Kathleen kissed his wet chest. "I know it's late, but she was so anxious for me to come now, I couldn't say no."

"Makes sense. She sees you as a mother figure. I'd bet all those girls do."

"Yes. And I wish I didn't feel like such a failure in that role."

"You've said that before. Why, I don't understand, but is it magnified being pregnant?"

"Something like that. Everything feels magnified, I guess." A small smile played at her lips. "I suppose this means a raincheck for any further fun."

"Plan on it, woman."

"Really? But why?" she teased. "I got what I needed, and even better, not for a second did

I think I'd get sick."

He laughed. "Is that the standard I have to live up to, now?"

"Pretty much," she said. She put her clothes back on as Thomas observed her appreciatively, the desire on his face clear even in the shadowy moonlight. Always, always, that look in his eyes, the look she was afraid she might not see again, and yet, here it was, burning brighter than ever. She wanted to cry at the inexplicable strength of the bond between them.

"Here," she said, handing him the towel. "Your turn to

dress." Her voice was thick with unshed tears. "And my turn to watch."

During the twenty-five-minute drive to Littleton Memorial, Thomas asked Kathleen more about the pregnancy, her nausea, and who her obstetrician was.

"Her name is Dr. Love, ironically."

"Good pick. I've heard of her before."

"She's Irish. Very no-nonsense, yet compassionate. Her practice is affiliated here, so this is where I'll be going, as well." She looked at him and corrected herself. "Where we'll be going, that is, if you can be—"

"There's no 'if",'" he interrupted.

They pulled in to the entrance road to the hospital, which was nestled in a hilly, forested area. Inside, they were met with a modern design, with glass prism sculptures hanging from high ceilings, and muted shades of aqua and sea artwork on the walls. The only thing unpleasant was the mild antiseptic smell typical of most hospitals, and Kathleen figured it was just her oversensitivity to odors kicking up again. As they made their way to the maternity ward, she asked Thomas if he'd ever been there before.

"Once, when Allie was born. Hers was a long, difficult birth."

"Were you there for all of it?"

"Up until the very end."

They approached the front desk, got the room information, and once there, Kathleen knocked softly. A young man wearing a Nike shirt and matching shorts opened the door.

"Are you Ms. K?" he asked.

"Yes. This is Thomas. Are you Matt?"

He smiled a shy, boyish smile. "Yeah." He waved and stepped back. "Come on in."

Thomas directed Kathleen to the hand sanitizer posted on the wall. "Old habits and all that," he said.

Brianne was in a rocking chair by the window, holding a tiny form swaddled in a blanket with pink and green stripes.

Kathleen rushed to her. "Hi! How's everyone doing?"

Brianne's face, devoid, now, of any goth makeup, revealed a vibrant, unblemished complexion, and without the heavy eyeliner, her eyes shone youthfully. "We're doing good. I'm tired and sore, but good." She craned her neck around Kathleen. "Is that *Thomas*?"

"It is."

Brianne's mouth crinkled. "I'm so embarrassed. He must've told you how we were at his show. I'm sorry about how that went down—"

"Shush, now. It's all good, trust me. We're here to celebrate *you*. I didn't have time to bring a gift, but I do have one at home for you."

"It's fine."

"Plus, I think Summer is planning on having a big baby shower for all of you girls, soon."

Brianne shifted the baby carefully to her other arm. "Ms. K, I don't care about that. Matt's overtime got us all that we need. I just wanted you to see her."

Kathleen leaned in for a closer look. "She's gorgeous. Look at all that black hair!"

"Yeah, between the two of us, she's definitely gonna be dark-haired." Brianne reached up and took Matt's hand, and the look that passed between them was intimate, tender. Kathleen averted her gaze, loath to interrupt the moment.

"Congratulations to you both on your marriage, too," Thomas said.

"Thank you." He was a good-looking kid, what Kathleen

guessed Thomas might have looked like at eighteen. A tall, almost gawky, athletic body, lots of hair, though Matt's was short and straight. "We're pretty stoked. Even if nobody in our families except her dad is."

"Is your dad here?" Kathleen asked Brianne.

"No. He will be, as soon as he's done working in the morning. He just started a new factory job and couldn't take time off."

"He'll fall in love with this little angel. Everyone will."

"My mom was gonna come with my sister, but mom said something lame and my dad lost it. Told her not to come if she couldn't be positive. That put a stop to any visit." She scoffed, "Imagine that, right?"

"I can," Thomas said. "Happened all the time after my parents split up, with us caught in the middle. I think when you've been through that, you become determined not to repeat it."

"Tell me about it. I could fill a book with all the crap I don't want to repeat," Brianne said, her eyes filling. "I'm so glad to see you, Thomas. Glad you are one of the first to meet our girl."

He brushed the baby's blanket back and smiled. "She's a beauty, all right."

"I see you've got some visitors!" A nurse wearing scrubs with cartoon babies and hearts came in, stopping at the sink to wash her hands. Her nametag read "JOCELYN." "Brianne was a real trooper throughout her labor. Did she tell you she never asked for an ounce of pain medicine?"

Thomas whistled. "No epidural? No Fentanyl or Stadol?"

"Nope," said Jocelyn. "A local for the episiotomy. That little eight-pounder fought her way out like nothing was gonna stop her."

"And the Apgar score?"

"She got a nine!" Brianne said proudly.

Kathleen heard the exchange, but she was intently watching Thomas as he rattled off more medical questions. His eyes were bright, inquisitive, animated, almost. Jocelyn appeared equally impressed. "I think we need you in our unit," she said, winking at Thomas. "Lemme tell ya, I'm fifty-nine and I'm ready to retire. There's a shortage already. Was labor and delivery ever a gig you entertained?"

Kathleen noted the irony in the use of the words "gig" and "entertained" in her question, but Thomas was unfazed.

"No. At the time, it was between psychiatric care and peds. And since I was basically certifiable, the mental gig won out. In hopes of curing myself, I guess."

Jocelyn laughed, her teeth a stunning white in contrast to her mocha brown skin. "Honey, ain't we all crazy on some level?"

Thomas laughed, too. "Maybe so."

"Dang, dang, dang," she said, a hand on her hip as she shook her head. "A smile like Elvis, smart like Dr. Spock, and easy on the eyes. You got it all, mister. Get your resumé in." She turned her attention to Brianne. "You beep me if you need anything, okay? We can take her any time, so you can get some rest."

"I will."

Jocelyn pumped from the soap dispenser and washed again, and Kathleen winced at the pungent odor. She swallowed the rush of saliva gathering in her mouth. This was always a bad sign. *Don't panic. Don't panic.* "Brianne, we'll be going, too. It's been a long day for all of you, and I'm starting to not feel well."

All eyes went to Kathleen and Brianne said, "Ah, no. What is it, the nausea again?"

"Unfortunately, yes. Smells can be—overpowering. This time, it's the disinfectant. I'm sorry. I feel like such a lily-livered sap."

Brianne laughed. "'Lily-livered'? I never heard that. I like it. Reminds me of my grandma."

"Speaking of grandmas," Matt gestured to the baby. "Tell them her name."

"Oh, God. Yes! Rosie, after my grandma. She died a couple of years ago. And her middle name is Kathleen, after you. You're still here, though, so that's good."

Everyone laughed at that, and Kathleen's nausea receded like a wave washing it to the shore. "I don't—I don't know what to say." She brushed her face and snorted-sniffed. "Other than, I don't feel so sick, now."

Brianne nudged her baby's chin. "See, little girl? You're gonna change the world. Maybe even heal people." She looked up at Thomas. "That's a special talent, isn't it?"

"It is," he agreed.

"Would you like to hold her?"

"Sure."

Thomas gathered her in the crook of his arm and her outstretched palm looped around his pinky finger. The pose was one for the ages, of masculine strength contrasted with fragility, one which Kathleen was certain would find its way into her sketches eventually.

Thomas walked a few paces around the room, and stopped at the window. He swayed gently with the baby and regarded the night sky studded with stars. "Welcome to the world, Rosie Kathleen. You're gonna have your work cut out for you."

They bid goodbye to the happy little family, and after a gas station stop where Kathleen was embarrassingly sick in the bathroom, went back to her place. Whereupon, the animals went circling, barking, and meowing with happiness upon seeing who came through the door. Thomas lavished them with attention as Kathleen beelined for the bathroom, once more. Afterward, she made herself a cup of ginger tea in the kitchen, and when she came out to the living room, he was gone. She found him upstairs, sprawled on the bed and asleep.

She got undressed and put on a tee shirt of his. A soft heather-grey one with holes, that he'd left behind weeks ago; one she hadn't washed because it still smelled of him. She lay down and fingered his hair that had fanned out on the pillow, and he stirred.

"Is that really you or am I dreaming?" he mumbled, one eye half-open.

"It's me."

He inched closer to her, touching her belly tentatively. "I'm sorry you've been so sick. I've been caught up in my own bullshit anxieties, not even thinking of how much it must suck."

She shrugged. "I am better, though. Little did I know hospital cleaning agents would be such a trigger."

"What did the doc prescribe for you, again?"

She told him all the different regimes and how the current one seemed to be the most effective.

"What about ginger ale? Does that help?"

"Vernors even more, but I can't always find it. And crazily enough, Krispy Kreme chocolate-filled donuts. All that creamy fat or something." She ran her hands under his shirt. "Now. Enough discussion about that. We've got some making-up to do."

He stopped her, clasping her wrists. He kissed the inside of one and then the other, and like falling dominoes, a crescendo of sparks travelled down her arms. "I'm thinking that might not be a good mix for an upset stomach."

"I'm thinking it's the opposite. Being with you is the best

medicine I could ask for. Just don't get offended if I lay here like a ragdoll."

He laughed. "You're the sexiest ragdoll there is. Puking or not. Though I've seen my share of that, and cleaned it up, too ..." He started a trail of kisses down her chest. "Nothing could make me want you less."

He pulled his tee shirt up and off, as did she. He stared at her body as if seeing it for the first time.

"What?" she said, all at once self-conscious of her new curves.

"I'm doing what you do. Sealing the image in my mind for future use." He traced down over the arc of her belly with an index finger. "It is a miracle, isn't it? How life finds a way."

"Yes." She reached for him, kissing him as hungrily as she ever had. He still smelled like suntan lotion, the intoxicating scent driving her even harder.

He chuckled softly. "Easy, there. Don't want to risk an untimely bathroom break, do we?"

She looked down at his torso, at the line where his tan stopped and pale skin began, where he throbbed with want.

"I'll be fine, believe me."

He smiled and balanced himself on top of her. He slipped into her slowly, as though they were both virgins, hesitant and trying not to end the party before it'd even begun. He waited, suspended, and she closed her eyes.

"No." His breathing turned rapid, his voice hoarse. "Look at me."

She did so. He held her gaze, the intensity and devotion close to overwhelming. He'd put all weight on his arms and none on her belly, shuddering with the effort. When he finally moved, it was in a hushed slow motion, an enviable picture of upper body strength and restraint above her. They'd had leisurely sessions in bed before, but not this drawn-out, delicate dance of exquisite ebb and flow, his eyes studying her intently for any sign of distress. She moaned in contentment.

He stopped. "Okay?"

"It's ... you've ... never been better. And that's saying something."

"I'll tell you what's something. I made it past the minute mark."

"Stop talking," she whispered.

The ragdoll leapt to life. She crushed herself to him, all languid movements abruptly transformed into frenzied writhing, and for a few brief seconds, it was as if nothing had ever happened before these moments of sweet abandon. No secrets, no painful pasts, no misunderstandings or ill-timed assumptions.

Just pure, unadulterated bliss.

When Kathleen woke up the next morning, Thomas wasn't next to her, which was unusual. Most days, she was the early riser, no matter what time she hit the pillow, whereas, he could and did sleep until noon. She yawned and stretched, then sat up and saw a folded paper sign at the end of the footboard.

"STAY IN BED. YOU WILL BE SERVICED SHORTLY."

She laughed at his wording and decided a trip to the bathroom would be allowed. When she came out, he still hadn't appeared, so she crept back into bed. She could hear him bustling about downstairs.

"Thomas," she called loudly. "What are you doing?"

"Be there in a minute," was his response.

She smiled to herself, her curiosity piqued, and propped herself up on a few pillows. The bed felt empty without the animals, and she knew they were undoubtedly circling his legs or at least in his proximity.

"Thom—"

He appeared at the doorway, looking nothing less than adorable with his mussed hair, naked chest, and pajama bottoms. Holding a tray.

She craned her neck, fully engrossed, now. "What kind of goodies have you got, there? Or are *you* my morning treat?"

He laughed. "We could make that happen." He walked over to the bed and set it across her lap.

"Oooh," Her eyes widened at what was in front of her. A cold can of Vernors, and next to that, what looked like a donut box. "Where on earth did you find this? You must've gotten up early!"

"I got lucky," was all he said. "There's more in the fridge."

She popped it open and sipped. "Sooo good. You can't even imagine." She reached over and kissed him. "Thank you."

He motioned to the box. "... And?"

"Krispy Kremes!"

She flipped open the flimsy cardboard lid, and lodged right in the middle of the chocolate-iced donut was a diamond ring. A sparkling, solitaire, oval-cut beauty.

Her breath stopped. Her heart drummed in her ears, and two kicks from below erupted, as if in joint celebration. *Omigod, omigod, omigod ...*

"Remember when I said I looked at rings while you were at Bear Lake? That I just looked, nothing more?"

She nodded, unable to speak.

"I lied." Looking boyishly embarrassed at the admission, he shifted the tray to the side. With that movement, his abdomen muscles twitched and rippled, much like her body's response to him. "I bought the ring that day, but I wanted to wait until the stars aligned, so to speak, before popping the big question. We both know that perfect timing stuff is bullshit."

She laughed and he went on.

"I was up about four and couldn't sleep, wondering when that right moment would come. So. I was watching you sleep and I decided it'd be whenever you woke up."

He picked up the jewel, held it between his thumb and pointer finger, and locked her gaze with his. She noted, for her journal or possibly a future sentimental purpose or even her art, that his ever-changing eyes were the same caramel color as the donut's frosting clinging to the silver rim.

"Will you marry me?"

She lunged at him with no second thoughts and, for once, no hesitation.

"Vernors and a donut. It's perfect." Cry-laughing, with her arms around his neck, she whispered into his ear. "Yes, yes, a thousand times yes. Yes, I will marry you."

15

When Thomas left later that afternoon, after a repeat performance of the previous evening's enjoyment, it was with great reluctance.

"I'll come to the last show," Kathleen said. "Near downtown Indy, right?"

"Yes."

"Okay. I'll get a hotel room."

"You mean I won't get to hole up with Caleb and Drew for one night?"

She kissed him lightly. "You can, but I think I'll pass."

"I feel like it's been a real ... rollercoaster of emotions the past week." He pulled her tightly to him. "And once again, I'm leaving you. I also realized I'm going to miss your birthday. I'm sorry."

She chuckled against his chest. "Of all the things to miss, that one is okay. Believe me."

"It's not okay, especially a milestone one."

"We'll celebrate later."

"That's just it," he muttered irritably. "I've thought about it constantly. How anyone can keep leaving their family over and over, missing out on things, and then summon the energy to please a crowd? Obviously, it wasn't an issue before, since I never had to think about anyone but me, and the band." He exhaled, stepping away. "My mom used to say people without a wife or husband and kids couldn't understand putting anyone before themselves. They didn't *have* to."

"I'd say there's some truth to that."

"She was mostly talking about my very single, childless aunt, who travelled over Europe at the drop of a hat, while my mom was stuck at home with us. At the time I said, 'Aunt Rebecca's life sounds pretty good to me.' After which an argument ensued about the selfishness of men." He smiled bitterly and shook his head. "I don't want to be that guy, rocking it out while you're up at three in the morning with two screaming babies."

She came up from behind him, resting her head on his broad back. "We'll figure this out. Maybe it means we go on the road with you. It wouldn't be so hard when they're little. We get comfortable with not having all the answers right away. Or, I should say, I do. You've never had that problem."

"No. Not with you. I knew from the first night we met."

"Knew what?"

He turned around. "It felt so ... I don't know. Right." He laughed. "Pretty unoriginal coming from a songwriter, but it's true. Not only did I find you extremely attractive, but there was—is—this acceptance. A feeling of coming home. Where I could be myself completely. And there was a voice inside my head that said, '*Ahhh. So, this is what it's like. The real thing. Don't screw it up.*'"

She wiped a tear away. "I heard the same voice. And I think I almost did."

He brushed another tear aside. "Of the two of us, the

chances of me blowing it are much higher. You haven't even seen me wallowing in one of my pits of hell, yet."

"When I do, I'll drag you out."

He kissed her tenderly. "I'm gonna hold you to that, Kath."

With that, he picked up his duffel bag and was gone.

"I'm just telling you right now, I'm throwing you a fortieth birthday party," Summer announced. She and Kathleen were in HopCanon's taproom, rolling up silverware in napkins. "I don't have time for all the dancing around, try-to-fool-you surprise crap. Plus, I know you're not a big fan of surprises anyway."

"True, but—"

"No buts. I also thought it would be the perfect family 'reveal.' You know, for *your* surprise."

"I suppose it might be." Kathleen paused in her rolling. "There's more than one surprise in store."

"Jesus God. I can't take much more. What now?"

"Hold on," Kathleen said, and went to her purse behind the bar. She fished the ring out of its box and put it on. She hadn't wanted to wear it at work, yet, worried about the water chemicals, but she knew it was irrational to believe it would start eroding before her eyes.

"C'mon. Sit down."

They both did and she held out her hand.

Summer's eyes popped. "Oh. My. God. Is this for real?"

"For real."

Summer scrambled across the table and hugged her. They were both crying by the time they sat down again.

"Is this what you want? I mean, really want, regardless of the circumstances?"

It was a point Kathleen had pondered often over the past few days, and she felt no ambivalence with her answer.

"It is. I never dreamed I would ever marry again, that much is true. Let alone, a man ten years younger. But I also never dreamed I would feel this way about anyone. To me, it's all new. A first. Lots of firsts."

To Kathleen's utter shock, Summer fumbled in her apron pocket and proceeded to light a cigarette.

"What are you doing?"

Summer waved the smoke away. "I'm sorry. Second-hand smoke is bad for the baby, and probably bad for your nausea, too. Should I move?"

"No. I'm asking why would you take up smoking again, after going so long without?"

"Because I'm weak and spineless."

"You are neither of those things."

"Kathleen, cut me some slack. The amount of stress I've been under, it's a wonder I'm not high as those guys in the kitchen. In fact, if I could figure out how to get some weed without asking them, I would."

"You know, maybe this isn't the best time for you to plan a party loaded with emotional bombs."

She took a deep drag. "Ridiculous. I'm deliriously happy for you. I want us to celebrate these babies, because you are a financially settled, mature adult who told me, when we were ten years old, that the only thing you wanted to be was a mommy. And you've found this incredible, hot, talented man who's already given you all you ever asked for. Compare that to my eighteen-year-old son who has five thousand dollars in his bank account, probably still whacks off to porn, and wants to marry the first girl he laid."

Kathleen whistled. "Honestly. Do you have any idea how terrible you sound? I think five grand in the bank at his age is impressive."

"What *is* it with you? You're always defending these kids!"

"In many ways, they're smarter than us. More perceptive than we give them credit for. Sam deserves kudos for working so hard, saving, and trying to man up. Why can't you give that to him?"

Summer exhaled smoke forcefully. "Because. Because I'm still mad. Disappointed. Fearful for his future."

"Fair enough. But it's his future, now. Not yours."

"Easy for you to say. Just wait."

Kathleen laughed. "I never professed to be a parenting expert. I know a good kid when I see one, though, and there's lots of them around us."

"I suppose you'll want them all invited to your party? Didn't one from your prestigious club just have her baby? What about the other two? The absolute last thing I need is someone going into labor at my house."

Kathleen thought she'd have to talk to Zack, see if he had a handle on getting some of that weed for his employer. "Calm down, girlfriend. Of course, I want them there. Yes, Brianne had a baby girl, and the other two are still two and three months out from their due dates. It should be safe from turning into a delivery zone."

Summer sighed and ground out her stub in an ashtray stolen from the back. "All right. Two weeks from now. My house. We'll get a growler of that cider and some wine coolers, and grease Mama Peggy up nice and good, ahead of announcement time. Too bad Thomas will be gone or he could work that charm on her again." She laughed. "What do you bet she's still tripping from his singing? And the kiss and hug."

Kathleen laughed, too. "Like mother, like daughter, I guess."

Summer touched her friend's cheek gently. "You haven't

stopped glowing from the moment you met that man. Let's hope it's a good sign for *your* future."

"Yes. Let's hope."

Thomas peeled his left eye open. His right eye was sealed shut, as if crusty residue from an oncoming case of pinkeye was imminent.

Except, it wasn't that.

He groaned and turned over in the lumpy motel bed, surveying the room. Crushed beer cans, an almost-empty bag of weed he could only hope had been smoked outside, and Styrofoam take-out containers with crumpled-up red-and-white checkered paper sticking out the sides. His stomach lurched. God only knew what substance was festering in his eyeball.

The turn in the bed sent pellets of pain raining down his side, temporarily immobilizing him.

"Count to twenty. Then do it again."

He could still see his father's guilt-ridden, dark-brown eyes pleading with him during the excruciating physical therapy Thomas endured after the accident. *"Come on, I'll do it with you. One, two, three, four ..."*

He practiced the counting often, and occasionally it helped. Then, not so much.

"Go away, Henry!" He'd scream at his father in the middle of a particularly wrenching session. Sometimes, he was merely frustrated; other times, he meant for him to leave. If Courtney was there, Thomas might ask for her, but she'd end up crying harder than he did, from witnessing his pain. Later, Thomas would wonder what the therapist thought of their three-ring-circus drama.

He shook away the memories, and with that movement came a fresh agony splitting up the middle of his forehead. *Jesus.* What had he done last night? The last thing he recalled was chugging a shot of fireball with Caleb. Likely, it was more than one. *Why?* He screwed his eyes shut and pieces of the night returned, foggy though they were. Someone's birthday.

He carefully lifted his head toward the bed adjacent to his. Caleb was there, sleeping on his side, clothing strewn about.

Clothes which included lace panties and a bra.

Thomas slowly lifted his head again, this time higher. Sure enough, there was a female form in the bed next to his bandmate. He rubbed his forehead. They'd all discussed this at the beginning of the tour, and it was agreed that any hookups were to take place privately. So much for that. He'd have to head to the lobby for some food, if he could handle it, and hopefully when he returned, the girl would be gone. That, or at least dressed. He was maneuvering out of bed when he spotted yet another prone body, her long blonde hair splayed out on the daybed's pillow.

"*Fuck.*" He croaked it like a protesting frog.

Additional bits of the previous evening sprinkled down, confetti coating his befuddled brain. The girls were friends of Drew's, who'd given them free tickets to the show, and it was the birthday of one of them. Dumb T names that ran together at the moment. Tianna, Tiffany? He frantically looked down at himself, and the quick motion sent another shard through his temple. He was fully dressed, thank God, unlike the girl on the couch. His gut contracted alarmingly. He sprang from the bed and made it to the toilet just in time, slamming the door behind him. In-between heaving, he remembered the T on the couch flirting, brushing up against him, having a fireball shot. He'd moved away, he knew it. He must've told her, at some point, he was off limits.

An engaged man. Soon to be a father.

Yes. *Yes.* He did tell her, and it hadn't gone well. She'd drunkenly and haughtily laughed in his face, her mascara smeared on her cheek, and said something to the effect he'd be missing out on the best sex he'd ever had.

He'd laughed right back at her. *"Hate to break it to you, sweetheart, but that's already been covered."*

So, what was she doing out there, half naked?

He tore off some toilet paper and wiped his mouth. He couldn't wait like a coward in a corner to find out. He stared at the white throne, at the water sweating on the tank's side.

This is what you call responsible? Shadowy recall of scantily-clad women in your cheap motel room?

Not his father's voice, but it might as well be. The bitch of it was, the show had been fantastic last night, one of their best sets and audiences yet. He could still feel the endorphin rush of all the smiling faces, pumping arms, and shouts for an encore. Heady. The telling part was what he *didn't* feel. Onstage, the ceaseless pain withdrew, like a needle pulling blood out of a vein. The relief was temporary, of course, but that didn't keep him from wanting to chase it down like any other drug. He raised up off the floor, lightheaded. He flushed the toilet, washed his hands, and unwrapped the plastic cup by the sink. He grimaced at the taste of the tepid water. Too bad. He was extremely dehydrated and had to recover before the show tonight.

When he came out of the bathroom, Caleb was awake and sitting on the edge of his bed, smoking. The others hadn't stirred.

"I think this is a nonsmoking room," Thomas said.

"It's a fleabag room. What are they gonna do, charge our

card? We paid cash. And there ain't no smoke detectors in here."

"We really need to not pay cash. It's harder to keep track of expenses. Will I go on to remind you of what else we shouldn't be doing?" He jerked his head toward the girl, who had one shapely leg resting on top of the sheet.

"I know, I know. I'm sorry. Not." Caleb laughed. "You can allow me one fuck-up before this whole gig is done."

"Forget about you," Thomas hissed. "What the hell happened with *me?* Why is whatshername over there?"

"Tanya." He gestured to the figure next to him. "And this is her sister, Teya. Do I have to spell it out for you why they're here?"

"Yeah, actually, you do. Because my mind is blank after that last damned shot."

"Relax, brother. Tanya tried, believe me. You blew her off like a strong north wind." He shook his head. "She is goddam fine, too. I don't get it. If it were me, I'd be treating the next coupla weeks like one long bachelor party."

"Fortunately, I'm not you."

Caleb twisted around. "Look, Thomas. Every night we play, I feel we're that much close to a big deal happening. I know you feel it, too."

He had. He also knew there was a real possibility he wouldn't be a part of any future break they might get. "Yeah? And?"

"And so, I know you. Don't screw it up with your little demented white picket fence fantasy."

Thomas reddened. "Fuck off. Maybe I like that idea more than band blowjobs and coke up my nose."

Caleb's pretty-boy face scowled. "Dude. We're on the edge of something big, something we've talked about for years, and you're gonna potentially walk away why? Because, like a goddam high schooler, you knocked somebody up? You shoulda stuck with nursing if all you wanted was to waste the prime of your *life* away cleaning up baby shit."

"How admirable of you to offer me career advice. From the guy whose last real job was delivering newspapers."

Caleb laughed. "Okay, you got me there, but people do that lowball crap so they can spend the rest of their time working on their dream. There's no chick, I don't care how hot she is, and Kathleen is pretty damned hot, I'll give you that, ain't none of them worth giving up the dream."

"Is that what you call this?" Thomas waved around at the mess in the room. "Yeah, we're busting our asses every night to some great crowds. But nonstop partying, eating junk food at four in the morning, and waking up with semi-clothed strangers in my room is not living the dream."

"You sure were singing a different tune a while back."

"Shit happens, as they say."

"Yeah. Good pussy will make shit happen, won't it?"

Thomas lunged, grabbing him by his grungy wifebeater tee. "Shut your nasty mouth," he snarled. "She's the best thing that ever happened to me. You only *wish* you could nail someone half as classy as Kathleen."

He let loose of him and got up. Caleb stared, shaking his head. "Man, you got it really bad for her, don't you?"

The ruckus had awakened the two dormant women, and Thomas pointed to them as they scrambled for their clothes. "I'm done talking. Right now, I'm gonna grab some food, and they'd better be out of here by the time I get back."

"Screw you, asshole," Teya piped up. "I don't take orders from anyone."

"No?" Thomas' fury was contained but palpable, his voice measured and cutting. "How about a friendly suggestion instead?"

She shrugged and rolled her eyes.

"How about the next time you get free tickets, food, booze, and drugs, *and* you decide, after all that, you wanna get laid, get your own room. Then you can do whatever the hell you want."

He pocketed his phone, took the room key, and stalked out.

16

"You've outdone yourself."

Kathleen looked around Summer's living room, smiling. Balloons hung from every crevice in black, pink, blue, and gold.

"Interesting color scheme," she added.

"I've covered it all, right? Getting old, getting married, giving birth." Summer pointed to a large "HAPPY FORTIETH BIRTHDAY, KATHLEEN!" sign hanging on the wall.

"Nice."

"Wait. After the first hour, I'll turn it around." She flipped the sign, which announced "CONGRATS, KATHLEEN AND THOMAS!" The message was decorated with wedding bells and baby paraphernalia drawn in among the bright letters.

Kathleen hugged her. "I love it. Thank you so much. This is gonna be interesting, I have to say."

"For sure. I'm drinking already. I wish you could join me. Or at least get my buzz vicariously, to take the edge off."

"I'll be fine. But very considerate of you to think of me."

"I'll make you some of that chamomile tea. Supposed to be calming, you said. I'd better try it, too."

"That would be great."

"Okay. Let me just check with Jeff to see where he is with the ribs."

Summer opened the slider door to the deck and Kathleen wandered to the kitchen. Sam was there, cutting vegetables for what looked like a salad.

"Hi," Kathleen said, sitting at the counter. "Look at you! I didn't know you had a culinary flair."

He smiled and returned her greeting. "I don't. But I figured I'd better learn how to do more than boil ramen noodles, though. You know, with the baby coming and all."

"Good idea. I'm sorry I haven't gotten the chance to congratulate you about that."

He looked up from his dicing, his mouth tight. "You'd be the first."

"I know it's been hard with your mom and dad. Just remember that they love you and want what's best."

"It's not my dad that's the problem." His knife made a thwapping sound as it sliced through a carrot onto the cutting board.

Kathleen sighed. "She'll come around, honey. She will."

"She has to. There's no changing it now. Chessa and me ... we're gonna make it work." He said it with an authority that belied his young years.

"Yes. I believe you will."

"Believe what?" Summer flounced in and proceeded to heat water on the stove.

"Nothing," Kathleen said quickly. "Sam and I were getting caught up."

"Mmm-hmm. Did he tell you they're discussing baby names?"

"Mom—"

"What? Kathleen won't tell anyone. I'm only telling her so she can agree with me about how dumb they are."

Sam stopped cutting. "Really? You're gonna start in now?"

"I'm not starting in." Summer poured the steaming water into two mugs and sat next to Kathleen. "So, the two top contenders are Kyrie and Finley."

"Ah. Meant for either a boy or girl?"

"Exactly. Gender-neutral is all the rage now. Asinine, right? *Finley?* You hear that and expect a border collie to come running with a frisbee in its mouth, for God's sake."

"Mom. We are still only *talking* about those names."

"Kyrie is pretty," Kathleen offered.

"Thanks. It means 'Lord' in Greek."

"Which I would translate to 'Lord help us,'" Summer said dismissively.

Sam slammed down the knife. "Okay. What names would make you happy? Right now, let's have it."

Summer looked offended. "I don't have anything in mind, *per se.* But why you two can't just entertain the idea of normal is beyond me. Everything has to be original or different somehow, in order to stand out. Meanwhile, the kid cringes his whole life and can't wait till he's eighteen to change it to Elizabeth or David." She sipped her tea, then went on. "Do you know how much I hated the name 'Summer' growing up? A hippie named for a season?"

"Your dad *was* kind of hippie-ish," Kathleen reminded her.

"I know, and I hated it. I wanted boring. I wanted to be Debbie or Kelly."

"This isn't about names." Sam turned and faced his mother. "This is another lecture about how stupid Chessa and I are, how this is never gonna work, how we barely know each other, which isn't true, blah, blah, blah."

"Sam, let's not. This day is for Kathleen."

"Shit, you started this! I'd also like to know why, when this happens to adults, it's a party, but when you're eighteen and get knocked up, it's a fucking death sentence."

"Watch your mouth! Have some respect for your godmother! And I never said this was a death sentence for you, ever!"

"Stop, both of you," Kathleen put her hand up. "Sam, honey, you've got a valid point. It might even surprise you to learn I've been through probably the exact same amount of shock, confusion and 'what do I do now' thoughts as you. It's called being human. Age has nothing to do with it."

He looked down. "Yeah. I guess it's not easy for you, either. I'm sorry."

"No apology needed."

"Oh, yes, there is—" Kathleen pinched her arm. Summer clamped her lips shut.

"The salad's done," Sam said, covering it with plastic wrap. "I got the recipe from that Italian chick on the Food Network. I hope it's good."

"Thank you," Kathleen smiled. "I'm sure it'll be delicious, and it means a lot to me that you're here today. You should also know I am about as nervous to tell my family about my pregnancy as you were."

His head snapped up. "For real?"

"For real."

"Well, since you always wanted a baby, they'll be happy, I bet. It'll be okay."

His concern for her amidst his own was touching. Kathleen got up and hugged him.

"It *will* be okay," she said softly. "For all of us."

Almost everyone who'd been invited came, with the exception of Kathleen's nephew, Connor, who was studying abroad in Spain. The atmosphere was lively, celebratory, helped with flowing drinks and the requisite party games. Kathleen wished, for the hundredth time that day, Thomas was there. He'd told her his absence looked terrible, which she couldn't argue with, but he was also nine hours away with a gig that night. The more they talked, the more she could feel him pulling away from his music.

Summer approached her now, beer in hand. "All right, I'm gonna herd the cats, now."

Kathleen took a deep breath. "Okay."

Some guests were outside enjoying an unusually mild July afternoon, and others were inside, so Summer asked Sam to round everybody up into the living room. She cleared her throat and whistled for their attention.

"First, I want to thank everyone for coming. We get that summer is a busy time. What you didn't know is that we're together to celebrate more than one occasion in Kathleen's life. I'll let our birthday girl explain."

Kathleen stepped in front of a cluster of balloons and looked out into all the faces of those dearest to her. Zack, Megan, her brothers and their families, her mother, Courtney, Sheila Gallagher and a handful of other parishioner friends from church, and the teen girls looking on expectantly, happily. Amanda was cooing and cradling little Rosie, as Brianne and Matt looked on. Allie was next to Amanda, trying to get close to the baby. Kathleen blinked back the tears creeping in and smiled as brightly as she could.

"Like Summer said, thanks, everyone, for being here. Before I go on any further, please know that Thomas wishes he could be here, too. You may have noticed the creative color combination of the décor and balloons—"

She stopped, momentarily, at the polite patter of laughter. "And the reason for that is, first, Thomas and I are engaged. Date to be determined."

There was a moment of silence, then the woohoos and whistles took over.

"There's more! People, your attention while I turn the congratulatory sign!" Summer said, and proceeded to flip it over.

"What's with the bottles and booties?" shouted Kathleen's brother, Mark, not known for his tactfulness.

"And diapers?" Megan chimed in.

Every head turned from the sign to the woman of the hour.

"Yes, about that," Kathleen said, her courage seeping away until she spotted Sam giving her a thumbs-up. "As you might guess, it means babies. Though this was completely unexpected, we're excited to announce we will be blessed with two bundles of joy. Arriving in December."

The hush that descended was tangible. It was Mark, again, who broke the awkwardness. "Holy crap! Dad always said go big or go home. I'd say you got it covered, Sis!"

Laughter commenced and she cast a grateful look at her brother. As irritating as he could be, he had a big heart and a way with putting people at ease.

"Our dad did like to say that," Kathleen continued. "I'd like to think he'd be happy for us. I hope you all are, too."

She looked pointedly at Peggy, who was actually smiling and holding a watermelon wine cooler.

Summer brought out the cupcakes. "Now, back to our regularly scheduled programming. Let's party!"

The music was turned back on and the mingling resumed. Kathleen sought out her mother. She was sitting on the couch, legs crossed, and this time sipping a strawberry wine cooler.

"Mom."

"Cheers to you, my daughter." She held her can up and Kathleen laughed. Peggy was definitely tipsy. "Rather a startling couple of curveballs you dropped there, wasn't it?"

"I know, I know. It was Summer's idea to do it this way. I was embarrassed to tell you—" She corrected herself. "Not only you. Everyone. I mean, who gets a surprise pregnancy at thirty-nine?"

Peggy giggled uncharacteristically. She sounded like a six-year-old, and looked like one, too, as she cupped a hand around her mouth as if divulging a secret. "Um ... me?"

"*What?*"

"Sorry ... that's not completely accurate. I was forty-two, not thirty-nine. You don't know about this because I lost the baby and we didn't tell anyone. I'd also lost one between you and Paul, which we kept quiet about."

"Really? Why?"

Peggy's eyebrows rose. "One simply did not advertise every life event, back then, and certainly not to one's children. And heaven help you if it involved anything remotely sexual, such as the conception of a child at an age considered scandalous." She took a healthy sip. "The idea that people would keep having marital relations past the optimal time to bear a child ... well, it wasn't done."

"Apparently, it was."

"I'll rephrase that. It *was* done, it wasn't talked about. Pardon me for saying this, but your father and I were *very* active in that department."

"Umm, I don't think—"

"Let me finish. With each miscarriage, I was hospitalized for heavy bleeding that nearly killed me. The last one, the doctor looked at my history and strongly suggested a tubal ligation." She leaned in and lowered her voice. "In a *Catholic* hospital, mind you. Utterly forbidden."

Kathleen smiled wanly, not sure if she was supposed to

be appalled or reassuring. "They made a medical exception?"

"Yes. In any case, Charles was so afraid I'd die the next time there might be a pregnancy, he absolutely insisted that I do it." Peggy laughed again. "The look on your face! Parents have their secrets too, you know. Anyway, once the guilt passed, we were never so happy. At long last, no more worrying in the bedroom, no more timing it all just so. Which was little more than silly guesswork. I don't want you to feel bad or take it the wrong way, but none of you were planned. Blessings, each of you, but nonetheless. Thank God for that doctor. Talk about freedom."

"Mother, honestly—"

"No, don't 'Mother' me. Enjoyable sex is critical in a relationship, though perhaps you've figured that out." She leaned forward, smiling. Her red lipstick had rubbed off onto the mouth of the wine cooler. "I'm quite sorry I didn't talk to you about these things long before you married Steve. It was so taboo. None of us knew how to even begin to approach the topic. It might have helped with him, too, since you were clearly a mismatch of needs from the word go." She patted Kathleen's hand. "Regardless, the reason I'm saying all this is because unplanned events can be gifts too. Your news is quite exciting. I didn't count on becoming a grandmother again, at this age."

Kathleen was reeling from the information dump her mother revealed in less than five minutes. Had Summer spiked her drink, somehow? Come to think of it, she'd been full of surprises the last time they'd met up at HopCanon, too. Could she have misread her mother all this time? Why had it never occurred to her to try to see her as a woman who'd had her own share of private pain, disappointments, longings? Were kids inherently that self-absorbed? She suspected the answer was yes.

"You're awfully quiet, dear, while I'm running at the mouth like the town crier."

"I thought ... I don't know. You're not ashamed of me? Worried about the church folks?"

"Pffft!" Her mother shook her hand in the air. "You're in love, that much is obvious, watching you two. And getting married. That's what matters once children are involved. The hard stuff comes later, which doesn't include worrying what others think. I spent way too much time dithering over that nonsense in my life."

Kathleen couldn't have been more shocked if her mother had jumped out of a paper birthday cake naked and started singing. Had she imagined the lectures over the years of making good first impressions, the importance of a spotless reputation, of following church doctrine to the letter? No. More likely, the passage of time had softened her mother's rough edges, like a crisp button-down that eventually ends up a well-worn work shirt, each stain telling an untold story. And Peggy seemed to have many of those in her pocket. Kathleen leaned over and kissed her on the cheek.

"Thanks, Mom. I can't express how much your support means to me. I think I'll be needing a lot more of it."

"Darling, I can feel my second wind coming on, thinking about babies in the family again. They keep you young." She elbowed Kathleen as if they'd just shared a dirty joke. "Lucky for you, eh?"

Kathleen laughed. "Yes. Lucky for me is right."

17

The next day, Kathleen relayed the day's events to Thomas. Hugo put his large head on her lap as she talked, which he normally did not do. "I think the dog knows I'm talking to you. He isn't the same when you're not here, I swear it."

Thomas was unusually despondent. "Tell him I've got the corner market on moping around."

"What? Are you all right?"

"Never mind," he said flatly. "Let's hear more about the party."

"It went better than I could've asked for. Peggy was genuinely happy for us, Sheila Gallagher didn't ban me from leading the girls' group, and I didn't vomit once." She thought that would get at least a chuckle, but it didn't. Nothing but dead silence. "Hellooo?"

"I should've been there."

"C'mon. We discussed this—"

"That doesn't change the facts. An absentee father before they're even born. They deserve better. You deserve better."

She jerked forward, annoyed and alarmed all at once. "Where is this coming from?"

"Nowhere." His toneless voice was utterly foreign to her ears. "Forget it. Listen, I gotta go, the guys are calling me. I'll text later."

"Okay—"

She stared at the muted phone. He'd hung up.

Damn you, Thomas Hart. You're handing the insecure baton over to me now? I'm tired of running that race ...

Hugo jumped off the couch, as if in unison with his missing master.

"I see how it is," she said to her departing dog.

She sighed. If only that were true.

Kathleen was feeling so much better that she called up each of the girls to see if they wanted to meet up. It was the second week of August and everyone responded they were available.

Brianne set out blueberry muffins on the community room table, sky-high jumbo ones with a glittery crumb topping.

"Look at those," Kathleen said admiringly. "How on earth did you find time to bake, with that little bundle to distract you?"

"Matt helped, just by holding her. She doesn't like to be put down. The nurse who's been coming to the house told me that's normal and it's impossible to spoil her. We've both been wearing that baby sling a lot."

"Boy, Ms. K," Mallory said. "How are you gonna hold *two* babies?"

"I suppose we'll figure it out as we go along."

"So, when's the wedding date?" Amanda asked, biting

the end of a pencil. “Like, when are you two for real tying the knot?”

Kathleen coughed. “We’ll see. He’s still touring and that’s keeping him busy for now.”

“Mallory and I might go see another show of theirs before it’s over.” She glanced up nervously. “I mean, we wouldn’t go to spy or tell him stuff this time. We’d go because they’re so good.”

“I’m sure he would love to see yo—"

“But anyway,” Amanda went on, oblivious. “I feel like engagement stuff is kinda stupid. Seems like a big loonngg time for people to procrastinate. Why not just *do* it?”

Kathleen clasped her hands in the steeple position. The rapid-fire way their minds switched topics required her own to work at a speed she didn’t have. Or maybe it was a clue she was inept as a leader, unable to rope in their focus and provide boundaries. She knew she’d failed miserably at that last part.

“Some couples do get married quickly, maybe by going to the courthouse. Others need time to plan, or to get Pre-Cana counseling.”

“What’s that?”

“When your priest meets with you and your fiancé to discuss things like compatibility.”

“Are you and Thomas gonna do that?” Francesca wondered. “Sam and I might.”

“I think it’s a good idea,” Kathleen said, proud that she’d deflected directly answering. “Why don’t we get started with our opening devotion?”

Francesca led the prayer and Brianne’s muffins disappeared almost instantly.

After cleaning up, they laid out their artwork. Amanda’s picture of Kathleen and Thomas was not only finished, it also stood out from the others’ work in its complexity and detail. She'd captured Thomas' expression perfectly, almost eerily.

"Look at that," Mallory exhaled. "Like, it's *exactly* how he looks at you, Ms. K. I think she drew him better than you did! If you don't mind me saying."

"Well?" Amanda looked at Kathleen anxiously.

"It's … it's simply stunning. Faces and body parts are especially difficult to get right. You've almost mastered what others spend years trying to perfect. And you told me you stopped taking art!"

"Ya. I didn't like doing pictures of fruit and wine bottles. Mr. Burke was sooo lame, I'm sorry. Droning on and on like that one teacher in the movie 'Fast times at Ridgemont High.' Putting us to sleep instead of letting us actually *draw.*"

Kathleen laughed. "I hope you don't think I drone on and on."

"You? Gawd, no."

"Good to know."

"Uh, I'm wondering though," Mallory crossed her arms as she talked. Kathleen noted she was wearing a billowy, tie-dyed shirt, this evening, a real departure from her usual grey and beige. "What exactly are you going to do with this artwork?"

"I've thought about it," Kathleen said, shifting her weight. The metal folding chairs were not the most comfortable. "With your input, of course, I'd like to get them ready to showcase somehow. For folks to consider buying."

"Oh, pfft," Francesca sniffed. "Who would want any of these pictures, except for yours, Ms. K? And Amanda's?"

"You'd be surprised at what people buy."

Francesca leaned forward dramatically and planted her palms on the table. "Speaking of surprises, do I see what I think I see, Mallory? Is that a piercing in your nose?"

Mallory touched her face shyly. "Yeah. It's small, but I

like it. Amanda and her grandma went with me, talked me into it. She even signed the permission forms."

"What'd your parents say?"

"They didn't notice. They wouldn't, though."

Kathleen knew so much teen behavior was about garnering attention, to stand out by declaring how different they were, with the irony that they ended up looking exactly like each other in the end.

"Does it bother you that they didn't notice?" Kathleen asked.

Mallory shrugged. "I mean, between my psychotic sister and dopehead brother, they've got a lot on their plate. I overheard my dad yelling to my mom, the other day. He said, "What the hell, Connie? We got one kid who a few months ago was saying she wanted to be a nun and now *she's* having a kid, another likely headed for jail, and another headed to the loony bin. Broke my back all these years to put food on the table and this is what we get in return?" My mom started crying, and I put my headphones on after that."

Kathleen brushed the last of the muffin crumbs away. "I've heard it said that a person really can't comprehend the struggles their parents went through, until they have a child of their own. There's a lot of sacrifice involved in raising a family. Seems we're all about to get schooled."

Amanda rocked backward in the chair. "Huh-uh. Not me. I don't *want* to understand why my mom would leave us. You don't have to be a rocket scientist to figure it out, either. She's a selfish drunk and we basically interfered with her hooking up with some barfly whenever she felt like it. And with finding her next sugar daddy."

"Amanda—"

"Sorry. The truth hurts. My grandma is the one who sacrificed for us."

"All right. My point was that sometimes we can't relate to something until it happens to us."

Little Rosie let out a booming squall, equal to that of a toddler three times her size, and seized all the attention in the room.

"Omigod, that's loud," Francesca gawked at Rosie's red face. "Is she okay?"

Brianne laughed. "She's fine. It took me awhile to interpret her cries, but this is the mad one. She hates waiting while I switch sides."

Francesca continued to gawk as Brianne latched Rosie onto her other breast. "Does ... does it hurt? The nursing?"

"At first, yes. It's better now, now that I'm toughened up there. It hurt a lot less than that episiotomy, let me tell you."

Francesca's lip curled. "Toughened up? I don't like the sound of that."

"Not *tough* like leather. Like getting broken in when something's new."

"Ugh! That's no better. I'm eighteen. I don't want to be broken in at eighteen."

"That's not all. They leak when she cries, so if I don't wear these pads in my bra, it gets all wet."

Francesca looked as if she might pass out. "Double nasty. I think it'll be formula for us."

"It probably also makes you sag later on, but I decided I don't care. Mine are pretty small anyway."

"Goodbye, perky pals," Mallory said, and everyone laughed.

"Why don't we reframe this as being appreciative of what our bodies can do," Kathleen said firmly. "There's nothing broken about giving birth and providing nourishment. In fact, it's the opposite. It takes a lot of strength."

"I'll probably go to hell for saying this, but I feel like the whole process from beginning to end is kind of parasitic,"

Amanda said. "It creeps me out, I can't help it. You guys are all naturals at this. I'm not. I can't even figure out my *own* cries, let alone someone else's." She nudged a finger under Rosie's clenched palm as Brianne balanced the baby on her lap, her eyes shiny.

"Lucky for my baby, I guess, that I won't have to figure anything out. It'll be up to her daddy."

"Same," Mallory said. "With the baby's adoptive parents."

The air was thick with silent sadness as they gazed upon the newborn in front of them. Kathleen said softly, "Girls, these are heavy loads to carry. I want you to know how proud I am of all of you, for each of your decisions. None will be easy, but nobody is going to hell, of that I am one hundred percent sure." She met Amanda's gaze. "Let's pray now for courage and fortitude in the coming months. Most importantly, for acceptance of our Father's will, and for his ever-watchful protection over us."

The prayer ended just in time. Rosie broke into her loudest protest yet, this one in reaction to having her meal interrupted by the timeless burping ritual, a cry that only stopped when everyone began laughing.

18

"Thomas. Hey! Wake up." Eli shook Thomas by the shoulder, but there was no response other than a slight grunt.

"Come *on,* bro," he said, louder this time. "We've got soundcheck in an hour."

Thomas squinted. "What?"

"Soundcheck. Remember what that is?" He sniffed disdainfully. "Jesus, it smells like a field of spraying skunks in here."

"It smelled like that at check-in."

"Sure, it did." Eli waved his tattooed arm around, the designs consisting of colorful Harry Potter characters. "Time to get moving."

"I'm so wiped, man."

"Yeah, well, boohoo. We all are. Hell, at least I brought you a double cappuccino. If that's not enough, drop some speed. Natalie has a shitload."

"That's nice, encouraging drug use to someone prone to addiction."

Eli yanked the pillow from under Thomas. "Dude! I'm not trying to get you hooked on anything. But it's make-or-break it time, and you're lagging like my grandma at the dollar store. This whole shindig, this tour, was your idea, in case you forgot, and now we've got to drag your sorry ass to every show."

"I know," Thomas mumbled, sitting up and rubbing his eye sockets. "I know, I know, I suck. Thanks for the coffee." He gulped from the green-and-white cup on the nightstand.

"Screw that. What we need is the Thomas Hart magic all lit up for showtime."

Thomas stood shakily. He looked at his reflection in the streaky mirror: the rumpled clothes, wild hair, and glassy, red eyes. "Oh, yeah, baby. I'm just a goddam glowstick, aren't I?" he said, and they both laughed.

Eli dragged from his cigarette and exhaled. "Hey, it's working. The chicks can never get enough of the hot-guy-on-the verge-of-collapse thing. I mean, think about it. Kurt Cobain, Scott Weiland. You just know they had an endless parade of half-naked, coked-out hand jobs waiting for 'em every night. And we haven't done so bad in that department, either. Thanks to you, our blazing wingman."

Thomas laughed again. "Now, that's what I call a true friend. Pushing pills, giving me heart attack-inducing caffeine, capitalizing on my imminent downfall. Plus, these nice comparisons to dead musicians."

"Okay, okay, my bad. Take Jack White, then. He's still kicking, isn't he?"

"Yes."

"That dude is, like, Halloween-scary, and he's probably doing some supermodel and laughing all the way to the bank. Just like Ric Ocasek from the Cars. I guess it don't matter who you are when you're behind a guitar. Or singing about screwing fans all night long."

"I don't do that."

"I said singing, not doing it. Feedin' the fantasies, man, that's the ticket."

Thomas finished off the cappuccino while Eli studied him with a critical eye. "You're also a damn good actor, because right now, you couldn't even shag the town skank, let alone the Playboy pinups you seem to be attracting. Not without someone propping your dick up for you."

"That's about what it would take."

Eli grinned slyly. "It wouldn't take that for your ladylove, now, would it?"

Thomas shuffled toward the bathroom. "She's my fiancé, so let's hope not. Oh, and thanks for the inspirational pep talk. I'm getting in the shower."

"Make it quick. Just enough to revive your man-whore vibe for the night."

"Right on, boss."

Eli yelled after Thomas, "You're a lucky bastard, you know that? I wish I could look like the walking dead and still get laid." After that got no response, he added, "And only a true friend would offer to prop up your limp dick for you!"

Thomas' muffled laugh came through the flimsy bathroom door. "I'll make sure to keep you on standby for the honeymoon, friend."

Eli screwed his cigarette stub into a plastic ashtray on the table. Picturing Kathleen and Thomas together in his head, he knew no such help would ever be needed. What wasn't so certain was the survival of the band in the face of upcoming domesticity. If the rest of them were smart, they'd get a Plan B together.

To be ready for whatever came.

September in Michigan brought more temperate weather and a dramatic drop in humidity, welcomed by even the most avid summer-lovers living there. Kathleen rearranged the pots of mums on her outside steps, admiring the multi-colored purple, yellow, and maroon shades. Fall was her favorite season, not only for its glowing colors, but for the symbolism the falling of leaves represented. Letting go. Hibernating. Preparing for new life. Her own cargo had grown exponentially in the past weeks, and were quite active when she most wanted to sleep. Probably some mystical conditioning for what was to happen in the future, she mused.

She snapped a wizened, crumbly bloom off its stem, and a few splotchy raindrops came down, making brown imprints on the cement under the plants. She went inside before it turned into a downpour. Hopefully, the weather would improve in time for the show, this evening. Four hours away could mean anything from sunny calm to tornado-like breezes, and given that it was in Indianapolis, possibly both within the hour.

She texted Sam to confirm the animals would be cared for, and packed an overnight bag. She debated throwing in the black oversized negligee found on clearance. She dug it out of her drawer and fingered the stretchy lace doubtfully. Why had she bought this? To make Thomas believe a ballooning belly was still sexy? All the black in the world wasn't going to make her look slim now. She laughed, imagining what he'd do or say. He'd slip a finger under a strap, stroke her shoulder and bend in to kiss her. *"Nice. Now off with it ..."*

A heady rush of anticipation hurtled through her at the idea she'd be with him that night. She folded the gown and put it in the bag, but her excitement was quickly tempered thinking about their last few exchanges. He'd been dismissive, with a dull ache in his voice she didn't recognize.

"Are you sure you even want to come?" he'd asked her last night, exhaustion coating every syllable. "This close to the end, I feel like I'm not on top of my game. At all."

"Yes, I'm sure. How could I not want to see my future husband? Even if you're wailing like the neighborhood tomcat, I'd want to see you."

This did make him laugh. A good sign. "That's me. I think I'm almost as attractive as one, these days, too."

"I'd take you any day of the week."

"I guess we'll see about that."

She gave a frustrated sigh. "There's no seeing about it. You're stuck with this misshapen mama."

"You're beautiful." He said it so quietly she thought she'd misunderstood him.

"Thanks. But I'm not feeling it."

He didn't answer.

"Hey. You still there?"

Nothing, except a hiccupping sound, and she knew then he was crying.

"Thomas?"

"I—honestly don't know what I'm doing here, and you're there. Everything seems so fucked up—"

"*Hey*. It's going to be fine. We can do this."

"Call me when you get here," he said, the flat tone back.

Two things were clear after they'd hung up. Thomas was not fine, and her weak assurances rang as false as they felt.

She zipped her bag closed and Hugo stared at her with ears cocked. "Yes, I'm going to see him." She scratched his neck. "Wish me luck, sweet boy."

Kathleen was late. She'd been stopped to a halt in backed-up traffic for at least an hour, and when the knot of cars loosened, she could see the culprit had been a terrible accident. Police and ambulance lights flashed distractingly as the responders hovered over the scene like people searching for elusive beach glass. A cold dread washed over her as she passed the cars crushed accordion-style into the dented guardrail. Survival of the crash didn't look likely among the mess of twisted metal and scattered shards covering the asphalt.

Fifteen minutes later, she pulled up to the Marriot and checked in. She quickly freshened her makeup, called Thomas, but got no answer, and after leaving an apologetic voicemail for her delay, she headed back out. She wasn't far from the venue, named "E Street Shuffle," which according to Thomas was a huge magnet for Springsteen fans (of which she was one) and students alike. She parked in an almost full lot and hurried across the asphalt. Twenty-five minutes till he was scheduled to go on.

As is common in nightclubs, the lighting was poor, but she could still make out walls plastered with photos, all telling the story of "The Boss" and his long career. From a mop-haired hippy to Eighties icon leaping into the air to seasoned performer on Broadway. She didn't study them in the detail she would've liked, due to the time constraint and trying to get her bearings. Later, on a break, perhaps. She searched for the will call booth, got her ticket, and a middle-aged man wearing a tie-dye headband guided her to where Thomas waited.

Further down the way, a door opened, light flooding the corridor, and Thomas stepped out with the lovely Natalie right behind him. As Kathleen opened her mouth to shout

out, she just as quickly clamped it shut. Natalie was shoving *something* into his back jeans pocket, and then patting him there intimately, all the while giggling like a smitten sixteen-year-old in a high school hallway.

Kathleen stood immobile and silent. He retrieved the something in his pocket, but her view was blocked by the rest of the band piling out. After a few moments, she turned around, went back to the general entrance, and managed to find an empty seat in the very crowded venue. She compartmentalized what she'd seen, telling herself there was likely a good explanation and she wouldn't let it ruin her enjoyment of the night.

What good explanation would that be, Brooks, of the beauty pageant queen pawing at your fiancée?

Kathleen closed her eyes. She had to trust him. She would calmly inquire as to what she'd witnessed and that'd be the end of it. Hopefully.

A manager of some sort appeared on the stage and introduced Thomas.

Out he came, his usual black ensemble making his skin look even more sallow than normal. What struck her was his gait. He appeared to be staggering a bit on the stage. The pain must be bad, she thought, worriedly. She waved like an overanxious groupie trying to attract his attention, and it worked because his gaze landed on her and he smiled. Not his usual dazzling one, but with that one facial gesture, her limbs went loose and her heart skittered in her chest. Questionable transactions were momentarily forgotten, concerns shuttled to the corners of her mind.

"Good evening, Indianapolis!" he shouted, and Indianapolis responded in kind. "We're excited to be here tonight. A big thank you to Midwest Hype for letting us open for them, and to the E Street Shuffle for having us. We'll get this party started with a nod to The Boss, an appropriate choice, I think, considering how we're surrounded by his spirit here. Hope you enjoy."

He launched into the opening lines of "Thunder Road" and the crowd erupted. They played four more songs, and he ended the set with the band by bringing out Natalie for one final tune.

Kathleen shifted uneasily in her chair. She'd prepped herself for watching them together again. Thomas had told her more than once the visual exchanges between performers were meant to be cues, as opposed to glances filled with yearning, but people unfamiliar wouldn't know the difference.

Natalie tossed her long hair back with the same Cher-like mannerism, this time the tresses landing on bare skin (because she was wearing one of those tops with the shoulders cut out), every inch as chic and alluring as before. She looked down at her own maternity shirt and a thousand definitions of frump crawled across her shrinking skin. What had possessed her? To think the mama and baby owl print, though it wasn't plastered all over the material, just a pint-sized picture of two birds on a branch across her chest, what had possessed her to think it was provocative or enticing in the least? To wear it out to a night club, of all places?

She sighed. She didn't dress with those goals in mind on a normal day; God knew pregnancy wasn't going to suddenly transform her into a fashion maven. She was a minimalist. If it hadn't been for Summer, she likely never would've ventured much past mascara and a little blush.

"So, I did a thing, recently," Thomas said into the mic. "I met this wonderful lady who's sitting out there, right now, and I asked her to marry me. And lucky me, she said yes." The crowd cheered uproariously. "This last one is for her.

Another good one written by Bruce. Here's 'If I Should Fall Behind.'"

Kathleen sat motionless, taken aback by his very public acknowledgement of her and their future. She strained to catch the lyrics, as it wasn't a song she'd heard before.

They went into the chorus, every word more perfect than the last, and she was on her feet by the end of the song. Applause thundered all around her.

"Thanks, ya'll," Thomas waved. "Stay tuned for Midwest Hype, coming up next!"

He and the others sprang into action like industrious mice, scattering and disassembling the considerable amount of gear onstage. She watched him in amazement. The missteps of before were nowhere to be found, and in fact, his lightning-fast movements had a manic quality to them. He'd be done soon, at that rate, so she wandered around the club, going back to all the walls studded with portraits and memorabilia. There were several autographed pictures of staff members with their arms around Bruce or shaking hands. Smiles galore.

"Hey there, sexy mama."

She turned around, laughing. "Yep. That's me." She glanced behind him. "Wow, are you packed up already? That was fast."

His face had a sheen of sweat from the laborious activity. "Yeah. We've got it down to a science, now." He pulled her in for a hug. "You okay? I gathered from your messages it wasn't a pleasant drive."

"It was long, that's all. There was an accident causing the delay. Glad I made it in time, though. I didn't realize your set was going to be an opener."

"They're definitely not the preferred gig, especially since

most people just want to skip right to the headliner action." He shrugged. "We take what we can get at the end of a run. Oh, except ... I didn't tell you."

"What's that?"

"Natalie got us some more dates. The tour's been extended."

"Really? Well, that's good." She took in the puffy bags under his eyes, and his eyes themselves. Something was off. "Right? A good thing?"

"Yeah. It is."

She knew what it was, now. His pupils were like a cat's, like Harriet's when she was seconds from pouncing a target. The black orbs all but obliterated the golden copper of his irises.

"Are you feeling all right?"

"You keep asking me that every time I talk to you," he said irritably. "As if I'm a kid away from home and I should go to the doctor. I'm *fine*."

Her head snapped back in surprise. "Maybe because you might very well need one, and it strikes me as scary that you can't see it. I'm sorry if that's being a nag before we've even made it to the altar."

He stared at a picture of Bruce clowning it up with sax player Clarence Clemons. "You're not. But I'm not gonna get into this here. Are you hungry? Want to go eat somewhere?"

She wasn't, but with one cursory glance it was clear choking down chain food wasn't the answer to what ailed him. She was sorry she hadn't baked a pan of his favorite lasagna. They could've heated it up in the hotel room's microwave. She could've brought tiramisu for after, like they'd had in the spring when she'd dropped a piece of creamy cake on her chest and he'd licked it off, both of them laughing as her body became a plate for the rest of his dessert.

Dammit.

"Let's do that. Let's find a nice place. My treat." She took his hand and they walked out of the E Street Shuffle. For now, the subject of unwellness was granted a short reprieve. She snuck a sidelong look at the perfect profile, careworn and less boyish each time she saw him, and her thoughts tumbled in apprehension. *Have I done this to you? Is this what engagement looks like? Is it too much to ask for excitement and not stress and dread? Or worse, apathy?*

There hadn't been this period with Steve. He'd proposed and she said yes at a French restaurant called *Très Bon* (literally, "very good"), topping off the dinner with crème brûlée. She'd dove into the rich custardy goodness, until she took a breath and noticed that, with every disappearing spoonful, his enthusiasm for a wedding celebration vanished, too. His preferred dessert was an old-fashioned cocktail. He'd cupped the etched glass and sloshed the ice around, his flake-less cuticles and manicured nails more polished than her own. *"Do you really want all the big fuss? A fancy dinner, dress, all that money spent for getting married to a divorced man?"*

She hadn't argued, due to his insinuation that perhaps wanting those traditions was superfluous. Crass, even. Additionally, the divorce made a church wedding out of the question. Her practical and his persuasive nature won out, and within two weeks, it was a courthouse done deal.

She inhaled deeply as she and Thomas crossed the street. *Your life has been one long compromise, Kathleen. No more.*

"Hellloo?" Thomas was waving his hand in front of her face.

"Sorry. Lost in thought. What'd you say?"

"Have anything in mind for where to go?"

"No. Just not fast-food."

She hoped that an accommodating restaurant could be found this late. They'd need sustenance for the long talk ahead.

They located an authentic Mexican place buried in a sketchy part of town, and filled up on beef burritos, with conversation contained to questions about the tour, work at HopCanon, and prenatal care. All of it safe, neutral ground.

When they got back to the hotel room, he showered and came out towel-drying his hair. The squeezing action caused the banded fibers of his muscles to go taut and protrude, and he reminded her of one of those pink-red pictures in an anatomy book. What humans looked like with the skin removed. Not exactly an amore-inducing image, but because it was him, it didn't matter. With his arms lifted, she could see a faint pattern of faint freckles underneath that made a triangle shape. She was fascinated and aroused by the discovery of new physical details in him, even as he appeared to be deteriorating right in front of her.

"You could be a model, you know. Did anyone ever tell you that?"

He laughed and threw the towel on a stiff, high-backed desk chair. "Uh, no." He laughed again. "Wait. I take it back. Once, in college."

"Do tell."

"Not much to tell. One of my roommates was an art major and asked me if I'd be interested in making some money as a nude subject. I respectfully declined."

"Why?"

"Really? With this eyesore of a leg? Of course, she didn't know about that, but still. There's no way I would've."

"It's not an eyesore. Imperfections are what make

someone uniquely attractive. You should've listened to her and taken the art gig."

He leaned down and kissed her. "I'm glad someone's turned on by my uniquely attractive imperfections. Since they are numerous."

With one towel rubbing and one kiss, her resolve unraveled, like kite string in the wind. *Focus, Kathleen, focus. Don't be so weak ... think of your babies, what they need ...*

That was it, that was the key, to remember this wasn't only about her, anymore. She pulled away and stood up. "I want to ask you something, and I want an honest answer. Tell me what Natalie put in your pocket right before the show, tonight. I was in the hallway and about to call out to you when I saw that little exchange."

His brow raised in surprise.

"The truth," she added, sharply.

"I don't lie."

"Okay. She just enjoys fondling your ass, then? I can't say I blame her."

He laughed. "Your jealousy makes me hornier than ever, if you can imagine that."

"You're wasting away and you think my concern is *funny*? Oh, but it's also irritating, apparently, according to your reactions earlier."

"Look, I'm fucking tired. That's it. I'm not wasting away—"

"You are. Your eyes, your skin, everything—is screaming for help."

"Hmm. How did I go from being model material five minutes ago to one foot in the grave?"

She paced around one of his guitar cases in the middle of the room.

"Answer the question, dammit. What did she do? What did she give you?"

His jaw was set, arms crossed against his chest. "Amphetamines. Speed. It's as common as candy in the music world and a hell of a lot less dangerous than some of the other things out there. Are you happy now?"

"No, I'm not happy. Not at all. It's so wrong—"

"Kathleen, you can't possibly get it, get what it's like. The chronic pain, for one. Which I did worry about, but it goes into hiding when I'm onstage. It's a double edged-sword. The night after night, having to be on top of my game, what it takes ... is so beyond what I expected. Call it naivete or flat-out stupidity, but there it is. And I can't do any less, because each audience deserves the same amount of effort every single time."

"In no time, the audience will see a stumbling skeleton unable to remember his own lyrics, if this continues. Or worse."

"I see. Because you have so much experience in these matters, Dr. Brooks? How much time have you spent treating drugged-up-musician patients?"

Kathleen whirled around. His uncharacteristically superior tone stung. "It doesn't take someone with a medical degree to see that you're in a dangerous pattern, but I guess it does take one to be in full-blown denial. Tell me, do you have a death wish? Do you *want* to end up as some modern-day Elvis caricature?"

"You know what? Asking me if I have a death wish probably isn't the best idea. Even if it's been a while since I had one."

"So, what happens? You keep going in this circle and I get to watch you wither piece by piece, because I 'don't understand,' because the band, the crowd deserve all of you?"

"You wanted this for me!" His roar was no doubt heard in surrounding rooms. "The tour, the tour, the tour! I was told we couldn't stay together because of the demands of the tour. You hid being pregnant because of the tour, to protect my 'dream.' And now you can't handle the reality of what that means."

"You're going to blame me for this decline? For trying to be supportive? For you abusing your body? And *you're* the psychiatric nurse!"

She bent close to his stony face. "I spent years with a man who was an expert at denying responsibility for his feelings, his actions, and transferring it all to me when anything went wrong. I won't do it again, even if it means I raise these babies by myself." She stood still, her face softening. "I love you, but what I'm seeing right now is not the man I love. What I'd like you to do is call it all off, cancel the rest of the dates Natalie so generously found for you—"

"I can't do that."

"Come back with me. Come back and rest and eat, let yourself recover—"

"That would be akin to career suicide, to say nothing of what it would mean to my band. What would that make me? What kind of dickless wonder throws in the towel before one small-potatoes tour is over?"

"Please! You said yourself the pace has been grueling. How do you know they're not ready to go home? Did the new band manager even consult with any of you before this surplus booking?"

"How did you know that?"

Exasperated, she said, "How did I know what?"

"That actually is true. Natalie is the band manager. As of a couple days ago."

She stared at him, then threw her hands to the ceiling, laughing. "Oh, my God. Of course she is! Here I was being sarcastic. Silly me!"

"It's a good fit for the band. She gets along with the guys, knows the business end of things. She's an asset."

Humiliation burned up her throat, creating an explosive minefield bubbling to the surface. Never had she felt this kind of rage. "Is she? Sorry if I don't think that a manager who gives her clients uppers, and probably wants bonus shagging in exchange, is the best hiring decision."

He laughed, which only fueled her outrage. "You're so off base."

"Really. Tell me, what other ways did you acquire her sweet stash? Did she stuff them in her bra, in addition to shoving them in your pants? You both seemed to find that amusing."

"Stop this. None of this is her fault. Furthermore, anything sexual is all in the past, and even then, it was weak at best. I suspected she was gay, and I was right. She's had an off-and-on girlfriend for years—"

"I don't give a damn if she has a dozen girlfriends from here to Zimbabwe! Maybe she swings both ways. All I know is what I saw in that hallway. Defend her one more time and I will seriously throw this engagement ring at you."

He looked down, his shiny hair catching the light, and the kite string resumed its stalled unraveling. She was torn between gathering him in her arms and stomping out, but she didn't move.

"I'm begging you to come home with me. Plain and simple."

"It's not simple. You don't just give coo-coo people hot compresses, chicken noodle soup, kiss their owies, and suddenly they wake up fresh as a daisy."

"Don't you dare patronize me. I'm not so ignorant that I don't realize that what you might need is more than a little R and R." She straightened and exhaled. "Regardless. Not only do I want you to cancel those gigs, but you need to fire your new employee."

He scoffed in disbelief. "What? What kind of demand is that?"

"A simple one, like my other request."

"Is that so? You don't think band life can be separated from personal life?"

"Right now, it's sure not happening. Because if you expect me to tolerate one more minute of you spending boatloads of time with a pill-pushing ex-lover trying to wheedle her way back into your graces, think again."

"Come on. That's awfully dramatic. You just can't handle my being friends with her."

"I maybe could've handled it if she hadn't contributed to your current condition under the guise of being 'helpful.' What kind of friend does that?"

"Gee, I don't know, one who's been in my shoes? Who understands what it's like to be in this pressure-cooker?"

She crossed her arms stiffly. "Not me, in other words."

"I didn't say that. But what I will say is there are people's lives to consider, here, rippling effects from decisions made frivolously. It's not fair to lay down these ultimatums."

"Frivolously? Are you blind? What about *our* lives together? You're sick and on the verge of collapse, and I'm what? Supposed to look the other way?" Tears edged in, clogging her throat. "What about what I want? Does that not matter?"

"Yes, of course it does. You know that."

Kathleen swallowed rapidly. Like a switch, her hot anger had turned to nausea, exacerbated by somersaulting protests in her belly at the unfolding turmoil. She gripped the office chair with the damp towel still draped across its back.

"What is it? Are you okay?"

She shook his hand off of her and through gritted teeth muttered the unthinkable, "Don't touch me."

"Kathleen—"

In minutes, she faced the difficult task of not choking while vomiting and crying. Looking up at the abstract grey-and-white wall picture above the commode, she made an unromantic comparison. There was little doubt love and fury could exist in the same maddening, simultaneous manner as what was occurring in the mundane hotel bathroom, and there was not a damned thing to be done other than to see it through.

19

She made him sleep on the daybed that looked too narrow and short for him. Fortunately, his objections were short-lived, for which she was grateful and sad. How could they be at this point already? Disregarding the quaint advice of "never go to bed mad," before it was even official? She needed the distance to remain firm. She told herself this as she slipped in-between the lonely, luxurious hotel sheets. Firm about what and why was a little blurry as she flipped about in the wide expanse of the king mattress. What would she do if he ignored her conditions? Could she walk away?

You are sorely underestimating him, Kathleen. Do you think he'll just stand idly by and let you disappear with his children?

No, Kathleen told the voice in her head, *I'm the one who's being underestimated, here.*

And with that declaration, sleep finally claimed her for a few solid hours.

She was up, showered, and had her bag packed early. Too early, for the shower nor a snack did nothing to refresh her energy. When Thomas awakened, she had a coffee and a full plate ready for him from the lobby breakfast bar. He looked no more well rested than she felt.

"Hi," he said quietly, sitting up.

"Hi. Here." She handed him the disposable cup and gestured to the food.

"Thanks. You didn't have to do that. I should be the one getting you breakfast."

"It's fine. I had a little something." She sipped her tea and gazed out at the grimy twentieth-floor window, where all she could see were grey rooftops. She surmised it was safer than watching him and ending up naked on the underutilized bed in-between them.

"Looks like you're all ready to go. I thought we'd spend the day together."

"I thought that, too, until last night."

"What? After one heated argument, you don't want to be around me, now? This isn't high school. We're engaged, remember?"

She looked away from the smokestacks and vents, to him. "You are so right. I'm not the one who needs to be reminded of that fact."

"I don't need reminding. I think about you constantly."

"It's actions that matter." She rose and stood over him. "Thomas, I need you. But I have one goal for the coming months, and that's to have a successful pregnancy and birth. Seeing you decline and in clear denial is tearing at me."

He was about to take a bit of the apple turnover, then reconsidered. "Jesus. You've got to cut me some slack, here. It's only three more months and then we're done! I can do it! Then I'm completely at your disposal. Where is your trust in me?"

"This isn't about trust. Nor do I expect you to be 'completely at my disposal.'"

He leaned back, looking at the ceiling. "Funny, it wasn't long ago you told me you were afraid of my resentment if I gave up my chance for a musical shot. Now you're telling me I have no other choice?"

"I'm more scared of the alternative if you keep on with this train wreck."

She was afraid of a few other possibilities, as his legs splayed in front of her, the cords and veins in his neck jutting out like a vampire's dream. Pleading to be caressed, kissed. Nourished. She quickly averted her gaze. "I—I'm not asking you to end your big chance. Far from it. I'm asking you to get healthy before something ends it for you."

"Is this your way of saying you're done? Presenting these demands or else?" His voice wavered, and in that fraction of a second, she did, too.

"What I want doesn't include a broken engagement." She gathered her things to distract from the tears that were flooding her vision. "I also don't want to argue. I should leave."

She turned away and he flew across the room as if he were that fictional vampire, landing deftly behind her. He gasped in pain from the impact, but still managed to brace his arms on the door, his palms spread out like Rocky Balboa encircling a reluctant Adrian. He pressed into her back, almost leaning into her for support. "Don't."

With one hand locked in place, he lifted her hair with the other and kissed the nape of her neck, raising every latent goosebump in her body as if by command. *Resistance is futile.* Her bags succumbed to him, as well, sliding to the floor in a thump. She laid her forehead on the door as she felt the last kite string of conviction coil into an imaginary corner.

"Give me some time. To regroup, make a plan—" He sighed deeply, his breath tickling the back of her ear. "I've said this from the beginning and it's still true. None of it—my music, my life, whatever—means anything without you." He pulled her around to face him and cradled her belly. "Or these two."

"Thomas—"

"I want to be at my best for us. I do. Every time I know I'll get to see you motivates me, makes me perform that much better. *You're* the only drug I really need, I swear."

"Hmmph. That sounds more toxic than romantic."

He laughed. "You know what? I don't think you've ever experienced real romance."

"I'm pretty sure it should be more than playing at being somebody's muse. Look at what happened with Eric Clapton and 'Layla.' I watched a documentary, the other night, about that."

"That song made Clapton a boatload of money. You might end up doing that for me."

She made a face and he kissed the tip of her nose. "Okay, okay, as long as we're talking famous couples, I'll be Johnny Cash, walking the line for you. My June."

"She gave him ultimatums. Because she loved him."

"Yes. And she was older than him, too. Must be something to that."

They both laughed and he wrapped his arms tighter. "I'm sorry for the arguing, last night. Please don't go. Not yet." He slid his hands up her back, under her shirt, his lips nipping at hers gently.

That silken mouth ...

She sagged against him. Warding off the inevitable seemed pointless and sophomoric. She extricated herself from their huddle, her knees like jumbled strands of spaghetti, and used the house phone to call the front desk.

"Hello. I'd like to request a late checkout, if it's possible. Mmm-hmm. Great, that'd be fine. Thank you." She hung up, turning around as she spoke. "They said we have until three—"

He was already in bed. He patted the pillow invitingly.

"You're not wasting any time, are you?"

He shrugged. "One thing you learn working in a hospital, you never know when the clock is gonna run out. Permanently."

There was no arguing with that universal truth, and fatigue and desire wiped out any other plan anyway. She laid down and he curled into her back, making an unhappy comment about her fully dressed state. She lifted her arms in the air like a sleepy toddler and he pulled her shirt off. He massaged her gently, expertly, the subtle warmth of his hands coaxing soft sighs of contentment.

"Ah, that feels incredible. You're learning."

"Only from the best." Her belly rippled under his touch and he paused. "They're very active. That's good."

"Yes. If only the somersaults weren't at four AM. And now."

"Let's see if a little humming quiets them." He rearranged himself even closer. "Hey, you two. It's naptime. Mmm, lemme think ... okay, here we go ...

"Mmm, I wanna rock her gypsy soul ... just like in the days of old ... mmm ... your mama's so lovely, like a deck of cards I fold...

I can't get enough

Your mama's so lovely

I can't get enough

I'm hooked forever

On her sweet, sweet drug ... oh, she makes me whole, rocking her gypsy soul."

She laughed in spite of her half-awake state. "What kind of lullaby is that?"

"A mash-up created in less than five minutes."

"Impressive."

After several more bars and repeat melodies, it worked. Everyone was still, pulses and breathing syncopated into the deep, peaceful rhythm of rest, the kind that only heartfelt music can evoke.

Kathleen dreamt her portrait of Thomas was burning. She was desperately trying to snuff the flames out when a fire alarm went off, which was not a fire engine at all, but her cell's ringtone of "Papa, Don't Preach." The persistent pleas of Madonna finally cut through her grogginess and she answered before it went to voicemail.

"Francesca. What's up? Is everything okay?"

Thomas stirred at the sound of Kathleen's panicked voice. Everything was not okay.

"Wait, slow down, I can't understand you." She waited, looking at Thomas. She became stick-straight, fully alert, and yet the words on the other end would not compute. She stared at a tag on the sheet in her lap and squeezed her eyes shut. "When ... when did this happen?" Silence, then, "I'm actually there now. I was planning on heading home this afternoon." She scrambled for the hotel pen and pad of paper, her hands shaking violently. "What hospital is she in again?" She scribbled the information down and leaned back into the headboard. "Okay, honey. I'll be there as soon as I can. Try to get an update on her condition. No, don't feel bad. You stay put. I'll talk to you soon."

She hung up and Thomas took her trembling hands in his own. "What's going on?"

"Amanda's in the ICU, and Mallory ..." She pulled her hands away, rubbing her forehead as if trying to erase the new information lobbed there. "I don't even know how to tell you this. Remember the reason I was late, last night? The terrible car accident and how I thought one of the cars looked familiar?"

His nod was just shy of imperceptible, like a tiny crack in pond ice right before imploding.

"It was *them*. Nobody knows what happened, but they crossed over the median—"

"Hold on. How do you know what you saw was the same accident? Why would they be coming in this direction?"

It was, Thomas. I'm so sorry.

She sunk into his chest. She pressed her cheek there to soften the planes, rigid with unease, and to breathe his scent in. Perhaps wisps of balsam and cedar pheromones had anesthetic properties, in addition to their other effects on her.

"Tell me," he demanded.

"Mallory was—was killed on impact, and Amanda's in a hospital somewhere close by. St. Vincent's."

"*What?*"

She looked up at his stricken face. "Francesca said they were coming here because they had tickets to see your show."

Rain pelted the waiting room's long rectangular windows, their watery path not unlike tears on the face of a patient's grieving or worried family member. The modern space surrounding the small group gathered now had witnessed many pacing feet and wastebaskets filled with tissues, but it was a far cry from the typical hospital waiting room of the past. No outdated Reader's Digests or plastic molded chairs with chrome legs, unfit for rest. This was more like an authentic living area, cozily decorated and minus the clutter of mail, keys, or scrunched-up homework papers. Two couches and loveseats that invited fifteen-minute catnaps were artfully placed, as well as a kitchenette with more chairs. And possibly most important, a decent coffee machine.

Mallory's family was absent. The funeral home had made arrangements for her to be taken back to Mount Simon, with services yet to be finalized. Nobody was certain as to the cause of the crash, other than witnesses had seen her car veer wildly seconds before impact, and thankfully the people in the other car escaped with minor cuts and bruises. At June's (Amanda's grandmother) request, Kathleen and Thomas had gone to the police station to try to talk to the first responders at the scene. One of the police officers who'd been there said the accident was likely due to distraction, such as reaching for a drink or adjusting the radio. Peter Bailey, as he'd introduced himself, expressed his sympathies. He appeared to be in his late fifties, tall with a slight paunch, and pinkish-red capillaries sprouting on the sides of his nose. Irish, maybe. Or an alcoholic. Or both.

"We go to the high schools, do the demos of what can happen, and you hope you make an impact. But these calls never get easier. In the back of your mind you always think, 'That could be my daughter.'" Peter's grey eyes glistened. He looked down at Kathleen's obvious baby bump, then at her and Thomas. "You'll understand, one day."

"Mr. Bailey—" Kathleen reached out, but her hand missed him by an inch because he'd already turned away, embarrassed. She sobbed in the car for the full fifteen minutes it took to get back to the hospital, at the injustice of a man never knowing the many lives he'd saved in his career. The power of carnage to blot out all the good.

She said a silent prayer for Peter Bailey and the havoc in his head.

Back in the waiting area, a muted wall television in the waiting room scrolled news at the bottom of the screen, where people stared without comprehending. One of them being June. Kathleen asked her gently, "Can I get you some more coffee?"

She shook her head, her straw-like hair immobile under a layer of hairspray. "No, honey, I got plenty. You don't need to be waitin' on me. Anyhow, I can fill up myself when I go out for a smoke."

Kathleen nodded. It occurred to her she was at her best waiting on people, but it wasn't always welcomed. Particularly for those who weren't accustomed to being on the receiving end. She glanced at the women's magazines on the end table and was reminded that not only was her proclivity for servitude outdated, but probably considered damaging to the current movement. The cover's blurbs read, "It's all about you! Embrace who you were meant to be," "The future is female: it's finally a thing!" and, "Ten-minute meals even HE can manage."

She sipped her own coffee, now semi-warm, which is about the level of inspiration she felt at skimming over the headlines. Politics, weather, cancel culture, Mel Gibson's newest baby mama. It all seemed so trivial in comparison to what was unfolding within hospital walls and police reports, every second of the day. What was happening right now in front of her. No visitors were allowed in the ICU, so the tension expressed itself in pacing, boredom, and hunger.

"Grandma, I'm starving." Riley, Amanda's eleven-year-old-brother, stood in front of them expectantly.

"Boy, you're *always* hungry. You got a hollow leg, I swear."

His freckled face crinkled in confusion. "Huh? My legs aren't yellow."

June laughed. "Never mind. Let me see here." She rummaged through her purse for her wallet. "That cafeteria food is expensive for a kid with a hollow leg."

"I was just thinking I could do with a snack," Kathleen said quickly. "You know, eating for two and all. Why don't we go together? My treat."

Riley's eyes were big, like his sister's, and he twitched in excitement. "Yeeess. I love snacks. Can your husband come, too?"

Kathleen merely smiled at his assumption. Thomas had spent the last couple of hours playing cards with Riley and entertaining him. Not surprising the kid was already smitten. "I'll go ask him."

He was propped against the wall, staring out at the rain, and the subdued light reflected angles and planes in the curvature of his cheeks. If mournful guilt had a physical expression, it was etched here in his face, as deeply as the curve of his dimple.

She sidled up next to him. "Hey, I'm going to the cafeteria with June and Riley. Want to come?"

"No, thanks. You go ahead. I've got calls to make. Explain what's going on, even if I can't understand it myself."

She knew that desolate tone. "Thomas. You're not responsible for this—"

"Don't." He lifted his hand in the universal stop gesture. "Not here, not now."

Wordlessly Kathleen backed away, over to June and Riley, who was still arguing with his grandmother that he didn't have a yellow leg, and she herded them out to the nearest elevator that would take them to food.

"It's that one, on the left." Kathleen pointed to a brick ranch home with a sloping driveway. Mallory's home. "Her mom said Google Maps always gets it wrong."

Thomas parked next to a dented van with letters on the side that read "ROMANSKI'S CONSTRUCTION." He took a deep breath, hesitating. It'd been a long trip from Indianapolis.

Kathleen stroked his hand. "You okay?"

"No. I have absolutely no idea what to say to them."

"They asked to talk to us. So, we respond by listening."

He lifted his head and looked at her. "How do you do that?"

"Do what?"

"Make something complicated simple."

She laughed. "Usually, I'm the one overanalyzing. C'mon, let's do this."

They went to the front, standing on a mat whose word "WELCOME" was almost rubbed away, when the door opened before they even knocked. A woman with hair the color of ruby-red oranges greeted them. Her eyes were watery and bloodshot, the hue of them nearly matching her head.

"Miss Kathleen," she said, ushering them in. "And Thomas, of course. Come, come. So good of you to visit. You'll forgive the messy house. And me. I look a horrible state, I know."

"Please, call me Kathleen."

The woman nodded as they entered the clean but cluttered living room. "Sure. 'Miss Kathleen' is just always what Mallory called you. Oh, and I'm Connie, and here comes my husband Phil."

He walked over, a big man wearing a ballcap, a well-worn Dickies work shirt, and painter pants. They shook hands and finished the introductions.

"Get you a beer?" Phil looked sheepish. "I know it's a little early. Something for the lady?"

Thomas said yes, while Kathleen declined. Connie went to the kitchen and came out with his beer, pouring it into a frosty glass. "Here's a nice cold mug for you. That's how Phil likes it." She handed it to him, smiling coyly. "My, aren't you every bit as handsome as Amanda described. And then some."

Thomas flushed. "Thank you. But I think girls that age tend to be easily impressed."

"Nonsense! Classic looks like yours never go out of style. I mean, I'm a beautician. It's my *job* to be in the know about these things."

Kathleen stared at her tangerine hair and pondered the mystery of professions. Everyone knew the story of the plumber with the running toilet, the manicurist with the broken nails. Connie was stocky and busty, and though she indeed did know enough to be wearing what was all the rage (among teens, anyway), the teal tunic and patterned leggings fused to her midlife bumps like permanent static cling. Her face was also meticulously made up, the eggshell blue eyeshadow reminding Kathleen of her mother's favorite shade. A Max Factor two-toned palette Peggy had kept in the bathroom drawer, which thankfully had only made appearances for Easter and Christmas services. Connie's eyeliner was smeared, presumably from tears, and Kathleen suppressed the urge to rummage for a tissue and whisper to her of the situation.

Instead, she nodded and said it was obvious Connie was in the know about all fashion-related things. Mallory's mother smiled.

"Isn't that kind of you to say. I do think Amanda was trying to show Mallory how to apply make-up and what have you. God knows she wouldn't hear it from me. It was okay, though, because those girls became pretty close friends the last few months."

"I'm glad to hear that."

"Oh, yes, Amanda was over here quite a bit, just hanging out, and they were always talking and laughing about you two. Especially you, Thomas." She cast a longing glace at him and choked off a sob.

Phil coughed loudly from a chair that was clearly his, a tattered-by-cat-scratches La-Z-Boy with a cupholder on the side that fit his beverage perfectly. "Jeezus. They're not here five minutes and you're embarrassing the young man."

"I know, I know. I'm little more than a running faucet, these past few days. I'm sorry."

"You've nothing to apologize for," Thomas said. "I'm the one who's sorry, and not only for your loss."

The two grief-stricken faces stared at him, puzzled.

"What I mean is, if the girls hadn't driven to my concert—"

He couldn't finish the rest. *Mallory would still be alive.*

Connie shuddered, her aquamarine spiral earrings dangling against her jaw. "Goodness, no. We *told* them to go. I asked you to come here to say thank you, for being supportive and kind to our daughter. You know, Kathleen ... until your group, Mallory had trouble making friends. I think she always felt like an outsider. The middle-child thing, all that."

"Connie, for God's sake." Phil's face had turned the same red as the ribbon on his beer can.

"What? I'm trying to make *sense* of it all." She dabbed at her eyes, helping the smudged liner to disappear. "I suppose she was lost in the shuffle, since we were constantly taken up with the other kids' latest crisis, and I blame myself for that happening."

"Raising kids today seems more challenging than ever," Kathleen said gently.

Connie's head jabbed up and down. "As you'll find out! But honestly, how are two people who work full-time supposed to keep it all together? I do hair, he builds houses, and there's always something pulling every which way. I'm sure that's how she ended up pregnant, for the attention, I suppose—"

"Enough." Phil waved a hand at his wife. "These poor souls ain't our counselors. Although, I'd venture to say they'd do a better job than those useless jamokes we were seeing every week. Them and their fancy degrees."

"That's not fair, Phil. It's up to us to make the changes."

He nearly choked on the Pabst Blue Ribbon he was in the middle of consuming. "Fair? I'll tell you about *fair.* There we were, shelling out top dollar, and all they did was lean back and push their pencils around and say, "Well, what do you think is the answer?" Gee, Einstein. If I knew *that,* I wouldn't be paying you schmucks half a days' pay, now, would I?"

"We're not therapists, that's for sure." Kathleen said it in the same low voice she used at the teen meetings. She hoped it was more calming than the one the schmuck counselors had tried. "I like to think we were people she thought she could trust. What I know is that Mallory was a sweet, smart girl who loved you. A typical teenager trying to figure out her place in the world."

Connie sniffed. "Yes, and now she's in another place. A better one than the world we live in, sent there for a greater purpose."

"Ah, Christ on a cross." Phil twisted the empty can, the crunched metal enveloped by his meaty hand. "More mumbo-jumbo bullshit, this time straight from the priest who was here yesterday. As if anyone can trust what those

SOBs have to say! Always hounding for more money, and how do we know that it ain't goin' straight to some Chester the Molester's pocket?"

"Phil!!"

His head hung down, and when he lifted it, defeat defined his every movement. He gestured limply to Kathleen and Thomas. "Sorry. Don't mean to offend. Thanks for all you did for Mal, but I got work to do outside." With considerable effort, he heaved himself up toward the kitchen and plucked another beer from the fridge. The screen door to the garage creaked and slammed shut a few seconds later.

"You'll have to excuse him." Connie's voice hushed. "He's gotten so bitter. We were having issues long before this nightmare, from family problems to the IRS hassling us. I don't see it getting any better."

Kathleen glanced at Thomas. "I'm so sorry. What can we do for you, if anything?"

"Oh, boy. Where do I start? Got a few thousand laying around for a funeral?" She laughed bitterly. "I don't mean that the way it sounded. Just ignore me. *And* him. We're literally certifiable."

"You're grieving. It's not craziness."

"Ha! You didn't know us before." Her scarlet lip trembled. "Still, I do want to talk about ... about the arrangements. Maybe you can spread the word we will have a memorial service at a later date. Possibly cremation? I just don't know. There's so much pressure to make all these decisions, none of which are affordable—"

"I'm wondering," Kathleen said tentatively, "Have you considered the possibility of starting a GoFundMe to help?"

"Heavens, no. Phil would *never* allow that. He's as pigheaded stubborn as they get. I can hear him now: 'We're no charity case.' We'll figure it out. Somehow."

Connie withdrew the tissue tucked up her sleeve and gave a great honk. "There is one thing. If you could keep me updated about how Amanda is doing. I don't want to bother the grandma."

"Of course."

"Is she still in the intensive care?"

"Yes, but it looks like she'll be transferred to another unit, soon. The doctors are saying it's going to be a lot of rehab and physical therapy."

The conversation went on a few minutes more, when it became clear Connie's attention was needed elsewhere. Her phone kept going off and she politely kept trying to ignore the dings.

Kathleen rose from the couch, thanked her for the drinks and talk. "I promise to stay in touch."

"I appreciate that."

Thomas lingered and turned around at the door.

"Mrs. Romanski, you should know something. If it weren't for your daughter ... Kathleen and I ... well, it would've been a longer and harder road for us if not for her 'intervention,' you might say. Sounds strange, but it's true."

"What do you mean?"

"Mallory didn't mind pointing out what we couldn't see ourselves. A gift of youth, that kind of honesty, but one we'd all be better off holding onto as long as we can."

Connie Romanski looked as if she might kiss him, whether from desire or gratefulness was anyone's guess. "She *was* good at that, wasn't she? And there we were, her parents, forever telling her to mind her mouth and be quiet." Her sad eyes had a faraway look. "When I think of the wasted time we spent on stupid, stupid things, the lecturing, the arguing and disapproval of her views. It makes me sick."

"You cared about the kind of person she was becoming,"

Kathleen soothed. "We're all trying to do our best, aren't we? All walking each other home, as the saying goes?"

"I suppose." She dabbed at her eyes once more. "You know, you have a gentle way about you ... now I see why she always made time for the meetings. Thank you both, again, for listening to her. For being her friend. For giving her a chance to find some, when she couldn't seem to any other way."

They hugged, amidst a fresh assault of tears, and as Thomas and Kathleen were leaving, Phil came back in to rummage for another beer. One more, he told them, as they bid goodbye, to help him get work done outside.

"That was ... interesting," Thomas said in the car. The rain resumed its gloomy drizzle.

"I'm glad we met up. They're just people trying to keep their heads above water, even before this loss. I guess it's make it or break it time for them, now."

"Yeah. Someone said that exact thing to me, recently, about make it or break it time. Caleb or Eli."

There was a long silence, and she turned to him. "Did you agree with him?"

"I dunno. Probably, in-between telling him to fuck off."

"Am I wrong? About the band, the tour?"

His hands stopped at the car's ignition. "What?"

"Did you make your calls? Cancelling everything?"

"Not yet, but—"

"Maybe you should just go do it. Finish your gigs, let the cards fall where they will. I'm thinking I don't have any right to tell you what to do."

"That's a three-hundred-and-sixty-degree switch if I ever heard one. What gives?"

She felt an arrow of desperation claw at her and she prayed it wouldn't turn into nausea. How could she explain the turn when she didn't understand it herself? Other than she didn't want to contribute to more regret and guilt? It was written so plainly on his face, and it scared her.

"I don't know," she admitted. "The events of the last couple days? Life is short and I'm crazy? Or everyone is, it's just a matter of degree, and if you find your kind of crazy, you shouldn't cling?"

He laughed and, looking over his shoulder, backed up the car.

She stared at the twisty column of his neck, at the whiskers like specks of black pepper on his jaw, until it all became blurry from the film of tears gathering once again.

"Don't you agree?"

He shifted into drive. "I think I need to go to HopCanon before we pursue any more of this conversation."

It was eleven forty-five. Apparently, not too early for Phil Romanski, or, for that matter, any weary soul, to kickstart one's coping mechanisms for the day.

20

HopCanon was already filling up when they arrived fifteen minutes later. They sat at the bar and caught Zack's eye, who smiled wide enough for his teeth to show. A sign he must be in good form, Kathleen thought.

"Hey, guys." He placed two glasses of water on coasters. It wasn't routinely done unless customers requested it, since there was a self-serve water cooler on the far wall.

"Thanks, Zack." Kathleen gulped from the glass. "I guess you knew I was thirsty."

Zack's eyes were somber as his gaze darted between them, sizing up the vibes the way he always did. "Hey, I'm really sorry to hear about what happened. Anything I can do?"

Thomas rubbed his weary eyes. "You can start by pulling me a pint of deliciousness."

"You got it. What sounds good?"

They read the taplist on the chalkboard. The new choices were "Ordinary Time," "Woman at the Well," "Pope's Pilsner," and "Sister Celia's Sour."

Kathleen laughed. "Oh my God, Sister Celia. She was

our old-biddy second-grade teacher! She hated us. I mean, not just me, Jeff, and Summer. Kids in general."

Zack nodded. "Thus, her namesake?"

"I guess so. It makes me wonder again why there are teachers like this, nuns or not. I mean, why? Why pick *that* for your job? Go sell steak knives door-to-door. Become a nurse and jab them with vaccination needles."

"Maybe career choices had something to do with limited options for women, at that time," Zack said generously.

Thomas clapped his hands. "Alrighty. Tell me about 'Ordinary Time.'"

"It's Jeff's effort toward producing a day-drinking beer. Coming in at four-and-a-half percent. So, not the most flavorful, but on a hot day or kayaking or whatever, it's good." He set a sample shot glass in front of Thomas. "Jeff said the name is a reference to the church's liturgical calendar."

Thomas sipped, then made a pained face. "Umm, not so much. How about I just go for it. A pint of Woman at the Well, please."

"Good choice. Our latest stout."

He put the dark brew with a healthy head of caramel-colored foam in front of Thomas.

"Zack, I'm coming back to work, believe it or not," Kathleen said. "For a little while, at least."

"Take your time. I can say that to you, as the new HopCanon taproom manager."

They showered him with congrats and questions. Yes, he was still going to bartend occasionally, and, yes, live music would still be featured weekly.

"I get asked at least once a day by patrons about when are you coming back," he said to Thomas.

Thomas unscrewed a bottle from his pocket and tossed a

pill, or pills, in his mouth, then washed it down with a swig. "That may be sooner than previously thought."

"Really?"

"I don't know about anything for sure, right now. Let's talk about it when my head is clearer. Like, in six months? A year?" He laughed mirthlessly. "Maybe never."

He drank the rest of the pint down, told Zack he wanted another, and excused himself to the restroom.

Zack's steady gaze set itself on her. "He's blaming himself for what happened."

"Yes, though he won't address it. Verbally, anyway. I'm worried. And I was worried even before this happened. Doesn't he look terrible?"

"He's a little gaunt."

She laughed. "How very tactful of you. Any advice, wise one?"

"You won't be able to convince him he wasn't at fault. So, my advice is to save your energy." He glanced downward at her belly. "You're going to need it. Obviously."

"That's it? That's all you've got for me?"

He shrugged. "I think he's gonna have a rough go of it for a while. Not that any of this is a walk in the park for you. But we both know who the stronger sex is."

"I've never felt less strong."

"You are. My guess is he'll make it through okay, knowing you'll be waiting there on the other side. Let's hope it's before the little ones decide to make their entrance into the world."

"Mmm. Let's hope." She shifted positions on the barstool, to relieve a worrisome pinch running down her spine. She'd had bouts of sciatica in the past, probably brought on by cross-country competitions and races as a teenager. It was the one sport she had excelled in. If, indeed, it'd been triggered, all the nausea she'd dealt with so far would feel like a walk in the park in comparison.

"You all right?" Zack peered at her.

"Yes. Just my lower back protesting a bit. I'll be fine."

Thomas was walking back toward her with Summer in tow. He took his seat as Zack asked him questions about the tour and band.

"Awe, girl." Summer enveloped Kathleen in a bear hug. "Are you doing okay?"

Feeling her friend's strong arms around her were enough to unlock another flood of tears, but they were thankfully short-lived. "We just came from Mallory's parents."

"How was that?"

"As you'd expect. They're shellshocked, and on top of that, trying to figure out how to pay for a funeral."

Summer grimaced. "The lovely afterlife industry. You know how I feel about that."

"I do."

Years before, Summer's mother, Carol, died after a brutal bout with cancer. She'd endured numerous rounds of fruitless therapy, her body withered to a grey husk, yet her mind remained clear when the painkillers weren't muddying the view. Carol's voice had risen above the beeping machines one late night at the hospital.

"Summer, dear, I'm sorry you've had to watch this."

Kathleen was next to Summer at her mother's bedside, and they both startled into wakefulness. Carol hadn't spoken in weeks, but her voice now was succinct. She struggled to sit, her toothpick arms shaking, and successfully hauled herself up against the headboard. "It's a load of cruel bullshit."

Kathleen and Summer exchanged glances. She'd never uttered a hint of profanity in front of them, not even when they were thoughtless kids tracking in mud on her clean floors or clogging up the vacuum with Barbie shoes half-hidden in the carpet.

"Mom?"

"I said what cruel bullshit it is, forced to witness your mother waste away like a starved dog at the dump. It's criminal, really, that animals get more compassion than humans crumbling from cancer. Where's Doc Kevorkian when you need him?" She rearranged a pillow behind her, grunting. "Father Flanagan sure wouldn't like to hear me say that, I can tell you."

"I don't remember a Father Flanagan," Summer said.

"He was the priest who married your father and I. A good man, gay as Liberace himself, which was obvious to anyone with working eyeballs. Married to the church, as they say." She coughed, a scary rattle, and Summer handed her water. "As if counseling cheating couples or baptizing babies brings any comfort on a cold night. I think he died of loneliness."

"How sad," Kathleen commented.

"Isn't it? The powers that be don't care, though. The so-called deviants can serve the laity, as long as they keep their pants zipped and their mouths shut—"

"*Mom.* Where on earth is this coming from? Is this the morphine talking?"

Whatever it was, Carol wouldn't be quieted. "Meanwhile, the parishioners are robbing the collection plate or cavorting with a best friend's wife. Then kneeling at the pews the next day." She sighed heavily. "You see these things firsthand when you're a part of committees, all that nonsense. I couldn't stand the hypocrisy. I sure won't miss that in the next world."

"Stop this, please. You need to save your energy—"

Carol's bony hand gripped her daughter with a strength

seemingly out of nowhere. "No. For what? I'm circling the drain, we all know it, and I'm going to say what I want to say. What am I saving my energy for? The big goodbye?"

"Don't talk like that," Summer choked through her tears.

"Honey, I know this is hard, but it's important. Listen to me, while I have the words, because we haven't discussed ... well, after I'm gone."

She hesitated as Summer's sobs echoed with the beeping machines.

Softer, this time, her mother continued, "This horrible disease has taken enough from me. You need to know I want to be cremated. Don't buy one of those eight-thousand-dollar caskets that likely fall apart five months after being in the wet ground. Hear me?"

"Yes."

Carol repositioned herself and pointed a twiggy finger at her daughter. "I want *you* to have that money, not some creepy caretaker. Don't let 'em railroad you, like they did me when your father died."

Later, Summer reported that plenty of sales attempts were made by Simon McAllister of McAllister and Sons Funeral Home. Each one expired midway through the pitch, like one of the bodies in the mortuary who'd met their end midway through dinner. Carol's ashes were buried in an inexpensive sealed container, next to her husband.

Kathleen had never forgotten that three o'clock in the morning hospital conversation.

"You think the 'afterlife' industry's a racket," Kathleen said to Summer.

"I don't think it, I know it."

"But even basic cremation is expensive. I don't think there's an insurance policy, either, the way Mallory's mother was talking to us."

Summer pulled up a barstool and asked Zack for a

drink. "Is there something we could do? Start one of those online fundraisers? Those seem to be all the rage, these days."

"I did bring that up. It was a hard pass."

They sat, contemplating various options.

Summer took a long draw of her Sister Celia's Sour. "Francesca asked me how they could help. She and Brianne feel terrible, of course. Sam, too."

"Yes. I need to meet with them—" Kathleen drifted off, staring blankly at the chalkboard taplist.

"What? What are you thinking?"

"I have an idea. Sort of."

"Let's hear it."

Kathleen groaned and rubbed her back. *Why* had she said anything? Summer could be like a bulldog with a chew toy, once she sniffed a scheme. She wouldn't let go. "I don't know. It probably wouldn't amount to anything."

"C'mon. It doesn't hurt to think out loud."

"Okay, okay. I was wondering if we could auction off our artwork and raise a few bucks that way. Sometimes, people really come together for a good cause. Plus, I'm telling you, Amanda's latest piece is stunning."

"You know what?" Summer's eyes narrowed. "We just might have enough artsy-fartsy second-homeowners around here that it could add up to more than a few bucks. And—" Her eyes inflated to their normal size, "—you, my dear, have tons of beautiful work sitting in that basement of yours. This could be an opportunity to finally dust off the cobwebs and get it out there!"

"Maybe. The next question would be the how and where."

There was a minute of exchanging various possibilities when Summer snapped her fingers.

"I've got it. How about we have it here? I was thinking

about doing a special Christmas celebration here. The auction would be a great addition to the festivities."

"Hmmm—"

"You two look like you're up to something." Zack placed another Sister Celia in front of Summer.

"Co-conspirators, that's us. Guess what? We've added an art auction benefit here to help raise money for Mallory and Amanda's families."

"Fantastic idea."

Thomas raised his glass for a refill, belatedly tuning in to the conversation. "What is?"

They explained to him and he nodded. "Ingenious. You'll have no problem getting people to buy your art. But I've told you that before."

Kathleen smiled. "Yes, you have. Many times."

Summer was in the middle of replying when six rambunctious young women came through the door, five of whom had matching white tees with "Bride Tribe" emblazoned in gold across the front. The presumed betrothed wore a low-cut, satiny white blouse and a mini veil.

"Our first booze bus of the day has arrived." Zack bowed out from the bar to greet them.

"Likely their first stop, so they won't be too obnoxious. Yet. Now, where were we?" She and Kathleen continued with the details of their plan, until the background noise became too loud to continue. "Sorry," Summer sighed. "I'd go tell Bridezilla to tone it down, but she's paying my bills. Do you wanna go in the back?"

"No, it's fine. We've got the basics covered. Thanks for your willingness to do this."

"Honey, it's the kind of thing Jeff and I talked about doing when we took this place on, hoping to be seen as an asset to the community. Not all of this town's leaders or congregations appreciate an old house of worship being turned into a tavern."

"It's more than a bar. I think that's obvious."

Summer laughed. "Don't you know it, ye who consecrated its grounds."

"Please! Will I ever live that down?"

"No. However, something about this joint *is* ethereal. So, I'm gonna say there's a good chance you were possessed that night."

Kathleen glanced at Thomas, who was now only paying attention to emptying his pint as fast as possible.

"Possessed, all right. By that dazzling creature guzzling your potions, trying to wash his pain away. And he drank down some pill when we first walked in. This night is probably not going to end well."

Summer patted her back. "No worries. We'll cut him off. Although I must say, after what he's been through, I can't blame the guy one bit."

Zack was behind the bar getting the party's orders when Bridezilla sauntered up. She leaned on the bar tipsily.

"Umm, sorry—Jack, was that your name?"

"It's Zack." He patiently asked if she needed something else.

"Yeah. Shelby and Hannah want to try the stout instead of that sour they ordered." She tapped a long, perfectly manicured nail (white) on the bar. "Oh, and we want an extra order of nachos, but leave off the gross white drizzly sauce that looks like somebody came all over the beans."

Ever unruffled, Zack simply said, "Got it."

She turned to leave, and upon spotting Thomas next to her, took a second look. She batted her fake eyelashes at him.

"Omigod. Aren't you that hot singer who used to be here on Friday nights?"

Thomas smiled slightly. "I did perform here on Fridays. They've had others, though—"

"It's you, all right. I wouldn't forget a face like yours. Or that voice."

"That's kind of you to say."

"Trust me, gorgeous. I'm a lot of things, but kind isn't one of them. Just ask my bride tribe!" She snorted, then hiccupped, observing him as well as she could in her current state. "What happened? You *rocked* it anytime we saw you here, and then you, like, disappeared."

"I actually went on tour."

"Yeah? Cool." She moved closer but didn't lower her voice any. "Listen, whoever has taken your place here is totally lame. It's a red-neck chick and her biker man singing a bunch of old country shit. Like Willie Nelson or something. You need to come back! Tell the owner Melanie said so!"

Summer rolled her eyes, while Thomas mustered a polite response.

"Thanks. We'll see. I've got a lot going on, right now."

She huffed, blowing her makeshift veil to the side. "Do you do weddings? Maybe you could do mine. And me." She giggled, then turned back to her group and yelled, "There ain't no ring on my finger yet. Is there, girls?" The girls hooted in excitement, and Melanie nearly fell in her too-high heels as she made her way back to the table.

Kathleen squeezed her forehead. "I'm ready to go home, hot singer from Friday night."

"Okay." He ordered a growler from Zack, who looked questioningly at her. She shrugged, too tired for a challenge.

"We don't do growlers of the stout. How about a crowler instead?"

"That's fine."

They said goodbye and were heading for the door when

Melanie's squeaky voice managed to make it across the room.

"Wait, are you leaving already? We didn't talk about my wedding, yet! Or my pre-wedding proposal!"

Thomas waved distractedly. "Congratulations!" he said, but it came out like, *"Congrashulashuns."* "Have fun, today."

He'd already opened the door with his back to them, but Kathleen did not miss the bride-to-be's disappointed pout, nor the sulky glare meant for her. "Yes, have fun!" she called out, laughing when the star for the day failed to return her thanks.

21

Kathleen spent a stressful afternoon staring at Thomas as he slept, watching his chest for movement like she suspected a mother of a newborn might. She studied the curvature of his face as she had so many times before, again, like a mother might, and wondered when he'd developed such a deep crease in-between his eyebrows. A line denoting pain. How much guilt and physical assault could one person take? She sighed, seesawing between frustration and empathy. The forehead line called to her, tugging at her like Lake Michigan's fierce undertow.

Rescue me. Shelter me from harm—

Like the splitting waves on the beach, she was divided by conflicting roles.

Except I'm not your mother. I'm going to BE a mother, of your children. How can I watch two babies and their father to make certain everyone is breathing? I'm not that capable. I'm not ...

The animals circled around the couch nervously, as if they sensed something was amiss. Hugo whined and Harriet tried to lay on Thomas' neck until Kathleen transplanted her to his feet. Her gaze went again to his chest, which seemed to raise ever slower. Was it her imagination? He twitched and moaned, occasionally, but he hadn't fully stirred once since they'd gotten home. As the minutes ticked by, she thought it was no longer sheer exhaustion contributing to his inertia. She shook him forcefully, panic climbing up her ribs. She put her fingers to his throat and detected a pulse, but still, his eyes wouldn't open.

"Thomas! Wake up. C'mon. You cannot do this, dammit."

She repeated his name, louder each time. Nothing. She felt pure hysteria rise and bubble through her, like overflowing liquid in a glass beaker, and along with it, two kicks in her belly.

She retrieved her phone and with shaking fingers punched 911. She prayed she hadn't waited too long to take action. When asked her emergency, her voice poured out in a mangled mess.

"Ma'am, slow down, I can't understand you."

She took a couple deep breaths, relayed the information, and was assured help was on the way.

Then she burst out with the most common request made to every dispatch operator in existence: "Please, hurry! Oh, God, please. Hurry."

Between her own brief visit and coming to see Brianne and baby Rose, Kathleen was getting a good feel for Lewiston Hospital. Even better, the antiseptic smell wasn't affecting her this time. She walked from the cafeteria to Thomas' room, sipping coffee, which tasted luxurious after not having it for weeks. A cup or two wasn't going to make a difference. Dr. Love had concurred, saying the idea of completely restricting pregnant Irish women from their tea was "frightful," and as such, she wasn't going to be hard and firm about caffeine with American patients, either.

She got to his room and was greeted in the hall by Courtney. Her pretty skin was blotchy under its late summer tan.

"Thank you for calling me. He looks and sounds absolutely terrible. Like when he was in the hospital after his leg—"

The memory was too much and Kathleen embraced her. "I'm sorry."

Courtney drew back and blew her nose into a tissue. "Forget about me. What about *you?* This is a stress no pregnant woman needs."

"I'm okay. If you want the truth, I'm just glad I was there. I've been worried about this exact thing happening for a while, and feeling powerless to stop it. The accident with the girls was the final trigger, I think." She relayed the details, some of which Thomas had told Courtney already.

Courtney nodded. "So awful, and it's not the first time he's blamed himself for someone else's death. I called my mom. Not sure how much Thomas has told you about all of our family dysfunction, but she's coming. She should be here tonight."

"That's good. And I don't know much about her specifically. I haven't pushed the issue."

"He's not happy about her coming, but I really don't care. It's time to put the past where it belongs. Thirty is too damned old to hold onto resentment, and now it's not just about him. Besides that, I believe there's a chance she can help him get healthy. Stabilized, at least."

"Do you?"

Courtney eyed Kathleen's coffee enviously. "I need one of those. Want to walk with me and we'll talk?"

The cafeteria was inviting as a hospital one could be,

with ergonomically correct seats and ambient lighting, and since it was still early in the day, it was mostly empty.

"Mom is a psychiatric nurse, too. It's how she met our dad, when he was a doctor at the same hospital."

"Ah. That's news to me, her being a nurse."

"Yes, and ... now, Joanne, my mom, has bought her own 'rehab' facility. Only, it's not your typical one; it's kinda woo-woo, I think. She's going to try to talk him into getting admitted." She exhaled deeply, staring into her cup. "God, I wish this was spiked."

Kathleen laughed. "Families are complicated. Always so many misunderstandings, hurts, wrong assumptions. I must be half-mad to be starting my own, I think."

"You're very strong. I sense it. In fact, in a lot of ways, you remind me of her."

"You're the second person to tell me that in less than a week, about being strong, and I've never felt that way about myself. Ever."

Courtney swallowed the last of her coffee. "Buckle up, buttercup. With twins on the way and all the baggage accompanying their father, you're in for quite the ride. Good thing you said you're feeling better."

"I am. But, also ... I'd really like to meet Joanne when she's here, if she's willing."

"Oh, God, yes. She's been grilling me nonstop. I'll make it happen."

At that moment Courtney's phone rang. "It's Jake." She talked for a few seconds, then addressed Kathleen. "I'm sorry, I gotta go pick Allie up. Talk to you soon."

She nodded and headed back to Thomas' room, her belly sinking with every step. He'd been conscious for a while, but not talking in anything other than monosyllables.

She found herself wishing her coffee was spiked too.

Thomas lay in the hospital bed like one of the patients from a Hollywood-imagined asylum: immobile, expressionless, his chestnut hair spilling out onto the pillow the only spot of color to be found in a sea of neutrals. His gaze was on the muted television, and it didn't waver when she sat down next to him. She stroked his wrist, amidst the IV tubes. "I just saw Courtney."

Silence, another reaction she was unused to from him.

"Thomas, I—"

"You shouldn't have called for an ambulance."

She stiffened. "Seems like strange advice coming from a nurse. What should I have done? Watch you die on my couch?"

He laughed scornfully. "After taking Norco and a few drinks? Highly doubtful. Worst-case scenario is a coma, which obviously didn't happen."

"It didn't happen because you got the medical care you needed," she said between gritted teeth.

"Yeah. Too bad for both of us, maybe."

She wanted to slap him, slap the condescending impudence off his face, until she remembered that this is what depression looked and acted like. She straightened her aching spine and unclenched her jaw. "You were unresponsive. And do you really think your children and I would be better off without you?"

He gave a barely perceptible shrug.

"We need you. How can you not see that—"

She should've known the lens he was looking through wouldn't allow for clarity of any kind.

Finally, he turned to her, anger radiating from his whole body. "You don't need a fucked-up drug addict and wannabe musician for a partner, who ends up hurting everyone he comes into contact with. I told you months ago this is why I'm not cut out for the domestic life. You can't say I didn't warn you."

She silently counted to five. Fury was better than his apathy, at any rate.

She leaned into the bedrail. "Guess what. *I* get to decide what I need. And, yes, that's a partnership, in which both people stay. Partners who don't turn with their tail tucked under when it gets rough."

"Then you picked the wrong guy."

"I don't think so."

"You should go." He went back to the screen, the anger hardening to cold.

"Fine. After you listen to my last speech for the day." She stood up and braced herself to sound fiercer than she felt. "I'm in this for the long run, and I want you when you're ready. I will be here, because, to quote you directly, 'what we have is stronger than any obstacles.'" She bent over and kissed him on his tepid forehead.

"I'll be waiting," she whispered, hoping he heard her through the lies in his mind.

Kathleen touched up her makeup at the stoplight and thought about what she'd say tonight. She'd set up a time with Francesca and Brianne to talk about her fundraising plan and a few other things, and she hoped it went well. Earlier, she'd contacted Connie Romanski, and to Kathleen's surprise, she'd received the idea with little hesitation. They'd had Mallory cremated, but that was all they could do, and even that had maxxed out what little credit that had left.

"The proceeds wouldn't be 'charity,'" Kathleen

explained, because Mallory had been a part of the artwork, and Amanda's family was also onboard.

Connie said, "Yes, I suppose that's true about the charity part. And every little bit helps," she added, as if she weren't sure adolescent sketches would amount to anything.

Kathleen wasn't sure, either, but they had to try. She pulled into the parking lot and unlocked the door to the church's community room. Within five minutes, both girls were there. Francesca, looking ready to pop, and Brianne already almost as slim as her pre-baby self.

Kathleen hugged them both. "No Rosie?"

"My dad is off from work today, and wanted to spend time with her. So, I got a lot of stuff done, and he gets to change diapers."

"That's what I call a win-win."

Brianne yawned. "What I should've done is take a nap. I am so tired, with her waking at night to nurse." She glanced over at Francesca, whose almond eyes did not have blue-tinged circles under them. "Want some advice? Sleep now. While you can."

"Oh, God, I wish. This child is caving into my back and I cannot get comfortable at night. The doc thinks it won't be long now. I'm two centimeters dilated."

Kathleen set out the banana-nut muffins Brianne had baked. "Are you all ready for the big day? Do you need anything?"

Francesca slowly eased into a chair. She wrapped her long hair up into a bun. "I think we're good. We're staying in the Airbnb house I told you about before, and between Summer and my aunt and grandma, we've got all the baby stuff. For the beginning, at least."

"Good. I'm glad."

They sat around the table and Kathleen lit a candle and put it in the middle. The empty seats staring back at them were a stark reminder of who was absent. The effect was much like when Kathleen sat at the first grief-filled Thanksgiving feast after her dad died. It was all her brother could do to carve the turkey, and even then, everyone picked at the food that had taken hours to prepare.

"No sense in ignoring the elephant in the room. Why don't we begin with special prayers for Amanda and Mallory?" Kathleen tried to sound upbeat.

"What does that mean, elephant in the room?" Francesca asked, truly puzzled.

"It means there's this big thing that's impossible to ignore, but people do it anyway, because they're stupid," Brianne offered. "Or they don't have the balls to face whatever it is." She looked quickly at Kathleen. "Sorry. You probably know a better way to say it than me."

Kathleen smiled. "Actually, you summed it up well. I thought it better to acknowledge this loss we are all feeling, off the bat."

They held hands, which they'd never done sitting around the table before, but now it felt right.

Somehow, she plundered through the words she'd prepared, between wiping her eyes and wrangling and laughing with the other two over the Kleenex box. They talked about the expenses involved in prolonged hospital care, and those involved in funeral services. Predictably, the girls had no idea how fast the costs added up, though Brianne had an inkling due to her recent stay.

"Thousands?" Francesca's bow-like mouth dropped. "It costs *thousands* of dollars just to get cremated or buried?"

"It can, yes. Depending on insurance policies and what kind of services people want."

Brianne said quietly, "I'm guessing Amanda's and Mallory's families don't have that kind of money."

"Truthfully, girls, it's not for me to say. But regardless of circumstances, I think we can do something to help, so hear me out." She went on to detail the art fundraising, and the skeptical expressions on the two of them made her laugh. "What? You don't like the idea?"

Brianne shifted uncomfortably in her chair. "No, that's not it. It's just ... who would buy our lame little pictures? Except for yours and Amanda's, that is?"

"For real," Francesca agreed.

"First of all, they're not 'lame little pictures.' They are well-done pieces depicting life as young people. And communities usually do come together to support good causes."

There were a few seconds of exchanging glances, and Francesca said, "Well, why not? What were we gonna do with them anyhow?"

Brianne shrugged. "Ya, you're right. I'm good with it. Especially if there's a chance it could help."

"It will. And thank you."

Kathleen talked about the auction being part of HopCanon's holiday activities, as well as other discussion points, then got out a journal and pen. "On another note, I wanted to ask you two something else. I've met with Sheila Gallagher to discuss this and she agreed. What would you think about taking over these meetings yourselves, for other pregnant girls?"

They stared at her, uncomprehending, with Francesca the first to respond. "What? Us, lead a group, you mean? I haven't even been to church in ages. Plus, what would we *do* with them?"

Kathleen laughed, remembering the very words out of her mouth to Sheila, months ago. "Those things don't matter, I assure you. It's having a safe space to talk, and caring people around, that matters. Wouldn't you agree?"

"Yeah," Brianne said. "But why? Don't you want to do it anymore?"

"It's not that so much, but there's a couple reasons for me to take a break. One is that girls might be more likely to attend and share if they are with older peers who have been through exactly what they are experiencing. The other reason is, two babies are going to be taking up a lot of my time, soon."

"Still," Brianne's brow wrinkled. "We really don't know much more than they would. Don't you think we need more time to have a little street cred?"

"Not at all. Look what you've learned in the last months, and are continuing to learn with your new baby. If it makes you feel better, Sheila said you could get a little training, and they would provide childcare for the meetings. I could also help out here and there." She looked with affection at their young and doubtful faces. "Please think about it. You're both mature and responsible, and there are two newly-pregnant girls in the wings we've just learned about, who might be interested in joining."

They promised to mull it over, and before they knew it, it was time to clean up.

"Once again, delicious muffins, Brianne."

"Thanks, Ms. K. Do you want to take that last one back for Thomas?"

Kathleen hesitated ever so briefly, but it was enough.

"Or you could just take it for yourself—"

"Thank you, honey. Thomas isn't—I won't go into detail, but he's not well. Physically, mentally. I think in a couple months, after getting some good care, he'll be fine."

"Like, he's doing a rehab thing?" Francesca asked.

"That's the plan. I don't know a whole lot, yet."

"But he'll be okay, right?"

Their empathetic eyes made her own water. "I hope so. I really hope so."

Brianne suggested that their closing prayer be dedicated to him, so Kathleen cobbled a few words together as they held hands again. It was the perfect way to end their night, and what might be their last meeting together for a long time.

"That's got to be her."

Summer jerked her head to the right, at an attractive, willowy woman who looked to be in her late fifties. She'd entered HopCanon and was being seated by one of the servers.

"Yes, I think you're right."

Kathleen smoothed her hair and put on lipstick. She'd worked an afternoon shift and had asked Joanne, Thomas' mother, if she wanted to join her afterward. Kathleen wasn't too sure how that would go over, given Joanne's vocation, but she'd insisted it'd be fine.

"Do I look forty? I'm ridiculously nervous."

Summer surveyed her with a critical eye. "Your hair is shiny, skin glowing, what every pregnant woman wishes she looked like. Or any woman, pregnant or not. She'll love you, regardless, just like her son does." She laughed. "Well, maybe not in the *same* way—"

Kathleen shook her head and approached the table. "Joanne?"

"Yes! Kathleen!"

Her face wrapped into a wide smile that Kathleen knew so intimately it was almost eerie. There was little doubt where Thomas' looks came from. She had the same lovely skin and thick red-brown hair, albeit with random streaks of grey and cut in a stylish bob. She stood up, a good four inches above Kathleen, and took both her hands and squeezed gently. "Oh, my. I just can't believe this. You ... you're stunning."

Kathleen chuckled. "Definitely not feeling it, but thank you, nonetheless."

"It's so good to meet you. Of course, I didn't know anything about *anything* until Courtney filled me in. Here, please, sit."

They did, and Kathleen took a deep breath. "I realize this is incredibly awkward. You didn't think the first time you met your son's fiancé she'd be six months pregnant."

"Well, no, but I'm lucky to be meeting you at all, I think. Courtney told you some of why, I gather."

"Some. I'm glad you're here. Thomas will be, too. Soon, I hope."

Joanne's hazel eyes clouded. "Maybe not soon, but I'm okay with that. He's been angry for a long time. It won't get worked through overnight." She blinked, and the bright smile was back. "But before we go there, I should have a look at the taplist. What do you recommend? I do enjoy a nice beer, every now and then."

"Let's see. I usually leave that to our illustrious bartender Zack, but he's off today."

They went on to discuss what styles of beer she preferred, and Kathleen went behind the bar and chose a new pale ale they'd tapped only hours ago. "Here you are." She set the pint down in front of Joanne. "Divine Providence."

Joanne's head reared back as she laughed, the wave of her bouncing hair reminiscent of Thomas, once more. "Bring it on. Divine Providence is something I could use right about now."

"Couldn't we all."

Joanne looked around at the remodeled church in wonder. "What a fantastic idea, to do this. Almost like repurposing."

"It's amazing what it's doing for our beach town. And its inhabitants. This is where I met Thomas."

"Please, do tell me."

Kathleen did, leaving out how quickly she and Thomas got acquainted, but still hoping to communicate the strength of their deep bond. They talked and talked, and it was easy. Joanne was warm, funny, and open about her family's difficulties.

"I always worried more about Thomas, even when he was a toddler. Courtney was just so much *tougher.* She was the proverbial duck, water rolling off her back at every challenge, while he—oh, how do I say it? The arrows of life stung him deeply from day one."

"How do you mean? Overly-sensitive?"

Joanne squiggled in her chair. "It was more than that, and hard to explain. He took everything in, whether we had a bad day, or he did, or a friend did. He couldn't seem to find boundaries. These days, he's what they call an 'empath.' That in itself has to be exhausting."

"Yes. From the minute I met him, I was aware of his pain. His struggles."

"And it didn't chase you off?"

"Far from it." Kathleen's ears grew hot, remembering how she'd stared in awe and lust at his scarred, naked body the morning after they'd first met. "I think he was surprised by that."

Joanne sipped her beer and said sadly, "Probably, because that's what he thought women did. They leave, like his mother."

"I don't know. If he does think that, perhaps it's time to move beyond it. And forgive."

Their server, Deirdre, came with the burgers they'd ordered. In-between bites, they discussed his potential treatment.

"It took a little angry persuading, but Thomas agreed to come to my facility, Pine Rest."

"Angry persuading?"

Joanne's lips thinned. "He's going to be a father and presumably a husband. Let's just say I had to remind him of those facts and it wasn't exactly pleasant."

Kathleen could only imagine how that scene had gone down.

"Anyway, I got through to him. That's what's important." She sighed heavily. "Pine Rest is a wonderful place. What you'd call holistic. Meaning, we treat the whole person and not just one facet of their illness."

"That makes sense." Kathleen nodded. "I'm curious as to what a typical day might look like."

"Typical varies for each patient, but it will likely be a combination of activities. Talk therapy, massage and other bodywork, meditation, exercise, and exploring various drug therapies."

"Will he go into withdrawal?"

Joanne shrugged. "To a degree. But it's important you understand that Thomas may never be able to be weaned off of pain pills completely. The fact is, opiates work, even with all the risks they encompass. What we will do is try to get him to a manageable state. Whatever that takes."

"Of course."

"Then there's the depression issue. He admitted to me he hasn't been on meds for months." She took another drink and her pint was gone. "Not to get too personal, but it's quite common. Young men who get into passionate relationships tend to go off antidepressants. Once they're flooded with all the ecstatic hormones a new love brings, they figure they can skip out. And they also skip out due to the ... em, side effects. You can hardly blame them."

"I've wondered about that. I've wondered if meeting me was ever good for him." Kathleen's chest tightened at the thought, at the idea their endless hours of pleasure had somehow led to this.

Joanne leaned into the table toward her. "No. Put that out of your head right now. Trust me when I say you and these babies coming are a very good thing."

"Well, it's not, if he doesn't take the medicine he needs to function."

Joanne pinned her with the intense gaze she knew so well. "His doctor will work with him on that, I promise you. There are so many new options, now. Or it may well be that once we get him on an even keel, without the external pressures he's been dealing with, he won't need to take them. The human body is a miraculous machine." She pressed her long, graceful fingers onto Kathleen's. "This is not your fault."

"Yes, but—"

She shook her head forcefully. "No. Thomas has much to work through personally that has contributed to where he is. Issues with me, with his father's memory, and in-between all that, his career choices. But, as fragile as I thought he was, he really isn't. It takes an enormous amount of will to both carry that emotional baggage and fight off daily physical pain."

"I agree. It's actually impressive, until it became too much ... the touring, this pregnancy, then the accident."

"I know. In all honesty I think that may have triggered post-traumatic stress for him. Of his own accident."

Kathleen sat up straight. "I never thought of that."

"You know what? For the next few weeks, it might be a good idea to forget it all. Focus on your babies, your own wellbeing." Joanne swallowed the last bite of her burger. "He'll get the best care possible, the best supports, and he'll come out of this. He might come out still hating me, but you and becoming a family is what matters here."

"He doesn't hate you."

"I can take it. He's had sporadic contact with me for, what, eight years? What's a few more months, if it gets him healthy? Or healthier?"

Kathleen whistled through her teeth. "Eight years. That's a long time. Too long."

"It is. And I won't pretend, it hurt. It hurt like hell, but I respected his wish for space. I prayed nonstop for answers."

"I'll bet. How did you ... manage?"

"I came to accept God had his own timeline, and I'm glad, because now it's been revealed." She smiled again, that same charismatic grin. "I've got tough skin and I'm a determined mother. I get the feeling you have that, too."

After more conversation about babies and parenting, they walked to their cars. Joanne and Thomas had a flight early in the morning, and Courtney would be dropping them off at the airport.

"One last thing," Kathleen said, "What about visits and phone calls?"

"They're encouraged, but not in the beginning. He's resistant to everything, at this point."

Kathleen's head dipped down. "Don't I know it."

Joanne gently put a finger under her chin and tilted it up. "Keep the faith, Kathleen. He knows how much you love him. I saw it in his eyes when I got him to talk about you, and it's going to save him. In a way that I couldn't, with his own father." Her finger dropped back down, as did her face. "That wasn't from lack of caring. On the contrary, our relationship was quite ... tumultuous. I used to romanticize it, thinking we were like Liz Taylor and Burton."

Kathleen was immediately intrigued. "That's a famous love story if there ever was one."

"Ha. Maybe for Liz and Dick, but the only place we were famous was the hospital where we worked." She crossed her arms. "Henry had women after him *constantly.* Hell, probably men, too, now that I think of it. Nurses, interns, therapists, orderlies. Just openly propositioning him, knowing he was married."

Kathleen was afraid to ask if he'd taken the bait. "I've never understood how people could do that."

Joanne laughed. "Trust me, it wasn't hard to see why. He was the total package. An extremely gifted doctor, compassionate with his pain patients, and God knows you'd never in a million years get tired of looking at the man. Here, I carry an old wedding picture around. You'll see."

She dug into her wallet and showed Kathleen. The photo was creased and faded, but there it was. The shape of Thomas' face. The dimple. His *hands.* And the way he was looking at his wife. "Oh, my God."

"Right? Then there was me. Young, insecure, insanely jealous, hot-tempered. And completely obsessed with him. Not a good combination."

Kathleen returned the picture reluctantly. "I can relate, to some extent. Except I'm not young. Or excessively hot-tempered." She looked sheepish. "Um, if you don't count when I told Thomas, in a raging fit, that he had to fire his Playboy bunny-looking band manager."

They laughed at this, and Joanne went on. "I do understand. Love, especially the fear of losing it, can make you irrational. We both behaved abysmally, and the constant drama was terrible for the children. That's my biggest regret." She sighed deeply and put the picture back in her wallet.

"Thomas thinks I left for another man, which isn't true. I

haven't dated anyone since his father. I have no desire to, either. A huge part of me died when he did."

"Wow. That sounds tragically unfair or something."

"It was something, all right. We never even got officially divorced. We couldn't bring ourselves to do it."

"That's just heartbreaking."

"Maybe. Still, I wouldn't have traded it for anything." She waved a hand. "I apologize for this silly background story. I have no idea why I said any of it."

"It's not at all silly. Thomas once told me we have a connection other people wait their whole lives for. While at the time I sort of dismissed it as corny, I think he's right. You had it, too."

Joanne smiled, but it didn't reach her eyes, glossy from blinked-back tears. "Perhaps. In any case, I feel strongly there's a much better ending in store for you, my dear."

They hugged goodbye, each promising to stay in touch, and for one second, Kathleen's longing for Thomas was eased.

His mother holding her was as close as she could get to him. For now, it would have to be enough.

22

October's colors faded into the usual grey-sky glum of November, but Kathleen hardly noticed. Her mindset was all about the famous nesting she'd read about in her pregnancy books. Turned out that, in addition to managing HopCanon, Zack also worked for his dad, a licensed contractor. He casually mentioned it one day, and delighted, Kathleen hired them to expand one of the upstairs bedrooms into a nursery. She was challenged and liberated by the array of choices to make. Designs, colors, different lines to pick from for this and for that. For the first time in her life, she alone got to make the important decisions. No consulting anyone, or arguing, or giving in to avoid a fight.

A small part of her was sad that Thomas wasn't a participant in this, but there was nothing to be done about it. She wouldn't let it steal her joy. She stood in the doorway looking at the debris. "I can have zebra stripes if I want," she said out loud, then laughed. That wasn't really her style. She'd already settled on a primary color theme, and had ordered two cribs that Zack and Megan offered to help put together. This was the fun part, she knew. The tough stuff was yet to come. The stuff that had nothing to do with décor, something Megan reminded her of at the baby shower Summer had hosted a few days before.

Megan was set to graduate in December, weeks from the babies' due date. "I was thinking about something," she said to Kathleen, in-between bites of chocolate cupcake.

"Let me guess. Starting your vet practice?"

"No, but that's definitely on the table." Her green eyes were wide and serious. "This is about you."

"Okay. What's up?"

"I guess I just want to say that if Thomas ... well, if he's still gone when the babies get here, I could easily move back in for a couple months. To, you know, be a big sister and help you."

The offer was so out of the blue, Kathleen didn't know what to say.

Megan laughed. "Don't look so shocked. I know I was never the babysitting type, but I'm a quick study. And I'm kind of a night owl, so I could take a shift of feeding, or whatever it is they need at three in the morning."

"Honey, what a sweet and thoughtful gesture. I may just take you up on it, if ..." Kathleen looked away. She couldn't bear to think about the alternative, but the fact was she needed to, and it seemed ridiculous it took her own step-daughter to make her see that. "If things don't work out."

Megan tsked. "They will. But a Plan B is always a good idea. Another Dad-ism."

"Yes. Along with Follow-up Plans C, D, and E."

They laughed. Kathleen knew Steve might not have approved of her current situation, but he'd be proud of Megan for trying to help cover the bases.

"Zack could stay, too, if it came to that," Kathleen said, grinning. "If you guys are still avoiding celibacy. Or not."

Megan hooted loudly. "I'll be sure to let him know.

Could be a good practice run." Before Kathleen could ask a practice run for what, Megan continued. "He does want the whole enchilada. Wife, kids, et cetera. I'll tell you something else, just between us. Good ol' wine, spiller of truth." She sipped from the glass that had complemented the chocolate cake quite nicely. "You won't believe this ... heck, even I can't ... but he wants me."

Kathleen scoffed. "What's so hard to believe about that? You're beautiful, smart—"

Megan's head dipped down and she whispered. "No, no. I mean he wants me as a *wife,* without knowing what I would be like. Physically. In bed."

Kathleen stared, not certain how far to probe with this unexpected turn in the conversation. "I see—"

"No, you don't, but I'll fill you in. At almost twenty-five, I'm still a virgin." She giggled. "Are you surprised?"

Kathleen cleared her throat. "No." Although she was, a little. Not that Megan had loose morals, but maintaining one's virginity, these days, past one's teens seemed unlikely. "I do remember dating never rated high on your list."

"Right. I thought something was wrong with me. As did Mom. Now I know it was the few losers I did date that were the problem." Another swig of wine and a snort. "The first time I was alone with Zack, I could barely restrain myself. *He* was telling *me* to stop, if you can imagine that. I think he's freaked out he'd be the first, and I'm freaked out he's talking marriage."

"Has he actually proposed?"

"No, but we've talked about the future. A lot."

"And other than freaked out, what are you thinking?"

She shrugged. "Before him ... it was a definite no, nada, never. He's the only guy I've met who gives me second thoughts. Like, major second thoughts. He says the same about me. Is that weird, after just meeting each other weeks ago?"

"Not necessarily." *Weeks? Try getting blindsided after one night ...*

Megan wiped the last bit of frosting off her lips. "I'm sorry for the TMI. I can't really talk about this with my friends. They already think I'm an oddball as it is. And they'd definitely think he was, if they knew. I mean, I always thought it was only holy-roller guys that wanted to 'wait' for the sanctity of marriage."

"I think Zack's highly spiritual."

"Yes, he is, but, you know, not so much in the traditional sense."

Kathleen gathered the torn wrapping paper on the table. "It doesn't matter one way or the other. People spend far too much time judging things they're clueless about. Let your friends think what they will. Their jaws will drop when they meet him."

"Ha! You're right." Her face lit up. "He is so gorgeously unique, isn't he?"

"In more ways than one. Sounds like you've got some tough decisions ahead."

"Ah, I dunno. I'm in love, not gonna lie. But let's be real, a couple months around crying, pooping twins, it could go either way. Fate's a funny thing, isn't it?"

Kathleen had agreed fate was indeed fickle, and then Summer signaled the shower's end by reminding all the guests to take their goodie bags home.

She wobbled over to the dresser placed in the hallway temporarily. Zack had laid out a dozen paint sticks in varying shades of white for her to peruse. She sighed and rubbed her belly, which she felt had gotten exponentially bigger in the last week. At her latest appointment, Dr. Love assured her the babies were a perfect size and in position for a routine birth. She'd asked if Kathleen wanted to know their gender, but without Thomas' input, she'd declined. The good doctor had, thank God, asked no more questions about him.

She picked up two sticks and frowned. Comparing identical-looking paint samples was still easier than contemplating labor, delivery, and the myriad ways life could go either way.

"*I miss you.*"

It was Thanksgiving. Kathleen was dozing in a post-turkey haze in her mother's living room when her phone dinged. She was quickly roused into wakefulness with Thomas' text, the first one she'd gotten since he'd left. Her fingers trembled as she returned the message, and her belly kicked wildly.

"I miss you, too. So much. I wasn't sure when or if I should reach out to you. How are you doing?"

"I'll be all right. Just had some kind of tofu turkey, here, and canned cat food would've been better. Ha! Mostly, the food has been good, though. Therapy and all the other stuff IS helping. Probably get a few songs out of this nightmare, anyway. Are you okay? Babies okay?"

The conversation went on briefly, with Thomas telling her he had to go to a yoga class, soon, and would be in touch. He sent her one more message.

"I'm sorry for all this, Kath. There's so much more I need to say to you, but our time is so structured even a phone call is hard. I'm sorry for how I was in the hospital and for being an asshole. You do deserve better, but please, please, don't give up on us."

The last phrase made her think of an old song and she laughed.

"Glad to see you smiling." Peggy sat on the couch with a plate of pumpkin and pecan pie. "Now, have some treats. We need to plump up my grandchildren. You were such a teeny baby I'm thinking they probably will be, too."

Kathleen ate two pieces loaded with whipped cream, and nothing had ever tasted so delicious. She picked up her phone.

"You forgot to add 'baby' at the end of your sentence. 'Don't give up on us, baby.' Another song from my Pandora playlist, by the guy who starred in Starsky and Hutch, back in the day. Credit my brothers again for that trivia."

He didn't answer, having left for his class, but she laughed at imagining his reaction, and from the utter relief at finally hearing from him.

Everything will be all right.

She believed it for the first time, with the same strength she believed God was good, that the sun would rise, and that Santa was real. She leaned her head back, pure gratefulness coursing through her, when her phone rang. It was Summer.

"Guess where we are?"

"Hmm. On the couch, digesting a feast?"

"No." Summer's voice was high and tinny with excitement. "At the hospital. Francesca and Sam are the parents of a boy, James Francis Martin. After her dad, and ..."

"And your dad, Frank," Kathleen finished.

"I'm sorry, I gotta blow my nose." She did, then said, "Can I tell you how much I miss my parents, right now? I'm bawling more than the baby."

"I know, sweetie. They'd be over the moon."

They talked details. James was a healthy eight pounds, born early in the morning after many hours of labor. Everyone was doing well and resting comfortably.

"It's such a miracle," Summer said. "I mean, you know it is, but you forget."

"I'm so happy for all of you. Can I visit, tomorrow?"

"Yes, but promise me you won't gloat."

Kathleen laughed. "What are you talking about?"

"You were the one saying, all along, Francesca and Sam were gonna be fine. You should see them now. They're like two cooing birds in paradise, holding this child. I don't think Sam's ever been so happy. Oh, God, I'm *never* living this down."

"Here's the deal. You stop rubbing my nose in the sacred events of HopCanon, and I swallow my told-you-sos with more pecan pie."

"Deal. And Happy Thanksgiving, my friend. I love you."

"Happy Thanksgiving. Back at ya."

She hung up and looked around, at her brothers and their families shouting over the football game, the kids fighting over Monopoly, at the normalcy that could be snuffed out in an instant by a twist of fate. Were the Romanskis having dinner now? Were they crying over an uneaten turkey and staring at the wall, uncomprehending? People at this minute were in rehab, recovering in a hospital, giving birth, and dying and grieving. It was the Ying and Yang of existence, the dark in the light and the light in the dark. Truths revealed.

She took one last forkful of pumpkin, savoring the velvety texture. Perhaps she needed to entertain the possibility the times she'd been accurate in her life were equal to the times she'd been mistaken. Maybe even outnumbered them, at some point. Had anyone kept count, other than those in the education world?

"You know so much more than you think you do."

Words straight from the mouth of Mr. Allen Harrington, a wise and kind math teacher she'd had in high school. He'd tried, on numerous occasions, to help untwist the stubborn mind blocks that stonewalled her as soon as a test appeared. It hadn't worked then, but it was working now, even if confusing algebraic formulas weren't part of the mix.

She smiled, thinking about the bespectacled, fussy-ish man with the wispy combover. Kids had made fun of him for being the stereotypical absentminded professor type, but she always remembered how he'd refused to give up on her. "Thank you, Mr. Harrington."

"What was that, dear?" Peggy was there with more dessert, which Kathleen took from her hands.

"Ah, nothing. Just thinking of something a teacher said to me a long time ago. Turns out he was right."

The Christmas rush was in full tilt, as was the fundraising party preparation at HopCanon. Summer and Kathleen christened the event "Advent, Ales, and Art!" The whole staff was involved in the planning and execution, from the servers to the back of the house. Spirits were high as the brewers tasted and named their new seasonal selections, and Jeff brought out a tray of samples for everyone to try afterhours.

"Here we go, folks. From the left it's Gift of the Magi, Oh Hoppy Night, Away in a Lager, All I Want for Christmas are Belgians, and Drummer Boy's Dunkel." He picked up the last glass and handed it to Kathleen. "And for all the child-bearing ladies and designated drivers, here's 'Mary's Mule,' a nonalcoholic brown ale."

Kathleen laughed. "How perfect. Thank you."

Once the sampling was over, Summer took out Christmas ornaments and laid them on two long tables, while Kathleen attended to setting up the artwork on easels.

She had to admit that, in addition to displaying the girls' pieces, it was a great feeling to have her work out of the basement and on display. Even if none of them fetched sizable bids. She surveyed Amanda's sketch, impressed anew with the shadowing and detail in Thomas' image. Indeed, she noticed something different every time she studied the canvas.

"Thank you for stopping by," Kathleen said to June, when she'd dropped off the picture. "Saves me a trip. How are the roads?"

June shook her head, her frayed knit hat sprinkled with melting snowflakes. "Ahh, they're fine. And thank *you,*" she said in her gravelly voice, before dissolving in a coughing fit. "Sorry. Gotta give up the damned cancer sticks. Anyway, I don't know what we'd'a done without all your support the last coupla months. Amanda is so excited for this shindig, wheelchair or not. She gets tired and cranky real quick, so we won't stay long, but it's all she can talk about."

June had left hurriedly. She needed to get home to take Amanda to another physical therapy session, and she was borrowing her neighbor's car because the battery in hers was shot.

There was a knock on the taproom door and Kathleen turned to find Brianne laden with a huge platter of cookies coming her way.

"Hi there. My, those look absolutely scrumptious. You made my favorite, thumbprints!"

"Are they? I'll have to remember that."

She'd also made the traditional sugar rollouts, gingerbread families, chocolate drops, peanut butter kisses, and some fun reindeer pretzel bites. "They *are* yummy, even if I say so myself. But I do want feedback."

"For your bakery in the making?"

Brianne smiled. "One day. Right now, I'm a little busy."

She took a deep breath and exhaled. "It smells so good in here, like pine—"

"Yes, look over there. Zack and Megan went to the tree farm and brought that beauty back." Kathleen gestured to the big spruce stationed in the other half of the taproom. The pointy top was mere inches away from the ceiling.

"It's ginormous! I told Matt I wanted a real tree this year, but it's just a tabletop one. We don't have room in our apartment for anything bigger."

"I'm sure it's lovely. Your first one as a family makes it special, no matter what."

Brianne caressed a blue-green branch thoughtfully. "That's kinda what Matt said."

Kathleen rubbed her back and sat on a nearby chair.

"Geez, you're really getting big," Brianne observed. Seeing Kathleen's expression, she laughed. "Sorry. Like you didn't know that. You must be close."

"Anytime, but technically, December twenty-eighth."

Brianne handed her a strawberry-filled thumbprint cookie. "Are you scared?" she asked bluntly.

"The unknown is always a bit scary." Kathleen bit into the cookie, making mmm sounds. "Can you offer any advice?"

Brianne laughed. "Now, that's funny. An adult asking a screw-up teen for childbirth advice?"

"You're not a screw-up. It's a legit question."

"I don't know, Ms. K. It hurts a lot, a hundred times worse than period cramps, so be ready? Especially that episiotomy thing, later on. Your boobs, too, when they suck, at first. So, you have to keep this ointment stuff on them in-between the times they eat." She shrugged dismissively. "Everything about it is painful, I guess, but you do forget right away. There. I didn't tell you a single thing you didn't already read about, did I?"

"Probably not, but it makes a difference coming from someone who's actually gone through the experience."

"I hope ..." Brianne brushed her black bangs away from her face awkwardly. "I hope Thomas will be there. With you."

God willing, Brianne. God willing.

She smiled faintly. "I do, too. I heard from him, recently. He's doing better."

Brianne's face crinkled with a huge smile. "Really? We all knew, or hoped, he'd pull through. Especially Amanda. She had total faith in you guys. How's she doing, by the way? I've been texting her, but she doesn't answer."

"I was trying to contact her, too. Amanda isn't purposely ignoring anyone. Her grandma said she gets easily overwhelmed. She *is* better, but even simple tasks like texting are a challenge."

"Will she be here, tomorrow?"

"Yes. June said for a little while."

"Oooh, good. I was hoping she'd be able to come."

"Just be prepared, honey. A traumatic brain injury can mean changes in a person's speech, memory, personality. The Amanda we know might be a very different version, now."

Brianne nodded. "I feel so bad for her. What about Mallory's family? Are they coming?"

"I don't think so. Everything is still too raw, at this point."

Brianne walked to the table with tree ornaments and picked up a gold one with a nativity scene emblazoned in the center. "I've been thinking a lot about something." She turned and held up the ornament. "Why does God let bad things happen? How does He *decide?* It's just bugging me so bad."

The spasm that came and went in Kathleen's back throbbed. She had neither the knowledge nor the energy for a deep theological discussion, but she remembered what Thomas said to her about listening. About how it was one of her gifts.

"I'll tell you this much. There's no explanation everyone agrees on, or even if God is responsible. What's bothering you the most?"

Brianne was silent for a few seconds. The glittery trim on the ornament caught the light and sparkled as she turned it in her hands. She said quietly, "I guess I wonder why I'm the lucky one. I almost went with them that night. I didn't go because I had to pick my dad up from work. He doesn't drive cuz of his old DUIs. Normally his girlfriend, Angelina, would've, but she was busy."

"Do you feel guilty that you weren't in the car, too?"

"Maybe. But isn't it bizarre how if only one thing changes, another thing doesn't happen? Like 9/11. The people who missed their flights for the planes that crashed. Or the ones in the towers that forgot something and left the area right before it went down. That did happen, ya know. I read about it for a school assignment."

"Yes. It is bizarre."

Brianne set the ornament down. "If God is supposedly in charge of it all, why is one person favored over another? Or is it all just random chance?"

Kathleen shook her head. "You know I can't answer that. And whoever does will be famous for eternity. When you think about it, though, not knowing makes it easier to surrender control to God. We spend so much time trying to orchestrate every minute, isn't it kind of a relief to give it all to Him?"

"But if you do that and He lets someone die, how do you not get angry?"

"Who says you don't? It's when the anger takes over and turns into bitterness is when it's a problem."

"I was on Facebook the other day, in this group for teen moms, and this girl said, 'If you worship a phantom king who lives in the sky, you've got bigger problems than worrying about your baby dying in a crib.'"

"That's her opinion, her belief system. Shared by many."

Brianne looked down at her chest, startled. "Crap. A sign I need to go. I'm starting to leak." She grabbed her wallet and coat. "Thanks for the talk. See ya tomorrow."

She was out the door in a flash. That's how teens rolled: from exploring the meaning of life to time to breastfeed in the span of five minutes. Kathleen chuckled tiredly and closed her eyes to rest.

"You doing okay?" Summer hovered over her in concern.

"Yep. Just recharging from a 'Big Question' conversation with Brianne. Hoping I didn't botch it."

"Not possible. Those girls think you walk on water."

"Ha! I'd float to the bottom in thirty seconds with all this baggage."

"I want you to go home, now, and take it easy. We've got enough folks onboard to finish up. And the artwork looks great."

Kathleen didn't need further convincing. "Aye, aye, Captain. Let's pray I don't go into labor overnight."

"You can't. But if you do, you'd better call me."

"I promise." She gathered her coat and purse and did her penguin walk out the door, talking softly to her babies. "Not yet, guys. You stay put for a little while longer."

The next morning, Kathleen was greeted by a fresh layer of snow, pristine and glittering in the sunlight, and Hugo leaped up and down in the backyard in delight. A day starting out this beautiful had to be a good sign for the evening to come. Or so she hoped. No word from Thomas since the text three weeks ago, and though she remained optimistic, it wasn't easy. Was he barely treading water? Getting stronger? Her last text to him was, "*I don't want to intrude on anything you're doing, so I'll wait to hear from you.*" She threw Hugo's ball for the umpteenth time, which landed and promptly sunk into white depths. He pushed his big head into the snow and ran back with the ball in his mouth. He deposited it at her boots and cocked his ears expectantly.

"Okay, boy." Her breath was smoke in the cold air. "A few more times."

Surely, Joanne would've contacted her if Thomas were worsening somehow. She'd gotten a couple of messages from her in the beginning. Nothing too descriptive, just that he was doing okay and not to worry. She'd actually listened, for once, until the tossing and turning in bed, last night. Anxiety rearing its ugly head, combined with end-of-pregnancy discomfort.

"C'mon, Hugo. Back inside we go." He bounded up ahead of her, making a trail for her to follow. Every few feet, he stopped to look back at her, and she laughed at his quizzical face. "Yes, yes, I'm coming."

Once inside, she made a cup of cocoa to warm up and looked out the kitchen window. Two cardinal couples flitted onto snow-crusted tree branches, their scarlet feathers dazzling against the white landscape background. One at a time, the males flew to the platform feeder and gathered seeds to bring back to their waiting mates. As it so often did, watching the birds brought back a memory of her father.

"It says cardinals mate for life, Kathleen."

She was ten, Christmas morning, and she was sharing her newest, most treasured stocking gift with her dad, "The National Audubon Society's Field Guide to North American

Birds." They were sitting on the couch in their pajamas, giddy from sleep deprivation and merriment, her head resting in the crook of his arm as they marveled at the bright avian pictures before them. Neither knowing this would be the last Christmas for such moments. By the next year, she'd declared cuddling was "for babies," and while he hadn't protested, she'd never forgotten the sad but resigned expression on his face.

One of the male cardinals chased a bossy nuthatch away, while she brushed a tear away, still reminiscing.

"So, if one of the bird couple dies, what happens to the other one, Daddy?"

"I don't know, honey. I imagine eventually they find another partner."

She'd cried inconsolably, thinking of all the abandoned birds in the world. He distracted her by making a cup of cocoa like the one she was drinking, except that his didn't come from a package, and it wasn't poured into any ordinary mug. He'd wiped her tears away and she sipped from her Grandma Eileen's delicate Irish China teacup, a Belleek piece that only made holiday appearances. She could still taste that creamy, slightly bitter chocolate flavor she was never able to replicate since.

She touched the windowpane as if she were touching the cardinal, mere feet away.

I wish you were here, Daddy, making me your special cup.

Just as she took one last sip of her grainy brew, the clumpy bits undissolved at the bottom, the birds swooped up and dispersed.

She craned her neck to watch and made a wish none of them would be unpartnered and lonely in whatever earthly time they had left.

23

HopCanon was decorated to the hilt by the time Kathleen arrived in the afternoon. Real swaths of greenery entwined with white lights flanked the windows, while the tree shimmered with red and silver trimmings, and a pile of staff presents underneath. People streamed in, gathering at tables and around the artwork. The auction wouldn't start for half-an-hour, but Kathleen's pulse raced with excitement. Much like it had the night she'd first met Thomas within these very walls.

She closed her eyes, the pungent scent of the tree wafting, relaxing her. *Please, God, let there be bids.*

"Hey, Ms. K. Merry Christmas."

Her eyes flew open. She whirled around to find Amanda wheeling up behind her.

At first, Kathleen couldn't speak, could only bend as far as her belly would let her to hug. She blinked back tears and straightened. "Merry Christmas! It's so, so good to see you."

"I'm pretty scary-looking, though, ya gotta admit, though not as scary as the last time you saw me. I can't *wait* for my hair to grow back."

She was wearing a red knit hat with a fluffy pom, to hide what wasn't there.

Kathleen grabbed a nearby stray chair and sat next to her. "I won't admit any such thing. You've been through more than enough for a young woman to handle. How are you doing? The truth."

Amanda looked down, shrugging. "I dunno. I just saw Francesca and met baby James. I'm happy for her, I am, but mostly, I feel so completely empty inside. When I'm not angry or feeling guilty, that is. The doc said it's gonna take time to adjust. Like, a long time."

"Your doctor is right."

"I didn't want the baby," she blurted, as cheery Christmas music played in the background. "Everyone knew that." When she finally met Kathleen's gaze, her eyes were dry. "I was the first to admit I would've been the worst mother on the planet. You guys were my witnesses. But I never wanted Krissy ... that's what I named her, Krissy ... I never wanted her to *die*. And Mallory—oh, God."

"I know." What Kathleen hadn't known was that Amanda's baby was a girl.

"I ... I ... sorry. I can't always get the words out like I want. It's like my, my, my mouth can't do it. And trying to write it down isn't much better. Other times, mean stuff comes out and I can't shut up." Her pretty face screwed up in frustration. "Then there's all these horrible hospital bills piling in. And nobody is gonna buy my dumb pictures, and even if they do, it'll probably be for throwing darts at them."

"Amanda—"

"No, *don't* 'Amanda' me," she said savagely. "I think sometimes it would've been better if I'd just died too."

"You almost did."

"Yeah, and why didn't I? Me, a white-trash nobody, I get to go on doing nothing, while Mallory ... she would've made a difference. She was smart. She had big dreams about saving the world." She shot Kathleen a scathing look before she could argue. "Don't. Don't tell me (her voice went up a notch), 'Oh, honey, how can you wish you were dead? Our heavenly Father doesn't work that way. He doesn't punish his faithful. He doesn't pick and choose who gets to live and die. It's all about free will.' I mean, how can I fucking forget that? Pretty sure it was free will that made me reach for my phone on the floor ... and, and poof."

"Do you remember reaching for your phone?"

"No. But I remember losing it in the car and panicking."

Kathleen sighed deeply. *Help me, Lord. The second such talk in two days that I have no answers for ... none that don't sound hopelessly trite ...*

"Okay."

"Okay, what?"

"Okay, I won't say those things."

If there was an expression that shouted both disappointment and relief, it was displayed on Amanda's face now. "Thanks." She shifted uncomfortably in her wheelchair. "I get these really bad mood swings, like, way worse than I ever had before the accident. So, if I sound like a jerk that's why." She flicked the fringes of her fleece lap blanket, the kind that required no sewing and tied together at the ends. "I've never been patient, but now *everything* stupid humans do irritates me."

"How so?"

"Social media, for one. The dumb stuff people argue about. It's like I want to scream none of it matters. Nobody cares if your BFF had sex with your boyfriend, or what political party your parents are in. I posted, the other day, 'So what if your dad's a Republican? If he keeled over tomorrow, you wouldn't give a damn who he voted for.'"

"I must say, your observations are pretty spot-on." Kathleen meant this more than she could convey. Her musings spoke of a maturity beyond her years, borne from great cost. A cost she herself had also incurred too early in life.

Amanda's lip curled in disgust. "But all any of my friends do is talk crap like, 'If your dad's a Trumpster, he deserves to die.' Or, 'If you like Hilary, you should be in prison, where she should be, too.' It drives me crazy, because it's all bullshit. None of them care about politics. They just want to act like they do."

Kathleen squeezed her arm gently. "The thing is this, Amanda. For better or for worse, you now have knowledge about loss that many of your peers don't. Simply because of your young age. And it's making you realize what's important."

"It's making me bitchy is what it is."

"Understandably so."

She crossed her arms. "I don't want to talk about it, anymore."

"Done. Tell me what Riley's up to, how school's going for him? And your mom? Has she been in town to visit?"

She peered at Kathleen suspiciously. "That's really it? You're not gonna go on about how lucky I am God spared me?"

"No. Should I?"

"Everyone *else* is. Why not you?"

"You asked me not to lecture you."

Amanda's head suddenly jerked around the room. "Oh, I am so sick of myself, sick of yak, yak, yakking about poor me. Where's ... where's ... you know, omigod, I *hate* this—"

"Thomas?"

"Yeah."

"He's been in a hospital, too. He wants you to know he thinks about you and hopes to see you soon."

"A *hospital?* Is he ... is he hurt badly?"

Kathleen hesitated. How much to reveal? As little as possible seemed the wisest course of action.

"Not the way you were. Now, how about a couple of Brianne's fabulous cookies?"

"All right. I get it. He went to some rinky-dink rehab and you don't wanna talk about it." Amanda spied the treat table. "I don't suppose Brianne made any Jamaican brownies?"

Kathleen laughed. Marijuana-infused treats were definitely not on the menu, as far as she knew. "That'd probably have to be a special request. But there's plenty of others. How does a frosted Santa sound?"

"Good, I guess."

Kathleen put two Santa cut-outs on a napkin and gave them to her. "Bon appétit. With that, I've gotta get to the ladies' room. We'll talk later, okay?"

Amanda clutched Kathleen's wrist and her eyes were no longer dry. "Wait. Thank you. For trying to ... for doing all this for us."

Kathleen smiled before stooping to give her one more hug. "Let's hope our work doesn't turn into dartboard material."

"Testing. One, two, three." Summer was positioned up on the former altar, talking into a microphone. "Attention, please, everyone!" The chatter of the taproom immediately reduced to a hum and she continued. "It's time for what we've been waiting for, our silent action! What a great crowd!" Polite applause scattered throughout the hubs of people. "I want to thank you all for coming to HopCanon's 'Advent, Ales, and Art.' I'll go over the bidding process, now. I also thank you in advance for your patience."

She laid out the details, which included putting one's bid on clipboards set out next to the artwork, and listening for the bell to signify the closing of the event. She placed the mic back on its stand and made her way over to Kathleen. "Nice turnout, don't you think?"

Kathleen pulled her hair into a scrunchie. "It is. And I'm a hot mess."

"I can tell. Your ears are red. They get red when you're uptight, did you know that?"

"Yes, Thomas informed me soon after we met, along with some of my other lovely tendencies. But thanks for the reminder."

"Your mom and Megan are here, too. Somewhere. Oh, and Thomas' sister introduced herself to me. She seems very nice."

Kathleen glanced around. "Courtney's here?"

"As of ten minutes ago, anyway."

"Oh, God."

"What? What's the matter?"

Kathleen wiped her brow. "Don't worry. No labor pains, yet. Just nauseous nerves, plain and simple."

"You want to lie down? You know we put a little couch in the breakroom."

"I didn't know that. Great idea."

"Yes, especially for when the guys have to be here in the middle of the night. But don't be thinking you can sneak away and conceive kid number three in there."

She laughed at the idea. "No worries. This is the end of the line, as far as I'm concerned."

"Jesus, you look ghastly. Come on."

"All right. For a little while."

Summer herded her into the room. "Relax. I'll go make you some tea."

"I'd love that." The couch there was a plush, inviting

loveseat, and she sunk into its comfort. Summer returned with a hot mug and Kathleen sipped it gratefully. "This hits the spot. Thank you."

"You're welcome. There's no reason for you to be out there, right now, stressing out. Just chill."

"Scout's honor, I will chill."

Summer left, and as she leaned her head back, she spotted a staff bulletin board with a tattered old flier pinned to the cork.

"Come check out our new Friday night music featuring Thomas Hart, 7 to 10."

A surge of loneliness for him engulfed her, triggering a patchwork of silent prayers.

Please be well and come home. Please, God, watch over him. Please be well ...

The words became meditative, and within minutes, she could no longer keep her eyes open. It felt like she'd drifted off only minutes before, when she heard a familiar voice telling her to wake up. She squinted in confusion, to find Summer shaking her vigorously. "Wh ... what? Why are you yelling? You told me to relax!"

"Okay, okay, I did, but it's been an hour." Summer's cheeks glowed, her excitement palpable. "Girl, you will not believe what's happened."

Kathleen struggled to sit up all the way, the cobwebs of her nap clearing. "Nothing bad, I hope?"

Summer snorted. "Dear Lord, no. *All* of the art has been purchased, by one man."

"Seriously?"

"Are you ready for this? You really might go into labor when you hear for how much." Summer leaned over. "*Five thousand for each piece.*"

"No."

"Yes! Your six pieces, plus the girls' four, for a total of fifty thousand."

"I … I don't believe it. This is some kind of joke. Who? Why?"

Summer laughed and hoisted her off the loveseat. "Santa's real, baby. Come out and see."

"Hold me. I'm not kidding, I feel like I might faint." Summer clasped her hand in Kathleen's, and together they made their way back to the taproom.

The new owner of the art turned around as she approached, and a fresh wave of shock washed over Kathleen. *Could it really be him?* Her mouth was sandpaper as she groped for his name, while at the same time the lyrics to "Angels We Have Heard on High" reverberated in the taproom. "Bill? Schmidt?"

His eyes, the corners crinkled already from age, creased even more as his face formed a rare smile. "Yes. You remembered!"

Bill hadn't changed much from that night at HopCanon, months ago, when Kathleen surrendered her table after a long shift of work. She'd been convinced to stay, to listen to a sexy songwriter perform, with no empty seats to be found. Quickly, it was clear an elderly, bickering couple had needed the space more than she did. She'd also helped his ailing wife to the restroom, because it seemed like the right thing to do, because they'd reminded her of her previous life with Steve. Bill's full head of gray hair was parted and combed precisely, his tall frame clothed in conservative leisure wear, with the exception of one item. Around his neck was a tie with a picture of Dr. Seuss' Grinch, his heart three times bigger, holding Max the dog.

Bill fingered the tie. "Whadaya think? I didn't want to, but Imogene made me wear it."

"I love it."

He gestured to her belly. "Look at you. Congratulations are in order, I expect. I didn't realize you were married, since Imogene went on forever about that singer having eyes for you."

Kathleen stammered. "As it, um, turns out, that singer is the father. Complicated, I know. About to get even more once they're born."

"*They're?* You're not kidding." He grunted. "Parenthood is a helluva thing. You do the best you can, work your fingers to the bone trying to provide, and then you're accused of being a neglectful SOB." He shook his head. "I'm sorry. I can hear Imogene scolding me from here. Hopefully it'll work out better for you."

Kathleen briefly recalled his wife's words to her about tension with a daughter. "Where is Imogene?"

"At home. She can't get out, anymore."

"That must be hard."

"Yes, but it won't be long, now. Before she meets her maker, that is." He looked away, sipping his beer.

Kathleen's eyes pricked, thinking about the woman confiding to her how she and Bill were married in the same spot when HopCanon was a church. How her husband was the "bee's knees," back in the day. "I'm sorry."

"Don't be. She's suffered enough." Another sip. "We've never forgotten your simple kindness to us, that night. That's why I'm here. We read about what happened with those girls, and then we heard this was going on, and ... Imogene sent me. She said, 'Bill, go try to buy it all, and be generous.'"

"What you've done is *beyond* generous. I don't even know

what to say, other than the families benefitting from your bids are in great need."

Just as those words came out, she spotted Amanda handing Riley pairs of mittens, which he then put on the tree. They were to be given to children at their local shelter. "I'm, frankly, stunned. I wish I was, I don't know, more worthy of your contributions. I'm not the kind of established artist who attracts these kinds of sales. I feel like a ... a poser, as the kids say."

He took a long look at her. "Hon, at my age, I've been around the block a time or two. Seen my share of humanity. Or lack of it, rather. I trust my gut, and I trust my wife. Sometimes, that's enough."

"But—"

"No buts. Even someone like myself, who couldn't tell a Monet from a dime-store poster, can see you're extremely talented. And here you are donating all your profits." He finished the last of his beer, scrutinizing her again. "Allow me to be perfectly blunt. I'm healthy as a horse, but even if I live to be a hundred, heaven forbid, I still couldn't manage to spend all of my money. That's not bragging. Just the God's honest truth."

She wasn't sure how to respond to such a statement. "*Wow, lucky you, lucky me,*" certainly wasn't appropriate. Instead, she said, "All the more reason for you to be selective."

He held a large, calloused hand up. "All the more reason for me to do with it as I see fit. I'm nobody special, you know. I built up my savings after putting in long hours, some investment luck, and by the grace of above. Over many years. Fact is, I don't care one whit about it without my Genie around. I did it for her and Beth, anyway. And my grandson, Billy. To make sure they'd be taken care of."

In that moment, Bill was the image of Kathleen's own

father. Charles McMillan hadn't accrued significant wealth, but as owner of a construction company, had labored the same way. The year her brother Mark was accepted to Michigan State, she didn't see her dad at dinner for months, because he'd taken on additional projects. All so that there'd be no unscrupulous college loans, unable to be paid back in a timely manner.

Did anyone ever thank you, Dad? Were we too busy—rebelling, too busy trying not to be like you?

She sighed and brought herself back to the present. "Your devotion to Imogene was obvious, and I'd only just met you. That's a gift in itself."

"She'd do the same for me. I realized a long time ago, being married to her makes me a better person. When she goes, so does anything good about me." He laughed. "I'll go back to being the bastard everyone thinks I am. Except for my Billy."

Kathleen reached out and touched his tie gently. "I don't believe that. Not if you honor her love for you."

He was looking at the tree, now, at all the mittens the community had placed on its branches.

His eyes blinked rapidly. "Maybe you're right," he said, his voice a raspy whisper. "Maybe."

24

Kathleen talked Bill into staying for some food and dessert. After getting him settled with nourishment, she headed to the kitchen to replenish the tray Brianne had brought. In all the chaos, someone had moved the box with the extra, so she was bent over rummaging around, trying to keep out of the staff's way, when she first heard the guitar notes. She leaned against the stainless-steel counter and banged into the container of cookies, on a shelf by her knee, and retrieved them, willing her hands not to shake. Slowly, she re-entered the taproom.

"It's so great to be back here, where it all started."

Thomas strummed some notes as he talked, but what he said was akin to the adult dialogue in a Charlie Brown cartoon to her. *Mwwaa, mwwaa, mwwaa.* She took his every detail in, her heart thumping in her chest like his fingers on a bass guitar, and it might as well have been that first night she saw him. The shorter hair, the filled-out frame clothed in that black sweater she'd so feverishly taken off his back, the pink color in his cheeks, the humble smile, the *voice.* It was déjà vu times ten, and no less intoxicating.

"Are you speechless?" Summer sidled up next to her.

Kathleen's eyes stayed on him. "I don't know how many more surprises I can take. I'm guessing you had something to do with this."

"I did not. He contacted me and I agreed to be quiet about it. Reluctantly." She laughed and someone turned around and glared. "Not my strong suit," she whispered.

They fell silent, and so was the taproom as it filled with his sweet sounds and words.

"... So, here I am, a little worse for the wear, but a little smarter, too. I learned that although playing for stadiums is fun, it takes a toll." Still strumming, he smiled. "I also learned there's nowhere I'd rather be, than next to the real star of the evening. The very gifted Miss Kathleen Brooks."

He pointed his arm toward her. Blushing furiously at all the head turning and clapping, she nodded in acknowledgement and mouthed the words, "*Thank you.*"

After the noise died down, he continued. "I've finally gotten some songwriting in, a thing I haven't done in a long time, and it feels good. Kath, this one's for you. Here's 'Never Leave You Behind.'"

He expanded on the previous chords and sang.

"I did all the things they told me to
I went away like you said I should do
I asked God about living in heaven, it's true
He said, Oh, no, my son, that you can't do
There's only room here for few
And you—still got work to do—
I went down the list like you asked me to
Tried to pack you up like a suitcase used
But I—couldn't leave you behind
Even if I tried a million times ...
You're the key I couldn't find
To the doors inside my mind
Won't you let me back inside

To heal in your sun and in your shine
Because I'm ... never leaving you behind
No, never leaving you behind ..."

The notes ended and the taproom erupted in applause.

"Thank you, you've been great. Thank you so much. I feel like this is a good time to lighten up. How about a few festive covers?" He launched into "Merry Christmas, Baby," and ended four songs later with "Baby, It's Cold Outside."

"And now," he said, when the applause died down, "it's time to greet my wife-to-be and have another Mary's Mule. Thank you for your support. You'll be seeing a lot more of me here, from now on. Cheers, and Merry Christmas!"

He set his guitar in its stand. As he walked off, several people cried out, "We love you, Thomas!" and he smiled and waved in return.

Her belly was fairly jumping by the time he made it to her. He circled his arms about her and laughed, backing away slightly as he felt the babies' kicks. "Wow. I guess that's a hearty hello."

She said nothing, afraid of exploding into tears if she did, so she clasped his hand and pulled him. "Come. This way."

She led him past Jeff and Summer, who stopped her. "Wait, where're you going?"

"Back to your new resting room. We need to talk," Kathleen said.

"Make sure that's all you do. I mean, unless you want to expedite this labor."

"For God's sake, do I really look like I'm in the mood for a toss on a too-small loveseat?"

Summer shoved her half-empty pint glass Thomas' way. "Maybe not, but he probably is."

Thomas laughed. Summer had clearly had her share of Away in a Lager. "I'll behave. I promise."

The room was thankfully vacant. They sank into the little couch together, her cheeks blazing, which did not go unnoticed by him.

"Why didn't you let me know what was happening with you? I mean, nothing since Thanksgiving. I came close to calling your mother."

"I'm sorry. It's part of the process, though. I did tell you not to worry if you didn't hear from me for a while."

She stiffened. "It seems like an upcoming birth would be enough to bend the rules. For *one text.* Do you know I had Zack and Megan coming to my prenatal classes with me? In fact, they were just about ready to move in at the house to help me afterward—"

He leaned over and kissed her, his lips undemanding and yet draining her body of every last ounce of rigidity. A fact which irritated as much as exhilarated her. She pulled back and tried to sound reproachful. "I've said it before, you can't manipulate your way out of things by turning me into a pile of—a pile of sloppy mush—"

He laughed, his hands roaming. "Oh, you definitely do not feel like a pile of sloppy mush. I missed you and literally counted the minutes until I could do this. Until I could see that lovely blush of yours." He was smiling, but his golden eyes were serious. "I know we have a lot to discuss. I have much to account for, to amend, and I will. Just give me these few minutes to soak you up."

She could hardly argue with that, since she needed the same of him. She touched his silky hair, his face, his stubbly jaw. The reality of his presence, combined with the adrenaline of the evening, proved to be a potent brew. She punched his chest, not with any real strength, but enough to send a message. "Damn you, anyway."

He rubbed the spot. "You're pretty strong, you know that? In more ways than one."

"Yeah, well, I had to be. If you think you can just waltz in here and sing these heartfelt songs and do what you do to me, and think everything is just gonna be hunky-dory ..." she took a breath, "you've got another thing coming."

"I don't expect that. I'll do anything you want to show how sorry I am. How much I love you. For as long as it takes."

She studied him again. "I suppose you thought you'd get bonus points for wearing that sweater."

He looked down, grabbing a handful of the material. "What? This old thing from Goodwill?"

"You don't remember, do you?"

"No."

"You were wearing it the first night we met."

He nodded, awareness dawning. "Okay, now I remember. And if it gives me an in, I'll take it."

She laughed, stroking him in the same spot she'd whacked. "You look good," she said softly. "More importantly, do you feel good?"

"I do. I started something called TENS. It's using low-dose electric voltage to treat pain, and it works. For now. We'll see."

"That's wonderful."

"I still take opioids for bad days, and probably will forever, but I've come to an understanding about that. Quite a few other things, too."

"Such as?"

He sat up, brushing her cheek with a finger. "We've got time to talk about all that later. Tonight is about *you.*"

"I don't like things to be all about me."

"You can like it for one night. Two little peanuts will take the spotlight soon enough." He wrapped his hands around her wrists. "C'mon, let's celebrate your grand entrance into the art world. You must've set some kind of record for those bids."

She heaved herself up. "I don't know about that. I'm just glad."

"*Glad?* Think of the impact. For Mallory, Amanda. It's what every artist dreams about, making a difference that actually amounts to something."

She stared at his animated face. "The song you wrote is beautiful."

"*You're* beautiful."

"I never lost faith, you know, that you would be okay. Even though I just yelled at you now for keeping me in the dark."

"I know you didn't. I could feel it. It's what kept me going, will keep me going."

She grabbed his neck and kissed him, until the door opened and they turned to see Zack.

"Uh, sorry to interrupt—"

"It's fine," Kathleen said. "We were on our way out, really."

"Not yet," a voice called, and Zack stepped aside. It was Amanda, and she wheeled herself in. She smiled a genuine smile at Thomas. "We've got some catching up to do, Mr. Rockstar. I gotta hear all about the loony bin, and you can hear all about the PT ward. Or the floor of pain and torture, basically."

Thomas embraced her, his long body folded over her wheelchair, and the tears flowed in the room like cracked vessels of holy water.

"Girl, have I got notes to compare," Thomas said. "I've been in both of those vaults of hell. And walked the journey to—" He glanced around. "To this. Shelter and grace, you could say."

Amanda's head tilted. "Sounds like an acid trip to me."

Everyone laughed, and he continued. “Don’t you think the notes of the fallen rockstar and his teen protégé has potential? Could end up being a song, or a book.”

He picked up her hands, which lay on her fleece blanket, and squeezed them.

“Or even a drawing that sells for thousands.”

EPILOGUE

Thomas had baby Henry (named for his father) in a swing and was feeding Maggie (Margaret, named after Peggy), when the doorbell rang. He propped the bottle in the crook of his arm and looked through the window, at an older man who looked vaguely familiar. He opened the door with one hand and cradled the baby with the other. "Hi."

The man coughed. "Hello. Sorry to be a bother, but is Kathleen home?"

"She's not, actually. She's at her art studio."

The art studio he referred to was housed in the newly refurbished HopCanon Annex, where the long-dormant catechism classrooms were now used for a variety of purposes. In addition to Kathleen's art space, Thomas taught guitar there (when he wasn't doing an occasional nursing shift or musical gig), Brianne honed her baking skills, and Amanda and Francesca led a support group for teens where they designed jewelry together.

"Ah, ah, that's good," the old man said, and put out a hand. "Uh, I don't think we formally met. I'm Bill Schmidt."

Thomas nodded in recognition. "Bill! Yes! How are you? Would you like to come in?"

"No, no. I don't want to intrude. But I have something for Kathleen in the car, if you don't mind making sure she gets it."

"No problem." Maggie had fallen asleep, so Thomas quickly put her in the Pack 'n Play that was set up in the living room.

Bill came back with a rectangular object wrapped in butcher paper. "This is the portrait I purchased at the auction. My wife, Imogene, passed, recently, and this was her wish. She said anyone who could create beauty like that needed to keep it, rather than let it sit in our lonely basement."

"I'm so sorry for your loss. Are you sure—?"

"God, yes. Beautiful or not, what would I want with a picture of you?"

Thomas muffled his laughter. "Good point."

"Besides, I'm having an auction myself. The whole kit and kaboodle's going, the house and everything in it, with the proceeds to benefit St. Jude's."

"Downsizing, then."

"You could say that. I'm doing what everyone over the age of sixty-five seems to be doing. Moving to one of those la-di-da senior facilities."

"Somewhere local?"

Bill snorted. "Hell, no. I'm getting out of this snow and wind, to Florida. My joints can't take another winter here. To think how I used to laugh at all the snowbirds taking flight."

"That'll be nice. It's kind of like one-stop shopping at some of those places, isn't it?"

"Son, to tell you the truth, it looks like a Mr. Roger's Neighborhood ... all these tanned people, smiling like they've had too much surgery, and about a hundred tennis courts, grocery stores, sports things. And a dancehall, if you can believe that. For us old codgers who've had every limb imaginable replaced. It's too much, but Genie said—" his voice broke at her name. "She said it'd be good for me." He pitched the package forward at Thomas. "Here, take it."

"Thank you." He gently placed the picture against the door. "Kathleen will be sad to have missed you. Do you have a forwarding address?"

"Sure, but do I know it? My mind is almost as useless as the rest of me. I'll look it up and send it later. Oh, and if anyone wants the other art, or anything else, for that matter, have at it before the auction begins. A week from Saturday, 1210 Acorn Drive, before noon."

"Great. I'll spread the word."

"I see the little ones arrived," Bill muttered. "Everything copacetic?"

"Yes. A healthy boy and a girl. They're keeping us busy, for sure."

"And those kids and their families, from the accident?" He winced, as if asking the questions pained him.

"Still healing, of course. Which you and Kathleen made much easier."

"Sorry for the third-degree, but Genie would want the lowdown. Every few days, I go visit at the cemetery and chat with her. I know, crazy. I've been called worse."

"I think a lot of folks do that. I wouldn't call it crazy, at all."

Bill squinted at Thomas in the sunlight and put one hand on the rail to support his weight. "I'll admit this is more than I've talked to anyone in months, and It's none of my business, but I hope you married that girl."

Without missing a beat Thomas said, "As soon as I could. And it wasn't soon enough."

“She’s good stock, as my mother would say. Not the sort to let get away.” He nodded approvingly as he turned halfway to leave. “I guess you figured that out, didn’t you?”

To his embarrassment, Thomas’ eyes filled. “I did. Before it was too late.”

“That’s what matters, isn’t it? That’s what matters.”

Without another word, the grieving old man shuffled down the steps, painstakingly made his way back to the car, and waved as he drove away.

ABOUT THE AUTHOR

Ellen Cassidy wrote in journals, crafted numerous letters-to-the-editor, joined writing groups, and ranted on her blog for years, until finally publishing an award-winning collection of short stories titled, "No Place like Home." She resides with her husband and tuxedo cat, Shadow, in Southwest Michigan. Her future life will include writing, living, and reading with her beloved granddaughter Ada Mary in Tennessee, where the rest of the family are welcome to join them if they bring Eric Carle and Pout-Pout Fish books.

WritingHurts.org
pintspawsnhalfpints.com